Us Three

Also by Jamie Berris

Whispering Waves

Carmen is at her wit's end with her rebellious teenage daughter gone train wreck . . .

Monica's conniving mother-in-law has moved in for the summer . . .

Gabriella is blindsided by an ultrasound picture belonging to her husband . . .

US THREE

Jamie Berris

Us Three

Jamie Berris

Copyright © 2019 Jamie Berris

Edited by Theresa Wegand.

Cover designed by Sarah Hansen of Okay Creations.

Great minds discuss ideas. Average minds discuss events. Small minds discuss people.

Eleanor Roosevelt

CHAPTER 1

Sometimes good things fall apart so better things can fall in place.

Gabriella

The black-and-white photo clung to the back of Greg's phone as he pulled it from his pocket to snap a picture of Gabby. His wife sat perched in a proud pose on top of a cardboard box, one of dozens to be unpacked in their new home. Gabby's wide, exaggerated smile turned puzzled as her eyes squinted to make out the fetus on the ultrasound picture before her.

"A baby picture is stuck to the back of your phone." Her voice hung between a statement and a question.

The confession was all over his fallen face before a single word came out of his mouth. He flipped his phone and tore the picture off with fumbling, nervous fingers, stuffing it into his pocket.

Feeling a sudden need for a barrier, she stood and picked up the box.

"I, well . . . I was going to show you." Greg flashed a presumptuous smile and then stammered, his face drained of color, while hers, she was sure, had turned a flaming shade of red. "Max from the office. His wife, I mean an ultrasound picture of their kid. It's his. Hers. I mean their kid. You don't know them." His Adam's apple bulged as he swallowed nervously.

Gabby's eyes darted to his pocket. She had half a mind to grab for the picture. An outlandish mix of dread and disbelief crept over her.

"Be honest with me, Greg," she said, although yearning for his bald-faced lie to dismiss any burden of truth.

"I never meant for it to happen, and now . . . Oh, Gabriella, I never intended . . . I tried to get out. I mean I am out. I was never committed . . . I can explain."

Gabby's arms jellied and gave out, sending the box filled with her grandmother's china to the ground, shattering on her feet. The pain that zoomed from her toes up her five-foot, five-inch frame was nothing compared to the sudden blow to her core.

1

"Excuse me, what?" Her heart bulged from her chest, each beat matching the throbbing in her toe.

Greg raked a hand through his hair and gripped his skull. "I never meant to . . . Gabriella, I'm so sorry. It's just that I don't know how I got into this mess. It's not my fault. I was lured. It started over business lunches. She pursued *me*. I would never intentionally do anything to hurt you."

Oh, but you did.

He moved closer for an embrace, and she put her arms up to stop him, or shove him, possibly hit him. Gabby couldn't grasp what was occurring, only that her world was imploding.

Leaping to the side to avoid his touch, she tripped over the box of broken teacups because, of course, she hadn't properly wrapped the china, nor taped the box. She was only moving the delicate set down the road from the rental cottage, so she hadn't felt the need to take such precautions. Silly her, she wasn't prepared for the lowest blow of her life from her husband.

Gabby hit the porch tiles with a thud. She lay on her back, sprawled over the broken glass, scrambling to sit up while frantically scooting as far away from Greg as possible.

In an instant, he was looming over her, pleading. "Listen to me, Gabriella. Please, listen. No one must know. We can keep the baby a secret. Holly has already agreed."

Gabby felt her throat constrict at the mention of the woman's name and gasped for air. Her entire body quivered in rejection as Greg got down on his knees, in her face, forcing her back on her elbows. He took hold of her cheeks like a mother trying to get the attention of a small child.

"Look at me and pay attention, Gabby. I can walk away from her and the baby. We can fix us." He pinched the bridge of his nose. "I know this is bad, but we can get past it. You, out of all people, know how to help others through their mistakes—clean up their messes and put them in the past."

She batted his hands away and saw an unrecognizable craze in his eyes. He was suddenly a stranger to her, despicable and threatening.

Greg's face went blotchy and red. Veins she'd kissed, lovingly traced with her finger a thousand times, were popping out of his neck. "None of this has any reflection on you . . . on our marriage."

"Get away from me," Gabby spat. "Get away from me, Greg," she repeated in a hasty snarl full of venom she never knew she possessed.

He stood, raised his palms in surrender, and took two steps back. Glass shards were stuck to her body as she scurried to her feet and wiped her hands on the thighs of her white jeans, leaving behind bright red streaks of blood.

Greg's gaze flitted over her and the remnants of the teacups. "I love you, Gabriella. I've never stopped loving you."

"You've gotten another woman pregnant?" she asked in clarifying repulsion.

"Yes. No. I mean it doesn't have to change anything." With his arms outstretched, he made another attempt at closing in on the space between them.

"NO! Stay away from me," Gabby warned as she threw the back of her shoulder into the front door. She searched for the handle, her eyes boring through him with ferocity. "Do not step foot into this house." She slammed the door, dismissing him with a flip of the dead bolt.

~*~

Gabby rubbed her hands over her eyes as if it were possible to erase the images of what took place on the porch, days ago. Why did it have to be here? She would never be able to walk through her front door or relax on the porch without reenacting the scene: playing it over and over in her head, analyzing what he said and what she said, and visualizing Greg's frenzied expression and her bewilderment.

Worst of all was the intense feeling that washed over her. Gabby had always shuddered at the thought of what it must feel like to receive abysmal, life-altering news: the tragic death of a loved one or a life-threatening disease. Gabby had always prayed for safety and health and had been grateful she had avoided such misfortunes.

Until now.

No, she wasn't dying, but something inside her had. Her day had come—her before-and-after event had occurred—the dividing moment in her life she would forever refer to as *then* and *now*.

She took the last sip of her coffee, stood from her rocker, and felt the familiar fiery blaze sweep over her. The vision of her clutching the handle and pushing through the front door to get away from Greg would remain crystal clear for the rest of her life.

Inside, their takeout dinner had been waiting in boxes on the coffee table: a bottle of Greg's favorite *Veuve Clicquot*, two plastic cups, and a pineapple-scented candle burning in a mason jar. The flame joyfully flickered, mocking her fairytale existence, as if she thought she could escape this life without mishap. The fact that the misfortune was intentional, caused by her own husband, only taunted her further.

Gabby abandoned the front porch and walked around the backside of the house to the water. A few fishing boats dotted the lake, and she wondered if the fishermen were in search of fish or merely escaping their own dire circumstances.

The rising sun was still low in the sky, a new day on the horizon, a day Gabby had no idea how to fill. For the first time in her life, she awoke and questioned her purpose. Even her work seemed shallow. The desire to spend her days counseling others through their dilemmas seemed comical. She couldn't cope with her own.

She could feel the weight of her cell in the pocket of her robe and contemplated calling one of the kids. No, she wouldn't put that burden on them, especially on Memorial Day weekend, the unofficial kick off to summer for Michigander's. She would never succumb and be the needy mother interfering with their plans.

Stella and Lottie were most likely on their way to Chicago for the weekend. Calvin and Klay probably hadn't rolled out of bed yet, no doubt sleeping off an underaged hangover that Gabby tried not to worry herself with. They were planning on roughing it in tents all weekend in the Upper Peninsula, fishing somewhere. Gabby felt guilty she couldn't remember where.

Wilderness State Park? No. Someplace in Marquette? Who knows? She'd been in such a fog. Considering the circumstances, she was going to let herself off the hook. The boys were twenty, perfectly capable of taking care of themselves, and they were in a group. Safety in numbers. They were fast runners—not fast enough to outrun a bear but fast enough to outrun their friends—a standing joke in their family that held zero laughable impact on Gabby at the given moment.

Her phone chimed in her pocket from a text. She smiled, knowing it was one of the kids. That's how it always happened. When she was thinking about them, a call or text came through. She would often say the name out loud before looking at the screen, praising her clairvoyant motherly instincts for her 90% accuracy.

Lottie, she guessed, before retrieving her phone.

> Can we meet for a walk? Please hear me out, Gabriella. I owe you an explanation.

Damn. Wrong. A percentage drop, statistically speaking. Seriously though, *owe* me? How dare Greg use manipulating tactics, acting as if I'm chasing his pathetic excuses. His motive to beg, scheme, and cover up was clearly obvious.

Her thumbs drummed a curt response.

Don't insult my intelligence, Greg. If you need to get your feelings off your chest, say so. I don't recall expressing interest in an explanation from you. I have the facts. You cheated. Your mistress is pregnant.

Gabby needed time to consider the facts. She was a therapist. It was her job to help people find out who they were, uncover the buried truth of their lives, past and present, confront, resolve, and figure out how to deal and move on from their quandaries.

This wasn't a situation coming from a new client where Gabby had to learn names, relationships, backgrounds, who was abusing whom, detailed scenarios, and the scarring emotions that needed healing. This was her life—a life she thought, perchance pretended, she knew inside and out. What a farce.

Gabby, what I've done is inconceivable even to me. Will you please give me the opportunity to clarify the situation and talk about our options? I need your help. I'm in a terrible state of mind.

What an ass. Did he really think conceive was a good word choice?

As expected, Greg, when I'm ready to talk to you as your wife, I'll let you know. If you need a referral for a therapist to talk to regarding your state of mind, I can pass along a name.

Gabby couldn't fathom going for a walk with Greg. Her emotions were running rampant. One minute she was engulfed in sorrow, the next livid, and the moments between she bounced from disbelief to disgrace.

Several minutes passed, and Gabby thought she had put Greg to rest. She kicked back in the lounge chair and started her own therapy session. She was going to be her own client.

First, she was going to feel the full weight of Greg's affair, own and sort out every emotion, logically deciding how to deal with the anger and hurt. Next, she'd figure out the questions she really needed answers to, which ones would be helpful and which ones would only cause her further grief.

Ding.

I understand that it's too painful for you to talk with me right now, but, Gabby, there are some time-sensitive decisions to consider. It's imperative that we communicate. We can avoid hurting more people by keeping this baby a secret. Our relationship aside, we don't have to go into that now. We do need to think of our kids and how this will affect them. I've done enough damage. It would kill me to hurt them to the depths I've hurt you.

Selfish bastard. What a coward move, placing this burden on me. Gabby silenced her phone without responding.

The kids. They *would* be crushed to find out their father had an affair and they had a half-sibling as a result of it. A mother protects her children. How do you decipher whether you should protect with truth or lies? Do lies ever protect or do they only delay the destruction?

Gabby's gaze landed on the Farnsworth's pontoon boat. They were floating close enough for Gabby to see that Jayda and Bryce Farnsworth were sipping coffee and enjoying breakfast and each other's company. Jayda's legs were extended across Bryce's thighs. He drummed his fingers on her shin to a beat Gabby couldn't hear. From time to time, Jayda would tilt her head back toward the sun, and Bryce would readjust his baseball cap to keep the sun from his eyes.

Their body language spoke of love, intimacy. However, that wasn't what Gabby was interested in; it was their conversation. She didn't know the Farnsworths well, but she knew their son was a senior in high school and their daughter a junior.

What piqued her curiosity was whether they were planning the next chapter of their lives as empty nesters. The scene in front of her mirrored the endless hours Gabby and Greg had spent floating on their boat, pondering just that.

With a cocktail in their hands, the waves rocking the boat, Greg and Gabby had dreamed for hours. Life with four adult children . . . For the first time in twenty years, their lives weren't going to be dictated by their kids' rampant social lives, academic agendas, and athletic calendars.

They'd decided to stay put in their forever house; leaving the lake was out of the question. They enjoyed boating, swimming, and the sunsets too much to ever give it up. They envisioned pulling their grandkids tubing and wake surfing around the lake for endless hours just as they had their own children.

Greg swore he would have enormous amounts of patience, teaching his grandchildren how to get up on the wakeboard. It had been excruciating giving skiing and surfing instructions to his own children. He'd get impatient when they ignored his direction, and they'd get tearful as they became discouraged—moments they laughed about as a family now.

They decided to demolish their existing house and rebuild. Gabby had spent endless hours on Pinterest, searching and designing the perfect serene lake house. She pinned boards upon boards filled with flooring ideas, tranquil paint colors in shades of blue, aqua, and green, all accented with grays and washed whites, coastal lighting, furniture, and décor flanked with plush rugs set onto durable tile floors equipped for sand and dripping suits.

The walls would be flanked with shiplap, wainscoting, or bead boarding. The ceilings would be both of color and white with beams or inset with a tray. The outside would boast colorful shutters, a wraparound porch, a three-season screened room, an outdoor shower, an outdoor kitchen and fireplace with cozy dining and seating, and giant outdoor ceiling fans shaped like palm leaves.

It would be grand, not so much in size—it was just the two of them now—but in amenities, Gabby decided. She had always loved decorating and designing, on the verge of obsessively searching and preparing for the day they would start over from scratch.

She envisioned a pergola with flowers climbing and swaying in the breeze. By night, the pergola would shimmer from strings of hanging lights. She and Greg would retreat to their outdoor haven and relish the peace of their slower-paced life. They would sip wine and reminisce of the frantic, crazy-busy days of raising two sets of twins.

Quite often they spoke about what they would do with their free time once the kids were in college. Stella and Lottie, twenty-one, had just finished their third year at MSU, and Calvin and Klay, twenty, had just finished their first year at GVSU. With two sets of twins, twenty months apart, they had gone from a full house to an empty house almost overnight.

It was no surprise that it took Gabby less than one month to meet with the architect, get the blueprints, and begin subcontracting the remodel. This was her project, her child, since she was hardly needed as a physical mom these days.

Demolishing the home they raised their family in was bittersweet. Gabby had spent every waking minute consumed with the construction. She feared someone would screw up her dream by putting a wall where one shouldn't be or run the bead board along the dining nook in the wrong direction.

Over dinner at Terra a couple of months ago, Greg was acting strange. In fact, he had been *off* for several weeks. He was suffering from insomnia, indigestion, headaches, and he reluctantly confessed to having a panic attack at work after a co-worker called Gabby, concerned.

He pawned it off to the extra mortgage on the house they bought in East Lansing for the girls, college tuition for four, feeling emptiness since the kids were all away, their rebuild, and work-related stress.

Work-related stress. What a charade.

When Greg presented Gabby out of the blue with a diamond anniversary band over dessert, she thought he was dying, the ring his last gift. Tears sprang from her eyes as she waited for the deadly diagnosis that would shine light on his erratic symptoms. Greg quickly assured her he was healthy, that he just wanted to celebrate this new chapter in their lives. All the changes had made him anxious, and he was ready to start fresh.

"We'll be like newlyweds again, rebuilding a brand-new home, a clean slate," he painted the picture. "Let's get away for a long weekend, possibly even renew our vows."

Gabby laughed. It was completely out of character for Greg to suggest something he'd normally describe as sappy. She declined without a second thought, claiming she couldn't possibly abandon the construction even for a few days. Greg persisted, dangling visions of balmy beaches, sparkling turquoise water, and shimmering sunsets into her mind until she reluctantly agreed to go.

Turks and Caicos turned out to be exactly what they needed: the break from work, building, and the frigid temperatures of a long gloomy Michigan winter. Greg booked a week at The Palms. He arranged every detail of their vow-renewal ceremony cruising aboard a yacht.

They went scuba diving, parasailing, and rode pink and yellow Townie bikes with attached baskets around the island. When they weren't being pampered with drinks by their personal butler, Niro, they would stroll the beach for miles, hand in hand, stopping at random resorts for drinks or an appetizer.

Gabby closed her eyes and rested her head on the newly upholstered Sunbrella pillow, the fabric far less exciting today than it was the day she fell in love with it. How a simple print became her mere focus that day. She'd snapped a picture, texted it to Greg, elated she had found the theme from which all other outdoor decorating would stem.

Had he received the text with Holly by his side? Sharing a bed, a romantic lunch? Had Holly reveled in Gabby's obliviousness?

The thought of their trip to Turks and Caicos, a mere twelve weeks ago, made her stomach recoil. Their conversations had been built on deception playing on repeat in her head.

A high-pitched laugh from Jayda Farnsworth echoed off the water, causing Gabby to curse both her first and second honeymoon.

What a sham.

Greg had made a disaster of their lives. Sure, Holly was also at fault, but Gabby was too grounded and knowledgeable to fall prey to solely blaming the other woman. Because of Greg's choices, she was alone in their brand-new dream home. Greg was alone in a city penthouse, or maybe he wasn't alone. Possibly he was with Holly, pregnant Holly. He'd lied to Gabby for months. How could she be certain he wasn't still lying?

Yes, quite possibly her husband was with his pregnant girlfriend. No, no, no, Greg had made it clear in text after text, over countless pleading voicemails, Holly was *not* his girlfriend.

Significant other, sleeping partner, stress reliever, mid-life lay, side-ride . . . what exactly was her status?

CHAPTER 2

A bad attitude is like a flat tire.
You can't move forward unless you change it.

Monica

Monica's short, jet-black hair stuck out from the bottom of her baseball cap. She adjusted it lower on her forehead to shade her eyes and focus on the figure approaching her.

"Hey, coach." Monica stood up from pulling weeds, brushed the sand off her hands, and stretched her seized-up muscles. "Your workouts are killing me, Gabby. This morning I ran six miles, biked ten, and swam laps around the floating docks for twenty minutes."

"Impressive." Gabby winked. "Don't forget tomorrow we're biking twenty-five."

Monica groaned in mock agony and parted her lips to protest the hilly terrain Gabby had mapped out, when a piercing scream bellowed from Kenzie. Without a second to brace herself, Monica felt the tenacious child forcefully barrel into her legs.

"Kenzie Kay Colburn," Monica said sharply, "that hurt Mommy."

"Beck frew sand in me eyes!" Kenzie screeched while slapping and clawing at her face. Then she shrieked louder as she scratched her chin, revealing the faintest speckle of blood.

Gabby's presence put a lid on Monica's agitation, keeping her somewhat sympathetic towards Kenzie, fully aware that if she hadn't an audience, she'd lose her cool. It wasn't even ten o'clock, and so far, between Kenzie and Beck, the two of them had managed to cry, or have some sort of mishap, at least seven times this morning. Monica had reached her empathetic limits.

First, it was tug-of-war over a toy. Then Kenzie stole Beck's Play-Doh, so naturally, he bit her, and she shoved him for it. Dex had spread pineapple cream cheese on Kenzie's bagel instead of strawberry, warranting an emergency worth calling 911. Beck's finger got smashed in the toy chest. Kenzie bumped her forehead on the unforgiving corner of granite, for the twelfth time in the last five days, while bounding kangaroo style around the kitchen.

11

Now, Beck swung a shovel, rather skillfully and powerfully for an eighteen-month-old, but regardless, sand was flying wildly, causing yet another catastrophe.

Would it ever end? At what point did logic kick into their tiny brains? A mother had only so much mercy.

"Beck, little buddy, easy with the shovel." Forced pleasantry laced Monica's voice. "Please stop swinging it. Now!" The words had barely left her lips before the shovel was sailing through the air. It bounced off Gabby's cheek and hit Kenzie's shoulder before landing at her toes.

Kenzie picked up the shovel and hurled it back at Beck with a shriek for emphasis. Fortunately, she missed; however, the entire episode had sent Monica's blood pressure soaring. Her already thin patience was sapped as she looked to Gabby, desperately.

"I'm so sorry. My children are crazy out of control." She went to scoop up Kenzie and stepped on a monster truck. "Ouch! Mother of truck!" Monica kid-cursed.

Gabby giggled and spoke reassuringly. "Your children are acting perfectly normal for their ages; they're seeking attention and testing their boundaries."

Monica rolled her eyes and scoffed. "I beg to differ. Day after day, post after post, I see all my friends with their perfectly behaved, overachieving children. Makes me feel like I'm failing as a mother."

"As if that's real. There's more truth in the National Enquirer!" Gabby rebuked. "Look. You seem a little on edge. Kids sense that and feed off it. Moms set the tone of the household, you know."

"No pressure in that, thank you." Monica grimaced but knew Gabby was right.

Monica raised her hand to Gabby's cheek. "You have a nasty welt forming."

Gabby brought her hand to her face and grinned comfortingly. "It's fine. It will give me something tangible to occupy my mind with."

"I can't imagine any of your kids had ever acted out the way mine do."

"Stop," Gabby warned. "You need to stop doing that."

Monica cocked her head to the side, anticipating Gabby's advice. She hungered for insight to guide her along in this mad world of parenting.

"What exactly?"

"Parenting means dealing with meltdowns, food wars, toilet issues, bedtime blues, and a host of other quandaries that change on a whim. Stop comparing yourself to other moms, your kids to other kids, fretting over the inevitable, and seeking perfection."

Monica knew Gabby was right, and she thrived on Gabby's forward, sometimes in-your-face, coaching. So often it was just easier to wallow in self-pity than it was to take off your lazy boots and be a mindful mommy, as Gabby coined it. How often had Gabby reminded her that her attitude and response to life was predetermined by mindset, so if you want change in your life, start with your head.

She made it sound so simple: stop reacting to your kids and let them react to your grace and mercy, which meant punishing without anger, reacting calmly, and following through intently. The list Gabby presented was long and exhausting. Exactly how Monica went through her days. Exhausted.

Beck had grabbed his shovel, attempting to bury his Thor figurine, but was mostly flinging sand dangerously close to where Kenzie had now begun digging a pool for Doc McStuffins.

Here we go again, thought Monica, and to boot, Gabby was observing. Monica retrieved a shovel from the crab-shaped sand box that was used for storing their beach toys and kneeled next to Beck.

"Beck buddy, Mommy will help you." Monica kept her shovel low to the sand as she scooped mounds on top of Thor. "Like this," she guided.

Kenzie stood with her hands on her little hips and watched.

"Hey, Kenzie, can you help Mommy teach Beck how to dig and bury Thor without splattering sand everywhere?"

"What a wonderful idea," Gabby complimented, grabbing a shovel herself and mirroring Monica's movements.

Kenzie eyed Gabby, then Monica, and finally rested her gaze on her little brother.

"You're three, Kenzie—"

"Free and half," she corrected.

"Yes, of course, three and a half, which means you're a skilled sand specialist. As a sand *specialist,* you need to teach Beck how to keep his shovel close to the sand so he doesn't accidentally fling it in people's eyes. When you were his age, this is how I taught you, and now you're an expert."

Monica kept shoveling the sand while sweet-talking Beck through the motions, repeating low and slow, while they buried Thor and moved on to Spiderman.

Kenzie moved closer and observed, finally getting on her knees next to Beck and mimicking her mother. "Like dis, Beck." Beck was in his glory, probably more than anything from the sweet tone of his sister's voice as she instructed him. Monica's eyes shot up and met Gabby's where they shared a silent understanding.

"Thanks for the lesson or mini session. Can you be my mommy mentor and stay by my side all day?" pleaded Monica. "You force me to be a better parent. Patient."

"We both know you don't need that. You're a wonderful mother. You only need to stay mind—"

"Mindful," Monica finished with a hint of charming sarcasm and an eyeroll for effect.

"Really though, this isn't new stuff for you. It's the same tactics you use in the classroom."

"*Used* in the classroom. I'm rusty and it's way different dealing with toddlers than it is teens. My patience these days . . ." She held up her thumb and pointer finger an inch apart and shook her head.

"Have you made a decision about whether you're going back in the fall?" asked Gabby.

Monica shrugged. "I used to cry when I left the kids every day, and now, sometimes I cry after being with them all day. Don't judge."

"Never."

"Staying home is harder than I thought, yet I'm not sure I'm ready to go back to school. I'll never get these years back, and I learned the hard way how precious and fragile life is." Her hand instinctively went to her belly, while her gaze hung on Kenzie and Beck, all annoyances dissolving.

Gabby nodded. "I do know. I also know how important it is to feel fulfilled. When you do, all other areas in your life tend to fare better."

"These days I don't know what fulfills me, or rather I feel guilt over what does, versus what should.

"I bumped into a coworker at the fro-yo shop last week, and she thoughtfully asked how I was doing. She commented that I looked great, which I took to heart, as the last time I saw her I'd been having a rough few days, wasn't wearing it well, and had embarrassingly been purchasing a box of cheap wine at the corner store.

"Anyway, we had a nice chat, one of those that had me longing for adult communication and intellect, stirring up my courage to return to work. Then, before we parted ways, she looked me up and down and commented how nice it would be to take a year off and hire a personal trainer to get in shape as I had."

The same intense, raw wretchedness still clung to Monica. "Apparently your free services, and friendship, warrant judgment," Monica said defensively.

"Then bam." Monica slapped her chest with the palm of her hand, getting more riled up as she spoke. "I gave birth to a stillborn baby, took a year off, and there I was justifying it."

Monica's head dropped; she intently watched her big toe draw circles in the sand. Gabby was right. The first several months Monica had been a recluse. Now she'd suddenly felt the need to post pictures of the crafts and learning activities she was doing with her kids, the grout she'd replaced in the bathroom, the closet shelves she'd rebuilt, the trips to the parks, zoos, and museums she was always hauling the kids to.

Why? So she could prove she wasn't abusing her leave of absence?

Tears burned the rims of Monica's eyes. "Another coworker, Kelly, asked me if I was done with therapy so I could come back to work. Then she carried on, saying she wished she could afford a therapist so she could kick back on someone's couch and bitch about her life without pissing anyone off." Monica's tone was thick with despair.

"I blurted in her face that I don't pay you. That you're a dear friend who happens to be a counselor and has helped me through the worst time of my life."

Gabby studied Monica's face the way she always did when Monica was snuggled on her couch in tears over the loss of Cade. The way she did when she wanted Monica to answer her own question. "One, you're too hard on yourself. Two, you don't owe her an explanation. Three, whom are those comments a reflection on? Her or you?"

"It's a reflection of her," Monica deliberated, "and I need to stop allowing others to make me feel inadequate."

"Envy is an ugly thing, Monica. It's a hostile obsession with what's positive for the people around you. You possess something Kelly doesn't, whether it be physical, material, or emotional. So even though you've been through something tragic, she feels jealous, threatened by the tiniest glimmer of fulfillment you've gained through your loss."

Gabby extended an arm toward Monica. "Giving birth to a stillborn is traumatic. Dedicating yourself to your family and your physical well-being the past eight months has been imperative. Don't allow jealous, insecure people to get in your head."

Monica's brain swirled with conflicting voices. "I feel like such a head case. I mean, before losing Cade, I had it all together. I didn't question my daily existence. I was confident in my decisions. Now, I'm full of doubt, everything seems so heavy, and every move I make is so calculated out of fear of doing the wrong thing. It's like I've gotten a handle on the grief, I'm not crying twenty hours each day, and yet I've brought on a host of issues I've never in my life dealt with. What is wrong with me?"

"Oouch!" Beck screeched and burst into tears. Kenzie had accidentally nicked his toe with the shovel, causing sand to coagulate in the dot of blood from the torn skin.

"Sounds like we could use a bubble intervention here," Dex said as he came bounding around the corner with a liter-sized canister of bubbles. He sucked in an enormous amount of air and blew gently through the wand, causing a spray of bubbles to dance around them.

Kenzie shot up and began catching the bubbles. "More, Daddy, more," she begged as she jumped and grasped at the iridescent suds.

Beck's cries slowed to a whimper as bubbles popped on his arms and nose. He looked to the sky with wonder and curiosity, squeals of glee escaping his mouth. The sight of her husband and children delighted Monica like nothing else. He was always a reminder of what was truly important, that they experienced far more of these moments than they did the disastrous ones. In times of sorrow, she chose to place her focus on the adverse.

Kenzie's excitement suddenly turned urgent, and she began dancing around Monica in circles, groping at her legs. "Bafroom, Mommy. Bafroom, now! My privates can't hold it!"

"C'mon, Kenzie. Run inside. Daddy will help you." Dex kept blowing bubbles as he backpedaled toward the house, Kenzie at his toes. Beck's arms stretched long, his little fingers opened and closed, and panic swept over his face as he watched Dex and the bubbles retreat.

"You're forgetting someone, Dex."

Dex obediently swooped in and took hold of Beck and cradled him like a football. "Don't freak, little buddy. Daddy's got you."

Monica inhaled the sweet scent of peace and quiet as the trio disappeared inside. Dex was a better parent than she. Her eyes welled up with both joy and sadness over that fact. "I would walk around the lake with you, but quite frankly, I'm somewhat of an emotional basket case today. I'm not so sure you want to entertain my foul mood." Monica half-laughed.

Gabby chuckled but didn't comment. She was good at that. A therapist's trait. They allowed your own words to hang in the air.

God certainly knew what he was doing by putting Gabby in her life. The timing was uncanny. Their friendship had been solid before

Cade's death. Monica had never felt more comfortable divulging to anyone in her entire life, and she'd taken full advantage of Gabby's open arms and steady stream of consolation. Whether it was curling in a ball on Gabby's couch in her counseling office, a midnight phone call, morning coffee, or a sweat session, no topic, concern, feeling, or worry was off limits.

Monica had been chugging along nicely, as best as one would expect after losing a child, reliably, kind of like her first car. The teal Ford Escort had a few dings, a tiny bit of rust over the passenger rear wheel, but Monica cared for it, oil changes, tire rotations, washing, even waxing it a time or two. Eventually, it started stalling out, always at inopportune times. Even though it was to be expected—the car was old, the mileage high—it frustrated Monica.

Not that she had expected to be unscathed, grieve over her son for a few months and never stall out. She didn't expect the onslaught of consequential anxieties, which really had nothing to do with her loss, to bombard her as they had.

The screen door to the deck slid open, and the chatter and giggles spilled out with the continuation of bubbles. Dex, being considerate, contained the kids to the deck to give Monica a break.

"Anyway, you know what's really bothering me? It's not all that deep psychological stuff."

A mocking trill escaped Gabby. "Good because I'm off the clock." She looked pointedly at Monica. "What, my friend, is *really* bothering you?"

"I know. I know. I should reel it in. Sorry, I don't know what has gotten into me this morning. Wait. That's a lie. I do."

"Janice?" Gabby guessed.

Monica nodded and looked over her shoulder to be certain Dex wasn't about to overhear her. Even though he knew she was furious with him for agreeing to let his mother move in for the summer, Monica didn't want to hurt his feelings more than she already had.

"Ironic how a broken pipe can cause a flood, warranting my mother-in-law to secure contractors for dry wall, new flooring, carpet, and countless other things like a pond in her circle drive stocked with Koi and adorned with a fountain," Monica said with pursed lips. "Yet for the life of her, she can't find a place to rent while the work is being done."

Monica's head shook in fury. "As if there isn't a single place to stay in Palm Springs." She motioned with one finger.

"Janice is always bragging about her *Cali friends* and their magnificent houses, the clubs they belong to, and the upscale boutiques they shop at while dropping hundreds on organic leafy lunch fare because, you know, women in California *take care* of themselves." Monica huffed and placed her hand on her jutting hip. "Well then, can't they open their homes and take care of their dear friend?

"She's just . . . I just," she stammered, "the ridiculing . . . I can't handle it, not now. She thinks because she miscarried with her first pregnancy, at seven weeks, only knowing she was pregnant a mere two, that we've gone through the exact same thing. She's constantly harping that I need to move past it, as if it's so simple to forget Cade and carry on.

"I consider myself a hospitable person and have welcomed her into our home numerous times for a week here or there. A couple of weeks is one thing, but I'm not in the right frame of mind to handle her for months on end. She butters me up with gifts, and under normal circumstances, I'd appreciate the gesture, but Spanx a week after giving birth, gift cards to the salon after ending a Facetime call where she remarked that my hair had lost its pregnancy shine, clothes a size too small, and even a gourmet meal prep service because she knows I hate to cook, but thinks I owe it to her son to prepare lavish dinners every night . . . all too much."

Monica flitted her hands in the air animatedly. "It's all about intention, and believe me, her heart is not in the right place. Janice's gifts don't speak love. How am I supposed to welcome a woman like that into my home for the next three months? Three months!"

Gabby sighed with sympathy. "Chase doesn't happen to be anywhere near California?"

Monica shrugged. "Last I knew he was in Costa Rica or maybe it was the Cook Islands."

Dex's brother Chase lived abroad. The exotic location and the exotic specimen under his arm changed frequently. Chase was a skydiving instructor who lived in a country for a year or so before relocating with his only asset, his plane, in search of fresh scenery and new clients.

So here they were with summer upon them and Janice weaving her web, guilting her son into agreeing to let her live with them for the next several months. It had nothing to do with wanting to spend quality time with her son and his family and everything to do with control and manipulation.

Monica tugged on her weeding gloves and vigorously began pulling the little suckers from the sand, thrusting them over her shoulder into the wheelbarrow.

"Janice will be zero help with Kenzie and Beck. Dex will dote on her to no end, I'll get aggravated, and we'll bicker," Monica seethed.

Moments later Dex stuck his head out the screen door. "I'm off to the hardware store, and I'll swing by the butcher's for chicken and charcoal for the grill."

Dex waved at Monica and Gabby, kissed his kids, and disappeared.

"Let me know what I can do to help. I've obviously got some free time on my hands these days since the remodel is complete and I'm, well, living alone. If you ever need a day away or a date night with Dex, I'd be more than happy to babysit."

"Ha! Thanks, I was thinking more along the lines of occupying one of your spare rooms this summer."

Gabby laughed reassuringly. "That's always a possibility."

Monica's fingers rubbed her weary head. "Listen to me. I sound like an ungrateful witch. I'm in a funk." She adjusted her tank top straps, feeling overheated from her outburst. Please accept my apology for my petty rant. As if Janice moving in for the summer is the end of the world . . ."

Gabby held up her hand. "Your feelings are far from petty, and sometimes a sounding board to get life off your chest is the best remedy. I adore my mother-in-law, and yet, months together under one roof would be familial doom."

"So, enough about me." Monica's forehead crinkled with concern. "Have you talked with Greg?"

"A bit. Mostly through texts, squaring away the last of the remodel punch list and settling a few concerns over the kids' apartments at school. I'm doing my best to ignore his countless pleas to work *things* out."

"Things, ha! That's a good one. What did you say to that?"

"Nothing," Gabby said grimly.

"Sorry, that was wrong of me to ask. It's private. I can be so nosy and inconsiderate."

"You're not nosy. You're a concerned friend, and I should be honest with you. All pride aside, I should be confiding in someone." Gabby's eyes shifted around the beach, making sure no one was in ear shot. "What I meant is Greg is pleading with me to keep it a secret and I'm not responding to his insistent texts to meet and talk."

"Wait. I thought you'd told some of your family about Greg's affair?"

Gabby's lower lip quivered. "My parents, brother, and sister were planning a visit to see the new house, so obviously I've told them why he's not living at home. However, no one knows"—Gabby paused and sucked in a breath—"the entire truth."

Monica's eyebrows raised in question. "The entire truth?"

"The woman, Holly is her name"—Gabby swallowed—"is pregnant."

Monica's mouth fell open in shock. "Get out of town!"

"I'd love to."

"Let me get this straight. Greg's mistress is pregnant, and he's trying to persuade you to keep it a secret?"

Gabby closed her eyes and slowly nodded.

"Holy Moses." Monica's face looked muddled. "Please tell me you're not seriously considering something so ludicrous?"

A piercing scream interrupted their conversation. Thankfully, Kenzie and Beck were safe, still entertaining each other in the confined area of the deck.

The scream came from two doors down, followed by a slew of obscenities. Monica and Gabby both jolted as a flowerpot descended from a second-story balcony, shattering its contents of dirt and gerbera daisies below.

"I hate you!" screamed the teenage girl after forcefully hurling the flowerpot. She then disappeared inside only to reappear seconds later, running out the ground-level door to the dock. She fired up the Wave Runner and sped away, the backend crashing into the floating trampoline as she sliced through the water.

"Get back here, Penelope," Carmen shouted as she ran out behind her daughter, but it was no use. Penelope was halfway around the lake.

CHAPTER 3

Some people are like storm clouds.
When they disappear, it's a beautiful day.

Carmen

"Well now, what a delightful way to start a sunny Saturday morning, and an even lovelier way to greet your neighbors. How are you, ladies?"

Carmen approached, beaming a bright white smile flanked by two generous dimples. Her long latte-colored hair was piled high on her head in a messy bun showing off streaks of caramel highlights. Her unmade-up skin was flawless, green eyes sparkling despite the debacle with her unruly daughter.

Monica and Gabby both greeted Carmen with a nervous laugh, offering to help her pick up the shattered flower pot.

"Thank you, but Penelope will most definitely be picking that up herself. I would apologize for her behavior, but to be quite honest, I'm over that. What you see is what you get. Penelope is a top-notch, entitled, unruly, disrespectful"—Carmen bit her lip and considered calling her daughter what was on the tip of her tongue and then thought better of it—"teenager."

Carmen exhaled loudly. "Despite all of that, I do love her. Really, I do. An abundance of love is flowing from me right now, yes, overflowing like Theresa's exquisite little bubble fountain, reeking of peace and love."

Carmen motioned with her hand to the statue a few houses down of a naked woman, her hair flowing over her shoulders and covering the nipples of her breasts, hands opened, her gaze turned toward the sun. Water sprayed and danced around the statue, creating a desire to stare at the stone woman and decipher who she was, as if once she had been a living, breathing creature, and this was now her afterlife.

While Carmen peered down the beach towards the fountain, Gabby and Monica looked to one another, eyes pleading for the other to speak.

21

Monica stepped forward. "I'm sure she just needs to calm down and get her aggression out. I see these outbursts all the time with my high school students. Teenagers are quick to overreact and be dramatic. An hour later, they're laughing and carrying on with their friends as if nothing ever happened."

No sooner had Monica finished speaking than the Wave Runner came careening around the bend, doing at least fifty mph, barely missing several docks, a mother duck, and her ducklings. Carmen locked eyes with her daughter and motioned for her to come in. Penelope whizzed past, wearing a sardonic smirk of defiance and yelled, "Make me."

"Whoa." Gabby gasped and covered her open mouth with her hand.

"Ouch." Monica cringed, fumbling for the right words again. "Teenagers, um"—her eyes darted to the spray behind the Wave Runner and back—"they mostly want to be heard and, well, understood." She nodded vigorously. "They often have unique ways of expressing their aggression."

"Well then, let's hope her unique expressions don't land her into a fishing boat, killing someone before her hour of aggression is up." Carmen rolled her eyes. "I'd hate for her actions to be misunderstood, because I'm not about to make up excuses for them."

Exasperated, Carmen covered her face with her hands and rubbed at her temples, her glow fading with the sun behind a cloud. Once again, Monica and Gabby eyed each other ineptly, willing the other to speak.

Fortunately, Carmen wasn't waiting for sympathetic bullshit. She threw her arms up in the air and turned towards Monica and Gabby. "I give up. I give up. I'm really, really, r-e-a-l-l-y giving up this time!

"Penelope will be the death of me. A mother can only take so much before she snaps and kicks her daughter out on the streets. She says I'm controlling, smothering, judgmental towards her friends, critical of her decisions, and unsupportive of her dreams.

"Funny, last I knew her dreams only occurred between the hours of two a.m. and noon and consisted of nothing more than new ways we could cater to her already posh lifestyle by swelling her wardrobe, filling the gas tank in the car we *gifted* her, handing out hefty sums of allowance for chores that weren't completed, and paying absurd amounts of money for private water polo lessons that she's decided to abandon.

"Oh, I almost forgot about the new iPhone we spent triple than our normal birthday allowance on, all so she could document every minute of her entitled life on social media."

Carmen flung a hunk of sand toward the water with her toes. The granules hit the water, a dozen tiny pebbles all making their own rings. All three women watched the ripples crash together, momentarily mesmerized by the sloshy mess.

"Penelope is also convinced I favor Amelia because I spend more time with her. Yet every time I ask Penelope to go to the mall, or catch a movie, or gasp"—Carmen's hand flew to her mouth—"have a conversation, she acts like I'm the evil villain in her enchanted life.

"Apparently, I've ruined her relationship with her father as well because he's barely home these days. Supposedly, I've driven him to become a workaholic who travels to escape the rotten wife and mother I am. Do you know where this accusation came from?"

Monica and Gabby vigorously shook their heads in unison.

"Because the service light in her car came on, warning her that she needed an oil change. Victor was out of town on business; therefore he couldn't change it for her immediately. Somehow that is my fault."

Carmen held up her hand and apologized for carrying on, but then started in again. "I'm also to blame that her boyfriend is on the brink of dumping her because I wouldn't allow her to break curfew rules and come home at 2:30 in the morning. Can you believe the audacity in even asking to stay out that late?"

Gabby's and Monica's faces scrunched in sympathy.

"Landon didn't want to leave the party they were at to bring her home. Obviously, he's *deeply* in love. So, Penelope hitched a ride with some other kid. Now word is spreading that she had sex in the backseat of this guy's car. The girl that likes this guy is mad and spreading nasty rumors about Penelope, and suddenly, at least five other girls are mad at her because, well, that's what teenage girls do: gang up and hate on each other for the sole sake of ostracizing . . . blah, blah, blah.

"All. My. Fault."

Carmen whistled and realized both Gabby and Monica had backed up a few feet. "Wow, that's an awful lot to digest. Sorry, ladies. I mean I hardly know either of you, and I'm spewing all this personal stuff, making it really awkward for both of you. Not my intention. Honestly.

"I realize I should be in therapy so I don't unload my family drama on the neighbors, but quite honestly, I don't need a therapist nodding at me and telling me they understand how I feel, feeding me complex lines about why my daughter is belligerent."

"Really though, wouldn't it all come back around to the fact that she wasn't given enough praise, or too much praise? As a working mother, I wasn't present enough, or the guilt of working persuaded me to give her too much attention.

"Possibly, I coddle too much, or maybe I'm too lax and expect her to be more independent than she's capable of. Yes, maybe I should still be folding her laundry, you know, to show I care, but then of course, I'd be stealing her independence."

Carmen folded her arms in front of her chest then lifted her pointer finger to her lips in thought. "I often wonder if being glued to her side every minute I wasn't working was too much, because I did volunteer to run centers in the third grade, never missing a class party in elementary. Yep, that's it, smother mother. In some way or another, I'm mothering her in a way that causes her to rebel and lash out. In one way or another, I gave too much of this, not enough of that."

Again, not waiting for comment, Carmen kept talking faster, her hands with a language all their own. "I could sit in a cozy, peaceful room and divulge every rotten thing that ever happened to me. I could acknowledge that I'm angry and resentful for my upbringing; therefore I overcompensate in countless ways, giving my daughter entitlement and authority to manipulate and reign over me. I'm an enabler, possibly a martyr. I deny nothing."

Carmen gave a lopsided grin. "I resent that by the way."

Dread washed over Carmen as she remembered Gabriella Bock was a therapist, some sort of wellness coach too. She had seen Gabby coaching Monica through workouts, and Monica, the chatty neighbor she was, had mentioned she owed her sanity to her sessions stretched out on Gabby's couch. Odd.

She slapped her forehead. "Nothing against therapists. I think they serve a fantastic purpose." Carmen briefly brushed her fingertips across Gabby's arm in a weak attempt to soothe.

"In fact, I see many benefits in paying big bucks to buy a friend that you can trust with your deepest thoughts, and that, per privacy laws, they can't disclose your skeletons around your social circle. Really, friends like that don't come without a hefty price tag," she joked, trying to lighten her sour mood.

"Truthfully, I had a session set up, but then I met my best friend Tiffany. Technically, her name is Peyton, and she's this stunning ice-colored handbag: smooth leather, draped in twenty-four karats of rose gold-plated hardware. For a one-time flat fee of two grand, I can tell Tiffany an-y-thing."

Carmen noticed Monica's eyes widen and the corners of Gabby's mouth relax and curl up slightly. Maybe, she hadn't completely offended and freaked these two women out. "Even though Tiffany will tell me I'm the best mother she knows, and she won't tell a soul about my family drama, I know she will spill to Peyton, but I'm okay with that, because I fully trust Tiffany and Peyton. They're just classy like that and technically one person anyway."

With that, an offhand chortle escaped from Monica. Quickly enough, she recovered, placing her hand over her mouth. Carmen picked up on the subtle look of surprise flashing across Gabby's face, and a hint of shame tugged at Carmen. She was flat out insulting Gabby, not intentionally, but still.

Gabriella Bock, out of all women, could see right through her—that she'd built up walls, or rather skyscrapers, to block out women like the two standing before her.

"Tiffany/Peyton, she really goes by either name, has never once let me down, never once gossiped or stabbed me in the back. And did I mention how much baggage she allows me to dump in her? Wow, even when I think she's full, that I can't unload more, bam, I unzip another pocket and dump the contents of my disgruntled life!"

Monica snorted and mouthed *say something* to Gabby as Carmen's glare blazed over the water towards Penelope. Gabby shook her head, dismissing any need for a response.

Carmen was sassy. A spitfire. Her mere existence rendered one to be intrigued with her every utterance. She had this throaty, yet velvety, Columbian voice and talked faster than one could comprehend.

Something mysterious about her sucked you into her aura. Somehow, she revealed this frankness about her personal life without seeking sympathy. Normally, her frankness came in the carefree way she lived. She didn't hide the outbursts of her children, nor make excuses or act as if they were the perfect charmed family, assuring other mothers how sweet her children were and how her kids always made the best choices. No. She told it as it was.

Despite leaving you feeling slightly shell-shocked, Carmen left you captivated, eager to not only be accepting, but a part of her dysfunctional world. The way she shared her misfortune left no room for pity or glee. One could only be *intrigued* by Carmen.

Carmen paused to take a breath and wipe the perspiration on her upper lip. She hadn't shared an ounce of personal information with these women in the decade she'd lived on the lake. She cursed her Columbian blood that had ruled her tongue, stealing her filter.

This rarely happened. She had to get a grip.

Maybe she did need more friends than Tiffany. No. Perish the ridiculous thought! Every time Carmen questioned that logic, she reminded herself how loyal and trustworthy Tiffany was. Gorgeous too.

The friend that complements your own beauty instead of overshadowing it, that's a true friend.

Vulnerability is a sneaky character flaw. It sinks its claws into you when you're weak and defeated, causing you to go against your cardinal rules, and for Carmen, that was disclosing her private life and befriending women. Female friendships didn't take residence in her life.

Women were exhausting, complex. They talked and felt too much. If Carmen were to have girlfriends, she'd have to listen to their sagas, give support, and act concerned. In turn, those nosy girlfriends would weasel their way into her personal vault as well. No, thank you.

They would take any private information and use it as ammunition to get their foot in the crowd of the "Who's who" in their town's society, upping their social status in the floozy club. Ultimately, isn't that why people gossip? Trash-talk to get a foot in the door to the adult sorority house? It's the connection that forms superficial friendships, the decrypting bond between women.

No, Carmen had no need for women who existed merely to meet at trendy restaurants in their small town, wear their most expensive labels, compliment each other on said outfit, all the while judging their friends' weight, hair, jewelry, children, houses, cars, and vacation destinations during the girls' night out of bonding. Puke.

Men. Men were far easier to befriend. Carmen spent her days surrounded by men. Talk was real. Their discussions accomplished actual matters, important issues. When Carmen met up with her employees after work for drinks, it was fun, not fake. They'd shoot the shit and then leave it right there at the bar, never to be passed around like the sinful tray of cookies women refrained from in public only to leave and devour privately in their pantry.

She didn't order the skinny martini because all the women did; she'd order a dry merlot when she was stressed, a dirty martini when she was on a high note, and a cold Stella when she simply felt like a beer after a long day.

Realizing she had fled the house scantily dressed in a tank and too-short shorts for the public eye, Carmen adjusted her wardrobe in a sad attempt to cover more skin.

Several neighbors had nonchalantly made their way outside to water flowers, sweep sand from patios, and take covers off boats. Carmen was fully aware it had everything to do with the ruckus between her and her daughter. The shattering ceramic, profanity, and scene that followed drew them out in search of a better view, to be within earshot of the performance.

Comical. If Carmen and Penelope had been outside playing Frisbee, laughing loudly, no one would have given a second glance. No story.

Carmen shielded her eyes from the sun and focused on Penelope. At least her daughter had stopped speeding recklessly around the lake and had succumbed to floating in the middle. There was a small splash as Penelope dove off the back of the Wave Runner. She came up and floated on her back, her T-shirt and shorts billowing out around her.

Carmen was hoping there was an ounce of truth to Monica's theory and Penelope would find the stillness of the water calming and come back apologizing for her behavior. Wishful thinking, she knew. Penelope had become a master rebel.

"I suppose it's best I duck back inside before I humiliate myself further." Carmen held up her hands as she started to back away, a weak smile on her face. "Please excuse me, ladies, while I go collect myself. I do apologize for any unintentional offenses. Lord knows we could tick off several."

Monica held up her hand. "No biggie, I've done my fair share this morning."

"Full moon." Gabby smiled.

Carmen hadn't taken more than two steps when Amelia came running towards her mother in tears. She had Carmen's cell phone in her hand, arm outstretched.

"I told Dad you were outside and you'd call him back, but he said it's urgent and he has to talk to you *now*." A sob escaped Amelia as she sprinted across the neighbors' beaches. "He's been arrested, Mom! Dad is in a Las Vegas jail!"

CHAPTER 4

Happiness is letting go of what you think your life is supposed to look like and embracing it for what it is.

Gabriella

Admittedly, albeit only to *herself*, Gabby ignored her gut. When Greg had coerced his way into their group at The Pit, charming everyone with his quick wit and one-liners, Gabby couldn't reject her immediate physical attraction. It had been undeniably intense, every millimeter of her body tingling, setting off waves of lust.

He had approached Mark, a guy in their group whom Gabby vaguely knew and, as it turned out, Greg vaguely knew, with a boisterous high-five and struck up an instant conversation, one of those conversations that led Mark to believe Greg was sincerely interested in being buddies rather than simply a means to Gabby. Gabby could see the situation for what it was. Greg's eyes lingered on her as he spoke to Mark, asking questions about some film class he had zero interest in.

When her drink was half empty, he placed another in her hand. And another. And another. Abandoning all rational judgment, Gabby filled with desire. Every millimeter of her body lusted for him, and vainly, Greg knew it.

"Damn, he's got it bad for you," Trisha had yelled in Gabby's ear over the roar of the crammed bar.

Yes, he does. Gabby glowed and willingly reciprocated the flirtatious touching, throwing her head back in laughter at his impersonation of a shared professor who resembled Marj Simpson.

When her sorority sisters called it a night, Gabby was reluctant to leave, nearly succumbing to Greg's pleading for a nightcap, a walk on a moonless mild fall night.

It was Sami who'd warned her that Greg was a player, that she'd wake up regretting being so easy, giving it up between the park benches, red maple leaves matted in her hair, dirt caked on her ass. The room was spinning, her heart swooning.

"College girls act blasé."

"Blasé?" Gabby questioned Sami. She was an English major and was always using these fancy words.

"Uninterested."

Gabby leaned into Sami. "Oh but I'm very interested," she slurred, "very, very interested."

She ditched her friends.

It was a full month before she'd crossed paths with Greg again. During those weeks, she'd accepted the truth. Sami was right. Greg had sought his way into her group and bought her drinks only to have sex with her that night.

~*~

Twenty-three years of marriage later . . . four children, a couple of dogs, one cat, numerous goldfish, family illnesses, the loss of close friends in an automobile accident, survival of the teenage years, sports injuries, social media sagas, failing grades, one suspension, and countless other issues that went along with raising children were followed by needy aging parents and most recently rebuilding a house.

Gabby and Greg had made it through many ups and downs in their marriage, always managing to come out stronger. They had it good. They were healthy, and they laughed, talked, dreamed, and loved—that alone defined a great marriage. Right?

Gabby could barely comprehend the news herself and couldn't fathom broadcasting that her husband had had an affair and had gotten his mistress pregnant. But keep it as a lifelong secret? What audacity. All for what? To protect their children? Save Greg's career? Holly's career? To preserve an image in their small town?

The clock was ticking. Holly was already something like twenty-two weeks along. The baby due in September, her husband would be a father to a fifth child. Technically, he already was.

Keeping herself insanely busy had been Gabby's coping mechanism. She scheduled clients back to back without taking a break, and after work, she'd hang pictures, decorate, rearrange, anything she could to completely wear herself out until the wee hours of the morning. It worked well enough, sleeping at least four or five hours before waking up to the nightmare her life had become.

When her tears woke her, she'd spend the rest of her waking hours obsessing over the last few months of their lives and looking for signs of her husband's infidelity, upset with herself for not seeing it coming.

Aggressively scrubbing floors, wiping every speck of dust from the baseboards, she scoured her mind of the past year of their lives, looking for clues as to how Greg smelled, whether they had been less intimate. Had he been working longer hours? Was he dressing differently, wearing new cologne? Where had his thoughts been as they were designing the built-in bunk beds for their future grandchildren?

Was he thinking of Holly every time they'd had sex over the last six months? How often had they slept together? Had he slept with Holly after proposing their renewal in Turks? Possibly he was with her the day before they left, the day after they returned.

What had Gabby been doing while Greg was in an ultrasound room, counting his daughters ten fingers and toes, verifying that her heart had all four chambers?

Was Holly on Greg's mind the morning Gabby slid the aqua paint swatch for the shutters and front door across the breakfast table to Greg, asking his opinion? He admitted he found the color hideous. "However," he mused over their lazy, Saturday morning cinnamon French toast, "you have impeccable taste, so I fully trust your selections."

Did his comment have meaning from the heart? Or was he so profoundly lost in Holly that he could easily detach himself from the concerns of their mundane, lackluster life. He had literally agreed to everything Gabby ran past him.

He loved the backsplash, thought the wainscoting gave *character* to the dining room, had never felt plusher, softer carpet, and agreed layering different textures and colors gave the house depth. It now infuriated Gabby how he complied with every little detail, most likely because he didn't want to ruffle any feathers.

As hard as she tried not to, she kept questioning herself. What had she done, or not done, to deserve his unfaithfulness? Was she too wrapped up in her own career, so consumed with helping others overcome their quandaries that she was blind to her own? Too exhausted and drained from her clients to put in the required effort in her own marriage?

Possibly she showed more interest in getting the boys settled in their freshman dorms and the girls situated with their roommates in their new house. She was driving halfway across the state, meeting the kids for lunch instead of her husband.

Over the past few years, she had slowly reclaimed her interests. She joined a book club, never missed Bunko, met up with girlfriends often, swam laps on the inland lake they lived on, and planted the organic garden she had always dreamed of but never had time to care for with four kids in the house.

Despite it all, Gabby knew it wasn't she who had been selfish. She'd been a counselor far too long and had advised countless couples stricken by infidelity. Infidelity was no one's fault but the unfaithful. It's a deliberate choice. Regardless, her mind wandered into dangerous territory. She was fully aware her husband could be rather smug, not the worst thing in the world, and she knew how to respond to it.

Gabby was filled with such rage that she shook with fury, as she ticked off on her fingers a slew of her present feelings. Resentment, bitterness, and anger currently topped the list. Tomorrow would warrant a new inventory.

She finished scrupulously arranging and rearranging the kitchen drawers and cupboards until they were Houzz Magazine material. Next, she took her time steaming her clothes before hanging them in a closet she now couldn't fill on her own. She supposed that was next on her agenda: go splurge on a ridiculously expensive summer wardrobe to fill up Greg's empty bars and shelves.

The house was eerily quiet and annoyingly clean without a streak or fingerprint on the windows, not a pillow out of place, nor a dish in the sink. Over the past couple of years, she had gotten used to no longer tripping on backpacks, finding dirty socks on the sofa, and constantly reminding the kids that the kitchen was neither an acceptable place to play sports, nor store sporting equipment. However, order like this was suffocating.

Now, she was alone with the neatness, peace, and quiet she had longed for at times while her life seemed to pass by in a blur. Tears sprang to her eyes. She longed for Greg's dirty travel mug with three inches of cold milky coffee to be waiting for her in the sink. At the same time, she cursed the thought and tossed the Yeti she'd had personalized for him in the trash.

She wondered how long it would take before the habit of keeping a six pack of Founders on hand would fade. How many times would she begin to prepare dinner for two before she realized Greg wouldn't be walking through the door, kissing her lips while giving her rear a gentle squeeze? He'd done that every night he'd walked in the door their entire marriage. Even during his affair, she realized, he came home and grabbed her butt. At least he was faithful in routine gestures.

Ding!

> Gabby??? Please respond to my texts. I don't want to show up
> unannounced.

Don't you dare. With her cell in her hand, Gabby ran to the front door and locked the deadbolt while peering out the side window panes. Greg had a key, but Gabby was certain he wouldn't barge in. He wasn't that disrespectful. Oh wait. He was.

Respect. What a mockery. They'd always followed the love and respect model in their marriage. The two were one. With love comes respect and with respect you felt loved. It was the same model she presented to her clients.

Countless clients Gabby had counseled with failing marriages, and she hadn't the slightest idea how she was going to get through her own hot mess.

Taking the steps two at a time, Gabby glanced through the upstairs windows for a bird's eye view of the property. It appeared Greg wasn't hiding in the bushes. Luckily, the new landscape wasn't mature enough to conceal a creeper. The thought made her snicker. There was satisfaction in knowing Greg was squirming. Gabby knew she was on a passive power trip.

> Gabby, c'mon. People are going to start asking what's going on. We
> need to communicate. We need to be on the same page.

This was true. The boat had been docked and covered, unused in this beautiful weather. Greg hadn't been out working in the yard, cutting the grass. She had hired a friend of Calvin and Klay's to mow the lawn, and she'd been either hiding inside or out shopping for accessories to avoid the neighbors. It was only a matter of time before they would be asking where Greg was.

Gabby started a text agreeing to meet Greg at the coffee shop or a park then deleted it, knowing such a public place was a bad idea for many reasons. She'd cry, they might yell, and someone might overhear. They lived in a small town. Rarely did Gabby walk the town square without bumping into someone she knew.

It was probably best that he came over. They would have no barriers to their conversation, and they could satisfy any curiosity the neighbors might have with his car in the driveway.

> You can swing by in an hour.

In the meantime, she needed to prepare her head and find something productive to do. She decided to wipe the layer of yellowish green pollen that had settled on the six rocking chairs.

Even the presence of the six empty rocking chairs seemed to poke fun at her.

Her life had revolved around doing everything to accommodate a large family. Sure, the kids were off at college, but they weren't far, and one or all showed up often enough. Even with everyone scattered, her family unit hadn't felt split or broken until Greg had cheated. His absence would ultimately divide their family.

The front porch wrapped around to the back. Gabby wiped away the grimy reminder of spring blossoms as she went. Her favorite additions were the two large porch swings that hung on either end, making it possible to view both the meticulous flower beds Gabby planted in the front yard, as well as the lake sprawled out behind the house, while swaying on the swing.

A few pats to the cushion sent her into a sneezing fit as a cloud of pollen engulfed her. Gabby realized she had yet to sit in the swing and figured now was the perfect time. She gave herself a small shove, raised her feet in front of her, and closed her eyes.

Boats were racing around the lake. Distant screeches of laughter filled the air as kids were flipped off tubes, skimming across the water's surface like skipping rocks. Small waves were lapping to shore. Sprinklers were spraying. Birds were chirping. Speakers played different beats. Life was ticking along all around her as Gabby felt hers had come to a halt.

When the car pulled up and the engine died, Gabby squeezed her eyes tighter. It hadn't been fifteen minutes since she'd texted Greg. If it were a lake neighbor driving by, stopping at the sight of her in hopes of a tour, she didn't want to explain why Greg's clothes weren't in the closet.

A car door slammed. "Mom, wake up or, better yet, open your eyes. We both know you can't take a nap to save your life."

Stella, with her raspy little voice that failed to match her appearance or personality, stood in front of Gabby, dressed in a simple gray tank dress and flip-flops. Her curly, white blond hair was piled high on her head, her purse slung diagonally across her chest, resting on her hip along with her heavily braceleted hand.

Gabby flew out of the swing so fast it flung back and hit the porch rail. She embraced her daughter like she hadn't seen her in years.

"What a surprise! I thought you and Preston were going to Chicago with friends for the weekend?"

"We were. He is. I decided not to." Stella wiped the sweat off her forehead with the back of her hand. "It's been a long drive. I need to use the bathroom before I leave a puddle on the porch."

34

Stella pushed past Gabby and disappeared inside the front door. Wonderful, thought Gabby. She and Preston must have had a fight, or they broke up and he took off to Chicago without her. Were they all doomed for heartbreak?

Gabby went inside and searched the fridge for Stella's favorite raspberry lemonade and the pantry for her much-loved trail mix, but she had neither. She really hadn't much of anything to offer.

Stella returned looking pale and sweaty.

"Sorry, sweetie, since I didn't know you were coming, I have none of your favorites on hand, unless you've suddenly grown fond of beef jerky.

"Ugh, you mean beef junky? That's Klay's favorite, not mine, Mom. Do you have any ginger ale?"

Stella roamed to the living room and plopped down on the couch without even bothering to walk through the house and see the finished product with furniture and decor. Hang over, guy troubles, typical college drama, Gabby supposed.

"I have ginger ale. It's in the outside refrigerator. Are you hungry?" Gabby moved contents around in the fridge. "I've got some fruit, cheese, and crackers?"

Stella had already wandered outside to the patio and was helping herself to a can of the ginger ale. "Crackers, please," she hollered through the open door as she slid into the lounge chair and turned her face toward the sun.

Gabby found her daughter's hangover slightly amusing since she was of legal drinking age. The burden of reprimanding was no longer hers. She had obviously punished herself.

"Want to talk about it?" asked Gabby as she returned with a box of crackers and Alouette cheese spread.

Gabby placed the contents at Stella's feet and plopped down in the lounge chair next to Stella and continued without giving her a chance to respond. "Let me guess. You were out last night, and everyone was drinking, something minuscule happened, like a guy hit on you, and Preston, with the help of some liquid courage"—she air-quoted with her fingers—"got upset and wound up in a bar fight."

"Or, scenario B, you and Claire had a fight, because even though she's a dear friend, she's needy, and she's jealous you're spending more time with Preston than you are her. She misses you and feels rejected."

Gabby caught Stella rolling her eyes, which only fueled Gabby's imagination. They used to play this game all the time when Stella was in high school. Gabby would conjure up wild tales of what had gotten her kids down in the dumps, and eventually they would crack. The easy camaraderie Gabby provided would eventually lead them to pour their hearts out to her.

"Or scenario C is that maybe you were out-of-control drunk, doing shots, dancing provocatively, embarrassing yourself, and when Preston tried to get you to leave the bar, you retaliated. I'm thinking you screamed a bit, and he tried leading you out by the arm, but you didn't want to leave, so you pulled back and his finger scratched you, drawing blood.

"You completely flipped out, screaming that he hurt you and he couldn't force you to leave. You cried and got so worked up you puked. Then the bouncers came and hauled you out."

Gabby noticed a small shake of Stella's head as she assessed her with an ambiguous look, quickly dismissing it because she was on a roll. "This morning you both woke up, argued about last night. You told him to go to Chicago without you, even though you didn't mean it, not one stinking bit"—Gabby waved her finger—"and because he's a guy and takes everything literally, he grabbed his bag and was out the door, without you . . . because you *told* him to."

Gabby paused, waiting for Stella to interrupt, but she remained transfixed on the lake, her expression flat.

"You're reeling because he overreacted last night and to boot, took off to Chicago for the rest of the weekend-with *your* friends. Clearly, he misunderstood that, when you told him to go without you, you actually meant put your arms around me and apologize.

"How close am I?"

Stella tilted her head, forcing out a loving grunt to her mother's analogies. "Will you forever keep doing this? Seriously, you haven't a clue as to how I, or my friends, act when we go out for drinks. We aren't a bunch of underage kids with fake ID's anymore, Mom."

Stella said this mockingly, the annoying tone in her voice from her teenage years gone. Fake ID's? Had Gabby known they had fake ID's? Did Calvin and Klay have fake ID's? Of course they did. How could she be so naïve?

Gabby placed her hand on Stella's forearm and sighed a giggle. "Okay, I'll attempt again. You were trying on your swimsuit to take to Chicago and asked Preston if it made your butt look flabby, and he paused just two seconds too long before saying no. You immediately went on the defense. You overreacted and accused him of inadvertently calling you fat and—"

Stella held up her hand and interrupted her mother. "Seriously, Mom, please stop. You're so ridiculous. Your humor may have done the trick in the past to loosen us up and get us all laughing before we broke down and told you what was wrong because we felt comfortable, loved, safe, and a bunch of other bullshit reverse psychology stuff. But really, Mom, I'm an adult now."

"Ha! Whatever, Stella." Gabby moved from her lounge chair onto Stella's, pushing her over so she could lie down next to her daughter and cuddle her, regardless that Stella was four inches taller than she.

"Shall I start counting down from ten now? I mean you wouldn't show up on my doorstep on Memorial Day weekend while your boyfriend and best friends are in Chicago if something major hadn't happened. By the way, did Lottie go to Chicago?"

"Yep."

"Did you two have a fight? It's not like her to take off with the group if something is upsetting you."

"Lottie and I aren't fighting, other than the usual bickering about her being a slob and not doing her share around the house." Stella pulled her hair tie loose, and her curls spilled over her shoulders. "Lottie's been great about the whole thing. I told her to go to Chicago and have fun. She agreed I needed to come home."

Gabby couldn't deny the slight pang of envy towards the deep bond Stella and Lottie had. She sometimes felt like an outsider. Stella and Lottie were as thick as thieves. They fought fiercely yet loved deeper. Gabby and her sister Mandi were loosely close and rarely quarreled, but never did they finish each other's sentences, share friends, or *choose* to share a bedroom since birth. She and Mandi spoke maybe twice a month, shared different hobbies and interests. So other than being related, there was nothing that brought them together.

Gabby and Mandi would catch up over a hurried phone call or a rushed lunch, have a few laughs, and that was about it. The intimate bond that Stella and Lottie shared was missing between Gabby and her sister, and Gabby took second seat with Stella and Lottie. So, the fact that Gabby had Stella to herself, even for a weekend, swelled her aching heart.

"Are you ready to tell me about this *thing*, the thing that has you needing your mama so badly?" Gabby mused, kissing Stella's bare shoulder, a gesture Gabby had done thousands of times to her girls over the years and feared the day they would push her away.

Stella retrieved her sunglasses from her purse, still slung across her shoulder, and covered her eyes. She inhaled deeply. "If only it were drunken bar scenes and miniscule bickering sagas that brought me here." Stella's voice shook on the verge of tears.

"Stella, honey, what is it?" Gabby tucked a loose strand of white blond hair behind Stella's ear and saw a tear slide down her cheek from behind her sunglasses.

They were smushed together in the chaise lounge. Gabby could feel the heat and dampness of Stella's skin as she reached across her middle and squeezed, pulling Stella closer. Stella flinched and swatted Gabby's arm away from her abdomen.

Stella sat straight up and clutched her belly. "I'm pregnant, Mom. Thirteen weeks pregnant!"

"Hey, Stella, what a surprise," Greg announced as he approached them from behind.

Gabby's heart plunged to her stomach as Stella sprang off the lounge chair.

"I thought you were headed to the city this weekend?"

Stella's eyes shifted to Gabby's, and she gave her daughter a reassuring shake of the head that her dad hadn't overheard.

"Change of plans. So here I am!" Stella said with fake enthusiasm that could easily fool her father. "Be back in a sec," she called over her shoulder as she took the patio steps two at a time up to the house.

Greg turned to Gabby, fear spreading across his face. "Did you know she was coming home?"

Instinctively, Gabby folded her arms across her chest in defense. "No, she only pulled in ten minutes ago, unannounced. And you're early."

"Good, so we'll act as if everything's normal until we can talk and figure this mess out?"

This mess. Not *his* mess. "She hasn't told me how long she's staying. For all I know, she could be spending the night."

Greg shifted awkwardly. "So, I should stay—"

"No, Greg," she interrupted. "You're not staying here, and I'm not playing puppet in your charade."

The French doors from the master bedroom swung open, and Stella barged out to the balcony. "Uh, Dad, why aren't any of your clothes in the closet? Where's *all* your stuff for that matter? Your toothbrush isn't in the holder, and the drawers that were supposed to be yours have mom's clothes in them."

CHAPTER 5

Never sacrifice your peace trying to point out someone's true colors. Lack of character always reveals itself in the end.

Monica

After making sand castles and splashing in the water with Kenzie and Beck for the better part of three hours, Monica was spent. She put them down for a nap and found her way to her beach chair with a tall Tervis of iced tea and a magazine she had no energy to browse through.

She reclined her chair and closed her eyes ticking off the day's accomplishments beginning with her morning workout, grocery shopping, scrubbing the bathrooms, washing the bedding, picking up toys four times over, playing tea time, building blocks, and drawing with sidewalk chalk. Her exhausted state was justified. She could relax.

Gabby's words replayed in her head. She had to stop doing this to herself. If she didn't conquer all the unrealistic expectations, she'd feel like a failure. Being home with the kids was hard. If she wasn't entertaining them, she felt guilty. After hours of entertaining, she often felt resentful that they expected it. Screw all of it. She was going to relish doing absolutely nothing other than enjoying sitting in the sun on a beautiful day.

It felt so good to be outside. Beck had gotten high fevers twice over the winter, sending them to the ER, and Kenzie had gotten the strep throat that had swirled around her preschool. Both kids had gotten croup, which meant sleepless nights spent in the cold garage to open their airways while they struggled to breathe.

Dex had been out of town more than usual, and Monica had crazy cabin fever from being on house arrest all winter. Kenzie had been crying and refusing to go to preschool, knowing her mother was at home instead of work. She would cry at drop off, and sometimes a tantrum would result in Monica having to go pick her up. Being a teacher, Monica was appalled that she had the cringeworthy, disruptive kid.

Finally, they had kicked the winter bugs, and Kenzie had graduated from the Thriving Three's preschool room. Miraculously, she was accepted into the four-year-old's program in the fall. Monica hated to think of the warning in Kenzie's portfolio that followed her.

Regardless, she was ready to frolic on the beach and watch sunsets with Dex. Monica envisioned having the energy to carry on a conversation with her husband for longer than five minutes after putting the kids to bed. She had also drafted her outdoor to-do list. First, she was going to power wash and restain the upper deck. Next, she was going to rip out the old brick walkway and redo it with slate slabs, and organize the garage, possibly attempt to build more shelving.

In the distance, she heard Dex plunging the sponge in the sudsy bucket and the gentle squeak of him rubbing the side of the Master Craft. He couldn't wait for the day he could pull Kenzie and Beck on a wakeboard. He'd had both kids tubing around the lake before their first birthday. Monica had held their little bodies in place while they putted in circles; most of the time it lulled them to sleep.

Monica was trying her hardest not to think about Janice living with them. Whenever she let her mind visit the possibility, she only got angry. Dex was fully aware of her feelings, but he felt trapped, or better yet, like the ping pong ball between his mother and his wife. Whom should he please? Who would be upset with him the most?

One minute, Monica was irate with her mother-in-law, knowing she was taking full advantage of them by moving in for the summer. Her excuses were lame. The truth was she thrived on control and desperately sought to steal Dex's attention from Monica.

Janice was used to her husband and sons doting on her, and since her husband had passed away and one son was continually halfway around the world, this left Dex in the hot seat. Janice couldn't handle being second seat to her son's wife.

Monica would go back and forth, empathizing with Janice one minute and loathing her the next. She badly wanted a mother-in-law that she was close to since her own mother was distant. She had envisioned a mother-in-law who tagged along with them to the park, who initiated puzzles and sat on the floor and played toys with her children. Instead, she was condescending, passive-aggressive, and quality time with her grandchildren meant watching from a distance while her son waited on her.

Janice was constantly correcting the way Monica did things, judging her parenting skills, criticizing her domestic abilities, and reminding her how lucky she was to have such an amazing husband who could put up with all her inadequacies.

When Janice corrected Monica's many shortfalls, she talked down to her, referring to her as Monica Dear.

"Monica Dear, this is how a proper table is set," she'd say as she flipped the knife so the teeth were facing toward the plate.

"Monica Dear, you fold towels vertically before you fold them horizontally. Monica Dear, this meat didn't marinate long enough. Monica Dear, these children will get sick if you don't put warmer clothes on them. Monica Dear, I didn't peg you as a mother who would dress her children in superhero and princess clothing."

Worse was that Dex didn't stick up for his wife. His mother had talked condescendingly to her sons like this growing up, and they just tucked their little tails and did whatever pleased her. Chase obviously retaliated and got out of Dodge. Dex, however, was lured into his mother's trap. Whether it was guilt, loyalty, or manipulation, Monica hadn't yet concluded.

"Ignore her. Smile, nod, and let it go," Dex advised countless times.

Sorry, that was not how Monica was wired. She pictured herself like a fire-breathing dragon, ready to throw her head back and spit flames. The thought of spending her days with Janice, always her shadow, while Dex escaped to work was enough to drive Monica mad.

Self-talk 101: I love my husband, so I will do this for him. I will extend love and hospitality to Janice because she's lonely and needs her family. I will react kindly to her bantering because this is her twisted way of showing she cares. I will not get angry when she challenges my parenting. I will not be offended when she ridicules my cooking, or lack thereof. I will not be annoyed when she reminds me (again) what an amazing husband Dex is and how lucky I am to be his wife.

"What are you mumbling about over there, Mon? You're white-knuckling the chair and working up a sweat." Dex dipped his hand in one of Kenzie's twelve sand pails filled with water and sprinkled a few droplets on Monica's chest.

"I was just getting hot and bothered drooling over your flexing muscles as you scrubbed the boat. In fact, I found it so sexy and alluring that I was thinking you could start washing the windows next. Do you have any idea how much it would arouse me to watch you wash windows? Wow, hot, like *really* hot!"

Dex flashed one deep dimple in his left cheek with his grin. He was boyishly cute, with a grin that spread clear across his face when he smiled, showing off an entire mouth of straight white teeth. His smile lit up a room, it was so contagious. Almost always a giggle followed, which wasn't what you expected from a six-foot six-inch beast of a man.

"Sure, but you need to come inside and show me where you store the window cleaner. It's somewhere in the bedroom, right?"

Monica pulled her sunglasses down to the tip of her nose and furrowed her brows. "That's seriously the sexiest line you could come up with?"

Dex sucked in his stomach and flexed his pectorals. "Yes, unless I simply ask you to go inside and get naked with me, that is the best I could come up with."

Monica shoved her glasses back up, snorted, and kicked sand at him.

"So . . . that's a maybe?" he asked.

"Now, Dex? Really? Can't I ever get a break from entertaining and serving everyone's needs in this family? I just got the kids down for a nap."

"Well, you're the one strutting out here in a bikini, plopping down in front of me, twirling your toe in the sand, and giving me that *look* while I was innocently trying to wash the boat."

Dex dribbled a few more drops of water on her chest and watched it run between her breasts.

"Ha! No such thing! I was purposely avoiding any, and all, eye contact with you for this very reason."

Dex plopped down in the sand next to Monica and pouted. "Aren't you attracted to me at all anymore?"

"Absolutely, but I like a little foreplay, and by that, I mean you sweeping the mounds of sand off the deck or clearing a walking path through the toys in the living room, or scraping the sticky, snotty goop off the glass doors. If you really want to make me go wild, you can prepare the kids' lunch and put them down for a nap, without being told, because you actually looked at the clock and knew it was time to feed them and get them down without any prompting from me."

Dex put his index finger over Monica's lips and shushed her. "Mon, you're killing the mood."

"Darn, not my intention. At all!" Monica couldn't help it: a snicker slipped out. She and Dex could go on and on with this silly banter. Their flirtatious bicker of sorts.

He grabbed the bottle of spray oil tucked in the side pocket of her beach chair and began spraying it on her legs, massaging her calves. Monica moaned in pain. She was so incredibly sore and tight from her workouts that every muscle in her body was seized up in knots.

"That's my girl. Relax and let your lumberjack work his magic," Dex purred teasingly. Monica had always told Dex he reminded her of a lumberjack because he was big and burly and he always cut wood for the fire pit with a handsaw the old-fashioned way. He misinterpreted this to mean she found lumberjacks sexy. She didn't, but she hadn't the heart to tell him otherwise. At this point, it was merely comical.

Monica gripped the arms of her chair in agony. She had been meaning to make a massage appointment to get a few knots worked out but hadn't gotten around to it. She sucked in her breath and flexed at the ankle.

Dex interpreted her anguished breathing as a pleasurable response and massaged deeper into the tissue until Monica's leg involuntarily jerked in pain, clocking him with her heel square in the nose.

"Holy mother of sand!" Dex screamed, accustomed to his kid-friendly version of swearing. Blood seeped between Dex's fingers as he cupped his nose.

"So sorry, so, so sorry, my love." Monica shoved her beach towel in Dex's face and pinched, trying to stop the bleeding. She littered his forehead with kisses and patted the back of his head.

"You broke my nose!"

"It's not broken, Dex. Don't overreact. Lumberjacks are strong, strong men." Although, Monica was ninety-nine percent sure the crunch she heard and felt on her heel was his nose breaking. She pulled him up and guided him inside to the kitchen sink. When she removed the blood-soaked towel, she gasped at the sight of the crooked, puffy spectacle of a nose.

His hand went up to touch it, and she knocked it out of the way. "Don't touch it, really. I think . . . Well, it's fragile. I mean . . . It may *possibly* be broken." She cringed.

"I can't believe you broke my nose. Seriously, I was only trying to show you some affection, and you hauled off and kicked me in the face. Who does that, Mon? Really, who does that?"

Monica couldn't help it; this strange trill escaped her. It was funny.

"Now you're laughing! You are so twisted!"

Dex turned and grabbed his key fob from the counter. "I'm going to the ER . . . and then the bar."

"No, no, no, Dex, please come back." Monica grabbed him by the arm and spun him toward her and buried her head in his bare chest. He smelled delicious, like her homemade sunscreen infused with citrus and coconut, almond and pineapple, mixed with boat cleaner, and wait. Was that chocolate she smelled? Had he eaten the last cake pop. She'd hidden it behind the tomato juice. "I didn't mean to laugh, not exactly. It's just that you hit a sore spot, and I didn't mean for my leg to flinch."

"Flinch? That was hardly a flinch. You hauled off and kicked me, Mon, hard!"

It was Monica's turn to put her finger over Dex's lips and shush him. "You're going to wake up the kids."

"Heaven forbid if you can't go back to your chair and relax while I'm off getting my nose reset or re-broken or whatever they'll do to fix my deformity."

Monica massaged Dex's upper arms and shoulders, digging her fingertips in his muscles while she looked up into his eyes. "Let's slow down, get a glass of water, some ibuprofen, an ice pack, and I'll drive you once the kids wake up."

"Ya, let's bring the kids and make it an official circus show."

"Okay, calm down. I'll see if Gabby can come over for a bit. First, we both need to change out of our swimsuits."

In one quick motion, Monica pulled the strings on the back of her bikini top and let it fall to the kitchen floor. Her hands immediately slid to the sides of Dex's swim trunks. She shimmied them from side to side until they fell to his ankles.

Still holding the towel over his nose, Dex's eyebrows perked up. She wiggled her way out of her bikini bottom and grabbed on to him. He growled at her in an ill attempt to sound irritated. Up on her tippy toes, she gave him tiny kisses on his neck and shoulders.

"Sympathy sex? It's not going to work, Monica. I'm hurt, physically and emotionally wounded."

She continued to caress and kiss him. "That's not what your body is telling me. It's begging for an up-against-the-counter escapade." Monica persisted, knowing all too well Dex was weak, that in a matter of twenty minutes she'd have him taken care of, they'd be dressed, a sitter arranged, and they'd be pulling out of the driveway.

Heck, this trip to the ER was a great excuse to extend a sitter and go out for a dinner date. Monica began thinking of a romantic evening away. She'd been craving sushi and a pitcher of sangria at Rockwell Republic. Yep, the enchantress and tarantula rolls were a definite. Although, last time Dex's scallops were amazing, and she'd been wanting to try the bulgogi tacos. Wait. Whoa. Focus. Dex is hurt. Seriously, reel it in. Thinking of a dinner date is out of the question. Although she could overmedicate Dex, put him in bed, and go out by herself.

Neither Dex nor Monica heard a car door slam, or a rapping at the door, nor did they hear Janice let herself in and dump her handbag on the couch and make her way into the kitchen . . . until she gasped and screamed in horror and disgust at the sight of her son and daughter-in-law stark naked, in the kitchen, Dex with a mangled nose and a fallen bloody towel next to them on the floor.

CHAPTER 6

It's easier to shape healthy children than it is to repair broken adults.

Carmen

Thank goodness Amelia had heard her father wrong. Victor was not behind bars. However, his business partner Ben was being held in custody by security at the Bellagio.

Victor was calling to let Carmen know that Ben had gotten into a bit of a brawl at the roulette table. In lieu of the scuffle, Victor had been tied up smoothing things over with security, and they'd missed their 6:00 a.m. flight home. He'd only told Amelia that Ben was in jail so she'd take him seriously when he said he needed to talk to Carmen immediately.

Carmen tried hard not to be annoyed. It wasn't Victor's fault Ben's bout caused them to miss their flight. It was just that Victor had been traveling more and more for the past few months out west to Nevada, leaving Carmen home to deal with Penelope's increasing drama and rebellious behavior and be sole chauffeur to Amelia's demanding schedule.

They used to be a team, but lately Carmen felt like she was sailing the ship alone and she was sinking. Victor had left real estate and, always an excellent golfer, started giving private golf lessons. He was booked solid April through October. However, when the snow began to fall, so did his clientele. Victor was bored out of his mind with only a handful of indoor lessons for months on end and took a job as a sales rep for Callaway. He traveled to conventions from the big PGA show in Orlando to clear across the country in Seattle.

A few months ago, he was at a convention in Las Vegas and gave lessons to a few prominent businessmen who asked him to fly out each week for lessons. Victor was over the moon excited. They paid his airfare, hotel, and expenses and thought nothing of Victor's hourly fee that he had doubled. He flew out every Tuesday morning, gave lessons Tuesday, Wednesday, and Thursday, and crawled in bed with Carmen just before midnight every Thursday evening. The schedule took some getting used to, but they had adjusted well and found their new rhythm.

Victor had returned from a trip, elated, explaining he had gotten an offer to give lessons to a rising .com company and wanted to resign from Callaway. He would only be staying in Vegas one extra night, arriving in Grand Rapids by 6:00 p.m. every Friday. Carmen had many apprehensions—it was risky, she wanted him home—but this was a dream come true for Victor, and who knew how long it would last. He could easily go back to sales. She'd never seen her husband happier and wasn't going to snub this opportunity.

Victor's business was booming, but their family unit was crashing, and Carmen felt defeated. She worked fifty-hour weeks herself. Her evenings were spent on the sideline, watching Amelia play field hockey or taxiing her to and from dance. When she was home, she was harping on Penelope about her sliding grades or arguing with her for breaking curfew or ignoring her chore list.

Amelia was struggling in school and required help from Carmen; most nights their heads were still hung over the books at eleven o'clock.

Carmen stood in the laundry room, folding five wrinkled loads from days ago, on the verge of a breakdown. She couldn't keep up the lifestyle anymore and pondered whether to hire someone to come in and help with chores. No! Her inner voice barked. Penelope and Amelia are perfectly capable of folding their own laundry. Carmen plucked her clothes out of the mound, leaving everyone else to fold their own clothes.

Maybe she should consider stepping down from the *Women At Risk* board she served on. No, her conscience responded. She was passionate about it. Possibly they could take a hiatus from volunteering at the *Kids' Food Basket*. No. Carmen knew the best way to overcome your own adversities was to help relieve other hardships, and she was adamant about passing this trait onto her children.

She could try and wiggle her way off the lake association board. However, she'd agreed to two years and never backed out of her commitments. Besides, she only had six months to go.

Yoga. Carmen finally made it back to yoga after a two-year hiatus. She had religiously been going three times each week. It would be the easiest thing to give up, but it was the one thing Carmen did for herself, for her sanity. Yoga couldn't go.

"Mom. Mom. MOM!" Amelia finally shouted, breaking Carmen's trance. "Why are you staring at Penelope? You know she's going to go ballistic on you and accuse you of nagging her that she's not raking the beach to your standards."

Carmen guffawed and took a step back from the window overlooking the patio below. "Don't we know her well!"

"I'm just saying . . . back off, save yourself the fight."

Amelia was basically pleading with Carmen. She feared her older sister flying off the handle and making another scene; she'd been very embarrassed after the flower pot launch.

Penelope and Amelia had been like glue when they were little. Penelope doted on Amelia, painting her nails, braiding her hair, holding onto her hand as they walked home from the bus, and as they grew older, Penelope would let Amelia hang out in her room when she had friends over.

Ever since Penelope's one-eighty from good girl to bad girl, she had been awful to her little sister. Penelope called Amelia names, refused to give her a ride to or from school even though it was on her direct route, and took her clothes without asking and inevitably got stains on them or let her friends wear them without returning them.

Last week she purposely ran over Amelia's rollerblades because she left them along the edge of the driveway. Penelope's latest stunt was to snag Amelia's sack lunch from the fridge, even though the brown paper sack was labeled AMELIA with a red Sharpie.

Carmen wrapped her arms around Amelia. "I was actually looking past your sister, thinking about trust and thankfulness. You need them desperately in this world. Trust will protect you from worrying and obsessing. Thankfulness keeps you from complaining and being critical. With that said, I'm focusing on the beauty and calm of the water. I love the way the late afternoon sun sparkles and dances. It reminds me of my summers as a kid on the Atlantic aboard my dad's fishing boat."

"How long do you have to stare at the water to be in a good mood?"

Carmen had always told her girls the secret to changing a sour mood into a sweet outlook was to list things you were grateful for. If breathing was the only thing you could come up with, then so be it. It was something.

"A few hours, I suppose." Carmen squeezed her daughter tight and inhaled the aroma left behind from her conditioner. "I'm sorry if you feel caught in the middle of your sister's erratic behavior."

Amelia shrugged and quickly dismissed the comment. Carmen sensed Amelia had loads of dirt she could divulge about Penelope but wouldn't out of equal parts loyalty and fear. "When's Dad going to be home? Is Dad's client still in hotel jail?"

"He'll be home tomorrow. Your smooth-talking father somehow finessed the police officers, and no assault charges are being pressed. Ben's getting off with a misdemeanor and a hefty fine from the Bellagio."

Amelia was already disinterested. "Will you go kayaking with me, Mom?"

Carmen didn't know if she had the strength; these days she felt perpetually drained. What she really wanted to do was go float on the boat, relax and bronze her winter white skin. However, Carmen couldn't say no to those insistent, loving eyes. She was lucky that Amelia, at thirteen, still *wanted* to hang out with her on the occasion she wasn't either glued to her friends or phone.

"Can we both fit in one? You do the paddling. I sit back and enjoy the ride."

"Ugh, seriously, Mom, it's not that hard. I'll even let you drift in my wake."

Carmen grimaced. "All the way around the lake?" she asked.

"No, Mom, let's go halfway, turn around, and come back."

"Now you're being sarcastic, Mealie," Carmen teased, poking her finger in Amelia's waist, making her giggle.

"Stop calling me Mealie," she said, swatting Carmen's hand, "and change into your swimsuit so we can swim too."

As Carmen pulled her kayak to the water's edge, she tried not to seethe at Penelope's poor attempt at raking the beach. The washed-up seaweed, snails, and weeds growing haphazardly seemed to mock Carmen, begging another fight.

She decided she'd hold her tongue and ask Penelope to take another stab at the beach after she returned from kayaking. Who was she kidding? She needed to build up courage for the backlash. Penelope would surely mouth off, saying she did the best she could. She would accuse Carmen of always nitpicking everything she did.

What Carmen wondered was how she could assertively run a business with a few dozen employees but, when it came to mothering Penelope, she feared confronting her own daughter. Penelope could kick you while you were sleeping and somehow the bruise would be your fault.

"Um, excuse me," a voice called from behind her. "You're wearing my baseball cap, and I'd appreciate it if you would ask first. Puh-lease take it off and put it back."

Carmen hadn't seen Penelope cozied up in the corner of the patio, basking in the sun. The sight of the string bikini she was wearing made Carmen cringe. She had repeatedly told Penelope she was not allowed to purchase anything that skimpy.

As if Penelope could read Carmen's mind, she hastily covered her bikini bottom with her towel, tucking it under her hips with a subtle wince as if it hurt.

Carmen noticed a small quiver in her legs and wondered if Penelope popped pills. Codeine, OxyContin, Methadone, Fentanyl, Adderall, Xanax, the list was endless. Kids could get their hands on anything these days. Maybe that's why her behavior was so erratic. Should she be stocking home drug tests?

Carmen's hand went to the bill of the hat. "This hat that I bought for you has been sitting in the mudroom closet for months, Penelope. I'm sure you won't miss it for one more hour." Carmen could see the detestation in Penelope's eyes and wondered where her jovial, fun-loving daughter had gone. More so, she wondered if she would ever return.

"It's a phase," Joel, her employee had said one day after he had overheard a phone conversation between Carmen and Penelope. Carmen had Penelope on speaker phone in her office as Joel hung out in the doorframe, waiting to talk to her. He apologized and comforted Carmen that it would pass . . . eventually.

"Ugh." Penelope's eyes lifted in disgust. "Why is it that, if I want to borrow something of yours, I have to ask, but if you want to borrow something of mine, it's a free-for-all?"

"I'm sorry, Penelope. I didn't realize that, beyond this one incident, I did that to you." Carmen took off the baseball cap and tossed it to her. It landed on her chest, giving Penelope another reason to growl. Carmen realized tossing the hat was childish on her part. She needed to work on that.

"You're right, Penelope. It's disrespectful to take something that isn't yours and wear it without asking. By the way, did your friend Grace ever return Amelia's sweatshirt?"

Penelope's face hardened. Carmen couldn't tell if the angst was because she felt a twinge of remorse or if she just despised her that much more for calling her bluff. Penelope dropped the hat in the sand next to a can of La Croix.

The last can of La Croix in the house. Carmen had placed it in the freezer door before changing into her swimsuit so it would be cold and slushy when she got back from kayaking. The fact that Penelope took it out of the freezer was a huge slap in Carmen's face. Penelope hated the drink. Everyone in their family knew Carmen chilled her can of La Croix for one hour before drinking it.

No doubt she had cracked it open with the intention of letting it get warm and dumping it.

"Are you coming, Mom?" Amelia yelled impatiently from the shore.

"I'll be right there, sweetie. I've got to run inside and grab a hat. Do you mind if I wear that wide-brimmed beach hat of yours?"

"No one wears a floppy beach hat to kayak in, Mom. I have baseball caps on the bottom shelf of my closet. Take your pick."

Penelope grumbled something under her breath as Carmen walked away, certainly something malicious, but she concentrated on keeping her mouth shut. She wasn't going to react. She had to stop chasing Penelope's bad behavior and trying to force her to be pleasant.

Carmen was more determined than ever to display all the love and affection she possibly could. Penelope made it near impossible most days, but Carmen powered through.

She came back out wearing Amelia's hat, sucking on a piece of cherry licorice. Penelope's favorite. Carmen took a few pieces and handed the rest of the bag to Penelope. Penelope accepted with a snort and tossed the bag down near her feet.

Love her. Don't like her at the moment, but love her.

Once Carmen got out on the water, she felt her stress slowly roll away with the waves. Amelia paddled as if they were being chased by sharks, triggering Carmen's arms and shoulders to burn as she tried to keep up. She was determined to match Amelia's speed and was concentrating so hard she hadn't noticed Amelia coasting, resting her paddle across her thighs.

When Carmen heard Amelia's scream, it was too late. The kayak crashed with a massive force that flung Carmen forward. She reached, trying to steady herself on the side of Amelia's kayak, but it only jostled the two of them further, and before Carmen knew it, she had not only gripped the kayak, but Amelia's arm as well. She tipped, Carmen tumbling on top of Amelia, sending them both in the water.

They came up sputtering, Carmen laughing so hard she was taking on gulps of water and choking. Amelia playfully shoved her mother under by the shoulders for revenge.

"Watch where you're going, maniac!" she teased, when Carmen came up for air. "You barreled into me at full kayak speed!" Amelia splashed water in her mother's face before swimming off to retrieve their drifting paddles.

It took Carmen a good five minutes to hoist herself back in the kayak. Her legs and feet were going numb, and she was certain hypothermia was about to set in. The water had not yet reached a favorable eighty degrees. Once they were safely situated, they made their way around the lake, hugging the docks, avoiding the wake created by the passing speed boats.

As they passed Gabby's house, Amelia voiced it was her favorite on the lake. Carmen didn't know Gabby well. They'd whizzed past each other numerous times while boating over the years, and she'd seen her hanging around Monica's house. Gabby attended the occasional lake association meeting, and they'd spoken a few polite words at the annual ice cream social. However, the most she had spoken to her was, embarrassingly, over Penelope's tantrum.

Now she felt like a heel for unloading so much personal information. What had gotten into her? Carmen knew Monica and Gabby were close friends. Monica, the gregarious creature she was, approached Carmen for idle chitchat quite often whenever Carmen was getting her mail or watering flowers.

It seemed Monica always appeared out of nowhere, ready to chat weather, kids, or careers. Of course, Carmen had always been guarded, not wanting to give Monica some false hope for a meaningful friendship. More often than not, Carmen avoided Monica.

Once, when they were both out raking the weeds from their beaches, Monica had walked over for her dose of babbling, and whatever it was they were talking about led Monica to share with Carmen that Gabby was not only her great friend but her physical and mental support system. Whatever that meant. Carmen thought it odd the way some women *needed* each other. She believed strong women relied on faith first, themselves second, never each other. It was so less complicated.

But as Carmen paddled by, she saw Gabby lying on a lounge chair with one of her daughters snuggled next to her. There was no mistaking one of the twins' long white blond hair. Carmen knew Gabby's children were all in college, and a twinge of jealousy stung her at the sight of their loving relationship.

These days Penelope would recoil at her mother's touch, and here Gabby's college-aged daughter was letting her mother hold her. Carmen was more than intrigued. First thought, did Gabby's daughters go through a rebellious stage? Second thought, Gabby must think Carmen has raised Penelope poorly for her to act the way she does.

"See, Mom. They accented their entire house in aqua, and it turned out so cool. Why won't you let me repaint my room that color?"

Amelia was right: the aqua trim and doors were stunning. When the painters put the first coat up, Carmen wanted to hate it. Who in their right mind would paint any square inch of their house aqua? As it turned out, it was the most dazzling, distinguished, yet peaceful house on the lake.

Carmen tried to hide her smile because she knew Amelia had already braced herself to be shot down. Her daughter expected Carmen to say, *No way, not ever.* Instead, Carmen gave her a studious look. "A better idea, you've never had."

Amelia stopped paddling and stared at her mother. "Did I seriously just hear you right? Are you on crack, Mom? Can I reeeally paint my room aqua?"

"Jeez, Amelia, no, I'm not on crack! You act as if I say no to everything."

"Well"—Amelia paused—"you kinda do. No dog. No hamster. No turtle. No Hawaii. No Disney. No Pop Tarts. No Jimmy Choo shoes. No Louis Vuitton handbag. No nose rings. No TV in my room. No new phone." She ticked away on her fingers.

Carmen only laughed as Amelia went through her short list. She had to give her daughter credit. She was determined to go after what she wanted. "If your requests were reasonable, they'd be worth considering, Mealie."

Suddenly, the new phone, Hawaii, Louis Vuitton, and hamster were insignificant to Amelia. She took hold of her paddle and pumped it in the air and chanted, "I get to paint my room aqua . . . aqua, aqua, aqua," in sheer delight.

~*~

"Dinner and a trip to the paint store?"

"Sure, if I can paint my room black," Penelope tested.

"Nope," replied Carmen as she closed the dishwasher with extra force and pushed start.

Penelope tossed a handful of Cheez-It crackers in her mouth and brushed her hands together, allowing the crumbs to disperse on the kitchen floor. Sad to say but Carmen was glad Penelope turned down the offer to go out with her and Amelia.

What bothered Carmen more than anything was the fact that she knew Penelope well enough to know that she'd never want her bedroom painted black. She only asked because she knew

Carmen's answer would be no. It was Penelope's ticket to start a dispute, future ammunition for Penelope to point out that Amelia was the favorite and always got her way.

"I'm taking off with Grace tonight."

"You mean may I take off with Grace tonight?"

Penelope sneered. "You know what I meant. Can I?"

Be kind, she willed herself. "Sure. Curfew is one o'clock. Where are you heading?"

"Don't know."

"Anyone else or just the two of you?"

"Don't know."

Carmen didn't have the energy to challenge and wished Victor was home to back her up. He'd tell Penelope to stop being disrespectful and that she needed to tell them her plans, otherwise she wasn't going to have any.

Penelope turned to open the kitchen cupboard for a glass, but Carmen still caught the eye roll.

Carmen felt her nails dig into her palm as she clenched Tiffany's strap. "Please check in with a text at nine o'clock and eleven o'clock and text me again on your way home at midnight . . . *before* you put your car in drive."

Penelope poured herself a glass of lemonade, left the pitcher on the counter, and turned to walk out of the kitchen without a response.

"Did you hear me?"

"I'm not deaf," she hissed.

Carmen reached for the pitcher of lemonade to replace it in the fridge and thought better of it. Instead, she typed out a text to Penelope, asking her to please put it away before leaving. She drummed her fingernails on the counter in thought. How had they gotten to this point? She wanted to give Penelope a hug and a kiss before leaving the house, telling her to have fun, to be safe. Instead, they were parting with animosity and it killed Carmen. Amelia honked the horn in a rhythmic pattern, signaling Carmen to hustle. At least one out of the two loved her.

After dinner and their adventure in the paint store, they pulled in the driveway, armored with cans of paint, tape, rollers, and brushes, determined to stay up until the wee hours of the night. To Carmen's surprise, Victor's car was in the garage.

"Dad's home. He can help us paint!" Amelia darted out of the car and inside before Carmen even turned off the engine.

A wave of relief passed through Carmen. When Victor was home, Penelope wasn't quite as nasty. Victor had her back and stepped in, sensing when Carmen was defeated, teetering on the verge of going ballistic.

Carmen had one foot out of the car when she heard the screams come billowing out through the open door. She gathered the paint and rushed inside, quickly shutting the noise in with her. The living room fell silent when Carmen entered.

Victor had Penelope and her boyfriend, Landon, sitting together on the living room sofa.

"What did you do now, Penelope?" Amelia didn't wait for her sister to respond. "Once again you ruin everything for me," she spat and ran upstairs and slammed her bedroom door.

Carmen felt the joy of the last few hours slip away in a matter of seconds. Sadly, it had become the norm these days.

An exasperated Victor kneaded the back of his neck. "I was able to catch a standby flight."

"What a lovely surprise, right, Penelope?" Carmen pinched the bridge of her nose, trying to prep for whatever was about to come her way. "Anyone care to tell me what's going on?"

She took a deep breath and prayed for the grace of God. She could already see herself lunging across the couch in an attempt to strangle Landon, so she squeezed in next to Victor on the oversized chair, securing herself tightly between him and the arm.

She gave him a peck on the cheek. "Welcome home, darling."

It seemed Victor always came home to a mess. His eyes were puffy and dark. He grabbed Carmen's hand and placed it on top of his knee and stroked it as if he was waiting for the genie to come out and grant three wishes.

Landon leaned back in the couch cushions and stared up at the ceiling, defiantly chewing on his bottom lip. Carmen couldn't tell if the boy was about to cry or fling the throw pillow he was clenching across the room. She loved that pillow and had searched long and hard for it. Would it be outlandish to remove it from his sweaty grip?

Sitting a safe distance from Landon on the couch, Penelope was hunched forward, looking down at her knees, digging at her nails. She reminded Carmen of the small child she once was. Long gone were the days Penelope melted into Carmen's arms and found comfort in her embrace.

Carmen broke the awkward silence. "So, what's going on?"

Victor started to speak and then stopped himself. "Actually, I think I'll let Landon and Penelope explain what happened."

Landon didn't move, only continued to examine the ceiling, then the wall, finally setting his gaze out the window as he fisted her beloved pillow. Coward.

Carmen inched to the edge of the chair. A dreadful ribbon of anxiety tightened around her. "Penelope, talk."

"Nothing happened," she snarled, her lower lip quivering.

Victor shifted impatiently. "Then why are we sitting here?"

"Because you made us sit here," she accused.

"Don't play that immature game with me right now, Penelope. You're only going to make things worse for yourself."

A million things were going through Carmen's head that she wanted to say to Penelope, yet, what about this little punk shrinking back into her couch?

"Actually, I think I'd like Landon to explain to me why *he's* here because he knows our rules." Carmen continued to look at him even though the thug couldn't meet her eyes.

"Landon, you're not welcome in our home when we are gone. I'm offended that you would disregard our rules and put Penelope in this position. You disrespected her, and both of you have disrespected Victor and me."

Landon's foot began thumping, his knee bouncing around like a kid on the verge of wetting himself, but he still wouldn't acknowledge the adults before him. That alone annoyed Carmen to the core. It took all her will power not to slap her hand on his thigh to stop the jerking.

A sniff and faint whimpering cry emerged from Penelope as she buried her head in her hands, obviously embarrassed.

Victor stood and opened the front door. "Landon, I think you should leave. As of now, you're no longer welcome here."

Penelope sobbed as Landon tossed the pillow and hurried from the sofa out the door, not bothering to mutter the slightest apology or good-bye.

"What the heck! You two love embarrassing me, don't you?" Penelope bellowed. "You're just looking for reasons to hate Landon."

Carmen couldn't contain herself one more second. "The reasons are right in our faces. What exactly was going on here? Did Dad catch you two having sex?"

"My gosh, Mom! No!"

"Drinking?"

"No!"

"Smoking weed, vaping, shooting heroin?"

"Nooo!" Penelope wailed.

"Then someone please tell me what's going on."

Victor cleared his throat and sat back down, this time next to Penelope where he could put his arm around her. He had always been better at remaining calm and disciplining with logic. Whereas Carmen often found herself short-tempered, flying off the handle with a ranting lecture and strict punishment.

"We were just fooling around. I swear, nothing more, okay? You guys freak out over everything and make such a big deal. I mean didn't you ever kiss your boyfriend when you were in high school?"

"You two were nearly naked, Penelope. Had I not walked in . . ." Victor ran his palms up and down his thighs uncomfortably. He lifted her chin so they were eye to eye. Penelope squeezed her red-rimmed eyes shut and jerked her head away.

"Are you high?" Victor gathered a chunk of her hair and sniffed.

Penelope's cry came out with a howl as she jumped and covered her neck with her hair in a panic. "What would it matter anyway?" she screeched. "You guys don't trust me. No matter what I say, you'll think I'm lying."

Carmen chose to ignore the hickeys Penelope was trying to hide since her blood was already boiling at the thought of her daughter having sex and getting stoned with Landon. The boy was shady and had never been able to look them in the eye or mutter anything more than a grunt in greeting.

"It *is* hard to trust you, Penelope, because you do lie, you do break the rules, and you continuously bring this upon yourself. You told me you were going out with Grace."

"You say that like you hate me."

"Don't be ridiculous, Penelope, or try and flip this on me. My emotions toward you have nothing to do with the fact that you disobeyed and broke our rules and trust."

Penelope looked at her with a deadpan stare, her eyes floating towards her lids. "You *are* high." Heat zoomed through Carmen's body. "Cool, Penelope. Really cool."

"Why do you humiliate me every chance you get? Why do you point out every wrong thing I do? I'm not perfect like you, okay! You're hypercritical and set unrealistically high standards that I'll never live up to."

"Ridiculous accusation, Penelope."

Victor shifted his gaze to Carmen, and they locked eyes for a moment. She knew he was pleading with her to keep cool. They were both fully aware Penelope was purposely trying to set Carmen off.

She was tired of Penelope twisting everything around and portraying herself to look like the victim in the situations she created. She had become this master manipulator and Carmen wasn't falling prey.

"Sorry, but failing classes, breaking curfew, smoking pot, lying, and breaking our rules is rebellious behavior. Asking you to abide by those rules is not setting high standards or asking for perfection, so please stop pointing fingers when you make a conscious choice to be devious." Rage edged Carmen's tone. She inhaled, begging herself to keep cool.

Victor cleared his throat as a warning to stay on track. Really though, she was the parent, and she was no longer going to succumb to feeling as if she always had to tread lightly around her daughter.

"The only involvement I have in this situation is that I'm your parent and I need to set boundaries and enforce them. I was gone for the evening; you created this situation. It's my job to steer you in the right direction so you learn how to make wise decisions by yourself. I will not enable you to throw your future away."

"So here's where you're going to lecture me on what a loser I am for quitting water polo. Go ahead, Mom. Make me feel guilty that I'm no longer your star player earning my free ride to college." Penelope spoke with vehemence, her sardonic pitch playing on her tongue. "Sorry I'm such a disappointment."

Thank God Carmen was so calloused to this accusation she had no qualms about taking the bait. Penelope was a superb and aggressive center-forward. Scouts were interested in her as a freshman. Unfortunately, she broke her leg wakeboarding over the summer before her sophomore year. Recovery was grueling; the down time and fear of losing her first-string position to her best friend Liz took a toll physically and emotionally.

Four months later, Penelope was given clearance to jump back in the pool, but she chose not to. She abruptly went from loving the sport to loathing the sport, as well as her teammates, many of whom had been her best friends since elementary school.

Penelope had spent her sophomore year, spiraling down to where they were now. Her grades slipped, and she began hanging out with a rough crowd, drinking, breaking curfew, being disrespectful, and now smoking weed.

"Oh, honey, we aren't—"

Carmen interrupted Victor. "That's nonsense," she said, waving her pointer finger back and forth. "I will not fall prey to your false accusations."

Penelope turned and buried her head in Victor's chest and continued to cry. He swept her hair back and tucked it behind her ear, kissing the top of her head. Boy, was she good. If Penelope played the poor-me card, Daddy would let her off with a warning.

Damn her. Carmen and Victor used to be a team, backing each other up. These days it seemed they were always second-guessing one another's disciplining and bickering ensued.

Carmen's tolerance was wearing thin, making her come down harsher. Victor, absent for most of the issues, was getting soft, enabling Penelope since he felt guilty being gone.

He was seriously falling for her act: hook, line, and sinker. She got caught half naked in her bedroom with her boyfriend, stoned to boot, and suddenly she was sobbing in his chest, and he was petting her like a lost puppy.

"I think it's time to get over yourself and own up when you screw up," Carmen said tersely.

"Landon is a bad influence, and I'm sure your father agrees when I say I don't think you should see him anymore."

Penelope's eyes flared. "First, you demean me in front of Landon now refuse to let me see him! Ya know, his parents treat *him* with respect. They aren't always in his shit!"

"Whoa! Watch your mouth," warned Victor as he sat upright.

Carmen walked over to Penelope and sat down on the ottoman opposite the couch. The sun hung low in the sky, casting light and dark shadows across Penelope's face, her delicate features taking on a harshness that chilled Carmen. Penelope twitched with annoyance and lifted her chin defiantly.

"Let's get a couple of things straight. Number one, you embarrassed yourself. I had nothing to do with that. Number two, boohoo, we care about you enough to have rules, let alone this talk, because I can guarantee you that Landon's super cool, uninterested parents don't give a crap about him.

"Secretly, he would probably love to have parents that care enough to even bother with giving him a curfew, encourage him to get good grades, visit a college campus, play a sport, or be a real go-getter and get a job."

It was building. Carmen was ready to spew, not only out of anger, but from the resentment she had towards her parents and her upbringing. When her kids acted out, it made her furious because they had no idea how good they had it. Curse her and her bitter heart. She'd be damned if she was going to say something she'd regret and go to bed angrier at herself than she was at her daughter's situation.

"Because we love you, we'd rather not see you ruin your life. I keep reminding myself to stay strong and firm with you. To you, that might mean we don't love you, that we don't understand you. You refer to the fact that you don't measure up. That is not true, and you need to stop making immature allegations.

"Our love is so deep that we would climb mountains and swim across shark-infested oceans if it meant keeping you on the straight and narrow. I feel like you are determined to self-detonate. For what? I don't exactly know."

Carmen took a breather and let her words sink in while she carefully pondered her next.

"We love you, Penelope, but you broke the rules, and there are consequences that follow. You're grounded for the next three weeks. No friends coming over, zero social obligations, and no leaving the house unless it's cleared with us."

Penelope pushed Victor away in one clean sweep. "I hate you! You're ruining my life! Landon is the one person that understands me and doesn't criticize and control everything I do. You can't stop me from seeing him."

She grabbed her handbag from the console in the foyer, slammed the front door, and squealed out of the driveway.

CHAPTER 7

Don't miss out on something extraordinary just because it will be difficult.

Gabriella

Greg locked eyes with Gabby, waiting for her to answer Stella. She pursed her lips, refusing to bail him out.

"Mom? Dad?" Their names were a stifled cry from Stella's throat, the pitch of her voice reducing her back to childhood.

"Why don't we talk about this inside," Greg said, heading for the door.

Stella disappeared from the balcony while Gabby stood, deflated. All her senses were on high alert, the sun beating on her back, the foul scent of the pear tree blossoms lingering in the breeze, and the one and only stand-up Jet Ski on the lake roaring around, desperately in need of a tune-up. Another day, along with its scents, visions, and sounds, would be etched in her mind forever and etched in Stella's mind forever.

Greg and Stella were looming in the kitchen, Stella perched on the bar stool, Greg anxiously standing at the island and pressing his hands into the quartz as if he could push his deceit through the stone and hide it in the cabinets below.

Gabby pulled out a bar stool next to Stella and realized she hadn't sat on one of them yet. Their once crowded and noisy kitchen, where the kids often did their homework and family and friends came together for meals, was now deserted.

"What's going on?" asked Stella bluntly. "You clearly aren't living here, Dad."

Greg fidgeted and leaned forward, placing his elbows on the counter, his head in his hands. "For the time being, I'm living in a penthouse in Grand Rapids," he spoke into his chest.

Stella's eyes shifted to Gabby with worry. "Why?"

Greg rubbed his forehead with his thumb and middle finger, stalling. Gabby half-willed him to break down in tears, half-willed him

63

to toughen up, lift his chin like a man, and look his daughter in the eye as he told her of his betrayal.

Silence hung in the air. Gabby knew Greg was waiting for her to step in and speak for him, be his advocate. This was the way their marriage had always worked when it came to the heavy stuff. She was the therapist after all. It was her role. Now more than ever she realized how she'd empowered him, forever his activist.

"Hello? I'm starting to freak out here! Will one of you talk?" Stella looked pointedly at Gabby, also expecting her to elucidate.

Not budging.

Greg cleared his throat. "We're having . . . some issues and need some time away from each other to sort them out."

"What kind of issues?" Stella demanded. "Is it about rebuilding the house? College tuition? Financial stuff?"

If only.

Greg shook his head shamefully.

"What then?" Stella questioned with urgency. "You just renewed your vows."

The roar of the Jet Ski flooded the kitchen through the open windows as it whizzed by the house again, buying Greg seconds to decipher how he'd plea for mercy.

Gabby's pain quadrupled for her children.

"The truth," Stella demanded, her voice rising.

Greg intently studied the gray swirls in the quartz. "I made a huge mistake."

Look her in the eye for goodness' sake.

"I had an . . ." His voice cracked. "I messed up," he whispered.

Gabby felt her stomach drop. Her entire body broke into a cold clammy sweat. They locked eyes, Gabby's stare willing him to admit what he'd done.

Tears filled his eyes. "An affair."

"What the hell!" Stella leapt off her stool so quickly it clamored backward to the floor. "You're sleeping around with other women?" Stella spat and stepped back. The distance she created between her and her father spoke louder than words. But words were on the way.

"Woman, not women," Greg defended.

Stella shook her head in disbelief. "You disgust me, you sick bastard! How could you do that to Mom? To our family? Who is she? How long have you been sleeping around?"

"Stella Rae!" Gabby was shocked by Stella's rage, her vulgarity. She was the calm twin. Pregnancy hormones or not, Gabby didn't expect Stella's outrage.

She swung towards Gabby. "Don't you dare defend him! I don't want to hear a single word that I'm speaking disrespectfully. *He's* disrespectful, despicable actually."

Gabby and Greg both flinched as Stella slammed her hand down on the counter. Stella had never flown off the handle like this. Tears streamed down her cheeks, which left Gabby vulnerable, her emotions too close to matching that of Stella's.

Greg moved towards his daughter with open arms.

She held up her hands and backpedaled. "Don't touch me!" Her foot caught on the edge of the rug, and she catapulted back into a bookshelf. A large ceramic vase teetered and fell, hitting Stella's cheek and crashing to the floor. Stella's cheek and the rug, both softened the blow to the vase, and instead of shattering to pieces, it split into three large chunks.

Greg wrapped his arms around her, but Stella wanted no sympathy and wiggled out of Greg's grip in a frenzy. "Dad, please don't," she said, the disgust in her voice evident.

He stepped back, and Gabby had to look away because, despite everything, the angst on his face was unbearable.

"I'm sorry. I'm sorry for everything."

"Maybe it's best if you leave, Greg. Give her some time to process. We can talk when we've all cooled off."

"Would you like me to leave, Stella?"

She nodded.

"Okay, but I can't leave until I know you're not hurt."

Stella's eyes pierced through her father, tears glazing her red cheeks..

He daringly cupped her face in his hands. This time she didn't object. "Physically. Are you hurt physically? Your cheek bone . . . it's swollen. Can I get you some ice?"

Gabby backed off and wrapped her arms around herself as Stella got to her feet. Greg and Stella stood, eyeing each other as they had during the frequent family stare-offs they'd had at the dinner table, the first to look away or break into laughter the loser. Only this was no fun game. Stella was determined to daunt and demoralize her father with her critical, unforgiving eyes.

Greg broke. His words choked on his tears. "I'm sorry, Stella. So, so, very sorry. I've hurt the five people I care about the most."

"Go," Stella whispered in a low growl before he could say more.

Gabby felt her heart split as the door clicked softly behind him.

"Lottie and the boys need to know, Mom. I think I should text them to come home. We can all stay here with you."

"Heavens no, Stella! There's absolutely no reason to ruin everyone's weekend. I see no need to call an urgent meeting. Besides, Calvin and Klay probably don't even have cell service in the U.P.

"Your hormones are on overdrive, and you're extra emotional. You need to settle down a bit." Gabby led Stella back onto the bar stool. "Let me get you some ice for your cheek; it's already turning blue."

Gabby filled a Ziploc with ice and wrapped it in a soft wash cloth knitted by Gabby's grandmother before she passed. She handed it to Stella and went to the cupboard for two glasses. Her hands were trembling as she filled them with water from the fridge. A tight chest, fluttering heart, and a wave of nausea swept through her.

Panic attack. Breathe. Ward it off. Gabby kept her back to Stella as she guzzled the cold water, begging her symptoms to subside as she stalled, refilled her glass, and retrieved a few slices of lemon from the crisper. Here they were, Greg out the door while she was left to tend the wounds of her children. Go figure.

"How long have you known, Mom?"

"Couple of weeks," replied Gabby as she took the stool next to Stella.

"Why did you try and hide it?"

Gabby tucked a damp piece of hair behind her ear and wiped the beads of sweat on her upper lip with a napkin. "I wasn't trying to hide anything. My hopes were to have you all over to the house for dinner next week. Explain things once."

Gabby saw the hurt in Stella's clear blue eyes, the eyes of her grandfather. "I know you're upset, Stella, but don't hate him."

Stella stiffened. "How can you say that? Don't you?"

Gabby bit the inside of her cheek. She could feel her entire body tense up, from her clenched jaw down to her curled toes. "I like the analogy of a deep wound. Right now, my wound is sliced wide open. It burns. If I don't treat my wound carefully, it's going to ooze, spread, and ultimately infect other people and leave nasty scars on all of us."

Stella was listening intently, showing how much she'd matured since Gabby had spoken to her this way as a child.

"Fortunately, my wounds aren't life threatening. Life will go on. I'm lucky enough to have my faith to rely on. A little wisdom too." She grinned. "It's far from the cure-all because I'm an emotional human being like the rest of the world. So even though I know *how* to deal with what's happened, doesn't mean I will always deal with it appropriately. No one does."

Gabby paused as she could hear her voice quiver. "I do know myself well enough that my way to fight is with my words, so that's why I need time alone, time to retreat with my own thoughts so I don't give a voice to an emotion that I'll later regret. I could easily sit here and rip your dad to shreds. My fear is that I'll infect others with my open wound. You kids. Does that make sense?"

Stella gave her a wry smile. "I get that." She paused. "But I'm still furious."

"I know. Me too." Gabby sniffed. "Let's go outside to the patio. I need fresh air."

Stella followed obediently, firing off questions as they sat at the large chunky table with seating for twelve. Gabby had searched high and low for the perfect set with no luck and ended up having the gray distressed set custom made. Silly but it was these reminders that seemed to taunt her: the visions of entertaining large groups of friends and their family as it grew over the years. All that preparation was now compromised.

"What's her name?

"How long has it been going on?

"How did you find out?

"I need to know everything, Mom. Please don't hold back." Stella looked at her intently.

Gabby felt like she'd been pierced by a needle filled with accountability for a crime she hadn't committed. Considering keeping the baby a secret would make her a liar and a hypocrite.

"Her name is Holly. Your father said the affair spanned over six months." As Gabby heard herself speak, she found herself sinking deeper into emotions she knew she didn't want to own.

"And how did you find out?"

"The evidence was in my face, but I don't care to elaborate." She cringed with the vision of the ultrasound picture and the scene on the front porch.

"Is she married?"

"I'm not sure."

"You didn't ask?"

"No."

"Does she have kids?"

Gabby's face smoldered. Liar was branding it's burn across her forehead. She answered with a shrug, "Not sure yet."

Stella eyed Gabby quizzically but went on, "Have you looked her up or tried contacting her?"

"No."

"How long did you suspect he was cheating?"

"Not long."

Stella sighed, prompting Gabby to continue. She was so close to divulging the entire truth, torn between right and wrong, truth and lies. Was it right to shield her children? Stella was an adult.

"So, the affair was over before you renewed your vows?"

"I'm not exactly sure."

"The trip to Turks was all Dad's idea though?"

"Yes."

"Could you elaborate a tiny bit, Mom?" Stella said with frustration. "I understand that every detail isn't my business, but is it okay to know the gist of what's going on? I mean you're not living together."

"Maybe you should ask Dad these questions. He had the affair after all." Gabby had an edge to her voice, which wasn't intended for Stella. "Look. Your father has all the answers. I'm not ready to ingest all of it yet.

"The thought that he was out sleeping with another woman while I was going along with our fairytale marriage, completely clueless, is so, so"—Gabby paused, embarrassed to say the word out loud—"so humiliating."

"It's like he woke up one day and just decided our past was meaningless, our present pointless, and our future insignificant. He made this deliberate, conscious decision to ruin over two decades of love and trust. To betray all of us."

Gabby transfixed her gaze on the water, sadness clouding her features. "Some people leave the doctor's office, blindsided by a terminal disease, or a car accident leaves you disabled, or against your best efforts, you lose your house to foreclosure, or a fire engulfs all your possessions, women have miscarriages, or you bet on the wrong horse. The list is endless and most often unpredictable. Adultery is *intentional*. You go along with it, even though the repercussions could destroy everything and hurt countless people.

"Don't get me wrong, Stella. I'm right-minded enough to know I'll get through this. Terrible things happen to people every single day. I have a lot of life yet to live. The hard part is accepting that my life isn't what I thought it was and my future that seemed so well planned out is now unclear. I've a lot of decisions to make."

"Why did Dad show up here today?"

"He's been asking to meet. I finally agreed. He was on his way over when you showed up."

Stella cocked her head to the side. "I still can't wrap my head around all the unanswered questions. I would have demanded answers immediately."

"Demanding answers doesn't change what he's done, Stella. For the moment, I know enough."

"Are you filing for divorce?"

"I haven't made any definite decisions. I was blindsided."

"What does your gut say, Mom?"

"Kick him to the curb."

"What does your heart say?"

"There are more people to consider than just myself."

"You mean us kids?"

"And the next generation," Gabby said while she patted Stella's belly.

"Makes me sick." Stella held up her hands defensively. "Don't stay married on my account."

"You're speaking in the moment, out of anger. What about ten years down the road when you're calloused, when your heart has had time to heal?"

"That's ludicrous. I'm never going to dismiss what he's done."

"You don't need to dismiss it, but eventually you'll have to forgive him, for your sake, not his. Replace your anger with peace. You can't allow his actions to fill your heart with bitterness and resentment."

"That's going to be hard."

"That's exactly why I'm choosing momentary distance. At this point, I don't know what I want to know. Some details may be better left alone if it means causing me further pain."

"Like if you won't be able to let it go, you're better off not knowing?"

"For my own sake, yes." Gabby abruptly stood from the table. "I'm starving." She wasn't, but the truth about Holly being pregnant was dangling at the tip of her tongue. "What sounds good?"

Stella didn't ponder the question one second. "Mexican or Chinese."

Gabby smiled. "Salt and grease. First trimester cravings."

"Second trimester actually."

"Right. Why'd you wait so long to tell me? I could have been your support for weeks now."

Stella cocked her head to the side and stared at Gabby, incredulous. "Touché."

"Damn. Fair point. Walked right into that one."

~*~

They sat on the patio at La Mexicana, indulging on authentic chips and salsa and burritos. The last thing Gabby needed was a brick of heavy Mexican food in her stomach on top of the ball of stress that had permanently settled there. However, the memory of being newly pregnant with the girls and devouring half a bag of lime tortilla chips and an entire container of salsa obliged her to sympathy binge along with her daughter.

Between mouthfuls, Stella revealed her surmounting anxiety. Stella hadn't divulged much to Gabby during her teen years, but once Stella went off to college, Gabby found herself on the receiving end of Stella's phone. Often the phone calls started out with either *I need Mom advice* or *I need a therapist,* and Stella was adamant that Gabby remain in the proper role.

Stella's mapped-out future was now vague. Since the early age of eleven, she'd been determined to receive a degree in broadcast journalism and land her dream job as a reporter for a national news company. Only a few short weeks ago, she'd started her internship at a local news station and was working with the dean of her department, applying for an internship in New York City with NBC, ABC, or FOX news for next spring.

Only now, next spring she'd have a newborn.

Watching her hometown hero rise to the top and land a spot as chief meteorologist on *Good Morning America* had always made Stella's dream seem feasible. Stella had stated the fact that she was going to be the most sought after anchor in the country so often over the years Gabby could visualize turning on the TV and seeing Stella's face fill her screen.

It wasn't only the big events of Stella's future that worried her. The here and now also consumed her every thought. Gabby and Greg had purchased the house near campus as an investment. Stella and Lottie had two roommates and the baby was due mid-December. Stella was concerned how Kesly and Brie would react to a baby living in the house. A baby was not in the housemate agreement.

They didn't throw massive parties, but they were college students, and newcomers came and went. Kesly brought the occasional guy home from the bar. Brie, the social butterfly, was always entertaining new people she'd met in her classes for study groups, Netflix binges, mixology parties, and her new obsession— soapmaking. Last week Brie and her soap crew pumped out eighty-seven bars in a single night, Stella explained. Brie was eager to have a stock pile for her segment on whichever network Stella would work for.

"How could I have a baby in a house with so much commotion?" Stella cried. Stella also knew her parents were counting on the rent money from Kesly and Brie, so if anyone were to move, it should be her, but where would she go? It all felt so heavy.

Stella twisted the wave-shaped ring on her finger that Gabby had brought back from Turks. "I was on antibiotics after our trip to Punta Cana for winter break. I never missed a single birth control pill. I also didn't pay attention to the warnings to use a backup method while taking antibiotics. Stupid."

Gabby reached across the table for Stella's hand. "Please don't feel like you owe me an explanation. You're an adult, a very intelligent adult, so don't beat yourself up. What's done is done. It happens, and lucky for you, you've got a family that can help. We'll figure it out, and I'll be right by your side."

Stella gave Gabby a grim smile and squeezed her hand. "Thanks, Mom. You're pretty amazing."

Gabby pushed her half-eaten burrito away and sat back in her chair. "How is Preston handling everything?"

"We'd only been together three months when I found out. I felt so irresponsible telling him because I ignored the fact that we should have been using condoms along with the pill. He never knew I was taking antibiotics. I came home with a horrible case of diarrhea from the Dominican Republic."

A chuckle escaped Stella. "It was early enough in our relationship that I was too embarrassed to admit I had diarrhea. Then bam, a few weeks later, I had to tell him I was pregnant."

Gabby had only met Preston a handful of times. The first time was over a rushed lunch between the kids' classes, an MSU basketball game, and Easter brunch.

Gabby liked Preston, especially when he brought her a dozen yellow tulips on Easter. He reminded her of Klay, mellow and easygoing. Gabby couldn't help but think Stella had chosen a boy just like her brother. Preston was good-looking, as expected, considering Stella's standards. She'd always landed boys that had striking features. Pretty boys, Greg had coined them.

"Preston was stunned at first. Then he freaked out a bit. Now he's kinda excited, I guess." Stella shrugged. "He talks about us with the baby in the future, but it's like he thinks life will go unaltered once the baby is born. It bugs me because I don't think he gets it."

"Do *you* see a future with him?"

"Ya," she hesitated. "Sure."

Gabby knew her daughter well enough to know she had serious doubts.

"I'm taking it one day at a time. I'm not throwing a wedding together for next weekend or even next year."

Gabby silently sighed with relief. "Has he suggested that?"

"Not really, no. He just makes references to us as a family in the future like it's a given, and sometimes it makes me feel claustrophobic like he's planning my future without asking me if it's what I want. Just because I'm pregnant doesn't mean I want a ring.

"At the same time, I feel like I'm the one looking at taking semesters off, or postponing my dream internship, or kissing studying abroad good-bye, and he's like, full force ahead as planned with kid in tow." Stella's voice rose as she got flustered. "He can't wrap his brain around the fact that it doesn't work that way."

"Was that the argument that landed you here?"

Stella pushed her plate away too. "Part of it. I know I'm stubborn and I don't like to be told what to do and he's truly trying to be supportive and loving. I guess I feel like my decisions aren't up to me anymore. Suddenly, I must consider Preston and this baby and"—Stella's lip quivered—"it freaks me out, Mom. I had a plan. A dream. I screwed up my plan, and my dream didn't have a baby or a guy in it for years down the road."

CHAPTER 8

None are so empty as those who are full of themselves.

Monica

Humiliated was an understatement, yet Monica was also secretly elated that Janice had walked in on her and Dex completely naked. It spoke loud and clear that this was Monica's domain and Janice was a guest in their house, not a key keeper to waltz in as she pleased.

The fact that she showed up unannounced, in her crisp white pants, four-inch wedges, navy-and-white striped sailor shirt, dripping in gold jewelry, with her Jaguar packed to the max, only added to Monica's fury. The woman screamed of privilege, perfection. Miss Hoity Toity.

"I thought you said your mother wasn't moving in for a few more weeks!" Monica pushed the accelerator to the floor as she weaved in and out of the cars on the Beltline. Dex held an ice pack on his nose with one hand and gripped the door in fear with the other.

"On Thursday she told me she was staying with her friend Harriet in Bay Harbor for a while . . . so I figured . . . I didn't think it would only be two days."

Dex flinched when Monica growled. "So it was a pipe dream that she would have an extended slumber party with her sixty-year-old girlfriend?"

"You make it sound like I was plotting against you. Besides, she's moving in for the summer. What's a couple of extra days?"

Monica held up three rigid fingers. "Three weeks, Dexter. Three more weeks than I had planned on."

Dex closed his eyes and leaned his head back. Monica felt a twinge of guilt for giving him such grief, but not nearly enough to drop it. Fifteen weeks instead of the twelve they agreed upon was a big deal.

"Your mother has loads of money. She can rent anything she wants, anywhere she wants, for months on end, and it wouldn't put a dent in her slush fund. The only reason she's staying with us is because she knows I don't want her to. Heck, *she* doesn't even want to. She doesn't even like me, only wants to show her authority by sauntering in our front door and making herself at home because she knows you won't tell her no. Janice thrives on being the wedge between us."

"You really think that's her ulterior motive, Monica? Her sole purpose is to make your life hell?"

"Yep."

"She's really excited to spend time with the kids."

Monica snorted. "This is no different from when she surprised me with the weekend away at the spa. For the first time, I felt like she was showing me a little love by doing something nice for me, until she showed up with her suitcase as I was on my way out. It was all a ploy to get me out of the house so she could have her precious Dexter all to herself."

"Seriously, Mon, we've hashed that out a hundred times, and we'll never fall for it again. Really, though, how bad can it be? She's already babysitting the kids. Can't you at least try and find a few positives in the situation? We'll be able to come and go as we please. You'll be able to use the bathroom without Beck barging in and asking to sit on your lap. You can light candles, lock the door, and take a relaxing bath, knowing she's right outside the door with the kids." He squeezed her knee, his expression pleading for her to chill.

"Dex, she was forced into babysitting because we needed to go to the ER. You dressed and bolted to the car to hide with your tail tucked because you couldn't face her after she barged in and caught us having sex in the kitchen."

Monica weaved right then left, cutting into the lanes with only inches between front fenders and back bumpers. "You left me standing there, mortified, trying to explain what happened to your nose, why there was blood all over, and apologizing for what she saw us doing in our *own* house."

"Technically, we weren't having sex yet."

"What?"

"Sex, we really weren't actually in the act yet, Monica Dear."

"Shush, Dex."

Dex dropped his head. "Okay, Monica."

They drove in silence the rest of the way to Urgent Care where Monica was pretty sure she was going to get arrested for domestic violence. Anyone that looked at her would clearly see that she was irate and Dex was this battered husband that took a severe beating from his wife.

Monica tried to act sympathetic to the fact that Dex's nose was broken in two spots and he was going to have to have surgery to reset it, but no, that little patronizing voice in her head was saying, *Serves you right for hiding the truth,* and another voice that ridiculed, *You're a horrible wife.*

With a prescription for pain meds and a surgery appointment scheduled, she drove home just as quickly, fearing their children would be scared when they woke up and found this stiff, strange woman, whom they were instructed to call Mémé, sitting in the porch, protecting her hair from any breeze that might move it.

Janice spent more time correcting Kenzie and Beck how to pronounce Mémé than she did talking with them about anything interesting like *Peppa Pig, Doc McStuffins,* or *Paw Patrol.* Even though she's only a quarter French, Janice insisted the kids call her Mémé because it sounds fancy.

It was quiet when they walked into the house. The slider doors were open, causing the sheer curtains to blow with the lake breeze. Monica caught a whiff of cigarette smoke and followed her nose to find Janice sitting in the three-season porch, puffing away on a Virginia Slim. Janice smoked four Virginia Slims each day. No more no less.

Call it territorial, but Monica liked to think Dex was more her husband than Janice's son. Dex had moved out of his parent's home at the age of nineteen, so in another few years, Monica would have lived with Dex longer than his mother had. With that, she reasoned, she would finally possess more tenure over him than his mother. Wow, did she really think that way? Yes, she did, but then again, only because she was forced to.

Janice was always trying to prove she knew Dex better than Monica did. If Dex was wearing a checkered shirt Monica had bought him, Janice would say, "Dex prefers stripes over checks, Monica Dear." If she saw him eating Cheerios, she'd ask why Monica didn't buy him Lucky Charms. "It *is* his favorite." If Monica handed him a turkey sandwich, she'd snap at Monica and inform her that Dex has favored roast beef since he was five.

Monica placed her hands firmly on her hips. "Janice, we don't allow smoking in our house."

Dex looked to Monica with wide eyes. Fine, it probably wasn't the best greeting, but Janice knew she wasn't allowed to smoke in their home or in front of their children. Monica matched Dex's scornful eyes then stormed off to check on Kenzie and Beck, leaving him to deal with his mother.

"Well." Janice jumped. "Are we just going to keep sneaking up on each other all day, calling each other's bluff?"

Dex ignored his mother's passive dig. "Mom, we'd appreciate it if you went outside to smoke and preferably not in front of the kids."

"I thought this room was considered outside since the walls are basically screens," Janice argued curtly.

"The smoke floats right in the house. Mom, please go outside."

"Where are the kids, Janice?" Monica shouted from downstairs.

"Relax, Monica Dear. They're playing in the sand."

"What? Where?" Monica didn't wait for an answer as she tore outside to the beach where she found both Kenzie and Beck, thankfully above water.

Dex was only footsteps behind her. He scooped up Beck in one swift sweep. The poor little guy's hair was sticky with sweat, and his pudgy cheeks were pink from the late afternoon sun. Kenzie had taken a shovel and cleared a road through the sand for Beck to drive his trucks and dozers on.

"Thank God they're alive! I can't believe your mother let them play by the water alone while she sat inside, smoking. No one in their right mind leaves children unattended around water."

Janice cleared her throat. "I can hear you, Monica Dear. If you must know, I haven't taken my eyes off them. My view is no different from that of a lifeguard. I'm only abiding by your rules. I knew you didn't want them to see their Mémé smoking."

Monica glared up at Janice's erect figure as she looked down on them through the screen. The porch may have had a bird's eye view of the lake, but it didn't have a door or steps leading down to the beach. It would take her a solid minute to reach the beach if one of the kids ventured out into the water or ran down the dock and fell in.

"Heaven forbid she actually sits on the beach and keeps an eye on them. As if it's so much to ask to give your grandkids some attention and play," Monica seethed under her breath to Dex.

Janice's tone was several decibels higher. "I can still hear you, Monica Dear."

Kenzie handed Monica a sandy, naked Barbie and asked her to play beach party. A lump formed in Monica's throat at the sight of the wet Barbie at the same time she noticed the bottom three inches of Kenzie's sundress were dripping. Monica forcefully wrung the dress out while eyeing Dex.

"Please don't ever, ever, never, ever go in the water if Mommy and Daddy aren't out here with you, sweetie." Monica got down on her knees and hugged Kenzie, wrapping her arms around her tiny waist. "Promise me, Kenzie."

"I proms, Mommy. I only did fer second. Trixie and Reese was washing their Barbie's hair in water, and they said me do it too. Kenzie no go past me belly buttons," she said while pointing to her belly.

Monica spoke loud and clear to be certain Janice heard, along with the neighbor that had comfortably sat himself on the edge of his dock, undoubtedly, to watch her unsupervised children. How embarrassing.

"It's against our rules for you to be in the water or playing on the beach alone. Please follow Mommy and Daddy's rules even if Grandma says she can watch from inside."

"Mémé," Kenzie corrected. "Trixie and Reese was with Kenzie. We's safe."

Monica smothered Kenzie with kisses, melting at the way Kenzie referred to herself in the third person.

Trixie and Reese were Kenzie's imaginary friends, and they were both a blessing and a curse. They were a blessing some days for hours on end as they were a never-ending playdate. Trixie and Reese kept Kenzie entertained playing Barbies, Polly Pockets, and cooking at her play kitchen.

Kenzie took Trixie and Reese to the park and out for dinner; they rode scooters and played sidewalk chalk together. At preschool, her teachers explained she played well alongside the other children, but mostly only spoke with her imaginary friends.

Several times over the past winter, a girl in Kenzie's class asked her over for a playdate, but Kenzie always refused, saying Trixie and Reese told her that they didn't want to go.

Both Monica and Dex had driven around town, trying to find the circus that Trixie and Reese frequently performed acrobatics in. They were the stars in the trapeze act. Countless times Monica and Dex had followed Kenzie's directions to the girls' house to pick them up for dinner and drop them off after playdates. They would twist and turn through the streets of town until Kenzie pointed at their house (always a different house but always white with black shutters). They would pull in the driveway, open the back door, and wait for the girls to get in. More than once, homeowners had come out, and Monica and Dex were left to explain they were picking up their daughter's imaginary friends.

On occasion, Dex had gotten suckered into buying two extra ice cream cones at Frosty Boy, two extra bags of Jelly Bellies at

Sweetland's, two extra dolls, and two extra Christmas dresses, along with tights and shoes to avoid a meltdown from Kenzie.

Trixie and Reese were as real to Kenzie as Beck. If Monica was being honest, Trixie and Reese seemed real to her as well. Monica found herself serving the two Dixie cups of Goldfish crackers at snack and setting their plates at the table on nights Kenzie hadn't asked.

"Let's put the kids swimsuits on," Monica said, inspecting Kenzie's red shoulders with a critical eye, and raising her voice, "lather them in sunscreen, and escape for a boat ride."

"And leave my mom here?"

"I'm sure she has unpacking to do, Dex. She'll be fine."

"Don't you think it'd be polite if we helped her unpack her car?"

Monica huffed. "Don't you think it'd be nice if we had an hour to ourselves to unwind a bit?" Monica chastised herself but spit the words out anyway. "Just because she's living here doesn't mean she needs to be glued to us every minute."

Dex lowered his head and walked toward the house as Beck begged him to stay and play trucks in the sand. Dex couldn't win. Was she being cruel? Possibly, but Janice was constantly out of line, she rationalized, and Dex, although upset, never stood up to his mother. Never stood up *for* his wife.

"Fine, invite her along," Monica called after Dex.

~*~

Janice shed the heels and rolled up her white linen pants to just under her knees. No denying she was beautiful, but in Monica's opinion, her personality overshadowed her looks, causing her features to appear harsh. Her nose was too pointed, her cheek bones too severe, her jaw a bit too square, but for sixty, her skin had very few wrinkles and her neck was as tight as a thirty-year-old's.

She wore a large pair of Louis Vuitton sunglasses and a navy-and-white wide-brimmed hat that matched her sailor T. She slathered sunscreen on every inch of exposed skin, leaving Monica baffled as to why she hadn't bothered with her grandchildren before shoving them out under the scorching sun.

Monica wanted to start fresh. She really did. Admitting she loathed her mother-in-law was disconcerting. She truly wasn't that type of person, fully aware Janice brought out her inner demons. She wanted to love Janice for the sole sake of her husband. Janice made it nearly impossible.

The tension was so thick on the boat, Monica couldn't relax. Dex was puttering around the lake, waving to those still hauling their docks from the beach into the water. Beck and Kenzie were sitting in the back of the boat, sipping on juice boxes, barely able to move their heads from the constraints of their life jackets. Janice was commenting, to no one in particular, about which houses suited lake living and which ones didn't meet her approval. This one had outdated brick, that one too few windows, unruly landscaping, ugly roof angles, and the hideous paint job that ruined the brand-new house.

When Monica reminded Janice that that was her friend Gabby's house, and stated that she loved the aqua accents, Janice tsk-tsk'd her, muttering it was gaudy. Janice was a master at making Monica feel like her taste was cheap and trashy, always asking her where she purchased her furniture, her shoes and handbags, even her cosmetics. She'd then shake her head and slip in a remark like, "What a shame you don't have higher quality stores nearby."

Monica needed to be alone, and with only twenty-one feet to work with, she resorted to the bow of the boat. Thank God Dex had packed her a Michelob Ultra in the cooler. She popped one open and took a long drag of ice-cold beer, fully aware Janice was watching her with distaste, because ladies didn't drink beer. They drank wine. Monica loved wine, but not when Janice was around.

Monica wished she could slather the icing on the cake even further by belching, but she was never good at forcing burps.

Dex cut the engine, dropped the anchor, attached the ropes to the tubes, and threw them in the water. He and the kids jumped from tube to tube like the old arcade game Frogger. Janice was getting soaked and equally irritated, but really, who wears such clothing on a boat with small children? Why couldn't she wear her swimsuit and a cover-up or at the least a pair of shorts?

"That's a nice color on you, Monica Dear."

Monica opened her eyes, a compliment? "Hmm?" She murmured in confusion; she was wearing a black bikini.

"What's *left* of your toenail polish. It's a good color on you."

There it was, the insidious dig. Instead of coming right out and saying that Monica's toes looked horrendous, she baited Monica into saying as much. Monica could respond in so many ways, stressing that her toes looked terrible, that she was embarrassed and in desperate need of a pedicure, exactly the corner Janice was trying to back her into. No. Monica was not succumbing to the insult. She would wear her chipped toenail polish proudly.

"Thanks, Janice, I love the color too. You can borrow it anytime." Monica guzzled the rest of her beer for effect and leaned her head back and closed her eyes, again trying to signal that she wasn't open for conversation. Unfortunately, Janice viewed this as a challenge.

"Whew! The breeze died. I'm getting rather warm out here."

Monica kept her eyes closed and only nodded.

"I do believe five o'clock is the warmest time of day."

Monica nodded again. Where was she going with this idle chit chat?

"Whew, had I known we would be sitting under the blazing sun for so long, I would have packed myself a drink or a snack."

Once again, Monica nodded. Good grief, the kids were less needy than Janice. Monica willed herself to show no sign of aggravation, knowing it only fueled Janice's determination to irritate her.

"You're warm too, Monica Dear. I see sweat dripping down your belly."

Okay, that did it! Monica's eyes flew open as she grabbed her towel and blotted herself. Janice continued to watch her in disgust, so Monica went for the cooler and helped herself to another beer. She twisted off the cap and gulped it down.

"Ooh, a cooler, I never realized you packed drinks for us, Monica Dear."

Is this woman for real? Where did she think I got the first beer from?

"I didn't pack the cooler, Janice, but feel free to help yourself."

"How sweet of Dexter. He does it all, doesn't he? Packs the cooler, entertains the kids for you so you can relax. All with a broken nose."

Yep, while I sit on my duff drinking beer, tanning myself, albeit trying to ignore his nagging mother. This entire conversation was building up to this moment. Is she insinuating that I'm lazy? A bad wife? A checked-out mother? A dirty, beer drinking, sweaty hog with chipped toenail polish?

Monica knew Janice was waiting for her to open the cooler, list the contents, and serve her a drink. Instead, she climbed to the back of the boat and tightened her top, gripping her toes into the vinyl as the boat rocked.

Janice huffed as she took the four steps to the cooler. "I'll bet Dexter packed a few Diet Pepsis, our favorite."

Monica knew better than to respond, but she lost all self-control. "Dex doesn't drink Diet Pepsi."

"He loves Diet Pepsi."

Monica whirled around. Were they seriously playing the *who knows Dex best* game? "No. He doesn't. Dex gave up pop years ago, right after we were married."

Janice turned toward Dex and the kids. "Figures."

Monica bit her tongue and propelled herself off the back of the boat, doing the biggest cannonball she could, dousing Janice with her enormous splash.

The kids squealed with delight as Dex stared in awe at Monica's sudden sense of playfulness. She swam under water and pretended to be a shark, pinching their toes and then placing her hand on top of her head like a shark fin as she swam towards them chanting, "Da-dum, da-dum."

After a half hour of playing shark, motorboat, and letting the kids dunk her, Monica waved to her family and swam away. "I'm swimming to Gabby's house. Pick me up when you're ready to go home."

As she swam off, she could hear Janice's scoffing. "What is she trying to do, get run over by a boat? Dexter, are you going to let her swim away like that? Does she think she's some sort of Olympian?" Monica dove under to silence the echoes of Janice's heckling.

When Dex's dad was alive, Janice wasn't nearly as condescending. She had never been exactly pleasant to Monica, but she was tolerable. Bob had congestive heart failure and passed away four months before their wedding. In failing health, Bob was adamant that he wanted the wedding and celebration to go on as planned. Janice didn't view the marriage as gaining a daughter. She viewed it as losing her son along with her husband and had resented Monica since the day they said I do.

She was bitter without her husband, angry with Monica that she must share Dex, and always trying to prove Monica didn't measure up, wasn't deserving of her son's love and attention.

Monica filled her lungs with air and went under the cool water. It was so peaceful she wished she could make it all the way to Gabby's without coming up to the surface. She could hear the whistle of speedboats from under the water and realized Janice was right: it wasn't a safe time of day to be swimming across the lake. She couldn't even think clearly in the presence of her mother-in-law.

Her lungs were burning, and her muscles were spent from her morning workout, not to mention she guzzled two beers on an empty stomach. She paced herself and focused on her breath as she fell into her usual rhythm. Before she knew it, the sand was beneath her feet.

"Look who washed up!" Stella beamed from the patio as Gabby closed the grill cover.

Monica trudged her lethargic body up the steps and helped herself to the platter of crackers and brie displayed with simple elegance on Gabby's custom table.

"I hope you don't mind. I'm starving." Monica took a sip of Gabby's sangria to wash down the crackers and apologized, "Sorry, I'm a little out of sorts. I broke Dex's nose, and then I was making it up to him in the kitchen when Janice barged in and caught us naked."

Stella threw her head back and let out a snort.

"Oh gosh, sorry. I probably shouldn't have said that in front of you, Stella. Oh wait. You're about to be a senior in college. Girls your age are having wild sex. Not you, I mean, but other girls."

Stella's face flushed, and Gabby rolled her eyes and snickered.

"I'll just keep my mouth shut and have another sip of your sangria if you don't mind, Gabs."

"You can have the rest." Gabby chuckled as Monica drained the glass. "Do you want me to get you a towel? Perhaps a bottle of water?"

Monica shook her head and helped herself to a four-cracker sandwich. She sat, dripping in her bikini, a puddle accumulating under her rear and two small puddles forming on the table from her breasts. She leaned back in her chair and licked the remaining cheese from her fingers. "So, Stella, what's new with you? Are you still seeing Preston?"

"Yep." Stella nodded vigorously and sipped her ginger ale.

"Whatever you do, don't rush anything," Monica said as she strode over to the drink fridge and helped herself to a bottle of raspberry hard cider. She cracked it open and took a sip. "This stuff is pretty good, Gabs.

"Anyway," Monica continued, sitting back down. "Before things get too serious and you're headed down the aisle and you've got a houseful of babies"—Monica missed the look Stella gave Gabby—"make sure, damn sure, you can tolerate his family because they can be tremendously stressful on a marriage."

Monica took a swig of her cider. "Once you have kids, you're tied to his family forever. For-ev-er."

"Oh look." Gabby raised a hand in greeting. "Dex is pulling up to the dock."

He tied a loose knot to the cleat and hopped off along with Kenzie and Beck. Monica cringed outwardly with a growl as Janice stood in the bow, her Louis Vuittons pushed down to the tip of her nose so she could scrutinize, unfiltered.

Please, no, sit back down, Monica willed Janice.

Gabby and Stella looked amused as Monica braced them for the encounter. "Please don't ask about Dex's swollen, bruised nose. Pretend not to notice."

Monica was pretty sure her mother-in-law would have enough class to hide her dislike for Gabby's accent color, but she rarely applied a filter to her mouth.

Janice was gushing, oohing and aahing, as she pranced up the steps to the patio. "I must have a tour. This is the loveliest home on the lake. The colors are splendid."

Barf. What a fake, but Monica supposed her mendacities were better than the alternative. Gabby, always the prepared hostess, handed Kenzie and Beck bottles of green Bug Juice, Dex a Coors, and offered Janice a glass of wine.

"I'm not a big drinker," remarked Janice as she eyed Monica, "but I'd love a glass of Sauvignon Blanc if you have any."

"Certainly." Gabby poured a sizeable glass for Janice and slipped Monica a sideward wink then ushered Janice inside for a tour.

"That woman gives me more than enough reason to drink," said Monica as she leaned across the table towards Stella. "Seriously, Stella, think with your head, not your heart. Don't go into marriage blinded by love."

Stella's eyes widened as she glanced towards Dex.

"Jeez, Mon, settle down. Stella hardly needs marital advice from you. She's a carefree college student."

Kenzie's and Beck's screeching interrupted, saving Stella from the awkward banter ensuing between Monica and Dex. They were on the beach squirting their Bug Juice at each other, running in circles as the sand flew in the air, sticking to their bodies.

Dex asked Stella what her summer plans were; however, the conversation quickly derailed when Beck burst into tears after stepping on a washed-up snail, embedding sharp pieces in his toe.

Monica cuddled him on her lap as Dex dug out the pieces only to have Kenzie trip on a step and scrape her knee as she was bringing Beck a fistful of seaweed to soothe his pain.

"You designed such a lovely home, Gabby. I admire your meticulous attention to detail," Janice purred as Gabby led her back outside.

"Did you know I'm currently upgrading my California home?" Janice didn't wait for Gabby to respond. She fluttered her hand. "An outdoor sanctuary is what you have here. I will too. I've hired the best landscapers in all of California. I believe the exterior furnishings should reflect the interior exquisiteness of a home."

Monica gave Dex an aggravated look, which he took a swig of beer to avoid. He was embarrassed with his mother's behavior but hadn't any idea how to handle it other than hiding behind his beer bottle. If they weren't careful, they'd both be alcoholics by the end of the summer.

Gabby opened the Weber and turned off the flame. "I've grilled plenty of chicken and fish if you'd like to eat with us?"

Monica opened her mouth to accept the invitation when Janice cut her off.

"I'm not the type to intrude. Dexter is eager to get home and prepare a lovely meal for us. Monica Dear isn't much of a cook, are you?" Janice gave Monica a smug smile, trying to embarrass her.

"Not really, no, I can think of way better things to do in the kitchen than cook." Now it was Monica's turn to reciprocate with smugness. "Right, Dexter?"

Dex choked on his beer and gave Monica a sideways warning glance.

Stella chimed in for Monica's sake. "Ugh, I hate to cook too. It's too time-consuming: the shopping, the prep, the cooking, and clean up. Way too much time invested for something that takes fifteen minutes or less to consume."

Monica pointed her finger in the air. "Exactly!"

Janice placed her hand on Dex's shoulder and squeezed. "My Dexter takes care of the family meals. He's a master on the grill. His specialty is thick-cut pork chops."

"Dex rarely grills pork," Monica contended.

"What a shame." Janice sighed. "I'll be sure to have the butcher select the best cuts for you."

"No need, Janice." Monica returned the smug smile. "Dex went to the butcher's this morning and bought organic chicken breasts so he could make my favorite, chicken lazone."

Dex drained his beer and pointed the empty bottle towards the grill. "Thank you for the beer, but we should go and leave you to your dinner. It was good seeing you, Gabby, Stella." He nodded in their direction.

Monica and Gabby shared a look that spoke a thousand words. She scooped up Beck in one arm, took Kenzie by the hand, and said her good-byes as she started for the dock, knowing all too well they were a spectacle to say the least. Gabby was probably analyzing all their behavior.

She fired up the boat as Janice climbed on and Dex untied the ropes. He was barely in when Monica jerked the throttle in reverse. Dex stumbled and fell back into the seat.

"Easy, Mon!"

Time for a thrill ride, Janice, thought Monica, cranking the wheel and plunging the throttle forward. They hit the waves head on, sending the boat bouncing and careening from side to side.

The kids bounded gleefully and screamed for her to go faster while Janice hung on, white-knuckled and petrified, her hair blowing back in one stiff clump.

CHAPTER 9

Always give a bit of your heart rather than a piece of your mind.

Carmen

There were only a couple of lights aglow around the lake, two of the night owls Carmen noticed being Monica and Gabby.

She was curious about the friendship between the two women. They came from two different stages of their lives with more than a decade separating them. She wondered what they talked about, what their friendship was like, how involved it was.

For the first time since high school, Carmen felt like she might possibly want a friend, or at least someone to share her frustrations with. She only had Victor and the girls. Tiffany was still a solid sounding board, but maybe it was time to communicate to a living friend, someone who could offer feedback and unbiased advice. She needed guidance, needed to know she wasn't alone in her struggles with Penelope.

Carmen was used to pulling through life on her own. She'd been thick-skinned since she was a child, protecting herself and being strong for her father. She couldn't figure out why, suddenly, after all these years, she felt like she needed more.

Kseniya, the sweet Russian woman who meticulously filled her eyelash extensions, couldn't figure out why Carmen insisted on a fill every ten days when all her other clients scheduled every three weeks. Carmen feared Kseniya rightfully suspected she was deliberately plucking the falsies out on day nine. Pouring out her soul three times each month on Kseniya's heated bed had been her saving grace. With her eyes closed and Kseniya's murmurs of acknowledgement, Carmen unloaded enough to feel like she wouldn't explode.

Monica, an overstrung peppy creature, had made several attempts to spark up conversation over the years. She had asked Carmen on walks, and if she saw Carmen relaxing in the sun, she'd holler down the beach, inviting her to lounge alongside her and the kids while they played in the sand. Carmen always declined, claiming she had to catch up on work emails or phone calls. There was always an excuse as to why she had to rush off when their conversation by the mailbox became real or personable. Carmen was defensive and realized she had snubbed Monica on more than one occasion. Yet, Monica's gracious determination never wavered.

In Carmen's defense, she had made her *ropa vieja* when Kenzie was born, again when Beck was born, and a third time when she had delivered Cade. Sure, she'd had the girls deliver the dishes with the arrival of Kenzie and Beck, but Carmen personally delivered the meal to Monica after Cade's stillbirth, along with *pastelitos de guayaba* for dessert. Carmen had even given Monica a hug, told her she was praying for her.

The urge was foreign to Carmen, but tonight she felt like knocking on Monica's door and taking that walk, even if it was almost 1:00 a.m. Penelope's bedroom light was faintly glowing behind the blinds, and Carmen pondered whether to go and try to talk with her daughter, hang out, make amends. The fear of rejection sprinkled with a layer of Penelope's nastiness kept her at bay.

They needed to start fresh, and Carmen didn't know what to do if she walked in Penelope's room to find that she had been drinking . . . or worse. Carmen knew it was a pipe dream to think Penelope would hang out with girls who spent their time watching Netflix and eating popcorn in a pink bedroom while painting each other's toes, but still, when had her parenting derailed to the point where Penelope thought getting stoned and naked in her bedroom was coolly appropriate?

Carmen was deep in thought when Monica stormed out of her house and down to the dock. She lowered the boat lift and fired up the engine. Carmen didn't understand what had swept over her and didn't take a second to ponder before she darted down her own steps, hurdled two kayaks, and sprinted down Monica's dock.

She leaned her head under the shore station cover, panting, startling Monica. "Um, excuse me, Monica. Are you going for a, um, moonlight cruise?

Monica's hand flew to her chest. "Jeez, you scared the crap out of me!"

"So sorry, it's just that I . . . I was sitting out on my deck and I saw you walk down, alone, and wondered if you, well, if you wanted some company. It's okay if you don't," Carmen rambled. "I mean I know I'm totally intruding and most people going for boat rides at one o'clock in the morning, well, obviously prefer to be alone . . ."

"Hop in," Monica interrupted. "I'd love the company."

Monica's eyes and white teeth glowed against her deeply tanned skin in the faint light adorning the posts along the dock.

Carmen had to admit she liked the edginess to Monica. She had jet-black hair that was styled in an array of messy chunks. Her features were dainty and petite, yet she had a killer strong body and this vibrant energy that radiated around her. She was kind of a tiny badass with her barbed wire tattoo and diamond stud in her nose. A showoff without trying. Carmen supposed that was why she felt a small kinship; maybe Monica was more like one of the guys.

Carmen climbed over the side of the boat, ready to elucidate her sudden intrusion when Monica put the boat in reverse, exposing them under the light of the moon. She slid the boat in gear and turned the bow out to the black water.

The stars and a half moon lit the lake well enough to see the docks and a few floating swim rafts, but the water made the night seem darker than it was.

They putted in silence for a couple of minutes when Carmen realized how out of character this was for Monica. She was usually so intense, high-strung, her mouth going a mile per minute.

"It's so peaceful out here," Carmen commented. "Makes me wish time could stand still."

Monica got up and tossed some beach towels to Carmen. "The nights are still so cold. Cover up."

Carmen wrapped up in a damp Dori towel that smelled of sunscreen. It reminded her of the way Penelope and Amelia would wiggle and squirm when she tried applying their sun lotion until Carmen turned it into a spa session.

They would both lie down and let her massage their little legs, arms, and back until the thick white cream had been absorbed. She couldn't imagine Penelope letting her touch her like that now.

"Do you often come out here late at night?" asked Carmen.

"Never, I'm not a night owl. Just a rare night I needed a breather."

Carmen looked up to the stars and located Orion's Belt. "Me too."

Monica's gaze followed to the stars. Halfway around the lake Carmen could still see the glow of Penelope's bedroom light. What was Penelope doing in there? She'd barged in just after midnight, bounded her way upstairs, and slammed her door so hard the house shook. Possibly Landon had snuck in? Perhaps they were now taking shots of vodka, smoking, vaping, and laughing about how naïve she and Victor were.

Heck, who knows if she was even in her room? For all Carmen knew, Penelope could have snuck out. She and Landon could be hundreds of miles away, runaways destined for the lives of junkies. She should have checked on Penelope. Good mothers check on their children instead of escaping on a boat in fear of them.

"I'm dreading the day Kenzie and Beck are teenagers and they enter the rebellious stage and cause me to lose sleep."

Carmen nodded in agreement, knowing Monica was giving Carmen an invite to talk. "When they're toddlers, you wish they were self-sufficient teenagers because you're physically drained from their constant demands. When they're teenagers, you wish they were toddlers because you're emotionally shattered."

Monica nodded. "I remember, when I was nursing Beck in the hospital, all the nurses were adamant that he be with me every second when all I wanted to do was put him in the nursery for two or three hours so I could sleep.

"They made me feel like a rotten, neglectful mother for asking. Then there was a shift change, and this nurse came in with a serious face and said she heard I requested a couple of hours of sleep. I geared up for a lecture and cried tears of joy when she whisked him from my arms, claiming her kids were in college, unscathed by the few hours they spent in the nursery their first two days of life.

"She brought him back four hours later, took my hand, and told me to hold and embrace my kids as often as possible. However, she warned me kids needed boundaries; otherwise, they go from sucking all the milk out of you to sucking all the life out of you."

Both Carmen's and Monica's laughter echoed across the lake. "It's the truth," confessed Carmen. "I'm sapped. It's so frustrating because I put my heart and soul into raising these kids and I felt like I had it all together when they were young. Then bam, you wake up one day and they are fighting with each other, with you, and there's drama surrounding their friendships. You catch them lying, sneaking around, breaking rules, and the worst—telling you that you're ruining their life and they don't love you."

Monica whistled. "Ya, that's gotta sting. I spend my days with teenagers, but I get to either send them to the principal or send them home and let their parents deal with the brutal stuff."

Carmen groaned. "I never imagined we'd enter the brutal zone and here we are. With eleven weeks of summer vacation looming in front of us, I'll have to worry about the trouble she's getting into while Victor and I are at work. She claims to have turned in seven job applications. Conveniently, no one has called her back for an interview."

"Can you ship her off to your parents for the summer?" Monica asked with a chuckle. "I've actually seen it a dozen times over the years, and sometimes those kids do a complete one-eighty. A different environment and some old-school boundaries sometimes make a world of difference. Not implying that you haven't set boundaries . . ."

Carmen cringed. "Not. A. Chance. The environment in my parents' home is less than stellar, and I haven't spoken to my—" Carmen cut herself off. What was she thinking? Getting on this boat was a mistake. Penelope had made her so weak and defeated that she was about to divulge forbidden personal information and seek solace from another woman.

Thank goodness Carmen didn't have to explain and was interrupted by a snarl slicing through the silence of the night. "You're a dirty bastard! How can you try and place the accountability for your actions on me?" screamed Gabby. "Have you forgotten who you're dealing with?"

Carmen gasped as her eyes focused on Gabby's house. Gabby was standing on the patio, animatedly arguing into her phone amongst the soft glow of a few scattered LED candles. Monica put the boat in neutral, cut the engine and running lights, hoping they could float in front of Gabby's dock, unnoticed.

"You gave me, our marriage, and our family up months ago, Greg. I didn't give up on us easily. You did. Do not flip the mess you created onto me. I will not take blame for hurting our children or breaking up our marriage." Gabby snarled and slammed her phone down on the table.

Monica grabbed Carmen's arm and squeezed. "He had an affair, and the other woman is pregnant," she whispered.

Even though Carmen didn't know Gabby well, her heart sank. "We shouldn't be eavesdropping," whispered Carmen, slightly panicked they were about to be discovered.

"It's okay," Monica whispered back. She switched the boat lights on and off to get Gabby's attention. "It's me, Gabby. Hop on," she whisper-shouted.

Gabby's frail silhouette moved down her dock. "What are you doing out here in the middle of the night, Monica?"

"I was going to ask you the same, but then we overheard . . ." At the same time Monica said *we*, Carmen gave Gabby an apologetic wave.

Carmen felt awkward for them both. "I'm sorry. I feel out of place. This is personal, and I don't want to make you uncomfortable."

"Nonsense," said Gabby as she pulled the boat closer to the dock and stepped in the bow. "It's only a matter of time before everyone on the lake knows my husband isn't living at home." She shrugged and shoved them off.

"At least you're communicating with Greg," offered Monica.

"More like Greg's insistently trying to guilt me into covering up for him." Gabby scoffed. "And to boot, Stella knows about the affair and she's irate." Gabby slapped her hands on the top of her legs. "Oh hell, I might as well tell you since you'll know soon enough." She sighed before going on, "Stella is pregnant. Her baby is due three months after Greg's."

A hush fell over the boat as Carmen and Monica processed what Gabby had shared. The slapping of their small wake hit the side of the boat, seeming to tick off the seconds they sat in stunned silence.

Carmen got up, joined Gabby in the back seat, and put her arm around her. She didn't know what else to do. It felt both uncomfortable and perfectly normal. Gabby shook under Carmen's arm.

Monica sat on the other side of Gabby, placed her hand on her leg, and did her best with a few consoling phrases before she began bashing Greg.

It was a small respite to Carmen that, although Penelope's behavior was wreaking havoc on their family, it was nothing life-altering, yet. She hadn't gotten in trouble with the law, nor was she pregnant, so Carmen had to be thankful that she wasn't dealing with irreversible matters.

The women floated under the stars and talked about their lives and the troubles they were facing—unruly teenagers, unfaithful husbands, a difficult mother-in-law, demanding careers—and Monica touched on the delicate subject of giving birth to a stillborn baby.

Crazy as it was, Carmen was beginning to feel at ease. Talking with Monica and Gabby was straightforward. Her guard was down, and her struggles seemed to erupt and flow from her mouth like hot lava. Both Monica and Gabby gave insight on how to parent Penelope with boundaries and love. For the first time in months, Carmen was feeling hopeful that Penelope wasn't lost for good.

While she was releasing her burdens and openly accepting advice and compassion, she was also feeling genuine empathy and companionship with these women. She cared and was open to hearing their qualms and being a shoulder to cry on. Something that didn't come naturally.

It was one thing listening to the guys at work hashing it out over sports, talking about nagging wives, and the occasional embarrassing topic of hemorrhoids, but nothing Carmen got overly involved in. Her guys at work held a special place in her heart. She genuinely cared for them, but she had never felt the emotional connection with them as she did with these two women over the past two hours.

At one point, there was a lull in the conversation as they all took a break and yawned. It was approaching three in the morning, and though Carmen would never admit it out loud, she didn't want the night to end. A snort escaped her, and Monica questioned what was so funny.

"I haven't talked to anyone like this in my adult life other than sweet, always agreeable, Tiffany."

Monica threw her head back and laughed. "I've thought about your handbag analogy a hundred times."

"You mean you've thought how pathetic I am."

"Hardly! More like hilarious! I wish I had the guts to ditch half my friends and splurge on a Tiffany," confessed Monica.

Carmen turned to Gabby, since she held the counseling degree, and was glad to see she was also giggling. "Do I dare ask your thoughts?"

Gabby pondered for a split second while she kept her gaze on Carmen. "It's incredibly safe."

Carmen waited for Gabby to go on. She didn't, and it left Carmen feeling shallow, like the women she avoided. Gabby was right though: Tiffany was safe. Carmen was defensive and went through life with her guard up. Befriending other women walked the fine line that led to exposure.

There was a shift in the mood, an uncomfortable truth, the buzz kill Carmen was waiting for. When her cell rang from the pocket of her sweater, she was both startled and relieved.

Victor's picture graced her screen. He was probably worried to death when he woke up and found her missing in the middle of the night.

"Hey there."

Panic laced his voice. "Where are you?"

"Boating with Monica and Gabby."

"Okay, whatever, just get home quick. It's Penelope."

Carmen's heart plummeted. "What is it? Is she okay?"

"I woke up and went looking for you and noticed her light was on, so I figured you were in her room. When I opened the door, she was lying on the floor, crying. There was blood all over her arms and the tops of her legs. She was cutting herself."

~*~

Multiple cuts grazed Penelope's hips. Two on the top of her left arm gaped open. Carmen's stomach recoiled. She'd always felt woozy at the sight of blood, and that unwelcome response only quadrupled when it was the blood of her child.

Victor and Penelope were sitting on the floor of Penelope's room, the first aid kit open with Band-Aids, ointment, and gauze littered about. He was cleaning out her cuts with a sudsy wash cloth, blotting her flesh ever so gently.

Carmen stood at the opened door, observing the foreign scene for a moment before entering. A razor blade and an old paring knife from the kitchen were sitting on the dresser, which she promptly, and discreetly, swept in the pocket of her sweater.

In the background, "Don't Let Me Down" by the Chainsmokers was playing from the Bose speaker on the nightstand. Carmen closed her eyes, relating to the words, "Crashing, hit a wall. Right now I need a miracle. Hurry up now, I need a miracle . . . I need you, I need you, I need you right now. Yeah, I need you right now. So don't let me, don't let me, don't let me down. I think I'm losing my mind now."

How fitting. Only she wasn't sure who the song was more fitting for, Penelope or her and Victor. She needed guidance. Please God, she begged. I need you right now. I'm losing my mind.

Victor's face was filled with concern as he wiped the blood and applied a generous coat of ointment. Penelope's eyes were closed, but Carmen could see the sadness in her features. Victor looked up to Carmen without saying anything as she moved closer and took a seat on the floor with the two of them.

They sat in discontented silence while Carmen searched for words. She had so many questions but no idea where to start, and she worried her delivery would come across as an attack. She feared Penelope would interpret anything she said as scolding or berating and put up even more barriers. She had to tread carefully.

As Victor continued to clean and bandage the cuts, Carmen rested her hand on Penelope's thigh. Penelope was sitting on the floor, her back pressed to the footboard of her bed, head tilted to the ceiling, eyes closed. Carmen figured this was Penelope's best attempt at keeping the tears at bay.

When Carmen kissed her cheek, she flinched. When she took Penelope's clammy hand in hers, she didn't squeeze back, yet didn't begrudgingly pull away. Let go of the defiance, yearned Carmen.

"We're here for you, Penelope, to listen. No lectures. Promise. Will you please talk to us? Please tell us why you're hurting so bad," pleaded Carmen.

A tear trickled from the corner of Penelope's eye, down her cheek. When Carmen wiped the drop from her chin, Penelope nudged her hand away. Victor locked eyes with Carmen and mouthed, *Be careful.*

Of course. Tiptoe. Tip. Toe. Carmen had all sorts of thoughts running through her head. Was this Penelope's cry for help? Was it for attention? Was it defiance directed at her and Victor for grounding Penelope? How long had she been hurting herself and what else had she done?

Carmen scanned her daughter's skin as she sat in her tank and shorts. She had a flashback of Penelope wincing as she covered her thighs with the beach towel the other day when she was lying in the sun. Carmen had assumed she was only covering the string bikini Carmen didn't approve of. She had been covering cuts.

"Are there any more cuts I should look at, Penelope?" Victor asked as he adhered the last piece of gauze. "We'd hate for you to get an infection."

Keeping her eyes sealed, Penelope nodded and leaned forward. Carmen's hand flew to her mouth as she choked back a stifled sob. Penelope had a cut on the back of her neck that ran parallel to her hairline measuring at least three inches. It wasn't a fresh cut, maybe two days old, but it was still red and puffy, infected. A trace of dried blood was caked in her hair from a spot that had reopened. So, it was cuts, not hickeys, on Penelope's neck she was trying to cover after Landon stormed out of their house.

As Penelope leaned forward, her tank top crept up, exposing a section of skin just above her tailbone. Carmen's eyes trailed from her neck down her back to three faint lines where cuts had healed over with scabs. These were low enough that Carmen wouldn't have noticed them even when Penelope had been wearing her swimsuit.

Carmen's mind was swirling in fear. Was this a precursor to suicide? Was she cutting with other people? Like in groups? A cutting cult? Had someone showed her how to do this or was this solitary self-destruction?

Instinctively, Carmen's hand went to the wounds. "Why Sweet P?" Carmen hadn't meant to call her Sweet P, her nickname from birth, but it slipped out. She had been respecting Penelope's wishes to refrain from calling her that for nearly a year and feared those simple words would be enough to send her into a fit.

"You wouldn't understand."

Victor closed his eyes and rubbed his goatee. "Try us."

Carmen was hardly a patient woman, and it was killing her not to demand answers, or rather, demand Penelope to stop this insane behavior. She couldn't understand it, and worse, she couldn't fix whatever it was that triggered the switch in her daughter.

When Penelope was little and she'd gotten a goose egg on her forehead from running into the doorknob, an ice pack, popsicle, and twelve kisses made it feel better. After their lizard, Norm, died, George the turtle helped ease her sadness. When she took second place in the spelling bee, Carmen's authentic Cuban sandwiches and a talk about perseverance gave Penelope encouragement to enter and win the next three consecutive spelling bees.

A slushy and a teddy bear soothed the stitches in her lip after a ski accident. In eighth grade, when Penelope's face began to break out, Carmen took her to the dermatologist; they put her on a regimen and watched the acne vanish. Day in and day out, at work and home, Carmen was used to fixing problems. What if she couldn't fix Penelope?

"Whatever it is, Sweet P, you can trust us. We promise not to get upset, punish, or scold you. Please just tell us why you're hurting so bad," Carmen pleaded, while ticking off eleven, twelve, thirteen cuts.

Victor continued to clean the cut on Penelope's neck as the three of them sat with the lyrics of "All Time Low" by Jon Bellion softly playing. She wondered if Penelope had thoughtfully put the songs together or if the playlist was random. Carmen chastised herself for being so oblivious to the depth of her daughter's pain.

Maybe it was time to reach out to Liz's mom, Brooke Jensen. Penelope and Liz were inseparable from second grade through ninth grade. During that time, Amelia and Liz's younger sister Piper, became best friends and still were.

The four girls used to alternate houses, giving Carmen and Brooke kid-free breaks. Carmen had a loose acquaintance with Brooke. They never hung out together, surprise, against Carmen's rules, but they always chatted for several minutes when exchanging children, always lingered next to each other at field trips and the ever-present classroom parties.

It had been awkward with Brooke now that Penelope and Liz were no longer friends, an unspoken impediment that settled deeper with time. They'd never said a word to each other about the friendship dissolving between Penelope and Liz, and since the days of field trips and class parties were over, along with the days of walking your child to the front door for playdates, Carmen and Brooke rarely shared more than a wave or hello or good-bye through the car window.

Carmen struggled with wondering if it was a good idea to ask for insight from Brooke. If she knew why the girls parted ways? If she thought there was a chance Liz could help Penelope with what she was going through. Or would that open an awful can of worms? Accusations of your daughter this, my daughter that. Would it cause more harm than good? Create bigger messes?

It had always been a struggle for Carmen, knowing how and when to get involved with her kids' social lives and when to let them navigate on their own. As the years passed, that line became thinner. You couldn't hold your child's hand and be her advocate as if she were a toddler.

"What the heck, Penelope? What did you do to yourself?" came Amelia's voice from the doorway.

Penelope's eyes snapped open. "Shut up and get out, Mealie."

"Hey now," warned Victor. "Your sister is only concerned."

"Hardly, and it's none of her business, so get out. Now!" Penelope seethed.

"Jeez, Penelope, I was on my way to the bathroom. Quit freaking out, you monster!"

"Girls, not now!" Carmen stood and held out her hand to Amelia. "Come on. I'll take you back to bed. We'll talk in the morning."

"No, you won't talk about it with her, Mom!" Penelope snarled. "She doesn't need to know anything. I don't need her running her gossipy, backstabbing mouth to her friends. Keep your trap shut, Mealie!"

Backstabbing?

Amelia's voice quivered; she was on the verge of tears. "Don't hate on me! I haven't done anything. I'm not the one that talks trash about you, Penelope."

Penelope jumped to her feet and in one giant leap was in her sister's face. "Get out!"

Victor was off the floor, between the girls before Penelope got physical. "Good night, Amelia," Victor said firmly.

Carmen ushered Amelia out of the room, stunned by what she'd witnessed between her daughters as Victor led a shaking Penelope to her bed, pulling the sheet over her trembling figure.

"In this house, we are a team, Penelope. People will come and go throughout your life, but whether you want us or not, we're family. We'll always be here, we'll always love you, and we'll always have your back."

"Ha! You're giving that speech to the wrong daughter."

"Elaborate, Penelope. I'm lost."

"She's a conniver, a sell-out, a bitch."

"Really, Penelope? Those are pretty cruel things to say about your sister."

"I'm tired." Penelope turned away from Victor, signaling the end to their conversation.

He kissed her sweaty forehead. "Try and get some sleep, and remember, Sweet P, every day is a fresh start. Difficult roads lead to amazing destinations."

Carmen was waiting for him in the hallway. "You were incredible with her." She kissed him and buried her head in his chest and let her tears soak into his shirt.

"I learned from you, the most incredible mother I know. I realize that was extremely difficult for you to not get crazy worked up and ask a thousand questions and demand a thousand answers."

Carmen giggled and sniffed through her tears.

"What's funny?" he asked.

"You're being so kind. What you're really thinking is I can't believe you didn't go into freak-out mode and tell her to get it together and knock this shit off."

Victor kissed the top of her head and squeezed her closer. "Okay, that too."

CHAPTER 10

Stewing in anger is like drinking poison and expecting the other person to die.

Gabriella

Memorial Day weekend and the following week came and went in a blur, leaving Gabby emotionally exhausted. She had been on autopilot while meeting with her clients all week, regrettably listening with one ear while tensely wrapped up in her own thoughts. The worst kind of trap.

A thousand questions plagued Gabby's mind. How long had Greg been checked out of their marriage? Was Holly some smart chic businesswoman? Was she wild in bed? Did they carry on interesting worldly conversations? Was she a strong, independent, well-traveled, and cultured woman Greg found fascinating? Did they share an instant fiery connection or was it a slow budding romance? Gabby wanted to know just as much as she didn't.

Was Greg welcoming his morning alone or was he waking up next to Holly? What had happened to her life? It had gone from a predictable harmonic rhythm to a volatile rock bottom. Holly was pregnant. Soon, another woman's child would be calling Gabby's husband, "Dad."

Would she make the call to a divorce lawyer? She'd already added the attorney to her contacts; all she had to do was make the call. If she divorced Greg, would that give him free rein to marry Holly? Did she want to hand him over on a silver platter?

Maybe Greg was right. It was going to be hard enough for the kids to deal with the affair. If they knew about the baby, it might sever their relationship with their father forever. As upset as Gabby was, she didn't want that. However, it was not her job to rescue him from that possibility.

Was she completely out of her mind for considering not disclosing the full truth of Greg's affair? Was Holly willing to go along with such a scam? Or was he feeding her other nonsense?

Gabby had counseled many clients through mind-blowing circumstances over the past two decades. There was the woman who had slept with her husband's stepfather, the couple who was swinging with two other couples in their neighborhood. That one got ugly when the wife from couple A fell in love with the husband from couple B, and he fell in love with the wife from couple C.

All three couples divorced, and four of the six individuals were forced to move to a new town. Families were broken, careers damaged, reputations and credibility compromised. And the kids . . . they always suffered the most.

There were always the couples that married for the wrong reasons and realized after five, fifteen, or thirty years that they'd never been in love. Some couples married because of a pregnancy. Other couples thought they could rescue or change their spouse. Physical abuse, emotional abuse, alcoholism, sex addictions, infidelity, narcissism, gas lighters, codependents, the causes to which a marriage failed were numerous, and Gabby had counseled them all.

Clients were either willing to accept the truth or they weren't. Too often one spouse was determined to change the other, to conform him or her into an image he or she was incapable of living up to. Often Gabby had to convince her clients that many people don't possess basic standards of trust, respect, and honesty, and never will.

Gabby wished she could say she hadn't seen Greg's betrayal coming. Quite honestly, she hadn't when it came to infidelity, but she was keenly aware of how often Greg trampled over people to get where he was going. They'd had their share of woes concerning the matter.

Her insides twisted with the memory of the day they closed on their house. Greg had handed the realtor an envelope thick with cash, she'd easily concluded, promising to send him loads of business for coming through for him. When she questioned Greg about why he felt the need to give him an extra bonus beyond his commission when they were already scraping pennies to purchase the house, she was dismissed with affection and celebration. "My bride wanted a lake house, so I bought her one."

Greg had kissed her passionately, and instead of driving home that Friday afternoon, he surprised her by detouring north to Petoskey, where they checked into the Inn at Bay Harbor for the weekend. Gabby's heart melted at the sight of the two large duffel bags in the trunk full of clothes Greg had packed: at least a dozen different outfits, several pairs of shoes, an assortment of jewelry, her cosmetic bag, and even shampoos, conditioners, sprays, perfumes, and gels so Gabby wouldn't fret about missing a thing.

Over dinner, she'd thanked Greg for the tenth time for his thoughtfulness, complimented him for being so kind to the realtor. "How much, exactly, did you gift the realtor?"

"Enough to put the key in *my* hand," Greg answered pompously.

Gabby hadn't appreciated the way he'd accentuated *my*. Their salaries nearly matched, they'd borrowed the exact same amount from both parents, but she let that go. What was harder to swallow was the sudden glare of the light bulb turning on in her head.

There were two other offers on the house. Until now, she believed Greg that the two other offers fell through because they couldn't get their loans approved. Whatever, she hadn't really paid it much thought, only that *their* offer was accepted.

Whenever memories like this popped in Gabby's head, she quickly dismissed them. Living in denial was far easier than accepting the truth. Besides, Greg had so many strengths. He was a great father. He was always appreciative of Gabby, going out of his way to run an errand for her, walk in the door with a bag of novels from Epilogue Books, or surprise her with a soft new robe or a bottle of her favorite wine and a bath bomb. Little things to make her feel special.

Gabby had scolded herself a million times over the years whenever she'd questioned Greg's motives. She shoved his little saying *Where there's a will there's a way* to the back of her mind, even though those words made her cringe and she wanted to dispute the means of the *way*.

Gabby's cell rang, and her heart immediately thundered in her chest at the probability that it was Greg. He had texted three times already this morning, saying it was urgent that they talk, and it wasn't even seven.

Relief washed over her as she saw Stella's face on her screen. "Good morning," Gabby greeted. "How are you feeling?"

"Awful. I screamed at Dad, spewed every nasty thing I thought of him and what he'd done."

"I never said he didn't deserve a good scolding. What happened?"

"He drove over, showed up at our house at one in the morning, called Calvin and Klay on his way, and told them to meet here too."

Gabby gasped, her phone shaking in her hand as she made her way to the wing chair by the living room window. She pushed the accent pillow to the side and sank into the plush cushion.

"Okay, wow. So, how'd it go?"

"He cried, told us he screwed up and did the unthinkable to you. To us. Klay was fuming and basically said he was disowning Dad. Calvin went ballistic. I thought he was going to throw some punches at Dad or hurl the chair through the window. Calvin needs to get fired up and release some anger before he can handle anything logically."

Gabby nodded to herself at the typical behaviors along with Stella's precise analysis.

"First, Lottie spewed all kinds of nasty comments at him while he sat there, never defending himself. Then she demanded answers, asking him how it started, why the affair went on for so long, if he loved Holly, and how he could take you on vacation to renew your vows when he was amidst an affair. She then topped it off by telling him he embarrassed our entire family and, by that, he proved that he didn't love any of us."

"Wow," said Gabby, at a complete loss for words.

"After an hour of crying and belittling himself, he left with his tail tucked between his legs. Lottie cracked open a case of beer with Klay and Calvin. Don't be mad. I know we shouldn't be serving our underage brothers, but they weren't going anywhere, and well, it's how siblings relate best at our age. Over cheap beer. I then had to explain to the boys why I wasn't drinking."

"Oh, Stella, to be honest, the picture of the four of you coming together like that swells my heart." Gabby paused, choking back tears. "I'm so sorry for all of you."

Stella huffed. "Don't apologize on Dad's behalf. We're pissed at him in our own right, disgusted actually." Stella's voice had an edge to it. No shocker, they'd been up all night, analyzing the affair through their own eyes.

Gabby was curious. What could they see that she didn't? Dad this (fill in the blanks). Mom that (fill in the blanks). What information did they have about the affair that she didn't? Did they want to stalk Holly as much as she did? Did they feel the same carnal need to pinpoint the allure?

"Dad's really fucked up our family. Sorry, bad choice of words, Mom. I know you hate it when we swear, especially the f-bomb, but seriously, he really screwed up. Ugh, another bad choice, no pun intended."

Gabby giggled through her sobs. "So, so glad you're not following in my footsteps and getting a degree in psychology.

"Please don't hate him on my account, honey." Gabby's voice quivered. "You kids have always had so much respect for him. It kills me to see that tarnished."

"We're adults now, Mom. We can see things for what they truly are. The last thing you need to be worrying about right now is us. According to Dad, you've completely cut off communication with him. He's been trying to get you to talk and see someone to help you through, but you refuse. Does that mean you're going straight for divorce?"

How dare he make such references. "I have no idea what I'm going to do, Stella."

"Well, for starters, we think you should find out how this affair started. We know where Holly lives, Mom, and I wouldn't put it past Lottie or Klay to knock on her door."

"What? Absolutely not! How disgraceful." A vision of Lottie and Klay knocking on Holly's door and being greeted by her bulging belly sent Gabby's heart racing. "Did they say they were going to?"

"They mentioned it last night. Calvin and I both told them it wasn't a good idea. The more I think about it though, the less I care. The wench has it coming."

Gulp. This isn't happening. They can't find out she's pregnant. Or should they? Gabby was so torn.

"Stella, don't let them. I don't want all of you caught in the middle of this."

"Since when are the four of us not part of the family? Dad cheated on us too." Stella's voice rose to an angry level.

"I agree, but what is there to accomplish by confronting Holly?"

"It will help us to understand, maybe dissolve some of the rage."

"Really, Stella, you think pounding on this woman's door, demanding answers, or chewing her out will erase the rage? It will only fuel it." Gabby's voice had risen to match Stella's. "I think it'd be wise to go to your father for answers and focus on how you're going to reconcile your relationship with him."

"She's to blame as much as Dad is. Klay and Lottie are both adamant that Holly needs to own up to her part in the affair by admitting it to their faces and apologizing."

This isn't happening. "Exactly what I was hoping to avoid, everyone getting in an uproar."

"Why not, Mom? Get upset, show some freaking emotion already. Stop plastering a fake smile on your face, trying to protect us all the time."

"That's the thing, Stella. As a parent, that's what you do. Your kids are an extension of yourself, your heart breaks when theirs does, and you care about the welfare of your children far more than you care about your own. You'll understand soon enough."

Stella sighed with recognition. "I only hope I'm half as remarkable."

With that, Gabby's tears began to fall. "Thanks, Stella, that means the world to me. You mean the world to me."

"Regardless of my circumstances?" questioned Stella.

"Yes, Stella, don't be ridiculous, regardless of your pregnancy. Speaking of circumstances, before I call your siblings and reel them in, you told Calvin and Klay you were pregnant?"

"Ya, they freaked out, naturally. Calvin guzzled his beer, belched, and said wtf is up with our family, without the abbreviation, obviously. Klay was concerned for my future, how I was going to finish school, and asked a bunch of questions about Preston."

"Wait. You told your brothers *after* Dad left? So, Dad still doesn't know you're pregnant?"

"Nope," Stella said proudly. "He's not worthy of that information yet. If he can keep secrets, so can I."

Gabby felt sick, recognition surely plastered on her face. "Fair point."

With that, Gabby hung up with Stella and broke down with the reality of her situation. As much as Gabby hated to admit it, she had allowed a tremendous amount of resentment and bitterness to fill her in a short period of time. It frightened her. She'd never been that type of person. But she'd never experienced this type of betrayal.

~*~

As Gabby waited for her next client, she peered across the lake to see three small figures on the beach she knew to be Monica, Kenzie, and Beck. Monica was most likely playing super mom, digging tunnels and building massive sand sculptures. Despite her overzealous parenting style, she was genuine.

A couple of doors down, Carmen's house looked quiet. She was surely at work, and Amelia and Penelope were most likely still sleeping. Poor Carmen, what a stressful time it was for her. Dealing with Penelope was going to be a long process.

The chime on the door sounded, alerting Gabby her client had arrived. The remodel allowed her to design her office space with its own entrance, keeping the feel of her practice professional. She loved bringing clients into the tranquility of the new space with its two full walls of windows facing the lake. The day was warm but not so thick that she had to shut up the house and turn the air on.

The breeze off the lake floated in the room and the faint sound of a ceiling fan whirred overhead. Gabby had put a few drops of stress reliever oil in the diffuser (more for herself than her clients these days) and refreshed the orange slices in the pitcher of water. So far, every client expressed that, if Gabby was trying to lure people into her office based on the peace and calming effect, it was working.

Sixty something Betty settled in on the down-filled couch and squeezed one of several throw pillows. She was a cancer survivor and had been meeting with Gabby through her treatments for both yoga workouts and counseling sessions to help her deal with the mental challenges that went with battling a life-threatening disease. Betty had been in remission for sixteen months. She couldn't understand why she was struggling with depression for the first time in her life when she should be doing cartwheels, celebrating.

Most days her counseling sessions brought Gabby the needed distraction from her own thoughts; other days it was difficult to concentrate on her clients and not let her mind drift. Betty seemed to foster both.

When Gabby felt like she was drifting, she went in repeat mode. She would repeat everything her clients said to stay engaged: "You feel hopeless when . . . You feel anxious when . . . You feel angry when . . . You feel your body has betrayed you because . . . You're struggling with your purpose because . . ."

She was beginning to despise the word *feel*. Wouldn't life be so much simpler if we didn't have feelings? Feelings muck up everything. Greg had *feelings* for Holly that he acted on. He certainly didn't consider Gabby's *feelings* while he was cheating. Now he has *feelings* of regret, but possibly *feelings* of joy toward his unborn daughter.

Feelings only got in the way of morals and values, triggering people to succumb to their weak flesh. Then, when the consequences catch up, we justify our actions with more *feelings*. Yet, there is no greater *feeling* in the world than to *feel* love. In the end, isn't that what we are all after? Gabby often pondered whether the root of all evil stemmed from not feeling loved and accepted.

After Betty left, Gabby took her spot on the couch and told herself she was going to mentally go through all her feelings. Work through each of them so she could react rationally.

Gabby lay on her couch, trying to deal with each emotion one by one: hurt, sadness, repulsion, disgust, humiliation, jealousy, bitterness, and rage. She tried to compartmentalize each feeling and then let it go, prayed to God that He would show her His way, but her anger was building, not subsiding. Who was she kidding? She completely understood Lottie's and Klay's need to lash out at Holly.

She didn't know Holly's cell number, but she knew the company she worked for, so she did the unthinkable tacky thing, especially for a well-minded therapist, and called Holly at work. She listened to the automated list of advisors and punched in Holly's extension when prompted.

"Good afternoon, Holly Nasser speaking."

She expected Holly's voice to be high-pitched and annoying. Instead, it was confidently strong. Professional.

"Good afternoon to you as well, Holly. This is Gabriella Bock."

A long pause followed while Gabby wound herself up for her rant. "I'm calling, I guess, to give you a chance to have a voice. You're a home wrecker, a liar, and a sneaky whore. Where did you get the audacity to intrude upon my family?

"I hope you realize Greg has no interest in any further relationship with you. You've meant nothing to him during this little tryst. In fact, he's begging me to pack up and move across the country to get away from you and this mess and start over fresh," Gabby lied, but considered the option for a half second.

"He has zero interest in the child and hopes that you will miscarry. How does that make you feel? He doesn't love you, despite what he's portrayed. He. Never. Has."

Gabby barely took a second to breathe before continuing. "Did he mention we just renewed our wedding vows in Turks and Caicos? Greg's idea. Not mine."

Holly listened quietly, so quietly that Gabby thought she might have hung up. The phone call felt like some sort of out-of-body experience. The words that were coming out of her mouth and the depths to which Gabby had stooped were so low and humiliating, part of her hoped Holly *had* hung up.

"Do you understand what I'm saying, Holly? Greg may have cheated, but he didn't give you his heart. He admitted you were the biggest mistake of his life. How does that make you feel?"

"Hmm, I see," Holly responded.

Wait. What? That's it? I see? Gabby wanted more. She wanted Holly to lash out and call her names in return, to get defensive and say equally cruel things about Gabby and bash her and Greg's marriage.

Surely, they must have talked about Gabby and her inadequacies, all the ways she didn't measure up. Holly must know why Greg went astray, the things he whispered to her after making love. Gabby shuddered. She was baiting Holly, trying to get her so upset that she would divulge something, spit it right back at Gabby, but she wouldn't even nibble the lure.

"Hmm, I see? That's all you have to say?" mocked Gabby. "You're happy being someone's second best, and you're fine with your daughter being second best to Greg's four children, his real family? You're even more pathetic than I imagined."

Silence. The seconds ticked by, and Gabby could have sworn she thought she heard typing on a keyboard. Was Holly sitting at her desk, the important businesswoman she was, pounding away at her keyboard only listening to Gabby with one ear while she made investment plans for her clients?

Or was she a panicked mess, dictating and emailing Greg the conversation as it unfolded?

"Holly. Do you have anything to say for yourself?"

Holly took a deep breath as the clicking of her typing subsided. Gabby envisioned her reclining back in her swivel chair with a smug smile on her face, looking out over the city in her posh office.

"Gabriella, you clearly caught me off guard at work. When discussing such private matters, I prefer to do it in a more suitable environment. I also like to take my time to get my thoughts together before speaking so I'm prepared and don't allow my tongue to get the best of me."

It would have been less demeaning had Holly thrown a few sucker punch phrases as Gabby had, called her names and told her Greg was bored with their marriage, that their sex life was dull.

However, Holly was being tactful, mature, and it sent Gabby's fury into a blaze. She was sitting in a pool of her own sweat, her heart thumping wildly.

"Perhaps it would be beneficial to both of us if we gathered ourselves for a few days and met to discuss the events in person," suggested Holly, her voice even and formal.

Gabby had to give it to her. Holly was being civil, exactly the way Gabby went through her everyday life. She coached and counseled people on how to be levelheaded, and here she was acting completely irrational. She had embarrassed herself immensely, and Holly was putting her in her place with composure and class.

"I have nothing left to say to you, Holly. I've never been put in a situation like this by anyone in my life, and I'm struggling with how to deal with it. What's done is done. There is no going back, no undoing.

"I have four children to think about. This affects their futures as well. That's the thing, Holly. Once you have children, you can no longer live a selfish life. If you do, they suffer."

"Yes, Gabriella, I understand."

Gabby could be imagining it for her own benefit, but she thought Holly's former, confident voice, now had a slight waiver to it.

"No. I don't think you really do. Maybe someday when your daughter grows up, something will threaten her world, break her heart, and you will think outside of yourself and do anything to shield her, but until then, you don't understand."

"Fair enough," agreed Holly politely.

Gabby felt a small victory, a slight redemption to the pettiness of her previous bashing. "Well, then, good-bye, Holly." She hung up as the dam broke and the rush of tears came.

CHAPTER 11

There's no need to be perfect to inspire others.
Let people get inspired by how you deal with your imperfections.

Monica

Monica loved mornings. She awoke with the first chirps of the birds, guzzled a shot of iced coffee from the fridge, laced up her running shoes, and was out the door two minutes ahead of schedule at 5:58 a.m.

She finished her six-mile course in forty-three minutes thirty-eight seconds, ditched her running shoes, socks, and tank on her way to the end of the dock and dove into the lake in her running shorts and sports bra.

She came up for air, realizing she had forgotten her swim goggles on the kitchen counter. As she swam back towards the dock, she saw them dangling on a cleat. Dex must have placed them there, exactly where she meant to before she left for her run.

An abundance of love filled her as she appreciated the small, yet significant, gesture. She hadn't pissed him off too badly with her behavior. Dex was a good guy. Monica never doubted his love for her. He wrapped his arms around her for a squeeze and told her he loved her several times each day. He was the kind of guy that prided himself on caring for his wife and family.

After all these years, he still opened Monica's door, unpacked the groceries when she returned from the market, made the bed the way she preferred, washed her car without being asked, and made her spinach-and-mushroom omelets every Sunday.

Bob had been an incredible role model and had done an amazing job of raising a respectful and honorable son. So why did Dex fail miserably when his mother was around? He was guarded, edgy—trapped. It was no secret he felt torn between the two women. Life would be so much easier if she didn't allow Janice to get under her skin.

Dex would pull out his mother's chair before she sat down at the table, and he would fluff a throw pillow before she sat on the

109

couch, hold her coat while she put her arms in the sleeves, even boil eggs and leave them peeled in the fridge for her. All those things Bob had done for Janice, and Dex now felt obliged to imitate.

Others would coo about these gestures and comment how sweet and respectful Dex was to his mother. Monica agreed. Under normal circumstances, it was, but not when Dex was forced into the acts because of his mother's constant passive melodramatic demands. Janice also kept a running score as to whom Dex catered to, her or his wife. Janice gloated at Monica's expense when she captured her son's attention.

Janice would probe Dex, saying things like, "These June mornings can be quite chilly. I should remember to get my robe before having coffee on the deck."

Dex would kindly reply, "Do you want me to go get your robe, Mom?"

"Oh no, dear, I wouldn't want to trouble you," she'd say as she shivered for effect.

"It's no trouble at all, Mom," Dex would call over his shoulder as he beelined inside to retrieve her robe.

"Your father made the best Arnold Palmers," she'd compliment as she sipped the iced tea with a single slice of lemon that Monica had made.

"Would you like me to add lemonade to your iced tea, Mom?" Dex would ask like an eager little boy.

"What a lovely idea, dear." Then with a crinkled face, she'd say, "I can't do bitter tea," handing it back like a toddler forced to drink medicine.

Monica saw herself as independent, hardworking, capable. Janice always made her feel lazy, incompetent, and not worthy of precious Dexter. Monica could have spent hours cleaning the house and playing with the kids, and Janice seemed to always catch her the moment she sat down to relax, weaving in some sort of lazy comment.

When Dex performed loving acts of kindness for his wife, Janice brought it to Monica's attention in a way that made her feel guilty, as if she wasn't deserving or didn't reciprocate. Monica could never do enough or be enough for Janice's son.

Knowing Dex had to get to work and the kids would be up any minute, she lifted herself out of the water, dropped, and did thirty push-ups. She stood and completed walking lunges up the dock and across the sand leading to the patio where she usually left a towel and a bottle of water before her run.

The table was empty. What was with her today? Had she left the house in a fog and forgotten to do everything?

On cue, a towel from above was tossed at her head. It came at her with such surprise it almost knocked her over. She looked up and found Dex peering down at her with a sexy smirk. She caught a whiff of his cologne and took in the sight of the big burly hunk of handsome he was. His surgery had been a success, and his nose was straight again. His left dimple showed with his wide grin, and after all these years, his smile still made her melt.

She wished she had time to go tackle him and bring him back to bed since the kids were still asleep. But surely Janice was in the kitchen, making her cappuccino with her larger-than-life Ninja Coffee Brewer that now took up half of their counter.

Dex rested his forearms on the railing of the deck and whistled down at her. "You're like a fine wine, Mon. You get better with age."

Monica patted her wet skin seductively with an Avengers towel, hoping none of the neighbors were watching. Living on the lake meant close quarters; one yard and beach spilled into the next.

"Take the day off, Dex. Let's get a sitter and go to South Haven. We can walk around the shops, have a relaxing lunch, and lie on the beach all afternoon."

Dex scrolled through the calendar on his phone. "I have meetings until almost two o'clock, but after that, I'm all yours. How about the beach and dinner at Taste or Clementine's?"

"Perfect, I've been meaning to ask Amelia, Carmen's daughter, to babysit so the kids could get used to her and we could get away more often. I'll see if she's around."

Dex winked at Monica. "Is she old enough to stay the weekend?"

"I wish." Since losing Cade, the only time they had left the kids with a sitter was to attend Dex's company's Christmas party. It was time to start getting out.

Janice, with a cappuccino in hand, walked out on the deck, wearing silk pajamas that looked more like a pant suit. "Good morning, darling," she greeted Dex with a kiss on the cheek. "Morning, Monica Dear," she spoke with disdain.

Thank goodness Dex picked up on the tone in his mother's voice. Monica often needed the validation to remind her that she wasn't being paranoid, that she wasn't conjuring up false contention. He looked at her with an understanding and empathetic eye, the eye that married couples share, bearing the weight of a thousand words.

It was the exasperated eye they shared when they were in public and one of the kids was having a meltdown and they needed to make a quick escape, or the rescue eye they shared across the room when it was time to flee a party tinged with mind-numbing chit chat, or the disgusting eye they shared when they were grocery shopping together and the woman in front of them farted, and then there was the irritated eye they shared when their friend's kid puked up red Gatorade and barbeque chips inside their boat, instead of leaning his head over the side.

Since Janice's arrival, they'd shared numerous annoyed eyes as Janice continually went out of her way to be . . . Janicy. The other night when Monica cuddled up to Dex and said, "I wish I had the luxury of a massage; my hips are super tight." Dex called her out and said, "That was a very Janicy thing to say. Are you asking me to massage your hips?"

To say Monica was caught off guard when Dex turned to Janice was an understatement. "Mom, would you want to watch the kids this afternoon while Monica and I take off for a few hours?"

Janice's face twisted in horrified disbelief at Dex's request. Her words came stammering out. "I um, well, I think possibly I was meeting Lila for lunch."

"No problem, we aren't leaving until two o'clock."

Monica caught a sideward glance from Dex and frantically shook her head no. He gave her the pleading, give-her-a-chance eye. Monica was all about second chances but not when it involved the safety of her children.

Dex shifted from one foot to another, and the movement was enough for Janice to catch a glimpse of her daughter-in-law. Janice's left eyebrow arched to a height Monica had never witnessed. She had to hand it to Janice. The way she arched that one eyebrow was impressive, a talent Monica was envious of and had practiced, unsuccessfully, in the mirror numerous times.

Janice lifted her chin and set her jaw. "Well, Monica Dear clearly doesn't trust me around the children, so I guess that settles it."

This was where both Janice and Dex would wait for the apology, for Monica to backpedal and say she completely trusted Janice but she wouldn't feel right asking her to alter her plans. Monica refused to cave.

A chime sounded on Dex's phone, and he excused himself for a meeting. "Gotta go. I'll leave the arrangements up to the two of you." He blew Monica a kiss from above and gave his mother a hug. "I left some scrambled eggs on the stove," he called over his shoulder as he left.

Monica threw a cover-up over her wet suit and filled two plates with eggs. She scoured the spice cabinet, eyeing the red pepper flakes, Cajun seasoning, and anise. All too obvious. She settled on the garlic powder and shook a generous portion onto Janice's eggs and mixed it together, then decided a few sprinkles of onion powder wouldn't hurt. This was cruel. Less than an hour ago, while running, she reprimanded herself for her lack of patience with her mother-in-law and told herself she was going to practice loving Janice wholeheartedly.

Always a big fan of different perspectives, she looked out the slider door and contemplated whether she should go through with her defiance. Forgiveness was free, she reminded herself, asking Jesus for it ahead of time. She completed the plate with a handful of raspberries, grabbed two forks, and silenced her rational, inner voice telling her she was a rotten person.

Monica took a seat next to Janice at the outside table. Janice, pouring over a hideous-looking $15,000 chair displayed in her C magazine, raised that damned left eyebrow in defense as Monica placed the plate of eggs before her.

"Look, Janice. It's not that I don't trust you with the kids." Monica dove into her eggs eagerly as Janice raised a forkful to her mouth. Janice's flawless features crumpled on themselves as she tried to swallow. Monica purposely stuffed an oversized bite into her mouth and spoke while she chewed, "You're right. Dex really is the best cook. He's on some crazy garlic kick lately. Hope it's not too much for you."

Janice spit the eggs on her plate and took a large gulp of her cappuccino. "The texture is perfect. I'm only sensitive to excessive garlic." Her face flushed as she daintily popped a raspberry in her mouth.

"Don't be embarrassed, Janice. We're family. From now on, I'll make sure to bring you a napkin to spit Dex's preparations in. It'll be our secret." Monica giggled.

Janice eyed Monica's eggs inquisitively. Monica shoveled in the last bite, while doing mischievous mental cartwheels for succeeding with her *harmless* prank. She was awful. Rotten. Elated.

"Look. You've only been here a short time, and maybe once you're more comfortable with Kenzie's and Beck's routines and the way Dex and I parent them—"

Janice held up her hand, shushing Monica. "I raised two fine sons, Monica Dear. You can fully attest to that as you married quite a gentleman. I'm perfectly capable of caring for my grandchildren as well. I'll even follow your generation's hypersensitive, enabling parenting style if you wish. All you need to do is ask me for help."

Help? So help me God! Monica clenched her fists and screamed inside. Here she was, about to beg Janice to be a grandparent when they both knew she had no real interest. How did this twist always happen? How did Monica always fall prey? And what the heck did she mean by hypersensitive?

~*~

As Dex and Monica pulled out of the driveway, her tongue let loose.

"Did you know she mocked me about my sunglasses? She did. She asked me if I purchased them from the drugstore because they looked like knock-offs."

"Are they?"

"Of course they are, Dex. When have you known me to drop four hundred bucks on sunglasses for the kids to scratch? But the point is, why does it matter? And who says that? Certainly my mother-in-law shouldn't!"

"Well, maybe she'll surprise you with those Ray Bans you want."

"Maui Jim's, but I wouldn't accept them," Monica snapped. "I don't need expensive sunglasses to prove my worth."

"Ouch! The claws are out."

"Your mother has a way of bringing out the worst in me," Monica shot back in defense. "Anyway, I made us all salads for lunch. Did you know Kenzie and Beck actually asked me to make salad?"

Monica waved her hand. "Anyway, I made salads, including one for your mom, complete with diced eggs, beets, orange peppers, celery, almonds, and sundried tomatoes. I'm not exaggerating when I say it took me almost an hour to prepare. I topped it off with the leftover tuna that you grilled last night, and the kids gobbled it up. Kenzie complimented me by saying the salad was 'awe-thumb, and Beck backed her up with, 'Yum!'

"Do you know the one and only thing your mother said about it? She said, and I quote"—Monica made air quotes before continuing—"'Dexter is a master on the grill. I've never had tuna cooked to this level of perfection. You kids are so lucky your daddy is such a superb chef.'" Monica huffed. "Master, superb, perfection! Really? For the life of her, she couldn't compliment me, only put me down through praising you."

"What's so wrong with that?" Dex teased. He rested his hand high on her thigh, pushing her sundress up to her panties, involuntarily raising his eyebrow like his mother.

She pushed his hand away. "Dex, don't. You're not being funny."

"C'mon, Mon, relax. Let it go. We are alone! Call me your master. Tell me I'm superb, perfectly pleasing. That's some seriously good flirting."

"Don't flatter yourself, Dex."

"Look. I get how awful my mom can be, but can we not talk about her this afternoon? Fun Monica is so much funner."

"Funner isn't a word, but you're right. We won't let her spoil our afternoon. I only hope our children are safe."

Dex slapped the wheel. "Monica, stop! The kids will be napping for the next two hours, so she won't even have to watch them that long. By the way, smart move delaying their naps, less time we have to worry about their safety."

Monica gave Dex the worried eye.

"Kidding, Mon, they'll be fine. Promise."

"I know they will. I've hired a second set of eyes. I asked Amelia to stop over unexpectedly and play with them."

Dex sighed heavily. "As if that's not incredibly obvious. Jeez, Mon, you've got to chill."

"It won't be obvious because Amelia is going to get locked out of her house, and she isn't going to have anything else to do but play with the little neighbor kids."

Monica was paying Amelia for the secret babysitting. She had explained to Amelia that Janice was easily distracted but was too stubborn to admit when she needed a break. Amelia was fine going along with the story and excited for the opportunity to babysit.

Amelia understood that Janice's feelings would be hurt if she knew the real reason Amelia was stopping by, so that was why Amelia was going to be locked out of her house until her parents got home from work.

Dex's eyes narrowed. "You're overreacting, succumbing to hover-mother status. The ones you always rag on."

"Yes, but we live on a lake, Dex, and I would never forgive myself if something happened to our children on her watch."

"Fair enough, but can we please forget about what we left behind for the next few hours? I want to enjoy my wife for a bit, not the mother of my children. My wife, the wild and spontaneous, live-on-the-edge, talk-dirty-to-me-in-French wife."

"C'est suffisant," she echoed.

The first hour they spent sitting in their chairs surrounded by a cooler of drinks and snacks, a bag overflowing with a football, Frisbee, and the paddle board game, but were so exhausted with their lives that they hadn't the energy to do more than bask in the sun. They both dozed and Dex drooled, until finally Monica mustered up some energy and swatted him with the paddle board, challenging him to a fierce game.

They tossed a football back and forth as they had when they were dating and then held each other in the water as the waves rolled over their shoulders. They entertained the idea of a summer vacation and reminisced about their carefree pre-kid years as they walked along the shore and to the end of the pier where they watched boats motor by.

They lingered over dinner at Taste, eating small plates of sushi, beef Wellington and fish tacos, Monica giving in to one too many martinis.

Monica had texted Amelia a few times, and their plan had gone perfectly. She had played with the kids, helped Janice prepare dinner, and set out their pajamas before going home. All Janice had to do was read books and tuck them in for the night. Monica could breathe a sigh of relief.

As they left the restaurant, Monica spoke with Janice and was assured that all was well. Kenzie had talked her into making model clay creations, but they would be off to bed shortly.

"See, nothing to agonize over," Dex said as they climbed back in the Jeep.

With no time constraints, they went back to the beach to watch the sunset. Monica rested her head on Dex's shoulder as they sat in the sand, taking in the blazing fireball about to dip into Lake Michigan. Orange bled into pink, pink into purple; it was stunning. Nothing beat a Lake Michigan sunset.

Monica grabbed Dex's hand and kissed it. "Thank you for today. I may not say it often, but I appreciate you, and I love the life we've created. Promise me we'll always remember to take time out to have fun together, even if it's forced."

Dex pulled Monica closer and squeezed her tight. She loved the way his enormity engulfed her. "It's not the Maldives or Bora Bora like I see you pinning on Pinterest. However, I promise to always be by your side, and I'll keep it fun. Because I am fun!"

"Don't let my pins threaten you. Pinterest is just a place to escape and live vicariously in a world where we don't have budgets. We'd have unlimited funds to travel the globe, and could craft anything with expertise, wear flawless makeup and stunning outfits while strolling down city streets with a latte in hand, and where calories didn't count, and every dish you prepared was picture perfect," Monica dreamed.

"I mean why would I want a complete pullout storage unit under the stairs or a mudroom with labeled cubbies, ten lockers, and no mud? Seriously, a guest house on the beach complete with a pergola and climbing vines with exotic flowers is so overrated. I was bored the day I pinned that one."

They laughed but, most of all, felt perfect contentment for the simple life they led. The sun was sinking fast, and the crowds of people on the beach had started counting down from ten as the last speck of orange disappeared into the lake. Dex kissed Monica as if it were the ball dropping on New Year's Eve.

They almost didn't hear Dex's phone over the clapping and whistles that often followed the sunset. After Dex answered, it took all of three seconds for Monica to register that the phone call was from Janice. It was bad news. Urgent.

Dex was on his feet, pulling Monica up with him in one swift move, yelling, "Who? How? When?" into his phone as he dragged her by the hand through the sand to the parking lot. Monica's tears were already streaming down her cheeks as she tried to keep up with him. Something awful had happened to her babies.

CHAPTER 12

The one who falls and gets up is stronger than the one who never fell.

Carmen

Carmen was aware of her headache before she opened her eyes. The sunlight was flooding in through the transom windows, a shining ray of hope. The clock read 8:12. Normally, this would count as sleeping in, but once again she wasn't sure if she even totaled four hours of slumber. Victor's side of the bed was empty, and she wondered if he'd slept at all.

Penelope had been holed up in her room, not speaking to anyone after the first night Victor had found her cutting. Since then, she'd become even more sullen, angry, and defiant. Carmen knew she had been sneaking out in the middle of the night, taking off in Grace's car and probably meeting up with Landon. Like a coward, Carmen pretended not to notice for fear of further cutting. She was going to pick her battles.

Big mistake.

Victor was in the girls' bathroom retrieving his shaving cream they'd suddenly grown fond of, when he found traces of smeared blood on the floor and splatters around the sink. He confronted Penelope and was on the brink of demanding a skin check, when she broke down in tears. One of Penelope's cuts under her arm was infected so badly he had to take her to Urgent Care.

Carmen shuffled out to the kitchen, pleased to see Victor had brewed a pot of coffee; it always tasted better when he made it. She poured herself a cup, added hazelnut creamer, and held her mug at eyelevel to take a closer look at the faces staring back at her. The collage comprised photos of Amelia in pigtails and Penelope with her crooked teeth before braces, the two girls in their Halloween costumes, the girls with a giant snowman between them, and a picture of them in leotards doing the splits.

The photo mug had been a gift to her on Mother's Day four years ago. She remembered opening it and telling the girls it was the best present she'd ever received. It still was.

She peered up the steps at Penelope's closed door as she passed through the living room on her way to find Victor on the deck. As Carmen opened her mouth to speak, Victor informed her that he had checked on Penelope earlier and she was sleeping soundly.

She kissed her husband, moved her chair close to his, and took his hand. They looked out over the water as if answers would roll in with the waves. It was time for a more serious discussion, a plan, an intervention.

Everyone in the family was suffering from Penelope's behavior, and Carmen didn't understand why Penelope couldn't see that. Or was it just that she was hurting, so she made it her mission to hurt others? At this point, Carmen feared a downward spiral from Amelia too. Would she grow distant and defiant as they poured their energy into helping Penelope?

Carmen feared her daughters' occasional bickering would only escalate into constant fighting and grow so intense they might never bounce back to the sisters they once were.

Amelia spent less and less time at home these days, shoving off in the kayak by herself for hours on end or escaping to Piper's house for sleepovers. Carmen had asked Amelia for insight as to why she thought Penelope and Penelope's best friend Liz had suddenly turned on each other. At first, Amelia blew Carmen's questions off, remarking that they'd simply grown apart.

Whenever Amelia asked to go to Piper's house, Carmen would suggest that Penelope should go to hang out with Liz. A couple of times Carmen had asked Amelia to urge Penelope to text Liz. Amelia shrugged at first then got upset at Carmen for asking. "They aren't friends anymore, Mom. Big deal, move on," Amelia had barked.

"What are we going to do Victor?" Carmen asked, sipping her coffee.

"I think we seek professional help. We can't do this alone. It's all so foreign, and it's blown way out of proportion."

Carmen couldn't help the fact that she immediately thought "*I*" when Victor said "*we*" since his presence at home was spotty. However, she quickly reminded herself of the fact that he *was* home that first night he caught her cutting, and thank God, because who knows what lengths Penelope would have gone to if he hadn't walked into her room. He had also been the one to confront her the second time and be there to take her to Urgent Care. Victor was remarkable with Penelope, the gentle way he took care of her without getting upset.

"Gabby Bock from across the lake is a therapist, and she's raised four teenagers." Carmen pointed towards Gabby's and thought of pregnant Stella. Just as quickly, she dismissed any judgment; it had nothing to do with Gabby as a therapist or a parent for that matter.

"Do you think Penelope would agree to that?"

"Nope." Carmen envisioned Penelope's refusing to go and the fights that would ensue. However, desperation suffused her. "I'll talk to Gabby today and see if she's willing to see her. Who knows? Maybe Penelope will be open for the opportunity."

"I don't get teenagers these days. We are supportive and loving parents. She has plenty of food, clothes, freedom, independence, and encouragement," Victor reasoned. "The basics aren't enough for kids anymore. It's almost as if their lives are so carefree they create stress for themselves."

Carmen nodded in bitter agreement, thinking about her upbringing. "Maybe we ask too much of her." Carmen's voice was thick with sarcasm. "Folding a random load of laundry and scrubbing her own bathroom *is* asking a lot."

"These damn kids have no sense of identity beyond social media." Victor rubbed the scruff on his jaw. "They're entitled and we enable it. Being grounded means she gets to sit in the luxury of her room, watch Netflix, and Snapchat all day. Penelope needs a purpose, goals. She needs to revolve around something other than herself and her small superficial world of screens."

Victor pounded his pointer finger on the table as he ticked off, one by one, what needed to change. Now. "What she needs is some laborious, meaningful work. Penelope needs to be told no. It's a free-for-all around here, the way she comes and goes as if this was a hotel."

Victor's cheeks flushed as he got riled up. Carmen sat back and let him because this was exactly what she went through in her head, alone, night after night.

When he called to tell her good night, she sensed his disappointment as she voiced her frustration that, the only chance they had to communicate, all she did was complain and vent about what was going on at home. He didn't understand the emotional drain because he didn't live it daily. He came home and got a small dose and set off again, receiving his break, while Carmen was left to manage on her own.

"The thing is, Victor"—she put her hand on top of his thumping finger—"I'm struggling too." She didn't want to start a fight with Victor. They needed to keep their focus on getting Penelope help, but she needed to get some bottled-up frustrations off her chest. The last couple of months he'd been extending his stay in Las Vegas an extra day or two, coming home sometimes for less than forty-eight hours before jetting off again. "I agree with everything you're saying; however, if this is how you think *we* should parent, then I need your help with the girls for more than a day or two here and there. I can't do this alone. I'm dog tired, on the verge of a breakdown, giving up. I can't be everything to everybody every second of the day while you're clear across the country."

Victor's tough-guy demeanor switched to an odd displaced apprehension. Carmen didn't understand where this awkward behavior came from. It was so "un-Victor" like. He had always been an involved, hands-on parent. Lately, he was absorbed with chasing success. Anything else was a distraction, even his family.

"I also run my own company, Victor—forty-eight employees that currently service sixty-four businesses. I have two full-time jobs, and the most important profession in the world is being a parent, and I feel like I'm doing a lousy job. We used to be this team; one of us was always available, always present. We both had the girls' schedules plugged into our phones. Have you any idea what classes they take, what papers and projects they are working on, or what days and times they have sports or clubs to attend?"

"We both know Penelope won't involve herself in anything since quitting water polo."

"And why do you think that is, Victor?"

"Heck if I know." He threw his hands up in the air. "She only gets pissed off at me when I ask, so I don't anymore."

"Exactly," Carmen said, nodding. "So, as parents, should we persist or check out?"

"Jeez, Carmen"—Victor sighed as he ran his hands through his hair—"are you really pegging all this on me? You admitted you thought she had been sneaking out and turned a blind eye."

"Not you, *us*. We have flourishing careers, each getting pulled in a different direction. I see what's going on at home. It's stressful and scary because we don't know how to make our daughter simply make good choices and behave. You've let yourself off the hook, and as many days as I'd like to, and threaten I'm going to, I won't." Carmen's voice wobbled. "Our family life needs to be our top priority."

Victor's arms shot up along with his voice. "It is!"

Carmen's eyes narrowed, shutting down any opening for argument.

Victor rubbed his jaw for the umpteenth time. If he wasn't careful, he was going to have a bald spot. "I know. My clientele has skyrocketed, and I don't want to turn people away. I don't know how long this will last. These companies want their employees to be good golfers for when they do business on the course, and I don't know how long they'll be throwing money out for my services. Once I navigate a solid clientele that will be in it for the long haul, I'll scale back. I'll be home so much you'll be wishing I was gone."

Carmen leaned forward and took Victor's chin in her hand. She looked directly in his eyes. "I doubt it. I miss you. Do you realize this is the longest we've sat down and talked in months? Months, Victor! It took our daughter slicing herself to get us to slow down and be present."

Victor inhaled loudly and exhaled much the same. His eyes shifted nervously away from hers, and a strange alarm went off in her body that she'd never felt before. Carmen was used to Victor calming *her* anxieties and giving her a reality check. The shift troubled her.

"You're stressed. I'm stressed. My business is doing well, the house is nearly paid for, and Penelope's and Amelia's college funds are full. We have a decent nest egg. What's wrong with scaling back now? One week you're gloating that we can retire when we're fifty-five and play golf all over the country; the next you're distracted, anxious, downright tense, and edgy. You can't wait to get back on the plane to Vegas, yet the schedule is wearing you thin."

Victor pulled Carmen from her chair onto his lap. "No wonder you're frazzled. You're bouncing from one dilemma to the next." He sighed and rubbed his forehead.

She reached up and ran her fingers through his hair. "So, are you involved in a dilemma?"

Victor scoffed and pulled her close, placing her head on his shoulder. To avoid eye contact? "The only dilemma is that I'm not turning anyone away. I can't yet. It takes time to navigate whom you click with and who is going to have longevity. In a world where your existence depends on reviews, likes, and word of mouth, I need to devote myself 110%."

Victor kissed Carmen tenderly and then traced his finger over her lips. He'd done did this on their third date while telling her she had the most beautiful lips he'd ever seen. To this day, it still worked to get him out of the doghouse.

"I promise to cut back down to three days each week as soon as I can. I feel awful I didn't realize how rough things were with Penelope. Teenagers, hormones, drama, defiance . . . Remember I grew up in a houseful of boys. I've heard the horror stories with teenage girls and figured her behavior was normal and would pass soon enough."

"She's a wreck." Carmen's voice trembled as a tear slipped onto Victor's shoulder. She let her weight sink into him. His familiar, muscular shape was protective and comforting. He'd let her down, but she didn't want to be upset with him. "Overnight she went from ponytails and American Girl dolls to black cats and voodoo dolls."

Carmen felt a smile spread across his face, his stubble tickling her forehead. He smoothed her hair with his hand. "We need to focus on getting Penelope straightened out and that starts today."

~*~

Victor woke Penelope and put her to work. The two of them mowed the grass, cleaned out the garage, washed and waxed the speedboat, and detailed Carmen's car, which sent Penelope fuming since she no longer rode in it and her own car sat filthy dirty in the driveway. Victor taught her how to change the oil in her car, branding her cheeks with a thick smear of Valvoline upon completion.

Her behavior went from sour to pouty, from argumentative to docile, and from tired to content as the day rolled on. Earlier, he had said he was going to make Penelope feel good about herself. He was going to work her to the point where she was proud of her accomplishments.

Every so often Carmen would sneak a peek at Victor and Penelope working side by side. Victor would be talking her through the steps of changing the oil, letting Penelope take charge and screw up. He would laugh, patiently redirecting her. As the day went on, Carmen saw Penelope's features brighten, her tone soften, and heard the sweet sound of laughter escape.

Carmen and Amelia set to work washing her bedroom walls and taping off the windows and trim. They slapped on the happiest color of aqua, each stroke clearing Carmen's mind, giving her hope that with time they could scrub the ugliness from Penelope and repaint her happy. What color would do the trick?

Taking the term "paint clothes" literally, Amelia took advantage of Carmen being lost in thought and took the paintbrush to Carmen's T-shirt, putting a large dot on each of Carmen's breasts and another on her belly with a smile underneath.

Carmen tried to keep a straight face—"Hilarious, Amelia"—but she cracked with laughter and gave Amelia her own aqua stripe across her chest and a dot of paint on her nose.

"Even," Carmen said proudly and turned back to the wall.

Amelia was only getting started and swiped the roller from the top of Carmen's back all the way down her butt.

Carmen swirled around—"Big, big mistake, little missy"—and slapped her brush across Amelia's forehead. From there it was an all-out war. Within moments, they were covered in paint, only the whites of their eyes left unscathed.

"First one to the end of the dock wins," Carmen challenged.

Amelia's eyes lit up. She dropped the roller in her hand and fled the room.

"Don't touch anything on your way out." Carmen ran after her in panic, fearing she'd leave a trail of aqua through the house.

Amelia burst out the door, Carmen on her heels. Playing dirty, she grasped for Amelia's shirt and tugged, only slowing her slightly as she wiggled free and kept sprinting through the yard.

They hit the sand and Carmen stretched out her arm again, this time snagging hold of Amelia's ponytail. It was a cheap move on Carmen's part, but she was determined. Amelia's head jerked, and she shrieked in pain, her arms flailing as she tumbled backward. Amelia rolled over and popped up like a cat, the aqua paint now speckled with sand.

Carmen gained at least four strides on Amelia, propelling herself onto the dock. She lost a flip-flop in the process, but it would not slow her down. She was going to win.

The dock shook behind her, signaling Amelia too, had reached it. Carmen kicked it into high gear; she hadn't run this fast since, well, never. Her heart was pounding from exhaustion but more so from the adrenaline rush. Ten feet of dock left, six more feet and she was going to make a leap for it.

Pumping her arms for maximum speed, she took her last step and leapt, felt the ball of her right foot victoriously catapult her into the air. For a moment, she was free, high above the water. Her arms rose overhead in triumph, until she was jolted. Her body jerked as Amelia's arms clamped around her waist, thrusting her backwards, Amelia's body slipping beneath hers.

They landed with a splat. The water rushed in around Carmen's face, up into her nostrils. Their arms and legs were a tangled mess. Carmen surfaced first, choked, and spat water.

Amelia popped up, inhaling a sharp breath, then yelled, "I hit the water first. I win!"

"You brat! That was cheating." Carmen flicked water in Amelia's face. "Play nice."

"Pulling my hair was playing nice? I was using strategy."

"Truce," Carmen growled.

They swam to the edge of the dock. Carmen, all energy sapped, was barely able to climb the three-rung ladder, and Amelia, hands on the dock, shot herself out of the water like she was weightless.

"Show off." Carmen nudged her shoulder, sending her back into the water.

"I wouldn't go there if I were you," Amelia warned.

Carmen squeezed excess water out of her shirt and lay back on the dock, closing her eyes. "If you push me in, I'll drown."

Amelia lay back next to her, a puddle forming around them. They looked like two drowned rats, Carmen wheezing, paint still stuck to their skin.

Carmen took advantage of the jovial atmosphere and nonchalantly asked Amelia for the umpteenth time, "Do you have any insight as to why Penelope's world flipped the way it did? Why she dropped her old friends?

Amelia tensed. "Nope."

"Mealie, why do you always clam up when I ask about your sister? Are you afraid of her being mean to you? Are you keeping secrets of hers? Is she blackmailing you? Or are you trying to be the loyal sister and not rat her out for taking drugs or something?"

"Mom, please stop. I don't want to talk about Penelope all the time."

The tone in Amelia's voice convinced Carmen there was something worth probing. Instead of the dismissive *I-don't-feel-like-talking-about-my-sister* tone, Carmen heard trepidation, the voice people use when they avoid a topic because they are apprehensive, protecting something or someone, possibly tangled up in it themselves.

"We need to help your sister, Mealie, before she gets worse. I know you love her very much and you're nervous she's going to flip out, because she usually does, but you can't be afraid. I get it. Dad and I are in the same boat; we're all walking on eggshells around her. But we're only enabling her, so if you know anything--"

"Seriously, Mom," Amelia interrupted. "I don't know anything except that she walks around pissed off all the time and she's mean to me for no reason. Like I had anything to do with it."

"Anything to do with *what,* Amelia?"

"Nothing! I've done nothing! Why are you accusing me for what she does?"

"Honey, no one is accusing you. I'm just trying to understand her. I think we both can agree that, after Penelope's broken leg, she hasn't been the same person. Water polo was her life, and now she won't even get in the pool. She doesn't hang out with any of her old friends, she's with a bad crowd, she's come home drunk and smelling of pot, and she's cutting. I want to know why."

"Then ask *her*."

Carmen paused as she remembered something Amelia had said to Penelope. "What did you mean the other night when you said, 'I'm not the one that talks trash about you,' to your sister. Are people saying nasty things about Penelope?"

Amelia growled and sat up, the heat rising to her cheeks, flushing them. Carmen had killed the breezy mood. How were these walls built between her and her daughters? One day they were fun-loving chatterboxes, and the next they kept secrets and sassed her.

Amelia stifled a sob. "Stop blaming me, Mom. I just meant I'm not the mean one. She is. She's the one always getting in trouble, and somehow I always get lectured too."

"You're right. I'm sorry." Carmen dove in for a hug, letting it drop for the time being, but she wasn't going to look the other way anymore.

Victor and Penelope came trudging down the dock toward them, each clutching a gas can.

"Let's spend the rest of the afternoon on the boat," suggested Carmen.

"Sure, I'll gas it up and go change," agreed Victor.

"No thanks, I'm tired." Penelope crossed her arms in defense.

"Please, Penelope, you can relax on the boat, take a nap," Carmen's voice sounded desperate and she was glad. She wanted Penelope to have empathy, to understand her attitude and behavior was also hurting others.

Carmen looked to Victor for help.

"We can't make her have fun." Victor shrugged. "She's been a trooper and worked hard today. I'm okay if she wants to hang back and take a break."

"Sorry, I'm not okay with her being here alone. I don't trust that she won't take off," Carmen argued; although she'd confiscated Penelope's car keys.

Penelope glared at Carmen. "I'm not going to take off."

Victor sighed. "We can't let our sixteen-year-old daughter out of our sight?"

Carmen's shoulders sank. "I'll hang out here on the beach. You and Mealie can go for a boat ride."

"No, Mom, please come with us," Amelia begged.

Victor held up his hand. "We're doing it, enabling her. Hard work and forced family time. It's how I was raised." He inhaled a sharp breath, no doubt gearing up for the battle. "Penelope, please change into your suit. We are all going for a boat ride."

Penelope spun so quickly her hair fluttered around her as if she were imitating a hair product commercial. Only, Penelope's features were far from the state of ecstasy that the hair models received from a bottle of suds. No, her penetrating glare was enough to make Carmen want to dive off the dock to avoid the darts shooting from her eyes.

"Please, Sweet P," Victor pleaded.

Seriously, Victor? Use your brain. Really, really bad time to call her Sweet P. Despite Victor's choice of nickname, Penelope's eyes shifted to her father's, which, Carmen noticed, didn't offend with the hatred Penelope reserved for her.

"Fine."

Carmen couldn't believe what she had just witnessed. Did they make a small step in the right direction?

They stood frozen until Penelope reached the house and was out of ear shot. Carmen turned to Victor and gave him a high five. "We did it!"

CHAPTER 13

God didn't add another day in your life because you needed it.
He added it because someone else needs you.

Gabriella

The sun had eagerly risen above the tree line as if it were anticipating the glory it would bring. A moment ago, she was chilly, but now Gabby untied her robe, revealing beads of sweat on her chest. Her coffee had gone lukewarm, but she didn't mind. Gabby loved cold coffee and usually reserved half a cup to gulp down mid-morning. She took the last swallow and stood on the front portico, admiring the beauty of her hydrangeas.

Gabby followed the porch around to the back patio facing the lake. She desperately wanted to absorb a bit of the sun's grandeur, to feel content, cheerful that it rose. That's the type of person she was. She went through her days appreciating the simple things in life. Only now, her sunshine had been stolen, and she hated to think how long it would take for the sound of the seagulls and waves, the scent of the water, or a pink sky to bring her joy. How long would it take to ease the pain that seemed to settle deep within?

She ran her fingers across the table, waiting to seat and feed an absent crowd. Leaning against the column, she looked out over the lake. Where are my people? They'd always entertained a crowd. Now, as the news circulated among their friends, they kept their distance. Sure, they called and texted, but it was a silent decision that neither Gabby nor Greg venture out to play golf or meet for dinner with their closely-knit group of couples, as if it were forbidden that one go and not the other.

Two fishermen were about fifteen feet from her dock, one of the best fishing spots on the lake for reasons Gabby was oblivious to. It was too early for motorized watercraft to be speeding around creating a wake, so the water sat flat as glass, serenely reflecting a few passing clouds.

She waved at the fisherman with her empty coffee cup dangling from her thumb. They responded by tipping their hats at her, one a baseball cap with a beer logo, the other a fishing hat with a bass on the front. For some bizarre reason, their gesture made her eyes well up with tears. She felt lonely, her morning company reduced to waving at fishermen.

"New friends?"

Gabby spun around to find Greg standing disturbingly close. Had he snuck up on her on purpose or had she been so absorbed in thought she hadn't heard him?

"Jeez, Greg, you can't just show up here unannounced." She clutched her robe with her fist.

"Why not? It's my house too, Gabby. You're my wife. Besides, would you have agreed to let me come by had I asked?"

"What do you want, Greg?"

He cocked his head to the side. "Really, Gabby? You, of all people, are asking such an imprudent question? I want to work on us. I want to fix us. I want to save our family."

"And how exactly do you think we should go about that, Greg? With secrets and lies? I'm not so sure you're concerned about us. I think your only concern is Greg. Greg and possibly Holly, maybe your unborn baby girl."

"I'm concerned about *you*, Gabby, about our kids. I've talked with them about the situation, which I'm sure you're aware of."

Gabby nodded. "Yes, Greg, I'm fully aware that you flew to your defense after Stella gave you a piece of her mind. On the verge of giving her siblings an earful, you wanted to beat her to the punch, explain your version."

"Unfair."

"True," Gabby retorted.

"Well"—Greg sighed—"now they know. It's out in the open. and I can start rebuilding my relationship with each one of them."

"Just like that, Greg? Tell them half the truth, or better yet, cover up half the truth. Wipe your hands clean and power on."

"That's what we need to talk about, Gabby. My relationship with Holly . . ." He paused, shifted from one foot to another uncomfortably. "I promise you the relationship is no longer physical. The affair is over, Gabby." He shoved his hands in a pair of light blue linen shorts Gabby had never seen before. Holly must be updating his wardrobe. Greg never would have picked that color out himself nor willingly worn them had Gabby urged.

Everything about Greg's mannerisms and words was unsettling. Like the old school movie reel, Gabby watched visions of Greg's character slowly spin in circles. Every so often the film would catch, the glitch on the projector screen insinuating when Greg faltered. Gabby, accustomed to disregarding his glitches, allowed Greg to keep the popcorn popping, adding extra butter to divert the audience's attention onto some other wonderful thing he had done. Or worse, Greg tended to fabricate falsities against others to divert attention away from his own wrongdoings.

When Greg flew off the handle at Klay, then thirteen, and called him a worthless idiot for denting the garage door with the snowblower, he made it up to Klay by buying him an $800 snowboard.

After he studied with Lottie for her chemistry test, she came home proudly waving her A- in the air. Instead of congratulating her, his first words had been, "How could you miss those three questions. We went over them a dozen times?" When her face fell, deflated, he backpedaled, convinced her to hop in the car to celebrate with ice cream and new shoes.

Greg seemed to have such a big, thoughtful heart, consistently going out of his way for other people, yet there was often an underlying compromise. Somehow, in the end, *you* ended up feeling guilty for getting upset over *his* manipulative behavior.

When he faltered, Gabby would try and talk to him about his behavior. Defensive, he had an uncanny way of reminding her of the boundless things he did for his family. He often dangled them over her head, whispered in her ear, leaving her to berate herself for being overly critical, analyzing her husband through a therapist's mind rather than a grateful wife's.

She stared at him intently, searching for clues, truth, insight.

"Holly is willing to part ways and raise our daughter alone. She's financially capable of supporting the child without assistance from me. I can walk away free and clear."

Gabby's face twisted in disbelief, her insides burning with his words.

"Free and clear, huh? So, life goes on as if nothing ever happened."

"That's not what I meant, Gabby." He took hold of her hand and brought it to his chest. His heart was thumping wildly, heat radiating through his shirt. "What I've done is wrong, horrendous. Will you at least allow me the opportunity to make things right with the people I've wronged?"

To point out he had a *habit* of wronging and then having to make things right with people was pointless. He couldn't see it.

"Do you think keeping secrets from our kids and walking away from Holly and your unborn daughter are the right things to do? You don't see that as wronging two more people?"

"My primary concern is for you and *our* children."

"Since when, Greg? Since getting caught?"

"Renewing our vows was my approach to starting over with you. I'm aware it's going to be a long road to get back on track with the kids too, but I'm willing to do whatever it takes, Gabriella."

Realizing Greg still had her hand resting on his chest, clenched between both of his sweating palms, she jerked away.

"What happens when your daughter starts asking questions about her daddy and she comes searching for you? When she's a teenager and demands her mother be honest? Will there be a difficult time down the road when Holly feels the pressure of being a single mother and suddenly feels compelled to reach out to you for support?"

Greg raised his hands and shook his head as if he couldn't bear the thoughts. "I guess it's possible we could remain open about the baby and still keep our family intact, Gabby. Blended families, sharing custody are the norm these days. If you're willing," he stammered. "I'll do whatever you want."

She narrowed her eyes at him in disbelief. "What are you suggesting?"

"If you think I should take more responsibility and be a father to the baby . . . we could figure it out, Gabby."

Gabby cocked her head to the side. "Right. We could start looking at a crib for the nursery on the weekends you have visitation rights. What a joke, Greg."

Greg opened his palms toward her. "What do you want from me, Gabby? Tell me what to do and I'll do it."

"I'm not giving you answers or a plan. I'm not giving you a way out. Nor am I giving you ultimatums. I didn't create this mess. What I will do is figure out what I want, *my* next steps."

"Gabby, give us and our family a chance. Knowing about the baby would kill the kids—"

"Hold on. It's not going to kill the kids. There's a possibility it could kill your relationship with them. That may be the risk you'll have to take. It's called taking ownership for your actions. You choose your behavior, but you don't get to choose the consequences."

Greg's eyes went wild. "So, you're going to tell them about the baby?"

"I didn't say that. I don't feel it's my place to do so."

"What are you saying, Gabby? You're going to force me to tell them?"

"Again, Greg, I'm not going to *make* your plans, decide your future, or give you ultimatums."

Greg was getting terse, impatient. Gabby couldn't help but feel slightly contented at his disposition. She had no intention of protecting Greg; her concern was solely for the kids.

"Please just say you'll give us a chance."

"I don't know yet, Greg. I don't know," she repeated softly. If she said no, would he go back to Holly? Did that threaten her?

"Forgive me. Please," he pleaded, his words choking in his throat.

She wanted to forgive Greg, not for him, for herself. She was a firm believer that forgiveness didn't excuse someone's behavior; it didn't wipe their slate clean of wrongdoing. Just as she'd told Stella, forgiveness replaced anger with peace. She wanted that. She wanted to let go of the rage, pain, and bitterness. More than that, she wanted to feel at peace with her decision. She didn't want to look back with regret, with the what ifs, or the if onlys.

"You should go, Greg."

He nodded, understanding he'd been dismissed. Gabby took a good look at him. Never had she seen dark circles under her husband's eyes, such worry in his features, or fear in his stature. The man standing before her was no longer the man she knew, the man she respected. His image was tainted so badly she wasn't sure if she could ever look at him and see anything else again.

~*~

Gabby dug in the dirt with force, hollowed a hole, placed the root of a basil plant in, and smoothed the dirt around it. While at the farmers' market, she had found the prettiest gardening box for her herb garden and scooped up dill, oregano, basil, mint, and cilantro. She situated the box on the patio near the grill and outdoor kitchen where she could easily access the herbs while cooking.

Over the past week, Gabby had been cooking up a storm. She refused to let the gorgeous outdoor space sit unused because she was alone. She was going to sit outside, enjoy the views of the lake, sip wine, and make elaborate meals for herself.

On a whim, she decided to invite both sides of neighbors over for appetizers and cocktails. No more than three minutes in, Bruce had jokingly asked if she'd kicked Greg out or buried him in the backyard. "I've never known Greg to travel for work." He eyed her intently, waiting for a response.

"I miss the competition with the grass," Jeremy cut in.

Melissa and Tracy, Bruce's and Jeremy's wives, trilled with fake laughter and respectively shared a swift look, poorly covered up. Gabby knew she and Greg had been a huge topic of discussion. No surprise.

"Buried in the backyard, now that's a thought." Gabby let her comment settle for a beat. She half wondered if someone on their street had witnessed their episode on the front porch. It would explain why not a single neighbor had knocked on their door for a tour or to welcome them back. "Greg is currently living in a penthouse in his office building."

"I'm sorry," Melissa spoke for the group while the rest of them nodded, their faces flushing.

"Thank you." Gabby smiled, the awkwardness of the moment heavy.

One by one they all reached for their cocktails, drinking in unison. Gabby held her glass in her hand, the condensation dripping down the sides onto the napkin she held underneath it.

The elephant in the room was big and fat, but Gabby was good at making people feel at ease, comfortable. It was her job. All she had to do was shift the conversation back on them. Men, like Bruce, liked to talk about themselves, so it was an easy task.

The awkwardness dissipated as the night rolled on and her neighbors helped themselves to far more cocktails than should be consumed on a Tuesday evening. It was fine though. Gabby enjoyed the loose conversations about who was doing what on their street: who was targeted as being responsible for bringing zebra mussels into the lake, who was paying big bucks to haul in truckloads of clean sand for their beach, and who was three years behind on their association dues.

Had they been gossiping when they left her? Absolutely. Gabby didn't care because her situation sucked, and Greg sucked, but *she* didn't suck.

Gabby finished planting the last of her herbs, stood, and clipped her shoulder-length hair back. Her thick wavy mop was out of control in the summer months thanks to the spike in humidity. She should have clipped it back before she did her planting, because every time she pushed her hair off her face she added another glob of dirt to it.

Gabby tossed her gardening gloves next to the planter, poured herself a glass of iced tea, and kicked back in a lounge chair. She closed her eyes, enjoyed the sun on her face until a shadow moved over her. Fear swept through her. Not again.

She opened her eyes, surprised, but relieved, to see Carmen.

"I'm sorry to barge in on you like this. As I was knocking on the front door, I could see your car in the garage, so, like a stalker, I followed the porch around. I hope that's okay."

Carmen stood in front of Gabby, looking all kinds of sexy dressed in a sleeveless yellow dress belted at the waist. She towered over Gabby in heels. Her caramel-streaked hair hung long with big soft curls, her makeup, heavier than Gabby had ever dared worn, looked professionally flawless. Gabby knew Carmen owned some sort of service company, heating and cooling or something.

Regardless, she looked the part of the high-powered career woman. Gabby wondered if Holly looked similar, if this was the type of authoritative figure that lured Greg to Holly.

"I'd love some company," Gabby responded while getting up to pour a glass of iced tea for Carmen.

Carmen dropped her purse on the table, the beautiful Tiffany, and Gabby wondered if Tiffany had finally reached her capacity, if the one and only friend wasn't enough anymore.

Gabby placed the iced tea down in front of Carmen, who was staring intently across the lake at her own house.

"I've always found it fascinating how the lake takes on a new shape from a different angle," commented Gabby.

"I agree. My house looks foreign from here. By the way, your place turned out remarkable." Carmen took in her surroundings. "It's so serene, so quiet." Carmen seemed to register what she said and apologized to Gabby. "I'm sorry. You're probably cursing the quiet."

"Don't apologize. It's beautifully quiet. Anytime you need a break, you're always welcome here." Gabby smiled to reassure Carmen. "Company gives me the needed break from my thoughts."

Gabby tilted her head to the side with a studious look on her face. "What brings you here? You're kind of a mysterious woman; however, it's no mystery dropping by for idle chit chat and tea isn't your style," she mused, assuring Carmen she was okay with the impromptu visit.

Carmen rubbed her temples. "Where do I start? Teenage rebellion, drama, the cutting . . . it's all mounting and I'm about to explode."

"Then you've come to the right place."

Underneath the meticulously put-together woman lurked a worn out, defeated mother. Gabby knew the look; she had seen it in herself plenty of times over the years while raising four children. There was always a situation with one or two or three of the kids brewing. She thought of Stella. There were still situations.

"Do you think you could help Penelope?" Carmen smoothed a strand of hair in front of her shoulder. "I'm at a loss of what to do. I've no authority or control over her anymore. I know that's not what parenting is about, controlling your children, but somehow her defiance has taken over our entire household. I want to get us back to where we were. Not broken."

"I'm willing to give it a shot. My only concern is that Penelope would hold back from me since she knows we're friends. I need to gain her full trust and that may take time. Teenagers are often tight-lipped for fear that whatever they say will ultimately slap them in the face."

Carmen nodded, looking fragile. Gabby always admired her beauty, but she had mostly witnessed the woman at home or on the lake in casual attire. No denying she looked sensual in a pair of sweatpants. She now saw the striking resemblance to Sophia Vergara that Monica had always pointed out.

"You barely know me, and you labeled us friends. Are you sure you want to own that? I mean . . . I know I'm not exactly a warm and fuzzy social butterfly, especially with women. Victor says I come across as brass and harsh."

Gabby patted Carmen's purse. "Tiffany is busting at the seams, Carmen. Why don't you give her a break and invite someone with a little flesh and bone into your world?"

A look of fear flashed across Carmen's face, leaving Gabby to wonder where it came from. Why was she so scared of relationships? "We all wear some type of armor. It's what's underneath the armor that counts. I pride myself on being a good judge of character, and I have no qualms about calling you a friend," Gabby assured.

Carmen looked down bashfully. "Thanks, I appreciate that. I never imagined Penelope becoming so defiant and never in my wildest dreams thought she'd cut."

Carmen went on to explain the past year of their lives: her struggles, her fears, all the ways she was feeling inadequate. Carmen's words flew out of her mouth faster with each sentence. Every now and again, Gabby detected the tiniest Columbian accent and wondered if her parents' accents were heavy.

"I saw Penelope and Victor doing yard work and waxing the boat. I think giving teenagers chores and holding them accountable is vital. I'm behind on paperwork and slightly overwhelmed with caring for the house by myself. What would you think if I approached Penelope and offered her a job? It would be a great way for the two of us to connect, build up trust, and ease into conversational counseling."

A stifled cry escaped from Carmen. She hiccupped a laugh to cover it up and wiped a single tear from the corner of her eye. "That's a fantastic idea, thank you. I feel so helpless."

Gabby leaned forward in her chair and gave Carmen an encouraging hug. Her arms reciprocated, hesitantly. "Family is generally the source of our greatest joy and our deepest pain."

Thoughts of Greg and Holly being intimate swirled through Gabby's head. She squeezed her eyes to abandon the image with no luck. A chill ran through her as she envisioned Greg's fingers tracing Holly's thighs, kissing the tender skin underneath her arm until it led him to her breast. Carmen started to speak in the nick of time. Gabby could feel her anger building, so she forced herself to concentrate, to extinguish the fiery surge, aware she'd broken into a cold nervous sweat.

"I swung home to grab a file"—Carmen dropped her head, ashamed—"and flew off the handle at Penelope. She was in the basement, blinds closed, watching a movie in sweat pants and a sweatshirt. None of her chores were done, dirty dishes filled the sink, the kitchen counters were littered with grease and crumbs, and the laundry I asked her to fold sat wrinkled in the dryer while the load in the washer sat wet, beginning to smell."

Carmen clenched her fists and gave a low growl. "I calmly asked her to get started on her chores and, without taking an eye off the TV or her phone, because one must manage both at the same time, she complained the air conditioning was set too cold."

A smile formed in the corner of Gabby's lips as she recalled a similar scenario with Calvin only last summer.

"Like any good mother"—Carmen sighed with sarcasm—"I blew up. I screamed at her from the top of my lungs to get off her lazy duff and go outside where the sun was shining. Good grief, it's eighty-four degrees!"

The declaration forced Carmen to take several sips of her iced tea and pat her upper lip with her napkin. "Instead of stopping there, I dug my heels in further and told her to find some ambition to make something of herself, to get over the pity party, and, prepare for the clincher"—Carmen closed her eyes—"to quit slicing her skin for attention."

Carmen covered her mouth with her hand. "I'm an awful mother. I can't believe I said those things. The worst part is that, before I even walked through the door, I knew I'd find her as I did. The civilized pep talk that I meant to deliver, that I had rehearsed, completely evaporated, vanishing into a vaporous stream sucked out of my brain. It's as if I lose all rationality, blow up to the point it's no longer her wrongdoing but mine. The fact that she caused us to get to the brink no longer the issue, instead, my reaction to it."

Grabbing fistfuls of her hair in her hands, Carmen lifted the long tendrils off her neck. "Gosh, Gabby, how do you do that?"

Gabby blinked. "Do what?"

"Get people to fall on their knees and spill their innermost, wretched secrets."

Gabby chuckled. If only. Seems my husband was rather skillful at keeping his secrets from me. Gabby pushed the thought aside before her inferno started raging.

"You're a wonderful mother who cares about her daughter. She's pushed you to the brink; you reacted out of fear and frustration. It happens. Don't beat yourself up."

Carmen let her hair fall, shaking her head in disappointment. "We've just begun to get to know each other, and I've definitely reversed the order of protocol. I'd feel slightly less inadequate had I revealed a few of my more flattering qualities before all the adverse ones."

Gabby frowned with empathy. "Stop. Teenagers are tough. They're like clever little aliens that trap you in their extraterrestrial forces, rendering you defenseless, breaking you to the point where you're all claws and fangs."

Carmen threw her head back with a trill. "And tongue. Don't forget my impulsive tongue."

Gabby eyed Carmen inquisitively, "Besides, who says you need to be perfect? Navigating through parenting is challenging, and you've laid a good foundation for your kids. Temporary derailment is bound to happen from time to time."

"I feel lost," Carmen stated simply.

"We may not always like *what* we do. What's important is that we like *who* we are." Gabby had sat opposite hundreds of women from all walks of life over the past two decades. Only a blind therapist would miss the concealed manner Carmen hid behind. The woman portrayed before her was obscured, her heart masked, different from the stealthy woman she presented. No doubt Carmen was confident and accomplished, but she was also carrying a deep hurt.

"Tell me about your parents. Siblings?" asked Gabby.

Carmen's eyes darted away. "Only child. My parents live on Bald Head Island, North Carolina." Carmen's tone was clipped, offering nothing more as her gaze remained fixed on the lake.

Bingo. Gabby was good at picking up on distress; she'd found it entailed in Carmen's family. However, now wasn't the time to probe.. It was time to earn Carmen's trust. "I love the Carolinas. We took the kids on a road trip to the east coast one summer: Myrtle Beach, Martha's Vineyard, Cape Cod, Provincetown." Gabby flitted her hand as she reminisced to Carmen.

Gabby recalled the excitement and awe on the kids' faces at the euphoric energy the Beluga whales radiated as their mouths opened wide to feed, as they crested the water, rolling, lazily plunging below the surface with a graceful force. Gabby had grasped Greg's hand while tears sprang to her eyes at the kids' elation as they ran back and forth from one side of the tour boat to the other, amazed at the enormity of the creatures languidly lifting their tails, splashing saltwater stories high.

There they stood, Gabby fully aware one of her fondest family memories was unfolding before her as whales larger than the vessel keeping them afloat were only feet below, elegantly displaying their supremacy.

Greg had gasped in amazement and pulled Gabby close. He'd felt it too. This was what mattered. The experiences they shared together a thousand miles away from home, free from the addictions of the crazy busy rivalry, the constant dings clamoring for their attention, the drive to achieve more, receive instantly. All that had robbed them from what truly mattered, tricking their minds into basing their worth on what they accomplished, success on what they possessed, and the obsession for attaining *it* faster.

There, they were home, albeit in the Atlantic Ocean. The six of them together had experienced a beauty only the hands of God could create. Sure, it was only a matter of time, dreadfully minutes, Gabby realized, before the kids would be posting videos and pictures. However, for a brief moment in time, they had surrendered the frantic, anxiety-provoking world that consumed them. Instead, they were experiencing life with heightened senses, captivated by the slapping of whale skin as it smacked the water, the spray shooting like a geyser out of the blow hole, glistening as the droplets caught the sun, a compelling awareness of the salt in the air as it settled on their skin, the gentle rock of the boat.

Gabby only hoped Greg and the kids could grasp the same perspective. An abundance of love for her family, thankfulness for the experience, joy for the moment, peace found within the creatures before her, contentment for her life, and a stillness of her soul in a world that seemed to despise just that.

Gabby exhaled a breath she hadn't realized she was holding and forced her attention back to Carmen. "Wow, I never knew I could be so philosophically descriptive. I'm scoring high on the emotional scale these days," Gabby admitted, but knew it made herself relatable and Carmen comfortable.

Carmen opened her mouth to speak, hesitated, then licked her lips and reached for her tea. She stopped short of taking a sip. "I'd like to do that with my family. Can't fathom it right now, but I'm determined."

"I say this not to sound harsh, but to give you encouragement. You're not the first mom to deal with rebellious teenagers. No matter what everyone portrays on social media, no one has it all together. Everyone has their issues. Some days you'll handle it appropriately; some days you'll screw up. You just do the best you can. The important part is that you stay true to yourself and don't ever compare."

Carmen quickly nodded, trying to look agreeable, yet her frown admitted she wasn't entirely convinced. Gabby felt an unexpected urge to reveal to Carmen her hideous phone call to Holly. Embarrassed, she hadn't confided in anyone and was hoping Holly wouldn't mention it to Greg.

"Shall I prove my own point?"

Carmen's eyebrows rose in question.

"Like a desperate high school girl, lashing out at the other woman"—Gabby paused with an exhale—"I called Holly and gave her a piece of my mind. Talk about shameful."

"Desperate times call for desperate measures," declared Carmen. "*You*, my friend, are not the one that needs to be ashamed."

Stunned, Gabby gasped for effect. "Did *you* just call me friend?"

Carmen shook her head and chuckled. "I did, what's become of me?"

The glass of iced tea turned into a pitcher, then a glass of wine, and another as the hours ticked by. Gabby pulled out chips and salsa loaded with fresh basil and cilantro from her herb garden. She loaded her chip and wondered why she hadn't forced a friendship on Carmen years ago. She was amazingly strong and smart. "I think we were put in each other's lives at the right time for the right reasons." Gabby winked.

CHAPTER 14

Strive to have eyes that see the best in people,
a heart that forgives the worst, a mind that forgets the immoral,
and a soul that never loses faith in God.

Monica

Monica felt as if she could vomit. She was sweating, hyperventilating, her body convulsing as she yelled at Dex to speed up, slow down, go around, get her to her precious daughter. They'd already lost one child. Losing another would undo her.

"This is what I deserve for wanting a kid-free day," Monica choked through her tears.

"Stop!"

"I forgot to lock the slider door, Dex, and now she's gone."

"Kenzie knows how to unlock the door and let herself out. It wouldn't have made a difference."

"What if she didn't walk out on her own? What if someone came in and took her? What if she was abducted by some child predator that walked right in our unlocked house?"

Monica had grabbed the phone from Dex as soon as they had gotten in the car. "What have you done, Janice?" When Janice had told her she found Kenzie missing, Monica's heart sank as she remembered going downstairs to lock the door and grab drinks from the fridge. She got the drinks and stood there for a second, trying to remember what else she was supposed to do. When nothing came to her, she shrugged and hurried back upstairs, excited to go to the beach with Dex. Had she not been desperate to get away from Janice, and undeniably her children too, none of this would have been happening.

Every scenario was going through her head, and she was verbally exploding to Dex. Had Kenzie been sleepwalking and walked right off the dock and into the water and drowned? Did someone kidnap her? Did she go outside looking for a toy and get lost?

Why did she entrust Janice with her children when she had such apprehension, doubting that Janice was capable of keeping them safe?

Monica's phone buzzed angrily with the Amber Alert for Kenzie Kay Colburn, age 3, height 3'2", 38 pounds, dark brown hair, with blue eyes, last seen in her bedroom. Monica thought she was going to die right then. Dex put his hand on her leg, and she squeezed his arm so tight she nearly drew blood with her nails. Her phone was blowing up with text messages from concerned friends. She called her mom and handed the phone to Dex, unable to speak through her sobs.

Two police cars were in the driveway. She was out of the car before Dex even had it in park. She ran around the house to the beach, frantically calling out Kenzie's name.

The entire lake was lit up. Every house had their floodlights on. The neighbors were walking the beach with flashlights, and dozens of boats dotted the lake, their spotlights illuminating the dark water. A constant call of Kenzie's name echoed in her ears.

Monica and Dex found Janice and a police officer talking near the shore. Janice dove into Dex's arms with a wail.

The police officer assured them that they had a team already searching the area and that, with the help from Janice, they were able to narrow the time frame she went missing to approximately seventy-five minutes thus far. Police dogs combed the area and police officers traversed the water on Wave Runners.

"I found your list of emergency numbers and called your friend Gabriella. She sent a mass e-mail to the entire lake and went door to door, pulling people out to scour the area. She's out in her boat, leading the lake search. Beck is sleeping in his crib, and Amelia is inside in case he wakes up or Kenzie comes wandering back in." Janice's words caught in her throat, and she buried her face in Dex's chest.

Gabby had been texting Monica as they drove, informing her that the search was exploding like wildfire, reassuring her that Kenzie would be back in her arms as soon as she got home.

"You did everything you could, Mom," Dex comforted, rubbing her back while Monica pushed a hundred contradictory thoughts out of her head. Every ounce of her wanted to lash out at Janice. However, she knew placing blame wasn't going to bring Kenzie back.

Janice's voice quivered as she explained again that she had put Kenzie to bed and went to check on her only ten minutes later and she was gone. After searching the house, she found the slider door open a mere inch and immediately called 911 and Dex after that. The police reassured them that they were doing everything they could, and thanks to the timely matter of events, the search had been under way for nearly an hour.

That didn't comfort Monica one single bit. An hour? An hour of looking for Kenzie was fifty-nine minutes too long. She feared the worst as she looked out into the dark black water. There was a continual, eerie calling for Kenzie. Her daughter's name was being shouted out near and far. Voices she recognized, Carmen's carried across the water urgently, along with male and female, adult and children echoes she'd never heard.

There had to be hundreds of people looking for Kenzie, walking the beaches, in boats on the lake, behind the houses on the road, and in the wooded areas. There wasn't a dark house among the more than two hundred surrounding the lake. Both hope and horror engulfed Monica as she reveled in the amount of people searching for her baby.

The policeman questioned Monica and Dex, asking if there were any secret play or hiding spots Kenzie often went to. Did she have a friend's house or a park she knew how to find? A tree house? A bike path? A well-known place they often went to picnic, look at flowers, or rocks?

"Anywhere she's familiar going that she could find on her own?" the officer asked.

Monica and Dex were wracking their brains and shaking their heads. "She's not old enough to go anywhere on her own, but we take walks around the lake following the shoreline. The streets behind the houses aren't connected, so sometimes we go to the end of our street and loop back around on her scooter or bike."

Dex hurried to the garage and came running back seconds later. "Her scooter and bike are there. News vehicles are pulling up to the house," he informed them with a terrified look.

"It's okay, Mr. Colburn," said the policeman. "The press can help spread the word quickly. You don't have to talk on-camera, and we'll keep them at bay." He looked towards Monica. "Do you have a recent photo of Kenzie?"

Monica had taken a picture of Kenzie this morning with her cell. Kenzie had gotten dressed by herself and had chosen to wear her purple sleeveless Easter dress with her pink winter boots and an orange-and-blue-striped scarf. Monica had put her hair in pigtails, and at Kenzie's request, she fastened little plastic flowers along her part. Kenzie topped off her look with a sparkly blue headband, green

Mardi Gras beads, and a dozen gold bangles that clinked as she played.

The crazy combination was so adorable that Monica had snapped a picture. What if it was the last picture she'd ever take of her daughter? No, she wouldn't allow such thoughts; everything would be fine. Monica swallowed down the fear that felt like a thousand snakes slithering up her throat, eager to wrap themselves around her neck.

As if the officer sensed Monica was on the verge of a suffocating meltdown, ready to crumble to the ground, he placed his hand under her elbow, steadying her. "Before you returned home, we took the K9 dogs into Kenzie's room for her scent. They've taken her pillow with them. Does she sleep with a stuffed animal, blanket, or doll that has significant meaning to her? Something she carries with her throughout the day?" His eyes flitted between her and Dex, searching for what Monica wasn't quite certain: answers, guilt?

Monica nodded eagerly. Numerous times butterfly blankie had gone missing only to turn up in the dishwasher, freezer, or in the yard. Certainly, they could find Kenzie as they always had blankie. "She has a purple blankie with butterflies on it. She can't sleep without it."

The officer held out his hand. "Leave your phone with me. I'll handle the reporters and give them Kenzie's picture to air. Go search to see if the blanket is anywhere in the house."

Dex nodded to Monica. "I'll stay here."

She ran inside on weightless legs, the moment surreal. This sort of stuff only happened to other people. How often had she flipped on the news to see pleas from parents to bring their missing child home safe?

Although she had always empathized with them, even gotten down on her knees and prayed for a child's safe return, in the back of her mind had always been that little doubt that they were inadequate parents. They weren't supervising their children properly; they were careless, neglectful. Sometimes those parents were found guilty of murdering their own child. Now she and Dex were *those* parents under scrutiny and criticism.

Monica went in the same slider door from which Kenzie had disappeared. As soon as Kenzie was back in her arms safe, she would be installing alarms on their doors and security cameras all around their house. She flipped on Kenzie's bedroom light and fell to her knees at the sight of her deserted bed, nothing but a pile of rumpled covers.

She had wanted Kenzie's blankie to be there, to hold it and bury her face in. To inhale the scent of her daughter. It was gone. Kenzie was gone.

Momentarily lost in a cocoon of grief, Monica jerked at Amelia's hand on her back. "Her blankie is even gone. She's gone," sobbed Monica engulfing Amelia in a forceful embrace. "What did you talk about when you played with her today? Did you play in some secret hideout? Did she talk about any strange people she'd seen? Have you seen any strange people lingering around the neighborhood?"

Amelia shook her head. "No, nothing. We played on the beach and made castles for her Barbies and went swimming. I put my hammock up between the two trees on the side of the house, and we lay together, played I Spy, and ate Popsicles."

"This is not like Kenzie; she doesn't wander off. She's responsible and always helps me keep an eye on Beck." Monica's hands flew to her head, her words sounding like that of a pack of wolves howling, "What if someone took her?"

Not waiting for a response, Monica stepped back from Amelia and turned to go back outside.

"Wait, Mrs. Colburn. I just thought of something." Monica held her breath in anticipation as Amelia's eyes grew wide. "When we were in the hammock together, I took a picture of the two of us and put it on my Snapchat story. I told Kenzie I wanted to show my friends how adorable she was. Kenzie then told me all about her two imaginary friends, Trixie and Reese."

Amelia tugged at her ponytail as if it were jogging her memory. "She told me she was going to go hammocking with them later and asked if she could borrow my phone to take pictures and *snap her story*. I laughed it off, a three-year-old and her wild imagination."

"I can't believe I haven't thought of Trixie and Reese!" Monica smacked her forehead. "Tell me everything she said about them. Did she say where they were? If she was going to go get them?"

"Well, as I said, she told me she was going to go hammocking with them because they both had purple-and-pink hammocks with blue dragonflies. She mentioned Trixie had gotten new rollerblades and Reese had gotten a new bike and they had texted her, on your old flip phone she carries around in her Elsa purse, and told Kenzie to meet them on the bike trail."

"Did she give you any details of where they were going to hammock? By the pond, the bridge, or resting bench? Sometimes she makes these plans, and we *actually* take her to these places, and she has a playdate with them." Had she been so stupidly senseless to cater these non-existent girls? "Trixie and Reese are very, very real to her."

Amelia shook her head. "No, I don't think so. I mean she talked about them for so long; only half of what she said made sense. She mostly talked about what their bedroom looks like, what she eats when she stays at their house, games they play, and that they are trapeze performers in the circus." Amelia grinned weakly.

Monica gave Amelia a quick hug and ran to Beck's room. He had kicked off the covers and was sprawled out on his back, his arms overhead, mouth wide open revealing a few small baby teeth. Monica leaned over the crib railing and kissed his parted lips, absorbing his hot baby breath. He smelled of strawberries and A&D ointment. "We'll find her, little buddy." Beck flinched yet didn't wake as a hot tear streamed down Monica's cheek, landing on his chin. "I promise we'll bring your big sister back to you."

Monica fled from Beck's room towards the door, telling Amelia to text her if she remembered anything else, any specifics to where Kenzie may have gone to meet Trixie and Reese.

Dex and the police officer were just moving away from the reporters. Thank goodness the police officer had told them they had to stay by their vans in the road and they weren't allowed on the property. Monica was in no shape to be questioned by a news reporter, her distorted, misrepresented face smeared across TV screens.

"Kenzie's butterfly blanket is not on her bed," Monica spat out so fast she was barely audible. She explained to the officer that Kenzie had imaginary friends and thought it might be possible she took off with Trixie and Reese to go hammocking, possibly meeting them on the bike trail.

"Do you think it's a good sign Kenzie's blanket wasn't in her bed?" Dex asked the police officer. "I wouldn't think an abductor would take the time to grab a blankie."

Monica cringed at the word abductor, but Dex's question gave her hope that Kenzie had wandered off to the bike trail and was sitting alone, patiently waiting for Trixie and Reese: Kenzie in her Unicorn nightgown, clutching her blankie by the rock where Tortie, the turtle, suns herself, or prudently waiting on the bench that overlooks Sunfish Lake, ankles crossed, swinging her feet back and forth, singing one of their made-up shower songs. Did she put shoes on? What if she was barefoot, her feet now blistered or cut from sticks or thorns? Her bare little arms getting bit by mosquitos and gnats?

Monica sensed the officer's reluctance to speak; instead he reassured them that it was a good thing Kenzie had her blanket with her. Meaning what? The dogs could trail her scent, or she had comfort?

Dex's strong arm pulled Monica close; he squeezed her so tight she felt like her ribs were being crushed. The last time he clutched her like this was in a hospital room after Cade's birth. The embrace was his. Monica needed to flee. She couldn't be held still when Kenzie was alone, in the encompassing darkness.

"What do we do? Where do we go? We need to be out looking. We can't just stand here and do nothing," Dex's voice rose impatiently, reading Monica's thoughts.

The officer nodded. "Yes, I agree. First, I wanted to make sure we were all well-informed." He put up his finger as he turned his head and radioed the search crew and instructed them to scour the Cannon bike trail."

"Does Kenzie know how to access the trail on her own?"

Dex and Monica both nodded. "We pull Kenzie and Beck in the Burley behind my bike to the trail all the time. She's a smart girl; she knows exactly how to get there from home," said Monica. "We rode there yesterday, and she knew we were halfway there when we approached the purple flowers in front of the yellow house. We frequently walk the shoreline of the lake and cut between the blue house and the white house."

Monica's thoughts were swirling. When Kenzie left, the sun was only setting, still giving off a glow. Now it was complete blackness. How far could she have gotten before people were shouting her name? Would she willingly respond? Or hide in fear of strangers or getting in trouble?

None of this sounded like Kenzie. She was cautious and smart. She knew not to run ahead in a parking lot, never to step foot on the dock, in the water, or in a boat without a lifejacket. Monica had drilled it in her head a thousand times, but then, the flashback of Kenzie wading in the water after they returned from Urgent Care as Janice sat inside the screened porch smoking, came flooding back.

Janice. Had she not been staying with them, none of this would have happened. Monica wouldn't have been so desperate to get away. She shook her head, dismissing the negative thought, banishing the pointless blame.

Kenzie was independent and curious. Monica and Dex often called her Curious George. Quite possibly she was on the lookout platform in someone's play set, gazing up at the stars with Trixie and Reese. On the other hand, she could be hurt, blindfolded, tied up in a stranger's house, shoved in a closet, a trunk, halfway across the state. Monica cringed and tried to dismiss the thought.

"We need to go find her, Dex, now!" She turned to Janice. "Stay put in case she wanders back." She pulled Dex by the arm, informing the officer that they were searching the bike trail and to call or text with any news.

Dex snatched two flashlights from the garage, only to find one of them was void of batteries. Outraged, he flung it towards a tree, the shatter reverberating, affirming a direct hit. The night seemed darker than any night they'd had in weeks. Where was the full moon, the stars to guide them? Why, on this of all nights, was there only a sliver of moonlight amidst heavy, suffocating clouds?

They parked in a housing development on a road that intercepted the trail about halfway between the routes they always biked. In the distance, Kenzie's name was being called, the resonance sending chills down Monica's spine.

Volunteers were combing the trail, wandering through the woods, the figures a blur as Monica desperately ran past them. She hardly recognized her own voice as she called out Kenzie's name, the urgency in her tone evident, the volume lacking. She wanted so badly to scream at the top of her lungs; instead, her tears choked her throat, reducing her calls to a weak croaking. Even the crickets trumpeted her.

It reminded her of a reoccurring dream she'd had her entire life in which she was being chased with neither the capability to run or scream for help. Her lead heavy legs, would drag limply while her faceless perpetrator followed only feet behind her. Her mouth gaped wide open, heaving for a breath, unable to summon a call for help.

Her mind was whirling. Had she had that dream her whole life as a prelude to this single night? Was there something going on with Kenzie's legs? Maybe she couldn't run fast enough to escape her kidnapper, or what if she fell and broke her leg? What if she was involved in a hit-and-run accident and she was lying in a ditch? What if Kenzie couldn't scream because she was gagged?

Monica's brain was gyrating with one horrific scenario after another. If she didn't find her daughter alive and well, it would be the death of her. She wondered what horrendous thoughts were going through Dex's mind as he bellowed Kenzie's name into the night. She feared the answer too much to ask.

Tears flooded her cheeks as she let herself go back to the day she gave birth to Cade: the baby who never took a breath of air, the baby Dex was denied the role of announcing, the child she would never hear cry or talk, see walk or play at the park, run off the bus into her arms, or peel out of the driveway at sixteen. Cade would never attain his daddy's height and kiss the top of Monica's head on Mother's Day. She'd never know his favorite food, his favorite color, whether he would grow to prefer blondes, brunettes, or feisty redheads.

Cade, whom they'd had a chance to love without being loved back . . . Holding him, knowing it was the last time she'd feel his skin, was the best and worst feeling of her life. What if holding Kenzie this morning had been the last time she'd feel her daughter's skin, smell her hair?

They rounded the bend, as Monica had hours ago on her morning run. They approached the bench overlooking Sunfish Lake, another lake to set off Monica's fanatical fears of Kenzie drowning. Monica highly doubted Kenzie would have ventured off the trail, through the trees down to the lake, but Monica never would have thought she'd be missing from their home in the first place.

She stood on the bench, cupped her hands, and yelled, "Kenzie, it's Mommy, can you hear me?" In what sounded like the most desperate and pitiful voice Monica had ever heard travel from her lips, she cried, "We're here, Kenzie. Mommy and Daddy are here."

Monica's flashlight traveled high in the trees and through the thick of the weeds and wild flowers lining the trail, the very flowers they had stopped to pick only two days ago when Monica pulled her kids behind her bike, secured safely with buckles, their heads protected with helmets.

Gleaming eyes from an opossum stared back at them, startling Monica as she cursed at it and jumped off the bench. Before she knew it, she was running, in her tank dress and flip-flops, at top speed, yelling behind her for Dex to catch up, her flashlight bouncing madly around her. She hadn't thought to change her shoes or her dress.

She still smelled of sunscreen and the beach, could taste their dinner on the back of her tongue. She wished the slight buzz from her martinis still lingered, helping her cling to the alcohol-induced illusion that she'd stumble on her daughter any moment.

Her throat hurt from trying to muster a scream, her head pounded from stress, and her eyes stung from crying. Dex was behind her, urging her to slow down. She ignored him, ran faster down the hill, rounded the curve, blowing by dark silhouettes, Kenzie's name booming around her. Her feet hit the bridge over the swamp, and she crumbled.

Grasping the railing, she collapsed to her knees. "Please, dear God, please, please, please bring her back to me. Keep her safe . . . bring her back . . . p-l-e-a-s-e," she yelped in desperation as the sound of a pack of barking dogs pierced through the night.

CHAPTER 15

Teach children to keep their feet on the ground by putting
responsibility on their shoulders.

Carmen

Carmen had a meeting bright and early at seven, in exactly fifty-six minutes. She quickly made the bed, turned the shower on, and rushed to the kitchen for a mug of coffee. As she hurried back to the bathroom, something caught her eye outside. Something was out of place, waving breezily in the tree.

As Carmen walked out on the deck, she had a bird's eye view of her yard littered with toilet paper. A closer look revealed small tire tracks, possibly from a golf cart, had entered the backyard from the driveway and flattened all the flowers. Eggs, ketchup, and some foreign thick substance, possibly syrup, decorated the side of the house.

She left her coffee on the outside table and went in to shut off the shower and change into clothes. Standing in the yard, she saw the state of her property was far worse than it looked from above. The grass was spray painted with graffiti: *cunt, whore, bitch,* and a few other choice words. The beach had three piles of what resembled human waste. Her chaise lounge chairs were tossed from the beach into the yard, also covered in the egg, ketchup, and syrup combination and topped off with what smelled like urine.

She recognized their boat floating in the middle of the lake, prompting her eyes to shift to the empty shore station. The lift was lowered, the ramps submerged in the water. A decent shove most likely sent the boat to where it now bobbed, looking cheerful, flooded with the morning rays of sun casting a shimmer off the metallic paint. A raging inferno ignited in Carmen.

The audacity of these little punks. Surely Landon and his friends were responsible, possibly even Grace and some of those trashy girls Penelope had developed a kinship with.

Carmen was livid. She dialed Victor and cursed him under her breath when it went straight to voicemail. It was three in the morning in Vegas, but still, what was he thinking silencing his phone at night while traveling? When you're clear across the country, you need to be available if your wife has an emergency. Cardinal rule. Okay maybe this wasn't an emergency, more like a crisis, or an urgent situation. Regardless.

Breathe. He promised by the end of summer he would be back to his old schedule. Now wasn't the time to get upset with Victor; he wasn't to blame for the mess before her, even *if so*mething was off before he left.

Zeroing in on a piece of toilet paper swirling in the breeze, her mind wandered to Victor. Why was he distracted and edgy lately when for months he'd been on cloud nine as his career flourished? The last few weeks he'd become tense, distracted.

Something didn't settle well with Carmen. She couldn't help thinking he was having an affair and quickly reminded herself she was only being hypersensitive because of Gabby. Victor was faithful. Right? She had no idea if he gave lessons to any females. Not that it mattered, he could meet a woman anywhere.

Focus. Reel it in. Now wasn't the time to analyze her marriage. She sent a text to her CEO, Jeff, asking him to push their meeting back a couple of hours. This account was huge. If Local Flair indeed signed the contracts, it would add eighteen restaurants to service heating, cooling, and refrigeration. Here she was rescheduling the most important meeting because of personal reasons, requesting six other people to rearrange their schedules because of her.

Carmen resented that Victor's career seemed to take precedence over hers. She didn't have the luxury of handing off the latest disaster for Victor to handle while she slipped away to run her company.

Her voice rose an octave as she spoke to the police and itemized the destruction. As she spoke, she wondered if she was wasting her time. What would they really do?

She felt needy as she texted Gabby.

> Me again, your bothersome neighbor. Can you help me rescue my boat from the middle of the lake?

Moments later Gabby pulled up to the end of the dock, and Carmen hopped aboard. Carmen saw Gabby wearing the same tired, puffy eyes that she was wearing, only for different reasons.

Gabby's jaw fell as she absorbed the scene. "Whoa, I'm guessing it wasn't a wild party. Any idea who?"

Carmen only shrugged. "My speculation would be a malicious boyfriend and his posse."

Gabby frowned. "I'm sorry."

"Me too. Did I wake you?" Carmen looked at her phone, 6:32 a.m.

"Hardly, I was sitting outside in my rocker, staring aimlessly at the flowerbeds with my coffee, mustering up the energy to face the day."

Carmen felt useless. She knew Gabby was hurting immensely but had no idea how to respond to someone in despair. She guessed it wasn't the same raw banter she could throw at the guys from her office. Besides, who in their right mind would offer advice to a therapist?

The easy camaraderie Carmen felt previously sitting on Gabby's patio evaporated, inspiring words eluding her. "Well, thanks for coming to my rescue." Carmen cringed at her own insensitivity, her lack of emotion.

Gabby sped away from the dock to the vacant speed boat. Carmen climbed in and fired up the engine. Except for a few dead bugs stuck to the seats with the morning dew and a dropping of seagull poop on the floor, everything was intact. Amelia and Piper's half-eaten bag of chips from yesterday lay open on the seat. In the bow, two empty cans of root beer sat in the cup holders. A heap of wet towels and a few hair ties lay scattered about.

"I'm nervous, Gabby. If Penelope figures out that I snuck behind her back and we concocted a plan for you to counsel her, am I setting myself up for more rebellion, future resentment?"

Gabby straightened and looked at Carmen assertively. "Penelope is in a very dark and destructive place. You need to keep reminding yourself that it's your job as a parent to keep her safe, to do everything in your power to get her help. All teenagers detest their parents at some level, at some point in time, during those neurotic years." Gabby chuckled. "And believe me. Whether she likes you right now or not is the least of your concerns. Don't make the mistake of trying to be Penelope's friend before her mother."

"I just don't want to make our relationship worse, to be the one that pushes her further into destruction. What if the cutting turns into other"—Carmen paused, bit her lip— "bigger attempts?" She couldn't bring herself to say the word suicide. It had happened three times in their district in the past five years.

"That, my friend, is exactly why you will do what's best for her and trust our plan." Gabby put her boat in gear and began pulling away, her eyes shifting towards Carmen's house. "Looks like the police have arrived. We'll talk later."

The police took pictures and filed a report. Since the damage didn't total an amount for felony charges, Carmen knew nothing else would transpire. Sure, they would talk to the neighbors, even visit Landon's house and question him; however, a torn-up yard, an insane amount of toilet paper, filthy lounge chairs, and siding that could be power washed, did not top their priority list.

The real damage was unseen; it cut deeper and would bleed longer than the wounds Penelope inflicted on herself.

Carmen entered Penelope's room quietly and sighed with relief at the sound of her deep breathing. Light flooded in through the doorway and from the two-inch gap between her blinds and windowsill. Carmen found herself scanning Penelope's room for anything she could use to hurt herself. Was this her new way of living? In fear of how her daughter might be harming herself while they slept?

Penelope's phone lay beside her as her stuffed animals once did.

They should have taken her phone away when they grounded her, given her the gift of freedom from the impending social doom it carried. But no, the device was permanently attached to Penelope, giving Carmen the opportunity to track her daughter's whereabouts. The lovely little app even warned Carmen when Penelope drove over the speed limit. Carmen hated to admit she couldn't fathom not having instant communication with her daughters yet simultaneously despised the device.

Just the other day, Penelope had posted her forty-fifth picture of her toes in the sand, waves crashing behind, not pausing for a moment to soak up and reflect on the beauty before her just for the sake that God had given it to her. Rather, she obsessively fretted over capturing a picture on a screen, to post, in place of appreciating the beauty in her mind.

Moments later she'd turned to see Amelia posting her eighty-seventh pose with duck-lips, Frappuccino in hand.

Carmen had instantly broken into a lecture. "What's the point? All your experiences are captured and released, not savored for the soul to treasure. Your mere existence is tied to a handheld device, living vicariously through the fabricated lives of others, depressed by the melancholy of your own."

Both girls scoffed at the speech Carmen had given, even teased her that she was outdated and being melodramatic.

"Stop using fancy analogies and even fancier words that I can't comprehend," Amelia said. Carmen told her if she were to put her phone down and read a book or sit quietly in nature with her own thoughts, instead of the constant pings of others, she'd not only understand what Carmen was talking about, she'd be able to close her eyes and *hear* the waves, *smell* the water, *feel* the sand under her feet, and be satisfied with the Frappuccino because of how it *tasted*, not yearning for the comments or likes for holding one in her hand.

"You're missing out on life," Carmen warned.

Penelope and Amelia argued that Carmen was missing out on life by isolating herself from social media.

Carmen wondered what part the device in Penelope's hand played in the eradication of her former self. Even when Penelope was in good graces with her friends, they had gathered in groups only to isolate themselves to feed their screen addiction.

Struggling to control excessive screen time always, *always*, brought about conflict. Carmen had tried to pick her battles wisely. Sadly, she caved to the battle of the phone and fed the addiction to avoid the fight.

Bad mom. She used to be a much better parent.

Carmen moved in, sat on the edge of Penelope's bed, and reluctantly woke her. As they walked outside together, Carmen could see Penelope was trying her hardest not to display emotion. Penelope's body deflated along with Carmen's heart.

Penelope took a few swift steps towards the rose bush and reached down for a gift box peeking out. How had Carmen missed it? A blue Tiffany box with a silver bow. How ironic.

Carmen moved next to Penelope as she revealed its contents: a razor blade and a box of Band-Aids.

Instinctively, Carmen's hand went to her mouth with a gasp. Had Penelope broken up with Landon and this was his way of getting back at her? Carmen remembered the very first time Penelope had Landon over. Carmen's phone was ringing, and Penelope had hollered in a teasing voice, *Tiffany's calling.*

Carmen took the call, a work fiasco unfolding, and when she hung up, she tossed her phone back in her purse. "Should have let Tiffany handle that one!"

Penelope and Landon were perched on the bar stools, sharing an enormous bear claw Carmen had brought home from a bakery her company serviced. Penelope giggled, and Carmen couldn't believe she thought her comment amusing, especially in front of Landon.

Landon clearly thought otherwise, his look revolting. Instantly, Carmen felt like she was being judged because of her extravagant, expensive purse, which she referred to by name, called her *friend*. It made her feel shallow, materialistic.

Penelope dropped the Tiffany box in the dumpster Carmen had wheeled around from the garage and bent over to pick up the shovel. Carmen met her face-to-face as she stood, placing her hands on her daughter's shoulders. Penelope diverted her glassy eyes toward the water, her face hard.

Carmen pulled Penelope close and squeezed her so tight she thought she might crush her. Tears burned the rims of her eyes as she became engulfed with more emotion than she knew what to do with.

"Sorry about your flowers, Mom." The sincerity in Penelope's tone made Carmen's heart swell with an abundance of love. A glimpse of the daughter she knew was wrapped in a few kind words. She stepped back and cupped her face, Penelope's appearance resembling a still portrait of a suffering girl.

"No worries. The only people to feel sorry for are the ruthless, pathetic individuals who did this. Those responsible are insignificant, obviously less-than-stellar representatives of humanity, victims of their own demise, not yours, not mine."

Carmen thought Penelope's eyes had welled up, but she was squinting into the sun as she looked up. She ached for her daughter to give up the tough-girl brazenness. Warped or not, Carmen wished she'd break down, cry, and ask Carmen for solace.

Instead, she backed away, bent over, and retrieved the fallen shovel and began disposing of the piles of feces into a plastic bag and tossing it in the dumpster. Carmen worked alongside Penelope, salvaging some of her flowers, letting the silence fall between them. She felt confident that Penelope knew she wasn't upset with her, that she wasn't blaming her for the destruction, giving her anymore reason to cut.

The wrapped feces landed in the bottom of the dumpster with a thud. Perfect, the trash was hauled away yesterday. It would be another week, in the heat of summer, the shit would sit, reeking.

Carmen attached the sprayer to the hose and turned the water on full force. The pressure sent the ketchup sliding down the house, but the syrup would have to be scrubbed. She was thankful the ketchup had rested on top of the syrup and hadn't stained the pale-yellow siding.

Penelope disappeared for a moment and came back with a scrub brush and the ladder. She opened it and set it haphazardly under the maple tree and began grabbing fistfuls of toilet paper.

Carmen went and held the base of the teetering ladder. "Don't get me wrong, honey. I'm not saying that all of this doesn't hurt. I can only imagine you're feeling sad, angry, embarrassed, and a slew of other things."

Penelope only kept working, forcefully tugging at the tree branches, leaves falling along with the tissue. Carmen picked her brain. What would Gabby say to Penelope?

"It's okay to be upset. What's not okay is giving into it." Carmen raised her arms and looked around her. "All this damage is a reflection on them, their character, not yours. Whoever is responsible is damaged. Do not let them suck you in."

"Okay, Mom, I get it!" Penelope shifted her weight, and the ladder tilted and sunk into the uneven grass. She didn't flinch. Carmen knew she had preached enough. She knew *why* she preached. Only she had to learn when to stop preaching.

"I'll go grab the lawn mower. Thankfully, the grass is long enough that, after it's mowed, most of the spray paint will be cut off. The words won't be legible."

When Carmen came back around with the push mower, Penelope was gone. It didn't take Carmen long to figure out where she was. The shouting from inside bellowed out the open kitchen window.

She quickly abandoned the mower to go play referee. As she got closer, she stopped. For once, she wanted the girls to keep arguing so she could eavesdrop.

Amelia was crying, saying she had no idea *it* was going to happen. Penelope was insistently yelling at her, calling her a traitor, accusing her of being superficial like her friends.

"Leave me alone," Amelia pleaded. "I'm not the one that hangs out with a bunch of laced losers."

"No, you hang out with a bunch of bloodthirsty, scheming, shallow little bitches," snarled Penelope. "Like I don't know about the Finsta and Spam accounts! As if pictures of our yard weren't posted!"

"Don't accuse me. I don't have fake accounts." Amelia growled. "Sounds like you're bitter since losing all your friends, the ones you so easily relate with."

Carmen didn't know whether she should intervene or hang back for insight. One thing was slowly dawning on her: Amelia was withholding information from Carmen and played some sort of role, albeit suppressing or abetting, where she should remain loyal.

"What goes around comes around, Amelia."

"What's that supposed to mean?"

"It means all your little friends are no different than their big sisters, and don't think for a second that your friendships are anything but superficial. They're sell-outs and will never think twice about wronging you. You're no better."

Someone stomped up the stairs and slammed a door, so Carmen rounded the corner. Amelia was sliding her feet into her flip-flops, her hand on the doorknob.

"What was all the yelling about?"

"Really, Mom, you have to ask? It was Penelope being Penelope. All I did was ask her what happened to the yard, and she blew up at me."

"Why would she blow up at you, Amelia?"

Amelia's eyes widened. "Exactly what I'd like to know!"

Carmen angled her head down and stared at Amelia for a few beats, hoping she would surrender something. Instead, she raised her shoulders in question and let them fall heavily with an irritated sigh.

"I feel like there is a lot more going on here than a sisterly spat. Do you know the real reason she and Liz aren't friends anymore? You and Piper are inseparable. She has to have mentioned something."

Amelia turned the doorknob impatiently, clearly wanting to escape, so Carmen fell into it with her shoulder, folding her arms over her chest.

"Amelia, I know we already talked about this but . . ." Carmen's voice shook, and she was a tad happy for the effect. Amelia couldn't stand to see Carmen cry. Carmen hoped it would provoke something out of Amelia. "Penelope is hurting deeply. She's not in a good place." Carmen sniffed. "If anything ever happened to her, and we knew there was a way we could have helped her, it would destroy me."

Amelia got all shifty and couldn't meet Carmen's eyes.

"She's cutting herself, Amelia. Don't you see how wounded she is? Every time she closes her door, I worry she'll end up slitting her wrists. She needs our help. If you know anything—"

"Believe what you want, but I told you I don't know what her deal is. I had no clue she was *cutting* till the other night." Amelia said the word with mocking disgust, keeping her eyes glued to a picture on the wall.

She's lying. Carmen was dumbfounded.

"Mrs. Bentley asked me to walk Lucifer. Can I go?"

Amelia's short and clipped tone got under Carmen's skin more than the fact that she was keeping secrets. It confirmed the animosity between the girls wasn't one-sided and Amelia's reluctance to divulge to Carmen wasn't about loyalty to her sister. She was protecting herself from something.

~*~

Carmen found Penelope in her closet, sifting through her clothes with one hand, her phone in the other. "What's up?"

"I have a job interview."

That's not what Carmen was asking; however, a quiver of nervous excitement replaced the anger running through Carmen. "Oh, really, where?"

"With Gabriella Bock. When I saw her at the search for Kenzie, she mentioned she was looking for an assistant to help her with organizing client data and files, spreadsheet and Excel stuff mostly, and some marketing."

"Wow, that sounds cool," Carmen said a bit too eagerly, so she faked a yawn.

"Ya, it won't all be glamorous. She said she needs help around her house too. Yard work and stuff."

Carmen nodded and tried to act nonchalant, but she was doing flips inside. Not only was part one of the plan working, but they were carrying on a conversation. Possibly this job would also give the two of them common ground, something to discuss.

"I guess her husband isn't living there right now."

"Yes, I know. It's a terribly sad situation."

Penelope looked at Carmen quizzically. Carmen knew the thought train that went along with the look, on the verge of comprehending that her mother had become friends with Gabby and had something to do with the job offer.

"Unfortunately, bad news seems to circulate the lake quickly." Carmen frowned. "Well, I won't keep you from getting ready. When is she expecting you?"

"In about forty-five minutes, so I better shower. I can work on the yard when I get back. I mean if she doesn't want me to start today."

Carmen giggled. "My, aren't we confident! I love it. What a go-getter!"

Penelope rolled her eyes with annoyance over Carmen's enthusiasm. Once again, she knew her choice of words was *stupid*. When the girls were little, she didn't have to try so hard. They spoke cheerfully to each other and smothered her with kisses, even when she denied them cookies.

"I know you'll nail the interview, Penelope. You're a perfect candidate for the job." Carmen quickly kissed her forehead and began to walk out of the room. "I need to go into work for a couple of hours. On my way home, I'll stop and get some cleaner, and we'll scrub the side of the house together."

"Mom, wait."

Carmen turned and saw a glimpse of her daughter she hadn't seen in ages: a confident, jubilant Penelope, only the bandages reminding her otherwise. Her lips parted to speak. Carmen stepped forward in eager anticipation. Then Penelope's body tensed up. Damn, she shouldn't have acted so fervently.

"Never mind."

"If you want to talk, Penelope, I'm all ears. I promise. All ears, not mouth."

"I don't want to be late." She gathered her clothes and blew past Carmen to the bathroom.

As usual, Carmen stood there, feeling like she screwed up an opportunity, doing exactly what she'd set out not to do. Now more than ever, she didn't know whether to push a subject or let it go. She knocked on the bathroom door. Penelope turned the shower on at the same time and hollered, "Ya'" over the running water.

"If you know who ransacked the yard, I'm not going to go after them."

There was silence on the other side of the door, and Carmen wondered if she had gotten in the shower and stuck her head under the water to intentionally tune her out.

"Penelope? Can you hear me?"

"Yep."

Tick. Tock. Tick. Tock. Apparently, that meant she had nothing to say, which only led Carmen to believe she knew exactly who was responsible, and she was protecting him, her, or them.

Carmen could picture Landon, the little punk, urinating on her lounge chairs and digging up her flowers. He couldn't T.P. their house to that extent by himself, so he probably had some of his Twin Shadies with him. She wouldn't put it past a few of the girls that had hung around over the last few months either, the ones that couldn't look Carmen in the eye when she asked simple questions such as, "How are you?"or "Do you have siblings?" or, gasp, "I was craving fro-yo, do you girls want to go get some with me?"

Their faces would twist, as if she suggested the most absurd thing they'd ever heard. Penelope would answer for them as they backed away towards her room. Later, Penelope would scold

Carmen for embarrassing her and treating her like a child in front of her friends. "Fro-yo, really, Mom?"

Carmen used to take Penelope and her old friends, Liz and Leila, shopping, to the beach, lunch or dinner, for pedicures, and she'd even gone snowboarding with them a few times. Penelope's new friends glared at her from the first time they met. She wasn't sure if the look of loathing was simply who they were or if Penelope had portrayed her as a horrible mother.

Whichever, it didn't settle well. In Carmen's eyes, any teenager that disrespected adults needed a reality check.

She had all but given up on the conversation and turned to go downstairs when Penelope spoke up through the door.

"I know you think it was Landon, Mom. I know you want it to be Landon because it will be another reason for you to shun him and prove he's a loser. But it *wasn't* him, okay?" Sure, the tone was there, but it was the waver in her voice that bothered Carmen.

They shouldn't be speaking about this through a door. Carmen wanted to see her face. She feared all the things in the bathroom Penelope could harm herself with—razors, tweezers, scissors.

"I'm not trying to point fingers at Landon, but it's obvious he was extremely upset and embarrassed when he left the other night. I'm only suggesting the vandalism wasn't directed solely at you. I think it was also to get back at Dad and me."

Carmen heard the shower door slam shut. Why couldn't they talk logically, have a simple discussion, without everything always going sour?

~*~

In and out thought Carmen as she entered the office. She felt an intense need to be home with her daughters and longed for the days when they were toddlers.

When the girls were little, Carmen had felt guilty for working. Victor frequently picked them up early from daycare. How she had wished for the day they were old enough not to go to daycare. So here they were, old enough to be home alone, and she felt as much guilt, if not more, that she wasn't with them.

Once in the office, she was bombarded with urgent affairs. She quickly delegated all her pressing matters, closed her office door, and relished the three minutes alone before her meeting.

When her cell rang, she was sure it was going to be Amelia asking if they were still out of kiwi, to which Carmen would answer yes, that she would have to eat the mango instead. Amelia would huff, but Carmen knew how Amelia apologized. She found and excuse to call Carmen, ask an impulsive question, to be right with her.

Amelia would then ask Carmen if they could go to the grocery store together and buy kiwi, another attempt at an apology, sort of, for the tension between them earlier.

Carmen's face lit up as she anticipated their evening, dining outside at one of their favorite local restaurants, followed by late night grocery shopping, a chance at reconnecting. Possibly she could entice Penelope into going, and the three of them would play basketball in the produce section, Penelope and Amelia tossing oranges and lemons in the plastic bag she held. The memories of those days were still vivid.

Instead, one look at the name displayed on the screen of her cell sent her heart into wild palpitations. Chet Moreno.

She broke into a cold sweat and thought of ignoring the call but figured if she didn't handle it now, she would be too distracted to concentrate in her meeting.

"Hi, Dad."

"Carmen, honey, it's so good to hear your voice. How are you?"

She softened; her body relaxed at the sound of his. It was far easier to hold a grudge when they didn't speak.

"I'm okay, Dad. How are you?"

There was a brief silence on the other end, just long enough for Carmen to feel the twinge that the phone call carried weight.

"I wanted to let you know that your mom . . . Mary . . ." His voice quivered. "Hospice is here, Carmen. She only has a few days."

CHAPTER 16

Guard your thoughts when you are alone.
Guard your words when you are with other people.

Gabriella

Gabby read and reread the text from Holly. She wanted to meet this morning. What for? Hadn't they said enough? Rather, hadn't Gabby spewed enough? She shook her head in disgust, appalled that she stooped to the shallowness, the depths of desperate idiocy, by lashing out at the other woman.

With a second chance for a civil conversation looming, Gabby wasn't sure she trusted herself to meet. She recalled Holly mentioning they should speak in a suitable environment after she'd had time to *gather her thoughts, so her tongue didn't get the best of her.* As Gabby's had. How humiliating.

What was left to accomplish? Was Holly about to divulge how the steamy affair started? Wasn't it enough that Holly was carrying her husband's child? Did she have to rub it in Gabby's face?

Gabby wished she could go to her in-laws, not so she could berate their son, but because they had always been her rock, especially since Gabby's parents lived in Colorado, and in truth had never been the nurturing type. Her parents had provided a loving and stable home for her, Mandy, and Rick, but their parenting style was utilitarian, based on raising independent, self-sufficient children to be released after graduation with a well-wishing pat on the back.

It was a basic, no-frills way to grow up. Her mother an orthodontist, her father a principal, all their needs were met. A four-bedroom house in a safe neighborhood boasting its own basketball and tennis courts, home-cooked meals, quality time, ample love and affection. However, they did not dote on their children, pave any special paths. They gave fairly and expected abundant returns.

Gabby had an easy, predictable childhood. Once her younger sister Mandy went off to college, her parents retired early, sold the house, and moved to Colorado. Boom. Their job of raising children was done.

It was Pete and Trudy who were alongside Greg and Gabby, giving bottles and changing diapers on their twin grandbabies at 3:00 a.m., who helped with carpool as all four kids were off in different directions with sports and social obligations, who showed up and swept the kids off to their house for the weekend, who drove across the state to sit in sleet and watch them play lacrosse and rugby.

It was Trudy who always kept a stash of dark chocolate on hand for Gabby, who hugged out of love rather than a perfunctory greeting. She hung seasonal wreaths on Gabby's door throughout the year and dropped baked goods on the porch for the kids, wrapped with big bows.

Pete never ceased to greet Gabby with a wink, asking, *How's my favorite daughter-in-law?* even if she was the only one. On the first Tuesday of every month, she met Pete for coffee. He initiated the meeting when she and Greg were engaged so they could get acquainted. That first meeting Gabby had been insanely nervous. With the windows rolled down, sunroof slid open in her red Sunbird, she tried to chill her anxious sweat as she rehearsed responses to probable questions Pete might ask.

Their first coffee date lasted three hours. He had cupped her hand, his sticky from the enormous cinnamon bun they shared, and told her, with a teary glint in his eye, that she was a godsend, that he and Trudy were honored to welcome Gabby into their family. Pete had also joked that he hoped Gabby would soften Greg's rough edges. She realized soon into their marriage how much weight the comment carried.

Pete suggested they keep a standing date. He never spoke ill of his son. However, he made it clear through various comments that he understood his son: his need to be right; the way he grew angry when he didn't get his way; how he could avoid accountability, could justify slandering others to lessen his own guilt, was a master in blaming, and raged when challenged.

Gabby yearned for her in-laws' support, their love, their never-failing acceptance. Pete and Trudy had both called. Gabby ignored the ringing but politely replied, via text, to the heartfelt messages they left. Gabby had agonizingly canceled on Pete last Tuesday, for the first time since their inaugural date twenty-three years ago. Pete had gone anyway, hoping she might change her mind. He texted her a picture of her empty seat, a *café miel* with a heart skimming the frothy top, a dark chocolate heart wrapped in red foil on the saucer.

She feared the loss of her in-laws if she were to divorce Greg. Would she have to give up coffee with Pete? Would a day come when Gabby's door would lack a springtime wreath, a ribbon-wrapped basket of peanut butter bars placed with love on her doorstep when she went to get the mail?

It was Pete whom she wanted to call and ask if it were wise to meet with Holly, but she wouldn't. For now, she had to go with her impulsive gut, the illogical decision to have an encounter with Holly. She needed to get a glimpse of the pitiful woman who sank her claws into her ruthless husband. Yes, of course, she had a burning desire to size her up face-to-face, read her body language, and squelch her growing curiosity. As much as she had tried to deny it, she craved details.

They agreed to meet at the Rockford Dam. A public place was best for keeping Gabby's temper at bay, outside where they were at less of a risk of being overheard. Holly could easily be dismissed as a client, and if the encounter went sour, Gabby would have an easy escape.

Gabby scanned the area, analyzing whether she should choose a bench or a picnic table. Should they be sitting opposite each other so Gabby could make eye contact? Interrogate and intimidate her? Would a bench ease Gabby's nerves? The last thing Gabby wanted to portray was herself as a victim, weak.

She made it a point to be early so she could watch Holly approach, dissect whether Holly walked confidently or with apprehension, whether she was a home wrecker due to superiority or insecurity.

Shit. She should have worn a double layer of deodorant.

Gabby needed something to keep her hands busy. She checked her watch and ducked into Sweetlands and ordered an iced coffee for herself and a large strawberry lemonade for Holly. She started analyzing the decision as she walked out with the two drinks. Buying Holly a drink might come across as apologetic for the previous phone call. It wasn't. Gabby would have gotten a drink for whomever she was meeting. Holly might be craving lemonade as Gabby had while pregnant. Would Holly view it as a silly choice for an adult?

With eight minutes to spare, Gabby was pleased the decision was made for her. All the picnic tables were occupied, so she claimed the last available bench overlooking the Rogue River. She sat and tried to calm her pounding heart. Thankfully, the bench was shaded. She could already feel the sweat beading on her upper lip and a few trickles roll between her breasts, pooling in her bra.

She took a tissue from her purse and dabbed her upper lip, nonchalantly swiping her chest from the V in her tank. She glanced over her shoulder, not sure she would recognize Holly as she only knew her from searching her Facebook profile.

Holly approached, on time to the exact minute. Gabby almost laughed out loud. How could she think she wouldn't recognize the tall, pregnant brunette scanning the area?

Holly was approximately 5'11" with heels, which Gabby was impressed to see her wearing. She was tall and slender, despite the pregnancy, dressed in a fitted black-and-white block sleeveless dress. She had a thick mane of silky black hair, loose curls bouncing when she walked.

She wore large hoop earrings, several bracelets in silver and black climbed her left forearm, and a long necklace with a black pendant dangled in the space between her breasts and rounded belly. A white blazer hung out of the large purse slung over her shoulder. Stunning.

Holly caught Gabby's eye as she stood from the bench. With a slight wave of recognition, Holly stepped off the pavement onto the soft grass, her heels causing her to wobble as they sank. Steadying herself, Holly smiled with a smirk. Naturally, Gabby smiled in return, painstakingly aware that she hadn't intended to.

The visions racing through Gabby's head were wild and fleeting: Greg and Holly being intimate, rolling around in silk sheets, exploring each other's bodies; the two of them laughing together, Holly's head falling back immersed in Greg's charm; Greg flirting, his hand lingering on Holly's arm or back when they met for business, dining in far off, candlelit restaurants, and planning secret rendezvous; Holly placing Greg's hand on her abdomen as his child kicked inside her. Her husband's hands had graced this woman's glowing skin.

Holly's hand extended towards Gabby several feet before she reached her. As expected, her hand shake was firm, but her voice was much softer than Gabby remembered from the phone. She was every bit the edgy, poised businesswoman Gabby presumed her to be, yet the fluidity of the way she carried herself also spoke gracefulness.

Gabby couldn't help but wonder what Holly's first impressions were. Did she find Gabby washed up and frumpy? Girl next door cute and naïve? For all Gabby knew, Holly could have been stalking her on social media for months, watching her in the grocery parking lot, following her while she picked up Greg's clothes from the cleaners. Did she feel the least bit threatened? Was she scheming to break up their marriage now that the affair had been exposed?

They sat. Gabby regretfully handed her the lemonade. "It's so hot. I hope lemonade is okay."

"Very thoughtful, thank you," she said and took a delicate sip.

Holly was exotically beautiful. She had flawless olive skin, large dark eyes, and lashes that were far too long to be natural. Her cheek bones were prominent and her nose sharp, but not overpowering. Gabby found her emotions conflicting, falling somewhere between allure and ferocity.

Gabby couldn't delineate how she felt about Holly being her polar opposite. Greg had always said Gabby's blue eyes sparkled like the Caribbean and her blond hair was like silk. How many times had he run his hands through the hair he claimed to adore? Grabbed a fistful as they made love?

"So," Gabby said, putting her counseling face on, allowing Holly to dictate the conversation. She didn't want any uncomfortable silences for fear of how she might fill the void. Her heart was already broken, her life turned upside down, and she was now sitting next to the Greek Goddess half responsible. Or was she Egyptian? Italian? Regardless.

Words momentarily eluded Gabby. She didn't want to ask how Holly was feeling, she didn't want to know if she had morning sickness or if she was sleeping well, if the baby was kicking, but in a nervous situation she might. She didn't want to come across as considerate as much as she didn't want to come across as caustic.

"I've thought about this day for the past few months. Dreaded this day actually," said Holly, breaking the awkward silence. She looked toward the dam. "Gabby, I need to tell you something that I haven't confessed to anyone, not even Greg."

Holly ran her hands down her lap, smoothing her dress over her thighs. "I would like you to respect my wishes by keeping this information between us."

The roaring from the water rushing through the dam took on a life all its own, and Gabby hoped it was loud enough to cover up the sound of her pounding heart, the blood racing through her veins like a runaway train, its horn blaring in distress. Holly was asking her to be her secret keeper too, really?

Holly's request confirmed the worst kind of intimacy in Holly and Greg's relationship, a bond other than sexual. Gabby had seen it numerous times with infidelity cases. When the relationship was more than physical, it never truly subsided, ever. Gabby had tried to deny this reality. Now it was staring her in the face. They were expecting a child together.

"I've done something I'm not proud of," Holly continued before Gabby's parted lips could respond vehemently. "It wasn't spontaneous. It was premeditated, well thought out and planned. I never fully anticipated the extent of the consequences."

"I don't want . . ." Gabby began to speak, holding up her hand to stop Holly from going further because she wasn't sure if she wanted to hear a bunch of warped lies, to be manipulated, blackmailed, but Holly had an agenda and kept on.

"I'm thirty-six. I've always wanted a child. I told myself a year ago September that by the following September I would give birth to my own baby."

Gabby's insides twisted. Her mouth even watered, vomit threatening the back of her throat. Holly was in fact due in September. "I'm sorry, Holly. Perhaps this meeting wasn't a good idea." Gabby stood and Holly took hold of her arm.

"Please, no, hear me out. Please, Gabby, you need to know this."

Gabby shook her arm free from Holly's grasp and placed her hands on her hips. She stood in front of Holly, saw the desperation in her eyes, and waited for her to continue without fully committing to staying.

"I decided I was going to have a one-night stand, or several, depending on how long it took me to get pregnant. At first, I was going to scout out some random, good-looking guy in a bar, but it felt sleazy. Then there was this guy in my cooking class who seemed like a good prospect, genetically speaking." She hmphed, both corners of her mouth turning up. "Turns out he was gay."

"I wanted no connections, so, after tracking my ovulation cycle, I booked a week in St. Lucia." Her head fell in shame.

Intrigued, Gabby sat back down. Holly turned her body towards Gabby and, for the first time, looked her in the eye as she spoke.

"I met a jeweler in St. Lucia. I gave him a fake name and, out of guilt, bought a ridiculously expensive ring I couldn't afford. We spent the next four nights together, and then I flew home and waited."

Holly looked down with embarrassment and played with her bracelets. "I was devastated when the pregnancy test was negative. I was about to book a short trip to Aruba for the following month"—Holly paused and closed her eyes—"but then I had lunch with Greg."

In her mind, Gabby found herself settling into her chair in her office. She needed to listen as a counselor, where people felt comfortable and divulged their innermost thoughts and feelings. She realized this might be the hardest confession she'd ever had to witness.

"I could barely focus. From the moment I met him, it was as if bells and whistles were going off. A maternal instinct I never knew I possessed came to life; the magnetic pull for Greg to father my child consumed me. For three days, I hardly slept. I couldn't think of anything else."

The hair on Gabby's body stood.

"I'm around men in my field every day, and I travel, so I'm always seeing different faces, but I had never encountered a man about whom I thought, *I want him to father my child.* I can't even pinpoint exactly what it was about Greg. It just felt right."

Gabby's mouth went dry. She swallowed hard and tried to keep her composure.

"Greg wasn't wearing a wedding band the first time we had lunch. He wasn't wearing a wedding band the second, or third; therefore, I didn't think he was married. Actually"—Holly paused and held up her hand—"that's not true. The thought crossed my mind dozens of times. I figured he was. However, I didn't ask because I was afraid of the truth, and he never offered evidence either way."

Holly stopped to take a deep breath, and Gabby did everything in her power to keep from interrupting. She was about to hear the specifics of the affair: the mood, the drive, the why. She had told herself over and over she didn't want to know, but she couldn't deny she was starving to hear.

"I kept setting up lunch dates and meetings, and he was reluctant, brushing me off, saying the business we needed to discuss could be handled over the phone or through email. I insisted on doing business in person"—Holly rested her hand on her abdomen—"especially as I got closer to ovulation."

They both looked away from each other, towards the kids eating ice cream cones and chasing each other around their picnic blankets. As if on cue, a pregnant mother pushing a stroller with a baby boy walked by. Gabby's insides blazed and churned.

"I'm sorry. The ovulating, that was inappropriate, too personal to share."

It's all inappropriate, thought Gabby. However, she felt compelled to hear this bizarre, mind-blowing narrative straight from her husband's mistress.

"Greg hadn't responded to my emails or phone calls for two days. The clock was ticking. I was panicking."

Holly played with her bracelets, twisting them, fretfully moving them up and down her arms. "I was waiting in the parking lot as he left work, an elaborate story of some dreadful thing that had happened to me, complete with tears, all planned out, ready to perform for the sole sake of getting him into bed.

"When I saw him, I didn't need to pretend. The tears came easily as the opportunity for a child approached me. I fell into his arms, sobbing, and he quickly helped me into his car."

Gabby made fists, welcoming the sting from her fingernails as they cut into her palms. She could picture Greg leaving the office, Holly, a damsel in distress, tearfully waiting. Their first embrace sucking him into where they were now.

"Greg was such a gentleman and suggested we go have dinner and talk, but I said I was in no condition to be out in public. I suggested we go to my place. I guess you could say I seduced him."

Holly reached into her purse for a tissue, and Gabby found herself doing the same, only it was perspiration Gabby needed to wipe. Holly blew her nose and dabbed the tears from the corners of her eyes, catching them before they spilled down her cheeks, smudging her makeup.

Gabriella should have been paying closer attention to Holly's body language like any good therapist, but she was too absorbed in the mental picture playing out in her own head: Greg's hands on Holly as he helped her into his car. Had he given any thought to where it would lead? It was the perfect opportunity for the bastard to explain that he was married and that going to her place was inappropriate.

"When did you find out Greg was a married man with a family?"

Holly drew in a sharp breath. "Several weeks later. By this time, I'd had another negative pregnancy test. I was too invested, determined to keep trying. I knew I should have ended the relationship immediately. It was wrong on so many levels, but I wanted a baby so badly."

Holly twisted the tissue between her fingers, white fuzz adhering to her dress. "I told myself I would try for three more months and, if I didn't conceive, I would break off the affair and volunteer to transfer to one of my company's other offices out of state."

Gabby focused on the ducks swimming about in front of her, quacking and diving below the surface for food, their only care, survival. She saw a mother with three young children standing on the dam, counting the turtles sunning themselves on the logs. A little boy jumped up and down in excitement as he declared to his grandfather that he saw a fish trying to jump upstream against the rushing water.

Suspicion tore through her. Gabby had never felt so inconsequential as her mind searched for the truth. On how many levels could she be played by both Greg and Holly? Was it odd that Holly was being so blatantly honest? Or was she lying through her teeth, all this one big scheme between her and Greg?

Gabby took a sip of her iced coffee for the sake of something to do with her shaking hands, even though it was wreaking havoc on her stomach.

"When I found out I was pregnant, it was bittersweet," Holly continued without warrant.

Gabby went numb. She was momentarily void of feeling, stuck in a transient gaze, perplexed by the cattails gently swaying in the breeze. Life was unfolding everywhere around her while hers seemed to stop spinning. Bittersweet.

"Meaning your guilt about sleeping with a married man, a father of four, didn't surface until you found yourself pregnant with his child?"

Holly's voice was no longer consistently soft and steady. It dipped low and rose high with emotion. "I had no intention of ever confessing to Greg that I was pregnant. The same day the pregnancy test read positive I immediately proposed a transfer to my boss and began house hunting in the San Diego area where I figured I would never see Greg again.

"We were having breakfast, a legit business meeting," Holly said with a hint of defense. "By this point, I was already pulling away from him, setting the tone to end the relationship. I thought for sure my boss was going to approve the transfer and I'd be relocated within a few weeks"—she looked over Gabby's shoulder—"before I started showing."

Holly's long hair fanned her shoulders. She gathered it and lifted it off her neck, attempting to cool herself. "I couldn't take a bite of my breakfast. The morning sickness had taken over something fierce, and I ran to the restroom to get sick. When I returned to the table, Greg immediately started asking questions. Why had I given up coffee? Why had I declined the glass of Pinot he offered me the other day after . . ." Holly caught herself, but not before Gabby understood what she was about to say. After sex. A glass of Pinot Noir after sex. Nice.

So, there it was. Over breakfast some cold February morning, Greg learned he had a baby on the way. Holly was still talking, explaining that she told Greg it was wise to end the affair and that she had approached her company, seeking a transfer. She would slip away quietly before anyone knew she was pregnant with no talk or speculation of who fathered her child.

But then, Holly's transfer to San Diego wasn't approved.

Gabby felt the piercing pain sear through her. If this was true, Holly was trying to end the affair and cut all ties, giving Greg no reason to accompany her to doctor visits, no reason to be carrying around an ultrasound picture. *Greg* was clinging on.

She did the math, leading her back a few months, the timing of Greg's preoccupied mood, his insomnia, and the unexpected trip to renew their vows.

"We both agreed the affair had to end."

Both?

"We are not in love, Gabby."

You might not be.

Holly turned her body toward Gabby so that their knees were touching and inhaled sharply. "Gabby, he's a good man, a responsible man who's merely trying to support our baby because he's trying to right his wrongs." She touched her belly.

Gabby scoffed, her body unexpectedly lurching forward. A good man doesn't commit adultery, keep secrets, intentionally lie and cheat for months on end. Greg was willing to risk losing his wife, kids, and the life they'd spent decades building and the dreams they'd created for future decades. Holly had been seeking a baby, but Greg? What was he after? His own cheap thrills.

She knew Greg was prideful; they'd had their share of arguments over the years concerning it. Greg always denied such accusations and would twist it to make Gabby look critical. Holly undeniably gave Greg the boost his ego consistently, desperately, sought.

"I encouraged him to recommit himself to your marriage. I apologized to him for being a homewrecker." Holly placed a clammy hand on Gabby's forearm, sending a ripple of chills through her body. "I'm sorry for what I've done, Gabby, and I hope that someday you can forgive me."

Gabby shook Holly's hand from her arm and looked at her pointedly. "You knew he was taking me to Turks with the intention of renewing our vows?"

Holly nodded, and in that instant, Gabby knew Holly had suggested it.

"We are not in love, Gabby," she reaffirmed. "His heart is committed to you. He did go astray, but I keenly led him." She bit her lip. "I used him at your expense, and I thought I owed it to you to explain the truth."

CHAPTER 17

As your mother, I will always be in one of three places:
in front of you to cheer you on, next to you holding your hand,
or behind you to have your back.

Monica

Monica and Dex embraced Kenzie in their arms as the rising sun beat through their east-facing windows, flooding their bedroom with a warm rosy glow. Kenzie was still sleeping, sandwiched between them so snugly that Monica's and Dex's noses were only an inch apart, their chins both resting on Kenzie's head.

Monica knew it was time for Kenzie to start sleeping in her own bed again but kept insisting she wanted to be beside her if she woke up with nightmares. So far, Monica had been the only one dealing with bad dreams from the night of Kenzie's disappearing act.

Through their closed door, Monica could hear Beck's pitter-patter as he ran through the house. Janice had convinced Monica to go back to bed when she had gotten up with him. Reluctantly, she agreed, knowing, if she could hear his little feet drumming across the wood floor, he was safe.

Janice fully understood Monica's wordless apprehension and reassured Monica she wouldn't take her eyes off Beck, that the doors *were* locked, and they wouldn't step foot outside. Monica caught both the sarcasm in Janice's voice and the accusation in her eyes as she commented on the locked doors.

Even though it had been two weeks since the worst night of Monica's life, the incident was still on replay in Monica's head: the images of her and Dex frantically chasing after the sound of barking dogs, her legs somehow infused with speed she'd never possessed, leading her to a crumpled hammock spread out on the ground littered with the remnants of a tea party.

The sight of six K9 dogs and a slew of police and volunteers, flashlights whipping wildly through the trees, and the sound of voices calling out Kenzie's name would most likely haunt her for the rest of her life.

To have a brush with the reality of losing Kenzie forever was so disturbing that Monica wondered if she was doomed to becoming an obsessive worrier. Would she succumb to the propensities of an overbearing, compulsive, smother mother like those she'd often mocked and loathed?

Kenzie had stuffed her purple unicorn backpack with her blankie, three plastic tea cups, one saucer, the musical lid to a missing tea pot, and Monica's old flip phone. She confessed to creeping out the basement door, sneaking into Amelia's garage to find her hammock bag dangling from the handlebar on Amelia's bike.

Feeling safe in the company of Trixie and Reese, Kenzie confidently ventured away from her home as the sun dipped lower in the sky. Kenzie claimed it was Trixie and Reese who led her far away from home in search of the perfect hammocking trees.

Kenzie explained in jumbled frustration that Trixie and Reese couldn't get their hammocks tied up, so she had spread the hammock on the ground where the three girls had taken *seffies* for their *Napitsory*. Tears rolled down Monica's cheeks as she envisioned Kenzie pretending to take selfies with the flip phone to create a Snapchat story with Trixie and Reese.

As dusk settled into darkness, Kenzie told Trixie and Reese they needed to get back, so they decided to take a short cut. The short cut led Kenzie off the bike trail, through a wooded area, a corn field, and eventually in the backyard of an elderly couple's home where the K9 dogs had led them to a curled-up, deep-sleeping, three-year-old.

Kenzie wandered to their patio, explained she had curled up in a lounge chair, and searched for the Big Dipper, but the clouds had swallowed it.

As soon as Monica heard her mention the Big Dipper, she knew Kenzie was trying to find her way home. On clear nights, the Big Dipper hung over the lake. Kenzie was always pointing it out, saying she wanted to go there, as if the Big Dipper were a destination they could drive to. Monica never bothered to squelch her imagination and hope, only told Kenzie, if she tried hard enough, someday she would surpass the stars.

The dogs had led their search party to the small mound nestled in an old woven folding chair, adorned with two French braids with strands of dark hair poking out haphazardly. Kenzie, in her pj's, clutching her blankie, awoke to the wet nose of a dog and a wolf-like cry from Monica.

The porch lights flicked on as the elderly couple, well into their eighties, opened their backdoor to a search party finale.

"Too tight, Mommy," Kenzie had chirped that following morning as Monica squeezed her, and Dex encircled his arms around both of his girls.

Monica had buried her nose in Kenzie's hair, savoring the lingering scent of mango shampoo mixed with the smell of the outdoors, dirt, and the early morning dew. Scents that would permeate her nose forever.

Dex's voice wobbled. "You had us so worried, Miss Kenzie Kay. We missed you."

"Are you okay? Are you okay?" Monica repeated several times, running her hands up and down Kenzie's arms and legs, inspecting her body for cuts and bruises, parting her hair, searching for ticks.

Kenzie was nodding, without a trace of a tear, scratch, or dent. Fearless. The little girl could have taken care of herself in the wilderness for days had she been forced to.

Monica had told Dex several times over the past few months that Kenzie was going to go places. She walked with a purpose. She spoke very matter-of-factly, and when she asked a question, she would ask it with the answer she wanted already included.

"Ice cream after green beans, yes, Mom?" or "Mom, think so we are going to have time for the park today, okay?" or "Thinks Dad wants me to skip nap, sure?" and Monica's favorite, "Kenzie's skin smells good, yes?" she'd say while holding out her arm for Monica to smell, and after Monica sniffed and agreed, Kenzie would say, "Thanks, no bath today, right, Mom?

Recently, Kenzie's new word was *actually*. "*Actually,* Kenzie not want butter and peanut butter, just peanut on me toast, okay, Mom? *Actually,* teeth clean and skipping toothbrush for day." If Monica were robbed of hearing these imperfect statements coming out of Kenzie's perfect little mouth, her world would cease to orbit.

"You're such a brave little girl, Kenzie Kay. Mommy and Daddy love you so much and were so worried when we couldn't find you. Promise us you will never, ever, leave our house alone, ever again."

Kenzie only nodded as her bottom lip slipped out and her face began to crumble. The only thing that would bring Kenzie to tears in this entire situation was the fact that she saw the fear on her parents' faces.

"We will take you and Trixie and Reese, anywhere. All you have to do is ask, sweetie." Dex swooped in and picked Kenzie up, and with that, they both began to cry.

Dear old Mr. Holden had given them blankets to wrap Kenzie in while Mrs. Holden gave her chocolate chip cookies and milk.

"Actually, my dad have me cookies please?" Kenzie asked, trying to soothe her father's tears with cookies. The rush of joy was overwhelming, and Monica knew she'd carry those precious minutes with her for the rest of her life.

Poor Kenzie had been asked to explain her disappearance over and over by the police. After a while, the tale coming out of her three-and-a-half-year-old mouth was getting twisted, her wildly unpredictable imagination taking over. Trixie said this. Reese did that. No, wait. Reese said this and Trixie did that.

Kenzie's curiosity was never dormant, for it was her imaginary friends that led her away from the house. It was her imaginary friends that piqued her inquisitiveness and drive for adventure, and it was her imagination that would prevail over her nighttime journey.

Monica had always encouraged Kenzie's relationship with Trixie and Reese, but now felt responsible for possibly taking it too far. Maybe driving to their house to pick them up for playdates was a bit much and possibly buying them ice cream cones was over the top. But Kenzie loved Trixie and Reese as if they were flesh and bone, and Monica wanted to support that.

Upon returning home, they were flooded with cameras and microphones. Reporters were asking how a three-year-old wandered so far from home without anyone noticing? Asking if there was foul play? If she was being hidden against her will? If she was harmed? Traumatized? Had she spoken of running away? Even what role Monica and Dex thought they played in her disappearance? What they could have done to prevent it?

Now, safe in their bed, Monica listened to Kenzie's steady breathing, yet couldn't help but let her mind wander into the muck, the muckiness of her feelings . . . the guilt mostly. She felt guilty for wanting so badly to escape with her husband for a day. She just needed a day away from her kids and mother-in-law, from the constant demands and scrutiny. Now she was convinced that none of this would have happened had she been home.

She couldn't keep Cade safe and healthy in her womb and couldn't keep Kenzie safe outside her womb.

Thank God Kenzie's eyes fluttered open, interrupting Monica's berating. Kenzie scooched up between Monica's and Dex's faces. "Good morning, precious. Monica kissed her forehead, nose, cheeks, and lips, welcoming the scent of Kenzie's stinky morning breath.

Dex, with his arms around Kenzie's waist, pulled her closer to him. "Hey, she's mine. Save some smooches for Daddy." He held up her little arm and kissed it from her shoulder to her wrist while making loud smooching noises.

Kenzie spun into a fit of giggles as they both began to tickle her. Monica would forever soak up every little laugh, sneeze, cry, and burp that came out of her children. She would memorize every scowl, grin, wink, look of wonder and delight that ever flashed across their faces, because in an instant it could be gone.

Janice knocked softly on the bedroom door while pushing it open. Beck, in her arms, greeted them with his wide, nine tooth grin. "This little guy has been loitering outside the door every chance he gets," she said in an unusually jubilant voice for Janice.

Beck thrust himself from Janice's arms and toppled on the bed. Bouncing, he landed on Kenzie's leg and toppled onto her, his tooth piercing the skin on Kenzie's cheek, leading to a frenzy of tears. They hadn't missed a beat.

Their front porch had been littered with flowers, cards, stuffed animals, boxes of doughnuts and gift cards to various toy stores and ice cream shops. The stockpile was still growing, trickling in weeks later.

Janice had made a quiche from scratch, Monica's favorite, and thick waffles piled with strawberries and whipped cream for the kids. Monica noted Janice had not prepared Eggs Benedict, Dex's favorite.

They sifted through cards and notes from neighbors, strangers, and Monica was graciously humbled by the number of stuffed animals and toys Kenzie received from her former high school French students. No doubt all their phones had sounded with the Amber Alert. She remembered faces of former students fervently searching.

The outpouring of love and support was mind-blowing. The blurred faces within the crowd around her yard, the lake, and twenty-mile radius of their home slowly popped into her head as she and Dex recounted seeing this person and that person. Countless people had been out into the wee hours of the night, helping to find their precious daughter.

Cheers, whistles, and clapping had greeted them when the patrol car pulled into their driveway, delivering them home, safe and sound. The tear-stained faces of Gabby and Carmen had smiled as they wrapped their arms around Monica and Kenzie and wept.

At the breakfast table, Janice doted on both Kenzie and Beck. Her gentle voice, although peculiar, was welcoming. For once, the over the top use of Mémé didn't make Monica's skin crawl.

Janice sipped her cappuccino and went on about how Beck had sat in his highchair like the perfect little boy and played with the extra dough from the quiche crust while she prepared breakfast.

She had diced up fruit for him to munch on, given him almond milk in his favorite sippy cup, bathed, and dressed him. Monica was impressed. A wave of emotion ran through Monica, opening her eyes to the good coming from a bad experience. She and Janice could start with a clean slate. Maybe there was a chance for a loving relationship after all.

Monica's hand floated to Janice's. She squeezed tenderly. "The quiche is amazing, Janice. Thank you."

Dex's eyes shot up in surprise over the top of his coffee mug, darting from Monica to Janice. He took a sip and set the mug down as if it might break.

"You're welcome, Monica Dear. A little comfort food can be healing."

Dex grinned at Monica, and she knew their thoughts matched. Although Janice couldn't ditch the Monica Dear, her tone was sincere and affectionate.

"Mommy, look!" Kenzie held up the plastic toys from the mound in front of her. "Doc McStuffins baff toys. Kenzie take baff, pease?"

Monica started to correct Kenzie's use of the letter f in place of th and stopped. She'd learn to use her tongue instead of her teeth to pronounce the sound eventually. For now, she was going to embrace the imperfection. "Sure, sweetie."

Kenzie interjected when Monica scooped her up, "No, Daddy take me." She stretched her arms toward Dex, so Monica handed her over while pretending to nibble at her skin until she erupted into squeals.

Dex and Kenzie took off down the hall. Monica felt this was her opportunity to make amends with Janice. They had been avoiding each other and it had been long enough. After all, life was fragile, and she needed to define this fresh start with a hug and a few heartening words. She still loathed Janice, but she loved her too, and it only seemed appropriate to tell her.

Monica turned to her mother-in-law with her arms outstretched, the words "I love you" on the tip of her tongue, when the stern look on Janice's face stopped her.

"Time to pull up the boot straps and get your head sorted out so nothing like that night ever happens again, right, Monica Dear?"

Monica was baffled. Her arms fell to her sides as her spirit plummeted to a new low. The entire morning was nothing but a show for Dex. She hadn't a second to react further before Janice spoke again.

Janice's posture stiffened. "You've become so self-absorbed in your own pity from the death of the baby that you can't even think straight. You've pawned Kenzie off to a couple of imaginary friends, putting her life in danger, and isolating her from the real world."

Cade, Monica began to say. His name was Cade. Her lips parted, irate that Janice always referred to Cade as *the baby*, with aloofness in her voice, never referring to him as if he was actual flesh, bone, and spirit, a child she and Dex loved. But Janice cut her off.

"Your decisions are reckless, and I question your mental health. Your obsessive exercise habits and lack of domesticity tell me you think of no one's livelihood but your own." She spoke with a hostile edginess uncanny for even Janice.

Janice's eyes bore through Monica. "You scarcely pay attention to Dexter and his needs. Instead, you loaf around the house and wallow in your grief while using your miscarriage as the means to manipulate him into taking care of you, playing damsel in distress while he waits on you hand and foot, when it is *you* who should be serving your husband."

~*~

Ever since that night, Monica had been sticking close to home, welcoming several consecutive days of thunderstorms as a gift from God. No better way to get rid of the lingering reporters and nosy gawkers driving by to stare at the house the little girl wandered away from. People were so weird that way.

Monica had avoided reading the local newspapers, tossing them in the recycle bin without taking them out of their thin, orange plastic bag. She declined the reporters' persistent attempts for an interview. She only wanted to be near her kids, not swept off, thrown under camera lights, reliving something she'd rather erase from her memory.

Janice had come and gone from the house to meet with her friends for lunch, then card night, shopping, tennis, and shuffleboard. They met for mani-pedis, coffee, and lit club. Monica wondered how much they gossiped about her. What an awful mother, wife, and daughter-in-law Janice portrayed her to be.

When Monica explained to Dex the nasty things Janice had said to her, Dex comforted Monica, assured her how ludicrous his mother was, and then made excuses for her, claiming she felt at fault for Kenzie wandering off under her watch, that she was only lashing out because she was on the defense, feeling inadequate herself.

"You know my mom. She can't stand being in the wrong. Even though we've told her it was Kenzie's free will to wander, deep down she feels responsible. Her way of letting herself off the hook is to blame everyone else."

"Say something to her, Dex. Can't you confront her and stick up for me?" Monica couldn't understand how Dex could go through life never reacting to his mother's condescending tactics. She wanted Dex to put his mother in her place.

"Responding only fuels my mom. Acting disinterested and indifferent is the only way to get her to stop. She only wants to be assured we don't blame her."

Monica frowned. "Being passive and silent makes it seem like you agree with her."

"She knows I don't agree with her." Dex held Monica's face between his hands and kissed her forehead. "Do you remember how bad my parents used to bicker?"

Monica shrugged. "I mostly remember your mom ordering him around and your dad having his tail tucked between his legs, waiting on her hand and foot, treating her like she was some sort of goddess."

Dex smirked. "That too, but my mom loves drama, and she thrives on adversity and confrontation, whether it's with her friends, the checkout lady, the restaurant server, or sadly, a family member. Conflict is my mother's drug of choice; it's her power trip."

A line appeared between Monica's eyes as she snapped her brows together. "Monica Dear, you'll get wrinkles," he teased as he placed his finger there to soften her scowl.

Monica growled. "Don't call me that. Seriously though, I don't get it. I feel like I try so hard to be the sweet daughter-in-law, and she just loves to hate me."

Dex drew Monica close and hugged her. "Look. My mom knows you are a strong, independent woman, and she feels weak when she's around you. She loves you—"

"Loves to make me feel like a peon," Monica interrupted.

Dex placed his finger over Monica's lips. "Either learn to ignore her and let it go or play her game."

"Play her game?" Monica's eyebrows rose in question.

~*~

After days of few words and avoiding each other, Janice endeavored a truce. She had put the sheets back on the kids' beds after hearing the dryer buzz, given Beck a bath after he decided to squirt his tube of Go-Gurt in his hair and lather it, and insisted that Monica leave the kids at home as she was strapping a screaming and stiff Beck in his car seat for a host of errands in and out of the rain.

Monica wasn't sure if Janice was enjoying spending time with her grandchildren or if she was giving Monica some sort of test— testing to see if Monica would leave them in her care.

Slowly over the days it seemed there was this unspoken balanced war. For every kind gesture, an undermining comment followed.

"This quinoa is excellent, although a bit heavy on the balsamic drizzle."

"Even with wrinkles, that shirt looks flattering on you, Monica Dear."

"Although it's a precooked rotisserie chicken from the deli, Dex will be thrilled he doesn't have to prepare dinner again tonight."

"Kenzie's hair sure would look nice if she had a trim."

Running her fingers through Beck's dark curls, Janice said, "I can't wait until the trend of long hair on boys has passed."

Monica was taking Dex's advice, trying hard to not respond to Janice's remarks. She'd shrugged, acted aloof, laughed at the ridiculing, plastered a fake smile on her face, and walked away. Janice, sensing Monica's falsity, the irritation flaring her temper, would follow on her heels, persisting in her interrogation.

Harbored rage gnawed at Monica, clawing, eager to get out. She wasn't a doormat, a scared little kitten who ran from barking dogs. Monica had little in the way of a filter on her mouth when she was provoked. She'd have to be careful not to succumb to the quarrels Janice sought. No, she had to be clever. Dex had mentioned playing her game. That was an intriguing challenge.

It was dirty, yet Monica felt little shame. She didn't bother moving Janice's white cardigan she'd left draped over the back of the chair while Kenzie painted, splattering a rainbow of color on it. Worse, when she found Beck chewing on a pair of Janice's Maui Jim's, she let him gnaw away until Janice discovered him.

Monica knew Kenzie had been eyeing Janice's fifty-dollar liter of shampoo with its pretty flower packaging and dreamy scent. She would never authorize Kenzie to pump fistfuls into her dollies' hair while she washed them, but she may have placed the enticing bottle on the shower seat next to Kenzie's shampoo while Monica busied herself on the other side of the curtain, polishing her toes.

After several consecutive days of thunderstorms, the weather finally broke. Monica skipped the kids' naps and escaped on the boat for the afternoon. Janice had been lingering in her shadow all morning, and Monica was going batty. She packed enough food to last days, toys for ten kids, and enough floats to create an island. Satisfied with her location out of the wind, Monica killed the engine and threw the anchor overboard with gusto.

For five hours, they were in and out of the boat, swimming, jumping on the tubes, squirting water guns, giving Polly Pockets and Spiderman swim lessons, and for a mini break to de-prune their wrinkled skin, Monica hauled out the craft bucket, and they molded clay while perched on the back of the boat.

On their return to the dock, both kids dozed off, so Monica slowly circled around the lake, relishing in the peace and the hot sun blazing down on her skin. When she closed her eyes, she reminisced of her teen years with a load of friends on her grandfather's Chris Craft, drinking Mellow Yellow, eating Funyuns, the music blaring, their skin an oily deep bronze thanks to Coppertone. Monica inhaled, recalling the coconut scent that hung in the air, clung to the interior of her grandfather's boat, and saturated her swimsuits and beach towels. To go back, just for a day . . .

Monica eased the boat between the bumpers and raised the lift. Dex texted her an hour ago when he got home from work and told her to stay out until the kids woke up, that he'd change into shorts and a T-shirt, start the grill and dig in the fridge for something to barbeque. From the smell of it, dinner was nearly ready.

Janice waited until Dex was seated at the dinner table before mentioning she had swept the piles of crumbs from the kitchen floor, tore down the cobwebs in the porch, watered the wilting flowers, and emptied the dishwasher all so Monica could enjoy a lazy afternoon on the boat and return with dinner on the table.

Monica beamed at her mother-in-law. "You're so thoughtful, Janice. I appreciate you doing those things for me, without being asked, so I can spend quality time with my children. Your support means the world to me. The benefits of being a present, hands-on mom far outweigh whether we have cobwebs and wilted flowers.

"I only remember the endless hours my grandfather spent on the lake with me. Thankfully, I was more important than cobwebs, and my memories don't include him running around doing meaningless tasks, making me feel like a bother."

Janice acted as if she didn't hear Monica. "How was your long, exhausting day at work, Dexter?"

"Amazing, some suppliers took us golfing, and I had a top-notch country club olive burger." Dex took a swig of beer. "Next week is a charter fishing trip."

Janice caught Monica's satisfied smile and chose her follow-up dig carefully. "Hmm." Her eyebrow rose. "Intellectual business conversations can be quite taxing, golf course or not. You must be exhausted."

Really? Good grief, woman.

"Nah, we talk business for ten minutes; the rest of the day is guy banter."

Monica looked at Dex lovingly. Without knowing it, he had just stuck up for her. After dinner, Dex and Monica did dishes side by side. Monica hadn't asked Dex for help, but she knew this was his way of showing his mother they were a team, and she was relishing it.

Kenzie and Beck were playing outside on the deck, and Janice had snuck outside with a Virginia Slim, so Dex took the opportunity to embrace his wife. "I'm sorry you have to be the one here with her all day. If I could trade places with you, I would."

"Liar!" Monica swatted Dex's butt as she buried her head in his chest, inhaling his fresh layer of deodorant along with the faint smells of his morning cologne and leftover sunscreen from an afternoon on the golf course.

He grimaced. "I admire your courage, and thanks for putting up with her. It's not much longer."

"Liar again, it's only been one month. We're only a third of the way through."

"Well, then, let's take a vacation, Petoskey or Traverse City." Dex planted a kiss on Monica, and another, and then burst into laughter.

"What?"

"The last time we were standing in this spot we were naked and my mom walked in."

"Sex every day for a month if you drop your shorts right here," teased Monica. She had that playful, yet sexy little smirk on her face that she knew Dex couldn't resist.

"Ha! Now you're the liar!"

Monica began massaging Dex's shoulders, then his biceps, and she then moved down to his waist. As her hands slid towards his groin, she looked him in the eyes.

"Which part am I lying about? The right here, right now, *or* the offer to rock your world for the next thirty days?"

"Both, and there are thirty-one days in July, and since its June 30[th,] you're technically committing to thirty-two days in a row."

Monica's hands kept sliding down. She watched Dex's eyes as they darted over Monica's head, scanning the windows facing the lake. "I think I hear the tire swing squeaking. My mom must be pushing them. That should buy us a couple of minutes," he said as he lifted his shirt over his head.

Monica rolled her eyes but knew anything more than that was too risky. She wasn't serious about any of this, yet her long lost days of spontaneity were overriding her judgment. Surely, she would hear the smack of the screen door if anyone were to barrel through. Four seconds was all she needed to dart out of the kitchen.

A quick shove and Monica had Dex up against the refrigerator. She slipped out of her dress and panties, undid the button on Dex's shorts, lifted her leg with graceful precision to his waist band, and skillfully slid them down with her toes.

Besides their bare skin sticking to the stainless fridge, it wasn't all bad. Anyone who says they had incredible sex while in an upright or awkward position is lying. Wild. Spontaneous. Kinky. Yes. Yes. Yes. But not mind-blowing. That would have to come tomorrow (and for the next thirty some days) in their own bed with no inhibitions.

Dex held true to his word. Minutes later they were searching for their scattered clothes. "Now that's the girl I married!" He held up his hand for a high five.

"A high five, really, Dex, you're so . . . so . . . " Monica was fumbling with the straps on her sporty little athletic dress, trying to untangle them, when she heard the familiar smack of the door followed by Beck's little voice shouting, "Wing, wing, Mama, me wing."

Monica snatched her underwear from the floor and balled it in her fist as Dex nudged her out of the kitchen toward the laundry room, but not before the trio rounded the corner. Kenzie and Beck were oblivious as Monica backpedaled and fumbled her way out; however Janice's scornful eyes locked with her own.

Monica felt her face flush and ducked into the laundry room just as Dex tossed Beck into the air, drawing all eyes on the flailing arms and legs above.

"Agin agin! Do gin!" shrieked Beck with delight.

"Once is enough, little buddy," said Dex as he placed him on his shoulders. "Let's go back outside to the tire swing for more wings!"

The smack of the screen door signaled the coast was clear. She supposed she'd lay off Dex's case about replacing the spring. The kitchen was turning out to be an ample place to knock a quick one out.

She sighed in relief and left her hideaway in the laundry room only to find Janice still lingering inside. Waiting. She turned her back to Monica and placed the last few dishes in the dishwasher, poured soap in the dispenser, closed the door with gusto, and pressed start as if she were killing a small bug with her index finger.

Seeing the table still needed to be wiped off, Monica snuck in next to Janice and grabbed a fresh rag from the drawer. "Thanks for finishing up, Janice. I appreciate it."

She wet the cloth, sprayed cleaner on it, and waved the bottle in Janice's face, "I love the sea salt lime scent; it actually makes me want to clean."

Janice snorted inelegantly in response, total distaste spread across her face.

"What, Janice?" Monica threw her arms up in the air. "What?"

Janice's face contorted. She made all kinds of huffing and tsk-tsking noises while shaking her head. Monica slammed the spray bottle down on the counter and waited, hands planted on her hips. It was a stare down.

Twenty seconds must have passed before Janice finally parted her pursed lips, raised her chin three inches. "I . . . I guess I don't approve."

"Don't approve of what, Janice?" She was going to make her say it. Make her uncomfortable. This was Monica's house, her domain.

"You know what you two *do* out in the open." She flung her hand for effect.

Monica couldn't help herself. She broke out in laughter. It was funny. It was seriously funny! "Loosen up, Janice. We were making love in our kitchen"—Monica gasped for effect—"with plenty of time to run for cover if we heard the door. Would you prefer us to be fighting, living in a loveless marriage?"

Janice shook her head. "Ugh, no, but there are things that can't be unseen."

"You could bleach your eyeballs," Monica mumbled.

"Bleach what, Monica Dear?"

"Nothing. Look, Janice. We are happy, in love, find each other desirable. Please don't be a buzz kill." With that, Monica hurled the dish rag clear across the kitchen, over Janice's head, crumbs flying everywhere. It hit the faucet and fell in the sink.

Monica pumped her arms into the air. "Three points!" she shouted, turned, and sauntered outside.

Dex was pushing the kids on the swing and gave her a questioning look to which Monica smiled her victory. "Mind if I go for a walk?"

"Me too, Mom?" Kenzie begged.

"Kenzie, no, let Mommy go so she won't notice when we leave for the ice cream shop." Dex flashed Monica his thank-me-later smile. "Better make a run for it."

"I may have to stop for a rest at Gabby's," she hollered over her shoulder as she fled.

CHAPTER 18

*Surround yourself by people who nourish your soul,
lift you up, and touch your heart.*

Carmen

Carmen had hung up with her dad and somehow still managed to shine in the board room. She'd been trying to land the account with Local Flair for nearly two years, and she'd sealed the deal on a less-than-stellar day.

After the president of Local Flair Restaurant left her office, she booked an outrageously expensive last-minute flight to Wilmington, NC for first thing in the morning, grabbed Tiffany, slung her over her shoulder, and told her crew they were on their own for a few days and to only call in case of an emergency.

Carmen didn't need an email pointing fingers at who left the hazelnut creamer on the counter in the break room all night.

Decades of smoking had finally caught up to Mary. She received the lung-cancer diagnosis a short four months ago. When Carmen had shared the news with Victor, he suggested they go visit her parents immediately, bring the girls.

"It could be the last chance you get to see her alive, Carmen." His caring eyes were full of concern. "Don't you think it would be nice if she got to meet her grandchildren before she passed . . . meet me?"

"No, no, and no," Carmen firmly replied.

The summer after high school graduation, Carmen moved to West Michigan to live with her dad's sister. Her Aunt Marta took her in graciously, helped Carmen apply to a local college, and gave her a safe and loving home for four years until she married Victor two weeks after graduating from Hope.

Carmen had cut off all communication with her mother the day she moved away. She spoke with her dad a few times each year and had only seen him a handful of times since she was eighteen. He'd snuck away when her mother was admitted for an extended stay in the mental facility.

Victor tried a different angle. "Don't you think you should go for your dad's sake? Give him some support in her final months? He's going through this alone."

Carmen thought about it from this point of view, but her answer was still no. Her father had tried to be there for her while she was growing up, he really did, and sometimes he was, but overall, she'd felt alone as a child.

"I really like the guy, Carmen, and maybe it will open the door for the girls to have a relationship with their grandfather, you know, after your mom passes."

"We'll cross that bridge when the time comes. And how can you say you really like a guy you've only met twice?"

Victor shrugged. "Twice I met him and twice I liked him."

"Ha, hilarious, Victor."

Victor respected Carmen's wishes and left it alone for three months. A few weeks ago, he asked if she had reconsidered taking a trip to North Carolina, and her answer was still a harsh no.

"I don't want you to regret your decision down the road," he had stated cautiously.

"How could digging up the demons of my childhood lead to regret down the road, Victor?"

Carmen closed her eyes, remembering the way Victor pulled her close and held her, apologizing for getting her upset. She didn't regret not going to see her mother sooner. Even the ticket she booked for tomorrow wasn't to say good-bye to her mother. It was the quiver in her father's voice that made her realize he needed her.

Her entire childhood, her dad had been her escape from her mother. The days spent on the Atlantic, tranquilly rocking on his fishing boat, *Hooked*, were her saving grace. On the water, she felt protected, safe; she could exhale and relax. It was no coincidence she settled on a lake. A far cry from the body of water she grew up on, but this small inland lake brought her peace, made her feel safe.

Ever since she'd hung up with Chet this morning, she felt an urge to take refuge with him on that old Boston Whaler. Work, the girls, Victor's traveling and odd behavior, her mother's death looming . . . it all seemed suffocating.

Over the years, she'd done a decent job of numbing herself from her past. Then Penelope's behavior switched. Penelope's retaliation stirred up the buried anger and resentment of her childhood. And now, with her mother's final days looming, Carmen's insides were on fire, and she was having a hard time keeping the flames from spreading.

Carmen thought of Gabby, how easy it was to talk to her, and wondered if, after thirty some years, it was time to deal with her feelings, to try and forgive her mother and let go. Carrying the hate was awful, and she felt ashamed that she still harbored those feelings.

Her mother was dying. The right thing to do was reconcile, forgive, but Carmen couldn't fathom the inkling. Her mother didn't merit forgiveness; she'd never spoken a single apology to Carmen. The hurt she had inflicted was so deep Carmen vowed to build barriers and never take them down. She couldn't entertain the thought of being at her mother's bedside, holding her hand, telling her she loved her. She didn't.

Her dad mentioned Mary only had days. Hospice had set up a bed for her in the great room, so she had a view of the ocean. Chet further described their surroundings and mentioned the heat was tolerable enough to open the windows, so Mary could hear the waves crashing to shore, allowing a salty breeze to fill the room. The description meant nothing to Carmen. She had never seen the house her parents had lived in for the past ten years.

When her dad had retired from flying cargo planes for FedEx, they moved to secluded Bald Head Island. Surely, it was easier on Chet to contain Mary in a remote environment without completely isolating themselves. Carmen was thankful her parents had moved from her childhood home. She refused to ever step foot back in that place and relive the memories that haunted it.

~*~

Carmen walked into an empty house. She checked her phone and saw Penelope was still at Gabby's. She peered out the sliding doors. Thankfully, only splotches of spray paint remained, the words *ugly bitch, loser,* and *slut* no longer legible.

She was thrilled that Amelia had offered to mow the lawn and scrub the chairs; obviously, Amelia's heart had softened toward her sister, and she was trying to make amends.

Amelia had texted while Carmen was in her meeting, saying she had been invited to Grand Haven Beach with Piper. Carmen couldn't help but feel sad that Penelope no longer hung out with Piper's sister Liz. She truly believed Penelope wouldn't be going through this awful phase if Penelope hadn't ditched sweet, outgoing Liz.

After changing into her swimsuit, Carmen settled in her sparkling clean, urine-free chaise lounge and called Penelope, surprised that it didn't go straight to voicemail.

"Hi, Mom," Penelope answered, uncharacteristically chipper.

"Hey, Penelope, how'd the interview go?"

"I got the job, and I'm working the rest of the afternoon." Carmen detected a smile in her response.

"Awesome, I can't wait to hear all about it."

"Yep, gotta go, Mom. I'm learning how to bill clients," Penelope said in the polite voice she reserved for when adults were present. "My boss is literally looking over my shoulder."

Carmen's cheeks rose with her smile. She heard Gabby teasing in the background, "Chop, chop, back to work! No personal calls."

"Wow, she sounds like a slave driver. I won't keep you."

"K-bye."

"Penelope, wait."

"Whaaat, Mom?"

"Congratulations, like, wow, way to go!"

"Yep!"

It was a short response, but the tone in her voice was sweet, rather than the usual clipped tone she reserved for Carmen.

"Also, of course, I'm proud of you, duh, but you should be too. That's a rather adult-like job you've got; most kids are scooping ice cream and clearing tables at your age."

"Yep, seriously, gotta go, Mom."

"Love you, Penelope."

Penelope was cheery even if it was forced politeness in Gabby's company. Carmen closed her eyes, allowing the scorching sun to penetrate her skin, and prayed Penelope would rebound, that Gabby could fix her broken daughter.

~*~

"Get up. Let's go!" called a stern voice that startled Carmen awake from a deep sleep.

She quickly wiped her mouth for fear she had been drooling and shielded her eyes from the sun, trying to make out the figure before her. Monica stood, hands on her hips, hovering over Carmen.

The angle of the sun told her she had been sleeping a long time. "My gosh, Monica, you scared me. What time is it?"

"Haven't a clue, six thirtyish, seven maybe?"

Monica's tone was far from the exuberant voice she normally spoke with. There was an urgent gruffness to it. Carmen grabbed her swim cover-up and pulled it over her head.

"I must have dozed off, for nearly two hours! I can't remember ever doing that!"

"Well, naptime is over. We're going to Gabby's for a drink."

"You okay?"

"No. Crappy summer, all things considered."

Carmen crinkled her face. "Sorry."

"Nah, don't be sorry. I'm really past the point of caring."

Carmen didn't buy it—otherwise Monica wouldn't be all riled up—but Carmen wasn't going to prod. She took a sip of her warm water and texted the girls to let them know she was going for a walk. Penelope texted back and said she was just leaving Gabby's and asked Carmen if she could stop at the drug store for nail polish and mascara on her way home. Carmen questioned her veracity and began a response reminding her that she was still grounded, but then she deleted it and instead asked her to pick out a new coral polish for her as well.

Amelia had sent Carmen a selfie with a slice of pizza hanging out of her mouth and texted she was still in Grand Haven and would be home after sunset.

"I'm a free woman. Let's go. Is Gabby expecting us?" asked Carmen as they started to walk through the sand along the shore.

"No, I took off in a hurry. She won't care"—Monica pointed towards Carmen's phone—"but maybe you should text her and give her a heads-up."

It took half an hour to walk to Gabby's house. They stepped over docks, walked through well-manicured beaches, weedy beaches littered with snails and dead fish, and rocky beaches they had to tiptoe through in pain.

Gabby was on the sprawling patio, waiting for them. She had a dozen candles lit, some smelling of citronella and some smelling like a tropical paradise of mango and coconut. Music piped through outdoor speakers, and she had a pitcher of homemade black & blue mojitos waiting. The concoction was almost too pretty to drink with blueberries, blackberries, and mint leaves floating about.

From the outdoor kitchen, she pulled a tray of chocolate-covered strawberries out of the fridge and placed them on the table.

"Do you have some sort of secret staff and chef who prepares all this glorious scenery and food for you?" Carmen took in her surroundings with a deep, grateful breath. Here she was with her new friends, all haphazard from sleeping in the afternoon sun, now sipping cocktails and eating chocolate-covered strawberries.

"Hardly, it took me two minutes to wash the strawberries and squirt Magic Shell on them." Gabby gushed to Carmen about how wonderful Penelope was, that she was a huge help, so eager and willing to learn, so efficient and polite. Carmen teased whether they were talking about the same girl, but she knew they were. Gabby had just described the daughter Carmen had raised, the one she prayed was only temporarily derailed.

They talked of the latest news around the lake, the weather, recipes, and their upcoming 4th of July plans. As they sipped, their conversations went deeper, their voices louder when the conversation swayed one way, then hushed when it swayed another, always on guard, knowing how well voices carried across the water.

Carmen and Monica jumped as Gabby slammed a hand down on the table. "Confession time, ladies. I need to get some things off my chest before I explode. Holly and I met in person," Gabby blurted after her second mojito. "She told me she used Greg to get pregnant. All she wanted was a baby. She doesn't love Greg and doesn't need him for any support."

"How awful—" Carmen began to respond but was cut off by Gabby.

"Confessions only. No responses yet. Go, Monica." Gabby pointed.

"My mother-in-law has caught Dex and me in sexual situations twice in the kitchen. Oh, and did I mention she is a passive-aggressive condescending witch?"

Gabby and Monica both pointed to Carmen at the same time. "Don't think. Just talk," said Monica. "This is how we play the game."

"I'm secretly addicted to pickled okra." Carmen licked her lips for effect.

Gabby and Monica both furrowed their brows in response. "Ya, no"—Gabby shook her head—"go big or go home. I've got pickled okra in the fridge. The whole jar is yours as soon as you spill your darkest confessions."

"Fine. My husband is a workaholic, I'm suspicious of his travels, and my daughter is a cutter."

Gabby raked her hands through her hair. "For the time being, I've decided to keep mum about Holly's pregnancy. I need to figure out who is playing whom. Who's hiding their true feelings about the other, denying, or lying about their emotions. Whether Greg or Holly are plotting something."

Monica's eyes widened. "What the—"

Gabby firmly held up her hand. "Don't break the rules. Your turn."

"Holy shit, Gabby, I'm biting my tongue, but okay." Monica's eyes filled quickly as she began to speak. "I could have lost my daughter forever when she wandered from our house, and as much as I want to blame Janice, I hold myself responsible for it because I've glorified her imaginary friends, I left the door unlocked, and I was selfish because it was one of those days where I couldn't wait to get away from my house, my kids, my mother-in-law . . ."

They all shuddered, thinking of those chaotic and scary hours only a short time ago. Carmen figured this was where they would stop—was hoping they would stop. Certainly, they had to console Monica, and how could they wait any longer to hear about Holly.

Carmen swirled the mint leaves in her mojito with her straw as the silence settled. Leave it to Monica to see that Carmen not be let off the hook. Monica cleared her throat. "Waiting."

"Right. Fine. My mother, whom I haven't talked to in twenty years, is on her death bed. I'm flying to North Carolina first thing in the morning to see her for the first time since I was eighteen."

Carmen looked out to the water where dusk had settled. Faint streaks of dark blue clouds mingled with smears of orange and pink. Countless times as a child she had rocked the waves, sprawled out on the deck of *Hooked,* and relished a similar saltwater-taffy sky.

"Thing is, ladies, if this confession game is all about honesty"— she took another sip of her drink, watching Monica's and Gabby's heads bob in unison—"I'm not exactly sad. I'm indifferent to her death."

Carmen hadn't shared information about her parents with anyone except Victor. Ever. She had even sugarcoated the truth to her dad's persistent sister when she took her in at eighteen. Confirming Aunt Marta's suspicions would've only made it that much harder to cut the cord.

Gabby folded her hands in her lap and met Carmen's eyes. "This is where confession ends and talk begins."

"Oh, is that how the game goes? It ends when the therapist feels the need for an intervention?" Carmen disliked the tone in her voice but felt compromised.

Gabby shrugged. "Pretty much, yes, but I'm not your therapist. I'm your friend."

Awkward, thought Carmen, and wondered why Gabby's constant declarations of friendship made her uneasy when it was so natural for most of the female species.

Carmen fidgeted uncomfortably in her chair. "A friend whose vocation is to analyze emotionally unhealthy relationships."

"Your words, not mine."

"Ooh, you're good. Threw that one right back in my lap."

Gabby opened her hands. "That's your perception."

"This is how you trick people into divulging, out of a need to explain their harsh comments rather than seek analysis."

"Interesting analogy. Why do you think you're defensive and guarded?"

Carmen wiped the perspiration between her breasts with the pretty little blue paisley napkins that coordinated with Gabby's outdoor cushions.

"Shit, Gabby, you've got me all worked up!"

Carmen saw Monica's eyes darting back and forth, now falling on a silent Gabby, her eyebrows arched in question.

"Fine, you win. I've got myself all riled up because I'm afraid of being judged. I'm a grown woman who was damaged by her mother as a child, and I've spent my adult life suppressing the demons and never dealt with it." Carmen sat up tall in her chair. "I loathe my mother, women in general for that matter. Admitting I'm indifferent to the fact she's dying sounds awful. I realize that. Quite honestly, it's freeing to speak it out loud. A burden lifted. How terrible and brutally honest is that for a confession?"

Carmen drained her mojito, fueling up on liquid courage, and continued with the raw, unfiltered truth about her mother and her childhood. It felt so good, exhilarating, to finally have the valor to share a complicated, abusive past.

Monica couldn't stop wiping tears from her cheeks while Carmen spoke, shockingly, with dry eyes. For nearly an hour, Carmen recalled painful events from her childhood, only skimming the surface, but really, that was more than she'd ever shared with anyone, besides Victor. Carmen had spent her adult life trying to forget, and you don't forget by constantly drudging up the past.

Unfortunately, her memories, the sights, sounds, feelings, and words came back to her as vividly as the day she experienced them. So much for decades of guarding her heart. Trying and failing, Carmen knew she had allowed her heart to become bitter and angry. She'd never permitted herself the simple gift of friendship. Instead, she'd allowed her mother's cruelty and brokenness to taint her own sentiments.

When she was too drained to continue, both Gabby and Monica held her. Had she ever felt a loving embrace like this? Yes. Aunt Marta had tried numerous times to hold her and love her, and

Carmen had allowed her, but it was unnatural, foreign on Carmen's end. She had already convinced herself never to trust or love another woman.

Monica was dotting her eyes when she started to laugh. "I hope this isn't completely heartless, but if you get to the point where you'd rather open up to actual human beings instead of a leather handbag . . . I mean Tiffany is simply exquisite, and I'd hate to see her snubbed. You could pass her on to me."

All three women threw their heads back in laughter. "Perfect example of why I don't trust women. They use you!" Carmen swatted Monica's arm with the back of her hand.

"Hey, at least I'm upfront and honest," teased Monica.

"Toast." Gabby held up her glass, and Carmen and Monica followed suit, only all three glasses were empty. Their gazes darted to the empty pitcher in shock. Gabby slid her chair back with such force it almost toppled over. She retrieved a bottle of Riesling, cold and crisp from the fridge, unscrewed the cork, and poured the wine into their Mason jars.

Gabby cleared her throat while Carmen and Monica leaned in for the profound, wise words Gabby was sure to deliver. "Friends!" declared Gabby.

Both Carmen and Monica waited for Gabby to continue; instead, she drank. Monica burst into laughter, and Carmen and Gabby followed suit once again.

"Why are we even laughing?" asked Gabby.

"Friends? That's it?" Monica trilled. "Here I thought you were going to drone on philosophically, say something monumental. Something inspiring. Something therapeutic."

"Jeez, it's a lot of pressure hanging out with you two!"

Carmen held up her glass. "Us three," she toasted.

"Us three. Now that's good." Monica smirked, clinking Carmen's glass.

Gabby playfully rolled her eyes. "Us three. Agreed."

"Us three," they cheered together.

"I have one more confession for you, Carmen," admitted Monica. "Dex thinks I have a girl crush on you because, every time you walk out of your house, I purr, *Sophia's out!* You know the actress Sophia Vergara?"

"Well"—Carmen flung her hair over her shoulder—"I, like Sophia, am Columbian, and if you think I look like her, then I have a girl crush on you too!"

Carmen helped herself to a chocolate-covered strawberry. "I'm starving. Let's order pizza."

Monica scoffed. "Order pizza when we could indulge on fancy wood-fired concoctions with goat cheese and a bunch of other toppings Gabby uses that I can't pronounce?"

They all looked at the beautiful stone fireplace equipped with a pizza shelf and wood stacked neatly by its side, ready and waiting.

Gabby stood. "I'll run inside and grab pizza dough from the fridge and raid it for toppings."

"I'll get the fresh herbs," announced Monica as she hopped up and began plucking oregano from Gabby's herb garden.

Carmen scoured the outdoor cabinets and placed a cutting board and knife onto the prep area and began chopping the herbs, washing and slicing a fresh tomato she plucked from a vine in a corner pot on the patio, and minced the large fancy green olives she found in a jar amongst the liquor.

Gabby returned with a tray of sauces, cheeses, pine nuts, leftover roasted eggplant, a jar of marinated artichokes, sweet peppers, and dough. They started the fire, sipped their wine, prepped three different types of pizzas, talked and laughed as the sun sank and the stars came out.

The fire was crackling, and the crickets were singing into the night as the three friends dined on their delectable concoctions. Gabby excused herself and came back out of the house with three glass jars.

"C'mon we're going to catch fireflies."

"Excuse me?" Carmen mused.

Gabby didn't answer, only shoved jars into their hands and motioned for them to follow. *Us three*, thought Carmen as they ran through the thick and humid summer's night air, each shouting with glee, "Got one, got another" as they trapped the glowing little bugs.

"You two are more fun than frogs in a pond," Monica announced.

"Hey, Gabby," Carmen yelled across the yard as she clamped down her lid on another. "Can my girls stay with you while Victor and I are in North Carolina?"

~*~

"I'm home," Carmen called into the quiet, dark house. She and Monica had walked home barefoot, splashing through the warm water as they trudged along the shoreline beneath the stars.

The air conditioning was continuously pumping cool air into the house while numerous windows remained open, allowing a warm night breeze to filter in, a bad habit Carmen passed onto the girls that drove Victor crazy. Carmen argued, wasteful or not, how absurd it was to live in a closed-up house all summer when you spent Michigan winters doing just that.

Carmen took the steps two at a time. Besides yoga, her exercise regimen was non-existent, and she felt inspired by both Monica and Gabby to be more active. Monica had walked so fast around the lake that Carmen pathetically had to keep jogging to match her pace, positive Monica could hear her gasping for air.

No surprise the girls' bedroom doors were both closed, their lights peeking out from under the door. Amelia's room was first, so Carmen gently knocked as she simultaneously let herself in. Amelia was sprawled out on her bed, hair wet and fresh from a shower, her phone in hand, music playing. Carmen inhaled a wide range of scents from Amelia's collection of sprays, lotions, bath bombs, and potions collected on her vanity.

Carmen counted on her fingers. "Do I dare say the scent of mango, pineapple, vanilla, orange, and sweet pea finally out power the paint fumes?"

Amelia giggled, her skin a deep golden brown from endless hours in the sun on their lake floating in Piper's pool and frolicking at the beach. A light dusting of freckles covered her pink nose and cheeks to which Carmen reminded her to be liberal with sunscreen.

"Your room looks cool," Carmen complimented as she took in the collage of canvas prints, distressed wooden wall hangings, and metal art all in a tropical beach theme. Amelia had used the level and pounded every nail into the wall and hung each piece herself.

Amelia crinkled her nose. "The letter A is a bit cockeyed, but I'll fix it."

"Never would have noticed. So how was the beach?"

"Awesome, we were in the water, boogie-boarding most of the day. The waves were huge. Piper's mom took us to Fricano's for pizza and Temptation's for ice cream."

"Sounds fun. Can you imagine growing up without Lake Michigan at our disposal? I mean, really, what do people in Kansas do all summer?"

Amelia shrugged. "I know, right?" Her eyes never left her phone. "I brought you something. It's in the freezer."

Carmen's heart melted at the gesture. "Coffee Toffee?"

Amelia nodded. "Two pints."

"You're the best, thank you. Someday this summer I'd like to skip out of work and take you girls to the beach in Grand Haven. Maybe we could go early and shop, get gyros at Mr. Kozak's."

Carmen paused, waiting for Amelia to show excitement; instead, her lip curled downward as she reluctantly nodded.

"Did Liz go along?"

"Yep."

"So, did Liz bring a friend along too?"

Amelia rolled her eyes and sighed. "Yes, Mom, Leila and Tara were with Liz."

Leila had been the third in the tight knit trio. Leila entered the friendship during water polo in sixth grade. Penelope, Liz, and Leila ice skated together in the winter, entered the talent show together every year, went through braces and first crushes together, and even got their ears pierced at the same time. Penelope ditched the threesome and was replaced by Tara last year.

"So, you five girls and Mrs. Jensen?"

"Yep."

Carmen had decided not to reach out to Brooke, at least not yet. She was hoping Penelope would be saved by Gabby. Still, she couldn't help but wonder what Brooke's take on the situation was. Had Liz bad-mouthed Penelope to her mother? Talked about her downward spiral at the dinner table with the whole family? Did they criticize and judge Penelope for quitting water polo? Were there rumors around school that Penelope was a cutter, she and Victor the last to find out? That her grade point went from a 4.2 to a 2.9? That she had been caught drunk and high?

"Does Mrs. Jensen ever ask about Penelope?"

"Nope."

"Do Liz or Leila ever ask you what Penelope is up to, like if she'd want to hang out at the beach or whatever?"

"Nope."

"Hmm, well, I'm going to get Penelope. There's something I need to talk to you two about."

Carmen entered Penelope's room the same way she had Amelia's, with a knock as she was already making her way through the door. She was holding her breath, slightly scared of what she would find her daughter doing but was happy to see her sprawled out in her chaise, ear buds secured, foot thumping to the music, with a notebook and pen in her hand.

There was a sticky note attached to the open page. *Respect yourself by being the best you can be. Reflecting who you want to be.* It wasn't Penelope's handwriting. Was it Gabby's? Penelope tucked the notebook under the throw pillow on her lap as she saw Carmen's eyes graze it.

She took her ear buds out. "You're still in your swimsuit and cover-up?"

"I was on the beach when Monica decided to drag me to Gabby's. Had I known we would be there until eleven o'clock I would have changed."

Penelope's face twisted with confusion and annoyance.

"Have you, like, become friends with them or something?"

"Ya, I guess so. We really had a fun time. So, more important, tell me about working for Gabby."

Shockingly, Penelope went on for a solid five minutes about her tasks and how Gabby allowed her to take complete control when updating her website. Gabby had listed all the necessary links and videos that needed to be included, but she left Penelope to be creative in the design.

"Tomorrow she said my time will be split doing office tasks and some yard work, but I'm fine with that."

"I'm glad you like it. You'll probably get a lot of good business experience too." Carmen paused, relishing in Penelope's poised mood. "Say, can you come in Amelia's room for a minute. There's something I need to talk to you girls about."

Carmen hadn't really thought ahead as to how she was going to inform the girls that Mary was dying. Or rather how she was going to avoid the questions that always followed the mention of their grandparents.

They all settled on Amelia's bed. "Grandpa Moreno called me today with unfortunate news." Carmen's head dropped. She couldn't even look her daughters in the eye when speaking of her mother, fearing the indignity would show through. Carmen was sure that someday they would resent her for denying them a relationship with their grandmother. In their eyes, she was probably a sweet old thing.

"Grandma is dying. I'm flying to North Carolina tomorrow, and Dad is taking a flight from Vegas and meeting me. Mrs. Bock has offered for you to stay with her for a few days while we're gone."

Amelia spoke first. "Um, okay. Sorry?" Her eyes questioned. "What happened?"

"Lung cancer. She's at home, but Grandpa said it's probably only going to be a couple of days."

"How long has she had lung cancer?" asked Penelope.

Carmen swallowed hard. "Four months."

"Why didn't you tell us?" Penelope scoffed. "I mean your mother, our grandma, is dying of lung cancer and you don't bother to let us know?"

Carmen looked at the two scrutinizing faces in front of her. They were all sitting on Amelia's bed, Amelia's knee touching Carmen's thigh, Penelope's toe grazing Carmen's shin. "I don't know. I guess I figured, since you don't know her, I didn't want to bother you with it. I didn't want you to worry about me."

Penelope's voice rose. "I find that hard to believe. Our whole lives you've made shady excuses for why you don't speak with your parents."

"I speak with my dad," Carmen said defensively.

"Hardly, we've only seen Grandpa twice in our entire lives, and you never give us a straight answer when we ask why we don't visit them," Amelia pointed out.

Well, this was new, the two of them siding together, ganging up on Carmen. "I'm sorry. It's complicated, nothing to concern you two."

Penelope locked eyes with Carmen defiantly. "Why do you hate your mom so much?"

Carmen gasped. "Penelope, that's inappropriate."

"Well?" she questioned. "Is it true?"

"I don't hate my mother. We are just two very different people and . . ." Carmen's voice began to quiver. She had suppressed her feelings to shield her daughters from the truth. She refused to allow her emotions to rule over her mouth.

Tears began spilling down Carmen's cheeks. Maybe she should have waited until morning for this talk when her head wasn't muddled from the drinks she'd consumed earlier. She only wanted to have a shower and crawl in bed.

"Girls, please respect my choices. They were made with good reason. I'll talk to Grandpa. Maybe we can set up a vacation to the Outer Banks and visit him in Bald Head Island for a few days in August."

"Why don't we go with you tomorrow?" asked Amelia.

"NO!" Carmen hadn't realized she shouted until after the girls both jumped.

CHAPTER 19

If you love someone, showing them is better than telling them.
If you stop loving someone, telling them is better than showing
them.

Gabriella

Now that Gabby had new insight into the affair, she couldn't banish
the smug feeling knowing Holly had deceived Greg. If indeed that
were the truth, he had no idea she only used him to father a child.
Gabby felt slightly vindicated in the fact that, just as Gabby had been
deceived by Greg, Greg had been deceived by Holly.

A part of her wanted to rub the deception in his face, but she
realized that could backfire. If she made Greg aware that Holly used
him only to father a child, he could use it to weasel his way out of
any accountability, play victim to his sin. She knew Greg. Knew his
thinking.

Amongst many garbled thoughts swirling in Gabby's head was
the reality that Greg hadn't spoken up from the beginning. From the
first time Holly came onto him, he didn't tell her he was married.
Sure, he may have pushed her away, with one hand, at first.

Ultimately, he failed to explain to Holly that he lost his wedding
band last summer in the lake after snagging it on a rope he was
untangling between the dock and boat. Yet, he slipped the new band
they purchased in Turks on his finger with ease and said, *"I do,"*
conceitedly, as if another woman wasn't pregnant with his child.

For months, he was sleeping with two women, leading a double
life, lying to Gabby. While they were rebuilding their house to
accommodate their future grandchildren, he was out destroying the
construction of the past twenty-five years. How many times over the
past few months alone had they dreamed about the trips they would
take after retirement—Bora Bora, Europe, Fiji, and Australia.

Greg was fully aware of his actions, and he had committed to
a relationship with Holly for months. Holly said she was not in love
with Greg; although Gabby sensed a fondness and wondered if
carrying his child would transform her feelings. She was forthright in

stating she felt an instant connection for him to father her child. If there was anything Gabby knew, it was people, especially women. Women rarely went into relationships without succumbing, entangling themselves in thick and complex emotional webs.

Greg, too, had looked Gabby in the eyes and told her he was not in love with Holly. She couldn't shake the faint notion they both could be playing her for a fool. She didn't think he felt for Holly this deep reverential love that came with being married to someone for decades, but he felt something; otherwise, he wouldn't have kept going back to Holly for months.

Was it lust? Did Holly look at Greg with adoring tentative eyes? Did she place him on a pedestal and give him the adoration he craved? Was it that Holly was ten years younger and strikingly gorgeous? Or did Holly and Greg's sexual relationship simply exceed the marriage monotony of her and Greg's? Was Holly wild and kinky, leaving Greg to compare Gabby as tedium?

~*~

Gabby's mind was so preoccupied that when her feet hit the cobblestone driveway, she barely remembered the five miles she'd run. Her watch congratulated her speed, thirty-six minutes. She found crescent pose and fixed her gaze on a fluffy, passing cloud, in an otherwise cobalt blue sky. The threat of rain on the fourth of July always made Gabby edgy; she was grateful for one less concern.

Last night Gabby prepared the kids' favorite dips for the endless supply of chips their friends reliably contributed. Stella and Lottie had helped her make the traditional fruit pizza adorned with strawberries and blueberries to create a flag. The girls made red velvet cupcakes piped with swirling blue and white frosting.

Calvin and Klay chipped in by husking corn on the cob and chopping the fixings for burgers while Gabby made a tortellini dish, an all-American potato salad, and baked beans. She cherished the time in the kitchen with them more than anything.

The boys, including Preston, disappeared for a few hours late last night and returned with boxes of fireworks, all illegal, she presumed. Would she ever stop fretting that this was the year someone would blow a finger off? Horrible to allow such a thought to enter her conscious, but she was a mother, and explosives worried her.

Preston was polite and helpful. He filled and hauled gas cans and shoveled piles of washed-up seaweed from the beach alongside Stella's brothers. Calvin seemed indifferent to Preston, compartmentalizing him as another one of his older sister's boyfriends that hung around for a few months to eventually disappear and be replaced. Klay seemed to pay more interest as he studied Preston and the interactions between him and Stella.

Klay had that intuition: he could read people, he saw and sensed things, almost without flaw. Gabby would wait a few days, and she'd ask for his impression of Preston. Klay wasn't one to criticize or judge. He was humbly clairvoyant.

Klay had been the one to voice which babysitter was a good fit when they'd interviewed a slew of new faces back when the kids were in elementary school. He'd warn them when Calvin brought home a buddy that was questionable, and he'd more than once gotten into a spat with his sisters after coining their boyfriends d-bags.

It felt like the old days when the Bock household had a revolving door. Carmen warned that Penelope and Amelia were slightly apprehensive about staying at Gabby's, so Gabby assured them they were free to come and go between their house and hers all day long but they needed to text their whereabouts and check into her house for the night by ten.

Gabby hadn't been wakeboarding in years and asked Penelope and Amelia, whom she knew were both crazy good, if they would take her and give her some pointers. She managed a couple of laps around the lake before hitting a wave and soaring through the air, landing on her back with a slap.

Gabby popped out of the water and heard cheering from the girls.

"Woo-hoo, Mrs. Bock, you almost landed that jump!" Amelia shouted.

Gabby clung to the board as Penelope steered the boat to her. "I hope it looked good because it didn't feel good." She held up her hand. "You're going to have to pull me in."

That first night they stayed up late, lit a fire outside, roasted marshmallows, and played board games. Amelia crushed them in Skip-Bo, and Gabby taught them how to play Bump. The constant flow of company kept Gabby's erupting emotions at bay.

To her surprise, they'd both arrived with their overnight things and hadn't left. Their preference to be at her house over their own had delighted and amused Gabby. Possibly they were in awe of the college kids and the constant activity.

Gabby had gone all out prepping for meals and snacks. She had the fixings to make anything from homemade macaroni and cheese, tacos, steak, or risotto. She laughed at the déjà vu when she could barely push the grocery cart around the corner from one aisle to the next.

Not only had she stocked up for the girls, but for her kids and their friends that were all rolling in for extended stays over the fourth. Gabby had asked the girls to share a room because of the accumulating guests, and they did so without a fuss. Carmen was shocked and pleased with the report.

Gabby had noticed Penelope seemed to bring different flavors of iced tea to work with her, so she had surprised her with a peach iced tea waiting on the desk with a sticky note and Penelope's name written vertically in bold letters. Next to each letter of Penelope's name, Gabby had written a single word, Passionate, Enthusiastic, Noble, Educated, Leader, Organized, Punctual, Eager.

Penelope had scoffed at the list and began to ridicule herself. Gabby silenced her, affirming to Penelope that she was every bit those words and more. She handed Penelope a journal, the letter P gracing the front cover.

"Own it. And while you're at it, I want you to come up with another positive word or quote to put in your journal every day. Declare the type of person you wish to be, and you will succeed. As a job requirement, we will periodically go through your journal together."

Penelope caught Gabby by surprise when she engulfed her in a hug and thanked her.

"No, thank you, Penelope." Gabby squeezed her in return. "I want you to know how much I appreciate your hard work and dedication. I'm going through such a difficult time right now, and you've really been a big help with keeping my business organized, helping around the house, and honestly, you've kept me sane."

The corners of Penelope's mouth turned up. "Well, I'm still learning, but I think I've got a better understanding of managing your books."

"When it comes to numbers, you know what you're doing. I'm impressed."

Penelope nodded. "Ya, I get that from my mom. When I was little and her company was small, she did her own books. I'd sit next to her with my mug of chocolate milk, and she'd give me a calculator and ask me to add and subtract things for her. She'd have me write it all out on a piece of paper, and each calculation had to result in the same answer three times before I could go on. We always played office together."

Gabby noticed the fondness with which Penelope spoke. "Your mother is a great role model."

Penelope's face switched on a dime to that of defiance, which Gabby noticed she tried to mask with a polite grin. Typical teenage behavior. It was far easier to focus on your parents' shortcomings than it was the decent, respectable qualities. The big picture behind the reasoning of their decisions would come much later.

"She's raised you to be confident and independent, important life qualities." Gabby knew a major component to gaining confidence was to consistently have someone remind you that you were confident. She had urged Carmen to also remind Penelope of this.

"So . . . a while back"—Penelope cleared her throat and fidgeted with the hair tie she had around her wrist—"when I um . . . you were . . . on the beach, I was pretty upset with my mom. The flower pot—"

Gabby held up her hand. "No need to explain. We learn from our mistakes."

Penelope bit her trembling lip. "I'm embarrassed. You and all the neighbors, you must think I'm such a brat."

A snicker escaped Gabby. "I don't think you're a brat. I also don't think it's a bad thing that you're embarrassed. It's a good sign you know right from wrong. Your conscience is working. I bet there'll be no more hurling planters off balconies!"

Gabby broke into a fit of laughter and Penelope followed.

"Don't beat yourself up for the past. Own up, make amends, and move on." Gabby winked.

"Saying sorry to my mom is hard. *She* can be so hard."

"I respect your honesty. Your mom might too." Gabby eyed Penelope and got the feeling the time was right. "I know you're cutting."

Penelope's face went pale, and her eyes diverted to the ceiling fan.

"I'm not going to berate you over it, Penelope. What I will say about the behavior is I feel like you're possibly doing it to punish yourself over something."

Penelope shifted from one foot to another.

"Nothing could be so bad that hurting yourself will make things right. Each day you're given a clean slate to start fresh. Make amends. The best place to start is with yourself because *she's* the one person you'll never get away from."

Gabby boldly took Penelope in her arms. "Let her shine. Let Penelope shine."

~*~

The temperature had soared into the upper eighties, and the humidity was thick. Stella hadn't been feeling well, insisting she was past morning sickness. Gabby reminded her to take it easy, stay cool, and drink a lot of water.

Stella had plopped down to watch the large crowd of college kids play beach volleyball, so Gabby pulled up a chair to keep her company. One thing Gabby noticed since the arrival of her children and their friends was how much Stella and Preston had recently matured.

They were twenty-one compared to Calvin and Klay's friends being mostly nineteen, but there was even a difference among Lottie's group, who were the same age. Her entourage was most likely overindulging in beer, so they were loud and a bit crazy, but they were safe, where Gabby could keep tabs on them. She'd had a lot of practice at this over the years, and it felt good to sit back and watch them as they led carefree lives.

Her heart sank at the thought when she looked to Stella. Stella and Preston came alone. Sure, Stella and Lottie's friends crossed over, but she and Preston had friends of their own they didn't invite. Gabby encouraged her to, but Stella wouldn't budge, and with the way Stella had been feeling, it was for the best.

Preston fit in with the present crowd and was having a great time, but Stella's wild days were swept away. Out of the graciousness of her heart, Lottie had made Stella a virgin piña colada complete with an umbrella and a sword-shaped skewer of pineapple.

Gabby knew her grown-up, baby girl's face, and she knew she was in agony, but just like when she was little, getting sick in the toilet while Gabby held her hair back and rubbed her shoulders, she would say to Gabby, "I'm fine, Mom. It's okay if you want to go back to bed." Gabby had that hunch that Stella was in far worse condition than she let on. Gabby pondered if it was physical or emotional.

Stella's full piña colada was in her hand, resting on her thick belly, which, at eighteen weeks, had yet to take on anything but the tiniest bump. She had moved her beach chair to the shore where the waves could crash over her ankles and keep her cool.

"Stella, you okay? Do you think you should call your doctor?"

"Nah, I have a raging headache. Things look blurry, probably because it's so hot."

Gabby took Stella's drink and helped her out of the chair. "Let's get you in the shade. Have you taken any Tylenol?"

Stella shook her head. Gabby figured as much. Stella had never been able to swallow pills. Gabby crushed up the Tylenol to a fine powder and stirred it into a glass of Cherry Coke just as she had when Stella was little. She agreed to a few bites of a peanut butter bagel and some watermelon, yawned, and said she was going to take a nap in the hammock.

Once Stella was settled, Gabby grabbed her phone with the intention of taking some pictures, only to notice Carmen had texted.

My mother's breathing is labored. The hospice nurse doesn't think she'll make it through the night. We'll have a few things to sort out but are planning to fly home within a day or two.

Gabby was concerned about Carmen. Thought it very odd that she would leave her father so quickly after her mother's death. Gabby texted back:

Are you free to talk?

No.

Gabby waited a few minutes for Carmen to expand, but she didn't, which really wasn't a surprise. It was apparent Carmen's relationship with her parents was extremely broken.

The girls are having a ton of fun, so feel free to stay as long as you need to.

Okay, thanks, Gabby. Please keep an eye on Penelope's skin for cuts.

Of course.

Moments later, her phone chimed again. She hoped it was Carmen saying they'd decided to stay longer.

Gabriella—I hear the kids are at home for several days, and it sounds like you're going to have quite the houseful. I've decided to be present as well. I think it would be great for us to all be together, keep the tradition, try and have some normalcy while we deal with the current situation. It's a great opportunity to get over the hump of awkwardness. If the kids see us together, acting respectful to one another, it will help them heal.

I'm their father. Although I've respected your need for space, I want to spend the fourth of July holiday with them on the lake as I have for the past twenty-one years.

It's still my home and they are my kids too. I'll be over shortly.

~*~

Gabby was stocking the mini fridge when Greg came up behind her. He had an armload of Oberon, his summer drink of choice, and a bag of oranges dangling from his finger.

Greg smirked. "I figured you weren't currently stocking this for me."

"Not really, no." Gabby took a step back, his familiar scent suffocating.

He had a fresh haircut and a tan, most likely from playing endless rounds of golf with his boundless free time.

"You look"—he paused, his eyes traveling from head to toe and back up—"stunning, Gabby."

Stunning? How many times had Greg ever told her she looked stunning? Beautiful, gorgeous, and even hot, yes, she'd heard that plenty over the years, but never stunning. It was probably on the tip of his tongue from saying it to Holly. An antagonizing ripple rolled through her at the same time she felt her stomach clench, flattery and fury all rolled into one.

She could have easily complimented him because Greg *did* look stunning. He always looked stunning, especially wearing the khaki linen shorts and white linen shirt he knew she loved. Greg was far prettier than she, he was far better looking than most people in general, with his pale gray eyes flanked with heavy dark lashes, but she felt no need to reciprocate. Instead, she brushed the compliment off and told him there was a little space in the fridge for his beer.

"The place looks incredible, Gabby." Greg looked at the lights strung above his head, the huge flower pots thick and lush, lanterns, candles, and tiki torches surrounding him. "I bet it looks *marvelous* at night." He used their inside joke with a flutter of his hand, mocking a male decorator who had helped Gabby for a short time years ago before she realized she had the talent herself. *Marvelous*, they had joked over the years, accentuating the r.

One corner of her face rose smugly. "Thanks." She was not going to play along with the joke just as she wasn't acknowledging the earlier compliment.

"Is there a punch list or anything you need me to look at? Any nail pops, cracks in the floor, electric, or plumbing issues?"

"Nope, all good."

Greg nodded, and Gabby was hoping he felt un-needed.

He looked to the lake. The speed boat was off the lift, out doing circles with someone wake surfing behind it, speakers blaring "Born Free" by Kid Rock, a July fourth favorite.

"Wow, there has to be fifteen people on the boat. I don't even recognize the kids they bring around here anymore."

"They've been great. I've enjoyed the houseful the last couple of days."

He asked about Stella, knowing she hadn't been feeling well. She caught him up on all the newcomers and which old-time friends of the kids were around. She thought Klay was quite fond of a girl named Bianca, Calvin was enjoying flirting with all the girls, and Lottie was semi-seeing a kid named Remel.

"Remel? What kind of name is that?" mocked Greg.

At least she knew the baby's name wasn't going to be Remel. Had he and Holly talked baby names?

Greg pointed to the floating trampoline. "Who are the young girls?"

"The Fletcher girls," Gabby went on to explain the situation. "Penelope is working for me, getting me caught up with the endless paperwork. She's having a rough go with friends and school right now, so I'm doing some secretive counseling at the same time."

Greg looked at Gabby adoringly. She looked away.

"You're an incredible woman."

Gabby held up her hand. "Save the flattery, Greg."

"It's just that you don't miss a beat. You've rebuilt this house from the studs, decorated it incomparable to any TV show, you spend your days encouraging and counseling others, and you graciously open our home to anyone, even while, through . . . everything that's going on."

He grabbed her hand and pulled her close, forcing her to look at him. "You're constantly sending care packages to the kids, being their rock for whatever they're going through, dinner had always been on the table for me, a secret stash of Golden Oreos hidden from the kids in the crock pot, a travel mug of coffee waiting for me each morning, spearmint Life Savers appearing in the center console of my car when I thought I'd run out, new socks in my drawer when I'd only just noticed a hole . . . " His voice trailed off.

Greg wasn't a mushy guy. He was always appreciative of Gabby, but he was never one to go around voicing his gratitude, instead gave off the aura that attention was expected, or rather, needed for his own security. Not that this was any sort of aha moment for Gabby. She'd been keenly aware from early on of her role in pulling Greg off his knees and putting him back on his feet.

He was easily offended, often blamed others for his own wrongdoing, and looked to Gabby for justification. Whether it was consoling minor things like placing near last on the golf course or reassuring Greg that he was in better shape than the guys in their group of friends, being married to Greg could be exhausting: playing mediator in his relationships, smoothing things over between him and the kids, and rationalizing his behavior to his own parents. *"Controversy chases you, Greg,"* she'd say jokingly, only hoping that someday he'd understand he was consistently the root of his own cause.

On the flipside, Greg had a way of taking care of his family, looking out for them fiercely. When the kids were young, if Gabby merely mentioned she didn't feel good, he'd insist she go to bed, and he gladly gave baths, read books, rubbed backs, sang songs, and tucked all four kids in tight. He'd taught the kids water sports, how to snowboard, drive, balance check books, use power tools, and told them he loved them every single day.

Greg's faults could get under Gabby's skin, as she was sure hers did to him. Only now, she was starting to face the truth that Greg's faults ran deep. Admitting it was those qualities that also led him to infidelity, behaviors she'd always known him to possess, made her acutely aware that Greg easily told bald-faced lies to twist and coerce people's thinking. Afterward, he'd soldier on relentlessly without a conscience.

Trust and loyalty were top on Gabby's list of vital character traits. Gabby no longer trusted Greg. And the only person he had remained loyal to in his life was himself.

He brought her hand up to his lips and kissed it, his eyes welling with tears.

"I've missed you so much, Gabriella. I've missed our wonderfully ordinary life and spending time together with our children. Shit, Gabby, I'm going crazy without you! I messed up. I can't live without you. I want our life back, and I'm willing to do anything to save our marriage. You've got to find it in your heart to forgive me."

"Greg!" she shouted in frustration. His sucking up only irritated her.

"Holly told me the two of you met," he continued. "She's still trying to get the job transfer."

"And if she doesn't get the transfer?"

Greg's eyes scanned the patio to be sure no one overheard their conversation. He sucked in a deep breath. "Holly talked with

HR and informed them of her pregnancy. She told them she was in a long-distance relationship."

More lies.

His hands found her hips before she had time to step back. He pulled her close and spoke, his lips brushing her ear with each word, "Gabriella, we've got a chance to let her go, start over. No one will ever know about the baby." His words came faster. "We can work on us. I can't let this tarnish my reputation with the kids. I can't lose all of you."

His shoulders slumped, and his head shook, reminding Gabby of the way the boys tried acting remorseful when they wanted to get off the hook easily. "The thought of hurting the kids further . . . I think we should avoid it at all costs."

Gabby's body stiffened at his touch. She felt like blurting the real secret to Greg: that Holly used him, and he was nothing more than a sperm donor. She couldn't decipher what repulsed her more, his arrogance that he could just erase the last few months as if it never happened, or his arrogance that he was just so fantastically good-looking and charming that he swept a gorgeous woman like Holly off her feet.

"The way you talk enrages me. You're trying to guilt me into saving your ass by putting the focus on the kids because you know I consider them before myself. Don't insult my intelligence with tricky reasoning, Greg." Gabby spoke through gritted teeth.

Greg took an intimidated step back. "You don't think it would hurt them further?"

"Of course it would, and it would hurt you as well. If I choose to remain silent about the baby, it certainly isn't about *protecting you*, your relationship with the kids, your image, or your career. Your decision to be honest with yourself and the children lies within you, Greg."

"So you're going to guilt me into telling them?"

Gabby's hand flew up. "Whoa, not a chance I'm going to be responsible for your feelings or what you do with them."

Greg's arms flew over his head and rested behind his neck. "Shit, Gabby, I need to know if there's any hope for us. This runaround is driving me fucking nuts!"

Gabby's head fell to the side. "Aw, bummer." Her insides were lurching, the urge to claw at Greg's pretty face overpowering.

"Klay! Dude, are you blind?"

Gabby and Greg both turned toward the beach, the boat was parked on the lift, and a slew of kids were disembarking down the dock. Klay made interrogating eye contact with Greg before picking up the volleyball that had dropped at his feet.

"We aren't doing this now," Gabby said. "If your intention was to come here today and make demands and offer a scene, then you can waltz right on out."

Klay missing the ball and looking towards the patio had also gotten Lottie's attention. Gabby saw them share a look before engaging in the game.

"Seeing us in a heated argument most likely won't buy you any favors with the kids."

"I'm sorry." He brushed her cheek with the back of his fingers.

Gabby flinched. "Please, I don't want to be touched, Greg."

He nodded. "I'm sorry. I'm scared of losing you and the kids." He looked around. "This, our lifestyle, Gabby, it means everything to me."

Gabby's face crinkled with disgust. "How presumptuous."

"Mom," Stella croaked from the hammock behind the hydrangeas. Her voice sounded weak.

"Stella's not feeling well. We don't need to add to her stress"— Gabby's hand flitted in the air toward the kids' friends on the beach—"or make ourselves the uncomfortable spectacle of the party, so either leave or play the charade for everyone else's sake."

Gabby put a hand to Stella's cheek; she was pale and sweaty.

"It's too hot out here. Will you help me inside, please?"

Gabby led Stella inside, force-fed her saltines and water, and placed a cold washcloth on her head before calling her doctor. She left a message with the nurse, stating her concerns, and was told to expect a call back from the obstetrician within the hour.

Stella gave Gabby strict instructions not to pull Preston off the boat to babysit her. "He means well, but if he asks me if I'm okay one more time today, I'm going to come undone."

Gabby sat with Stella until she fell asleep. Not knowing where to go, other than knowing she'd spend the rest of the day avoiding Greg, she helped herself to a plate of appetizers, surprised by a rather beautiful platter of pinwheels and fruit kabobs. The girls were getting domestic in their early twenties, Gabby mused.

She took the opportunity to immerse herself in the festivities. It was odd not having half of their usual crowd in attendance. Gabby couldn't remember a fourth of July without their closest friends. They could have come and pretended everything was normal, but Gabby hadn't the energy, and she feared her friend Chloe would have a loose tongue. These were couples with whom, together with their families, they'd vacationed, celebrated birthdays and holidays, watched each other's kids play sports, and comforted each other as their children left for college.

Gabby missed their friends. How do you keep those relationships that are tied by strings of matrimony? Sure, Gabby had been invited to play golf and have dinner with the group, as she was sure Greg had been invited on a different night, but she declined. Being with shared friends only invited animosity, opportunities for friends to take sides and speak words that could never be undone no matter the outcome down the road. Gabby found it far easier to avoid all that for now.

As she made her way down the patio steps to the beach, she took in the wealth of activity. A few boys were fishing off the end of the dock, and another boat load had gone out on the lake to do some extreme tubing that Gabby only prayed wouldn't result in serious injury. Two girls were playing Frisbee in ankle-deep water, a few dotted the beach chairs in the sand, and a slew were floating on rafts. Greg was acting busy, tinkering with the boat lift, most likely because his sons snubbed him and didn't invite him on the boat as they most often did.

Without her own friends to hang out with, Gabby didn't know where she belonged at her own party.

As if reading her mind, Lottie yelled over the commotion, "Grab a raft and join us, Mom."

"Ya, c'mon, Mrs. Bock, chill with us," Breckon called.

Lottie dangled an empty Corona bottle in the air. "Would you mind grabbing me another beer on your way out, pleeease," Lottie hung sweetly on please for several beats.

Gabby gave Lottie a wry smile. Although legal, fetching her daughter a beer still felt wrong.

"Me too, please," shouted a few others.

Gabby played servant, teasing the girls that she missed the days where she was handing out juice boxes. She eased herself onto a raft next to a bunch of bikini babes with more piercings and tattoos than she and her friends ever would have dared at their age. She helped herself to a Jell-O shot as the tray passed by and settled in easily with the dozen or more girls talking rather candidly about guys, mostly bad dates. At one point, she realized her cheeks and stomach hurt from laughing so hard.

The spread of food was enough to feed one hundred. As always, Gabby watched it disappear in a fraction of the time it took her to prepare. The boys ate two or three burgers a piece and still managed to empty the side dishes. There had always been an odd satisfaction in watching the mounds of food she served to her children and friends be greedily consumed.

The barges took their place in the middle of the lake and set off a display of fireworks that gave Gabby goose bumps. Greg had cozied up next to Gabby, and as much as she longed for him to put his arm around her shoulder and pull her close, she repulsively left the blanket, tears welling in her eyes, and found an open chair on the grass.

Klay had noticed the interaction and moved his chair over by hers. She smiled at him—"Hey, kiddo"—and nuzzled his shaggy mop with her knuckles.

"Hey." He nuzzled her arm with his knuckles and then took her shoulder in his palm and squeezed.

The gesture filled her with immense joy and pain.

After the fireworks, they were tidying up in their usual fashion. Greg turned on the floodlights, folded the extra chairs, and scraped the grill. He handed out the brooms for the kids to sweep the sand off the patio and dock. Trash bags were dispersed to collect the fragments of explosives that littered the beach and rakes to comb fresh sand over the remnants left behind from spilled food and drink.

A bonfire had been started, and Gabby double-checked that all keys were in a bucket and all guests were spending the night. Now all she needed to do was see Greg on his way and curl up in bed.

Greg kept trying to make small talk, asking about the neighbors, her family, obviously fishing for how much she'd divulged of his affair and questioning her about various petty things to stall and linger.

"I'm worried about Stella." Greg closed the grill cover and boxed Gabby into a corner where she was tucking plastic silverware away in a drawer. The floodlights were on, casting shadows over his tired face.

"Are you sure we shouldn't bring her into emergency? At the least, they could check her vitals and listen to the baby's heart, possibly do an ultrasound?"

The way he talked confirmed to Gabby that Greg had been attending all of Holly's doctor appointments. It had been so long since she was pregnant he wouldn't have remembered these simple tests that monitor mom and baby. Gabby knew the look on her face must have shown the revulsion of his words.

He fidgeted nervously. "She seems rather ill to just pawn off."

Gabby pushed past Greg to gather a pile of wet, sandy beach towels. "No one's pawning her off. Since she didn't have a fever and wasn't vomiting or dehydrated, her doctor thought it was fine to wait until tomorrow for an office visit. If something changes during the night, I'll bring her in." As I've done since the kids were infants, she thought, call the doctor and stay calm.

Gabby exaggerated her yawn. "Speaking of, I'm off to bed. We have to be at the doctor tomorrow at eight. Stella will text you with an update."

She turned her back on Greg to make her way inside when a wail interrupted.

"Mom. Mom!"

Gabby looked up to find Stella standing in the doorway, stabilizing herself with the handrail. Preston held his arm around her waist, looking frightened.

"I'm bleeding, Mom."

CHAPTER 20

*Don't marry a man unless you would be proud to have a son
exactly like him.*

Monica

There were eleven kids under the age of six between Dex and
Monica and the other four families they had invited over for the
fourth of July. The adults were constantly counting heads, spraying
sunscreen, clipping life jackets, changing swimmy diapers, and
filling water balloons and water floats.

Portable beds were set up in various rooms of the house to
accommodate the young nappers and small gated play areas on the
lawn to contain the crawlers.

How, in the last five years, had their group multiplied from ten
adults to now include eleven offspring? They were outnumbered.
The racket amongst the group had quadrupled with babies crying
and toddlers screaming and splashing with delight.

The guys stood in the water, beers in one hand and either a
baby or a football to toss in the other. They were shouting as they
tried to carry on a conversation over the ruckus of their children.

The women reminisced of the days they kicked back with a
cocktail and enjoyed the sun and engaged in uninterrupted,
meaningful conversation. These days, no one sat down long enough
to spit out more than a couple of words. Someone was always
jumping up to dig sand out of a mouth, rescue a shovel being swept
off down the shoreline, nurse or fix a bottle, put a tike down for nap,
or retrieve a crawler who'd ventured to the water's edge. The
endless needs of small children . . . a mother's eyes never received
a vacation.

After losing Cade, Monica had had no intention of trying for
another child. She'd been content with the two strong and healthy
children she had. Lately though, she felt a nudge. Her mind flip-
flopped from fantasizing of another child to remembering the fateful
day during her ultrasound when the technician's face went flat,
excusing herself and returning with the obstetrician.

She and Dex learned their twenty-week baby boy had a less than eight percent chance of being born alive. His little heart had holes, along with transposition of the great arteries, a congenital heart malformation where the pulmonary artery and the aorta are switched. He had one lung.

At twenty-four weeks, Monica went into labor, and Cade was born. The hospital room was somber as the nurses spoke in hushed, sympathetic tones. They wrapped his little body in blankets so she and Dex could hold him, welcome him, and say good-bye, in the same moment.

Deep down she knew she was nuts. If she were to conceive, she would be a nervous wreck her entire pregnancy. Besides, she really should go back to work in the fall. Could she handle being pregnant while living life in a blur, dealing with daycare and preschool? Rushing through their morning and nightly routines made Monica anxious just thinking about it. Being pregnant on top of all that was foolish.

Trying for another baby would be a reckless move, it would push her over the edge, and she'd push Dex over the edge. But she couldn't stop thinking about it. She couldn't stop aching for the kicks against her stomach, the feel of soft infant skin on hers. Another chance.

Monica looked at Jolee with yearning. She was reclining in her beach chair under the umbrella with nine-week-old Nya sleeping on her chest. "Is Nya sleeping through the night?"

"Beautifully, she only gets up once, usually around midnight, so I pump before I go to bed, and Jake gives her a bottle. They get daddy-daughter time and I get some sleep."

"That's awesome. So, she's nursing well?"

"Couldn't be easier, she'll take breast milk or formula from a bottle too. She's so easy, rarely fusses. The most chill little baby."

Ugh, Monica wasn't so sure that was what she wanted to hear. She was secretly hoping Jolee would complain about the lack of sleep, a raging diaper rash that kept Nya screaming for hours on end, possibly some reflux that sent projectile vomit across the new carpet, anything to taint the picture for Monica. But Monica was getting sucked in, infatuated with the bald bundle.

"That was Kenzie, so easygoing. Beck, on the other hand, wouldn't take a bottle." The sitter had to bring him to school twice each day so Monica could nurse him during her prep hour and again at lunch. Thank God she was able to wean him to a sippy cup and solids at thirteen months.

Monica would remind herself of how difficult the first year of Beck's life was. Exhausted didn't even come close to describing how she felt, constantly being at his beck and call. That was her and Dex's joke, that they cursed themselves by naming him Beck, deeming him to be needy.

"I have to run inside to use the bathroom. Will you hold her for a minute?" Jolee asked, already placing a sleeping Nya on Monica's chest.

For real? She had just been convincing herself how ludicrous the idea of a baby was, and now, with this precious little one in her arms, the urge was undeniably strong.

"Look at you!" purred Kendra. "You and Dex should try for another." Her eyes were sympathetic. "You're such a good mom, and now you've got Janice here to help out. What a blessing."

"Ha! Hilarious, Kendra! More like a curse. Janice is like having a third child, a mouthy, disrespectful toddler or teenager. I'm not quite sure which."

"Oh, come on, she can't be that bad."

Monica kissed the top of Nya's head to prevent herself from rattling off spiteful remarks. She didn't want to get herself all riled. Janice had *skedaddled* for the day and went to visit a friend on Lake Macatawa. Monica had shouted, "Let Freedom Ring," as the door closed behind Janice. She wasn't about to compromise her freedom by going off on a tirade.

~*~

As much as Monica loved hanging on the beach, playing on the lake, the boat parade, and the all-American feast that came with the fourth of July, the very best was sitting in lawn chairs cozied up with her family, gazing at the bursting fireworks. They had traded their sunscreen for bug spray, their swimsuits for stars and stripes.

Lingering in the air was the smell of the hundreds of grills that had barbequed dinner around the lake. Now the faint smell was mixed with the tang of explosives.

Everyone had lit their two flares and placed them on the beach, creating a red glow outlining the lake. The barge containing the fireworks floated in the middle for an unobstructed display. Young kids ran around with sparklers, dangerously waving them in the air inches from each other's hair and faces. How was it in their safety-crazed generation that sparklers were even on store shelves?

The adults, men, also played with much bigger explosives on the beach. For hours on end, the continual piercing sound of booms, crackling, and whistling persisted. Mothers covered the ears of their young, muffling the sound while affirming their safety.

Monica looked around her yard. Some families sprawled out on blankets, others reclined in their chairs, but everyone's heads tilted to the sky with faces aglow from the bursting colors. Maybe it was the beauty and the awe that stole her thoughts, but the single most prominent thing on her mind was conceiving another child.

She didn't want to feel this way. She wanted to be content with their doable little family and couldn't fathom the stress and uncertainty of another pregnancy. Besides, they were done with bottles, and Beck would soon be potty training. Why would she want to go back to all of that?

Monica looked to Dex, Kenzie on his lap in the chair next to hers, and took his hand. Beck jumped at the boom and flashing white of a massive firework and buried his head in Monica's chest.

Dex rubbed the top of Beck's head. "You're okay, little buddy."

At the sound of his father's voice, Beck leaped to the security of his lap, barreling into Kenzie. Monica took hold of Kenzie and pulled her from Dex's lap, brushing her sticky hair off her face. Kenzie smelled of sunscreen, lake water, bug repellant, and the sweetness of the twelve desserts she ate instead of dinner.

Monica leaned in close to Dex's ear so he could hear her over the continual blasts. "We should do it again."

He nodded. "Of course, we do this every year," he agreed.

"No, I mean this." Monica pointed at the kids.

Dex's brow crinkled with confusion. He looked to Monica, not fully registering. "You mean . . . another kid?" he asked, leaning in so that his lips tickled her ear.

Monica nodded, feeling a firework display ripple through her body, and a smile engulfed her face. Dex's expression immediately reflected hers.

"Ya, most definitely," he agreed. "Yes."

~*~

The sweat trickled down her forehead and stung her eyes. She wiped it away with a dirt-streaked forearm. Monica was on a mission. It was already July, and she hadn't tackled anything major on her summer to-do list.

This morning she power-washed the deck and hoped to restain it sometime in the next week when Dex could give her a hand. Now, while Kenzie and Beck were blowing and chasing bubbles around the yard, she dug out the old brittle bricks from the walkway her grandfather had meticulously laid decades ago.

Thank goodness the bricks weren't cemented in. Her grandfather had carefully placed each brick in the dirt in a herringbone pattern and allowed the grass to haphazardly fill in the cracks. Although the bricks held sentimental value of her grandfather's handiwork, the kids had been stubbing their toes on them, and several bricks were missing large chunks, creating sharp edges. It was time to let them go, save a few to outline the firepit.

She and Dex had picked out some beautiful, smooth slabs of stone from the landscape nursery, and although Dex suggested she wait until he got home from work to start on the project, Monica was eager. She relished the hard labor, the sweat, dirt, and aching muscles as she dug and hauled wheelbarrows of brick to the dumpster.

"Monica Dear."

The fretful voice came from above. Janice peered down at her from the deck. She was in her tennis dress and visor, her hair meticulously styled around it, sprayed stiff to resemble a headdress. The ensemble was admittedly flattering on Janice, but Monica couldn't muster up the effort to compliment her.

The kids cheered, "Mémé *watch me*," as they ran around the yard. Janice gloated, acting highly interested in their play. The scenario irritated Monica, Janice's distance continually proving the lack of depth in their relationship.

Monica stood and stretched her back, one hand on the shovel, one on her hip. "Yes, Janice?"

"My, aren't you quite the busy bee today!"

Here it comes, thought Monica. Janice would surely dish out a few pointers on how to properly dig up the old bricks, even though the woman had never engaged in physical labor that required getting dirt under nails. She wouldn't outright tell Monica that the way she was currently doing it was wrong; she would only point out a better, more efficient way, less messy . . . something.

Monica didn't respond to the busy bee bit; she wasn't three years old. For once, Kenzie and Beck had been entertaining themselves for a solid forty-five minutes without asking for a snack, fighting over toys, or Monica having to assist Kenzie in the bathroom or change Beck's diaper. There had been no tears to soothe, owies to kiss, or Band-aids to stick. They hadn't even asked Monica to blow bubbles with them.

It was Janice that was going to squelch her productivity.

"I played pickleball by that new little deli in town and brought back lunch for us. Hey kids," Janice shouted through cupped hands, "Mémé brought you chocolate milkshakes for dessert!"

Kenzie and Beck deserted their toys and darted for Janice.

"Save the milkshakes for after nap!" Monica called up after them.

"Nooo, Mom, please! Kenzie want it now!"

Beck jumped up and down, pumping his fists, "Nowww!" he mimicked.

As soon as the words left her mouth, she regretted it. She hadn't meant to disappoint Kenzie and Beck. She threw the rule out there for authoritative reasons over Janice, and it only backfired with meltdowns.

"Fine," she called back up, "make sure you eat your lunch too."

"I brought lunch for you as well, Monica Dear. I ordered us all some veggie hummus wraps. I figured *that* was something you'd approve."

Why did Janice have to spit the word *that* with venom? Really, why did she have to throw that last line in at all? Monica had to get a grip; she was stooping to new lows because of Janice. Her head was constantly filled with nasty thoughts. The underlying gesture of Janice surprising them with lunch meant she was trying; it was thoughtful. She could have really pissed Monica off and brought back chicken nuggets and fries and sent Monica into a tizzy.

Monica let the shovel fall and went inside to wash her hands and splash water on her face, double-checking in the mirror for dirt smudged across her cheeks. Anything to avoid a scornful raised eyebrow from her mother-in-law. Beck's and Kenzie's shakes were nearly gone when she sat down at the table, not a single bite taken from their wraps.

Janice had gotten Monica an iced tea and sweet potato chips to go with her wrap, Monica's favorite. The gesture softened her.

"Yummy!" Beck gloated with hummus all over his face.

Monica agreed, "Thanks. Janice, this is great."

Kenzie snuck a sip of her milkshake, peeking at Monica as she did. "Go ahead and suck 'em down before they melt," Monica caved while devouring her chips.

"Since everybody approves of lunch, I'll get takeout next time I meet the girls for pickleball."

"Milkshakes too?" Kenzie asked.

"Milkshakes too, Kenzie Dear," Janice agreed jubilantly.

Kenzie Dear! Monica choked on her chip, coughing, and finally washing it down with her iced tea. If Janice began calling her daughter Kenzie Dear, she'd lose it. Sure, there was sweetness in Janice's tone, but still.

Janice looked disgustingly at Monica, her hand resting on her chest. "My, slow down, Monica Dear."

Kenzie touched Monica's arm. "You okay, Mama?"

"K, Ma?" Beck echoed.

Monica nodded as she cleared her throat and dabbed at her watering eyes.

"Mommy was shoveling her chips in her mouth too fast, Kenzie Dear. She'll be fine, but that's why you need to use good manners and eat slowly so you don't choke."

"And die?" Kenzie asked, fear taking over her face.

"Not die." Monica wheezed, patting her chest with her fist.

Kenzie placed her little hand on Monica's forearm. "Manners, Mom, pease."

Wait. What? Monica was screaming inside. One chip, one single chip lodged in her throat!

Monica's eyes darted to Janice. Her mother-in-law's face rested, victoriously smug. Winning her grandchildren over with milkshakes, demeaning Monica, orchestrating the show, would it ever end? And she couldn't say a peep about it to Dex without looking like the irrational, ungrateful one that didn't appreciate Janice surprising them with lunch.

CHAPTER 21

I never knew how strong I was until I had to forgive someone who wasn't sorry and accept an apology I never received.

Carmen

Bald Head Island was a serene island with its beaches bordered by grassy dunes, marshy streams filled with wildlife, and a simple, slow-paced life. Once you arrived to the island by ferry, transportation was either golf carts, bikes, or your own two feet.

The salty ocean air and sounds of gulls overhead made Carmen feel like she was home; although she'd never lived on the island. She couldn't help but dream of escaping there with her family for the next several years until Penelope and Amelia were both in college.

Her parents needed the solitude for different reasons. Her father enjoyed the peace and scenery after flying FedEx Boeing 777F cargo planes for thirty-two years. Her mother, well, she functioned better when removed from stressors, mainly everyday life and people.

Carmen and Victor hadn't been on the island more than two minutes before agreeing they needed to bring the kids for an unplugged vacation—a vacation where they would ban screens, savor the quaint restaurants, stroll the shops, ride bikes, visit Old Baldy lighthouse, and walk and relax on the beach.

There was only one hiccup. Carmen went back and forth with whether introducing a stronger relationship between the girls and their grandfather was something she wanted to pursue.

Deep down she knew the girls would instantly click with their grandfather. They both resembled him in personality and character. She'd spent a lifetime praying they'd never acquire a single genetic trait of her mother's. Whenever she caught a glimpse of a familiar mannerism, she cursed it. Penelope's current behavior concerned her.

Once, while fishing on the Atlantic, Carmen's father confessed he had wanted to name her Amelia, after Amelia Earhart, but her mother wouldn't allow it because she knew he had a fascination with the woman, however minimal. Out of defiance, Carmen had done a report on Amelia Earhart in the fifth grade, and in her research, she'd discovered that Amelia Earhart's middle name was Mary. *Don't you think that's ironic, Dad? That Amelia Earhart's middle name is Mom's first name?*

Had Carmen named her daughter Amelia out of spite? A slap in the face to her mother? Be it the name or blood, Amelia was fascinated with airplanes and talked of getting her pilot's license. She had even written a paper for school a few years back about her grandfather, the FedEx pilot. It was one of the few times Amelia had spoken to her grandfather on the phone at any length while she gathered facts.

No doubt Penelope would be drawn to the harbor and the fishing just like Grandpa Chet. It reminded Carmen of the endless hours she had spent with her dad as a child on their Boston Whaler, fishing from sun up to sun down.

Those were the best memories of Carmen's childhood, the only memories worth remembering really. Chet had tried, tried to sweep her away, tried to make up for what his wife wasn't, or was. The boat was their saving grace, but it hadn't been enough.

Carmen had wished, prayed diligently actually, that the two of them could abandon her mother and live on the boat. They could catch their food, travel along the coast, and not have to deal with the woman they both feared.

Chet always reminded Carmen that he needed to work, and she needed to go to school, and that it wasn't realistic to live on a boat. It was very realistic, argued Carmen, and she suggested they live in a marina down the coast. She could switch schools, and he'd only have a short drive to work.

The winters were too cold, and the threat of hurricanes loomed in the fall, he reminded her, even though she saw the longing in his eyes. Mostly though, Carmen knew those were excuses. He needed to take care of his wife. Carmen loved her dad feverously but resented him at the same time for always putting his wife before her, for loving her more.

Carmen's stomach was twisted in knots as she stepped foot into her parents' coastal home. The spectacle of her mother's deteriorating body in the portable hospital bed made her want to vomit for numerous reasons. She stood, one step in the bright sunny room facing the Atlantic, and stared, unable to move closer to her mother.

The windows were open, allowing both the scent of salty air and the sound of crashing waves to fill the room. She took in her surroundings, soft white upholstery over two cushiony sofas layered with light and dark shades of blue-striped pillows. A large sisal rug anchored the room and three large bluish green glass vases filled with sea glass and shells towered on a coffee table. Carmen pictured her parents, on Mary's good days, scouring the beach for the shells.

An antique whitewashed rocker was next to the bed, but Carmen wasn't ready to be that close. In fact, the sight of her dying mother, whom she hadn't set eyes on for more than half her life, filled her with immense pain.

Mary was no longer conscious, which meant her mother would never be able to speak words of remorse or regret. Deep down Carmen knew she only craved the apology so she could throw it back in her mother's face. Too little too late. Words of acceptance or forgiveness would never pass Carmen's lips.

Carmen walked past her mother to the window, allowing the embers in her belly to cool. In the distance, she saw two people kitesurfing, hurtling the waves with forceful grace, and added it to her bucket list. She saw the typical sunbathers, seagulls, and boats dotting the water, but what stole her attention was the elderly man sitting alone under a multi-colored beach umbrella. Her heart strings were pulled at the realization that that was going to be her father at the young age of sixty-three. Alone.

She heard Victor and her dad in the kitchen, her dad most likely offering Victor one of two things, sweet tea or whisky, neither of which Victor liked but would accept graciously. She hadn't heard them come into the room, only felt her father's large hand on her back. He pulled her close, and Carmen caught a glimpse of his sea-weathered face and hands.

Time and distance had made it easy to bear a grudge. However, within moments of being in her father's company, seeing the memories they shared on *Hooked* between the wrinkles on his face . . . her heart softened. She missed her father, along with the deep bond the two of them had once shared.

Always a loving father, he tried to make up for an unstable mother and a violent childhood, but he had ultimately chosen his wife over his daughter, and to this day, it panged Carmen to the core.

Her tears came easily from the touch of his hand, the tenderness in his eyes. She would keep to herself that the tears were not for her mother, but for the years she had lived without her father, missing him.

He led her by the hand to her mother's bedside.

Chet put his arm around Carmen. "She hasn't spoken in three days, but she can hear you, and periodically she squeezes my hand."

To the world, Mary was a beautiful woman. Carmen saw through the bronzed Columbian skin, dark hair, plump lips, and high cheek bones to the ugliness hidden behind her features. The devil in disguise, she'd often called her as a teen.

Her once long hair was now cut to a bob, and the thick shiny brown mane was heavily streaked with gray. Void of makeup, her lips glistened from the tube of balm on the table next to her. Carmen hadn't witnessed the transformation through which her mother had aged: the occurrence of crow's feet by her eyes, the deepening of the crease between her brows, the hollowing of her cheeks, her bony frame.

Carmen was fully aware that most daughters would be holding their dying mother's hand, telling her how much they loved her, how much she'd be missed, and reminiscing over all the fond memories they'd created. Carmen wondered what it would be like to tell her mother she had appreciated her, that she'd been a great role model, that she only hoped she was being half the mother she had been.

The seagulls squawked, filling the silence. Carmen felt like she should say something kind, something consoling, solely for her dad's sake; however, nothing but venom rested on her tongue.

"You must be Carmen. I'm Ritzy, your mother's hospice nurse," said a voice from behind. Ritzy came at Carmen and hugged her as if they were longtime friends. Carmen hugged briefly in return and let her arms fall, but Ritzy wasn't ready to release her.

"I'm so, so sorry, dear," Ritzy spoke over Carmen's shoulder as she rubbed her back, embracing tighter. "Please don't worry. Your mother is comfortable, and I'm sure your presence will put her at ease even more."

Carmen's eyes shifted towards Victor and her father. Chet's eyes glassed over as he turned his gaze away, out the window to the ocean.

After another minute of tight southern hospitality squeezing, Ritzy stepped back and took hold of Carmen's hands.

Ritzy looked to be in her late fifties. She was short and round, comfy to hug. She rubbed the top of Carmen's hands with her thumbs, her skin was soft, her hair a golden blond cut to her chin, and her smile seemed to be a permanent fixture on her face. Ritzy's voice was chipper yet calming.

Her head fell to the side. "How are you holding up, dear?"

What *did* she feel exactly? In lighter, simple terms, anguish. Everything else that came to Carmen's mind wasn't anything she should speak out loud. Instead, she bit her lip and shrugged.

"Oh, honey, you don't have to say a thing. Sometimes it's simply too hard. There really are no appropriate words to sum up the devastation we feel when losing a parent, especially a young beautiful woman like Mary. I'll bet she was the best mama ever. She hasn't spoken in a few days, but she's been so kind these past few weeks, more concerned that I was comfortable in her home than about her own suffering. I've enjoyed caring for her."

Ritzy snickered, looked to Chet and then back to Carmen. "Believe me. I've had my fair share of cranky patients. I've had a patient or two go a little rash on me, screaming, demanding, even trying to scratch and hit me and their loved ones. Not your mother, not a nasty bone in her body, she's been the sweet compliable Mary I'm sure she's been her whole life."

Carmen hadn't meant for the squawk, bark, whatever sound it was, to escape her. Ritzy confused the sound as a stifled cry and pulled her close again, shushing her like a small child. Carmen felt her airway constrict and this time placed her hands on Ritzy's shoulders, stepping back, breaking their bond.

She restrained her true emotions, all the ravenous wolves wrestling inside her, clawing to get out. "Sorry, I . . . I need a minute." Carmen swiftly excused herself and snuck out the back door. She sucked in a deep breath of salty air, slipped off her shoes, and stepped into the sand. The sound of the waves rolling and crashing to shore called her home.

The feeling the water gave her felt indescribable even to herself. It was as if the Atlantic Ocean was her family, welcoming her back. The body of water had been the only stable thing in an uncertain childhood. She stepped in up to her shins, feeling the waves caress her calves.

As the water retreated, the foam gathered around her feet, tickling her toes. The ocean was her safe place, the tide pulling and begging her to surrender. Her eyes fell shut, opening the vision to her time spent on the bow of their old boat, dipping and cresting with each wave, rocking her while singing its sweet lullaby. The sea slapped the side of the boat, like a mother's hand lovingly patting, soothing her child.

Why had she come? Seeing her mother only filled her insides with ugliness. Images she'd spent her entire adult life trying to erase from her memory, came flooding back with a vengeance. Her mother didn't deserve her presence, her father didn't deserve her pity, but she loved him. She loved him so much it hurt.

Victor's sudden presence, his arm collecting hers, sent a flood of tears streaming down her cheeks. He knew her well enough not to say a bunch of meaningless, comforting phrases. Instead, he entwined his fingers in hers and stared out to sea alongside her.

"I want it to be over so we can go home. I can't even feel sorry for my dad. Victor, he chose her over me, and I've become so bitter that I'm indifferent to his feelings." Carmen inhaled sharply to diffuse the tightening in her throat.

~*~

The seashell nightlight lit the hallway well enough for Carmen to find her way in the unfamiliar house to her mother. The stars hung low over the ocean, the moon casting a glow across Mary's face.

Carmen settled into the rocking chair. "I grew up afraid of you. Rejected. Most days I felt inadequate, ugly, stupid, unaccepted, like nothing more than a pesky insect you swatted out of your way."

Carmen leaned forward so she was inches from her mother's ear, the hostility in her voice thick. "I spent my childhood trying to be a perfect, flawless child, my days spent tiptoeing around in fear of upsetting you. Do you have any idea what it was like sitting in my third-grade classroom, consumed with worry over whether I squeezed the tube of toothpaste from the top, leaving it in the cupholder without folding the bottom up? Whether I would walk in the door and be chastised for not putting your pillow shams on the correct pillows, or for replacing the orange juice in the refrigerator with the label facing to the side?

"Then there were the days you'd meet me at the bus stop, a bag of saltwater taffy in your hands and a glass bottle of Pepsi. You'd kiss the top of my head, and the other kids would mention you were the coolest mom as you handed each of them a piece of candy. The girls admired your beauty, and the boys' jaws dropped over your large chest, lean legs, and the elegant way your cigarette hung between your long red nails.

"We'd get home, and you'd ask for help in the kitchen, frying the fish dad had caught, or you'd teach me how to perfect Colombian empanadas. Singing to Madonna, we'd make Dad's favorite cornbread and fried plantain, or your famous *Carne Bistec* recipe. One minute you'd be singing "Papa Don't Preach" into the wooden spoon, the next . . ."

Mary's index finger began to tap wildly.

"Did I spark a memory, Mother?"

Mary's chin jerked to the side.

"We have a connection after all."

A deep moan came from Mary, her lips pressed together, thinner than Carmen remembered. Mary's shoulder twitched. Then her entire arm seemed to convulse.

"I'm glad you remember because I haven't been able to forget. You had everyone fooled, including my teachers, friends, even the neighbors. Sure, they felt sorry for me from time to time when I had to lie, vouch for your extended absences to Barranquilla. How exotic it was that my mother flew home to Colombia so often to visit, when in truth, you were in a mental health facility only miles away.

"I even fell prey to the flattery and attention, in fear of being exposed for the life I actually lived. I'd lie and embellish them, paint you in the grandeur they all misinterpreted."

Carmen moved to the edge of her seat. Her heart was thumping wildly, shocked by the rage that harbored inside her. "I didn't come here to tell you I understand why you abused me, that I forgive you. Not once have you reached out to me, sought forgiveness, showed remorse."

"Then why did you come?"

Carmen jumped at the sound of her father's weary voice from behind. Her cruel words made her no better than her mother, and she instantly regretted her father overhearing. Carmen opened her mouth to speak when they were both startled by a deep labored breath that filled the room. It had been twenty years since the three of them had been together, and the dark, stormy clouds still loomed.

She was hoping he would wrap his arms around her and tell her he was sorry that he let her down, that if he could do it all over again, he would do it differently. He would whisk her away, keep her safe.

"Obligation," Carmen spoke truthfully.

Chet walked in the room past Carmen to the window. He unlatched the lock and turned the crank, allowing a strong breeze to flood the room. A storm was brewing, how fitting.

"I don't remember stressing it was your responsibility or duty to be here in your mother's final moments. I only called to give you the opportunity."

Chet spoke to the window, his back to Carmen.

"You don't *want* me here?"

She stressed "want" in a tone her girls would have used. What was it that parents brought out in children, regardless of age?

"Of course I do, Carmen, more than anything."

Yet he didn't move away from the window, nor turn to her as he spoke. She had to stop seeking his approval, his love and attention. Her parents, two opposite personalities, both had left her to chase after the same thing.

Carmen was about to speak the words *show it* when a struggled gasp for air filled the room. Realizing that was the first breath Mary had taken in what seemed like a full minute, Carmen's pulse quickened as she stood. Chet was between his wife and daughter in a split second.

I'm killing her.

Chet took Mary's hand. "She squeezed." He turned to Carmen, giving her a look between a warning and a plea. "She can hear us."

Chet unexpectedly dropped Mary's hand and turned to Carmen. A muffled cry escaped him as he wrapped his arms around her. His body shook as he rested his chin on her head and wept.

Over the next two hours, Mary's breathing became shallower and less frequent. Carmen called Ritzy and left her dad to say his good-byes and took a walk on the beach to wait for the sun to rise.

~*~

Carmen was refilling her coffee for the third time when Penelope walked into the kitchen, sleepy-eyed. "Good morning. There's not much food in the house. Maybe when Amelia gets up, we could go out for breakfast?"

"It's eleven, Mom."

Carmen glanced at the clock and wondered where the morning had gone. Sure, she was on her third load of laundry and had sifted through and responded to the urgent emails awaiting her from her absence, but she was still in her pajamas.

"Right. Lunch then?"

Penelope took some foreign-looking substance from the fridge labeled Kombucha and headed toward the stairs. "We'll see."

"We'll see?" questioned Carmen. "Do you have other plans?"

Penelope stopped halfway up the steps. "You said I wasn't grounded anymore."

"No, you're not. I was only thinking of eating a meal together as a family."

"I might hang out with some friends since I don't have to work."

"Oh, like who?" Carmen didn't pause long enough for Penelope to respond. "Any chance you'd be interested in having Liz and Leila over?"

Penelope's face contorted. "Mom, stop!"

"Sorry, what's the harm in asking?"

"You know I'm not friends with them anymore," Penelope shouted. "And I never will be, so quit trying to force it!"

"Okay, okay, I'm sorry." Carmen rushed over to the bottom of the stairs. "I wish you would talk to me. Why do you get so upset? What happened, and why don't you feel like you can trust me to talk about it?"

Amelia walked out of her bedroom, interrupting the slim chance Carmen had of a conversation with Penelope. Trapped at the top of the steps, Amelia hesitated, peering down at the two of them with a look on her face that suggested regret for waking.

"What's up?" she greeted cautiously, avoiding eye contact with Penelope, and it dawned on Carmen how rarely they looked at each other, and if they did, it was with scrutiny.

Carmen couldn't help herself. "I don't get it with you girls. Why is there always drama, fighting, and gossiping? If you two would talk to me, then maybe I could help. It kills me. There's this unspoken air of peevishness amongst you two, and it contaminates the air in our house."

The girls disregarded each other in a way Carmen had never seen. There was this division, this uncanny separation of their once strong tribe. For the longest time, Carmen blamed Penelope for shutting out her little sister. She was the one who'd done the one-eighty, and Amelia was taking the brunt of it for no reason, but now, Carmen sensed Amelia wasn't free of fault.

Amelia folded her arms across her chest and mumbled something under her breath while Penelope took the elastic band from her wrist and began piling her hair on the top of her head.

"Girls!" Carmen pleaded. "Stop ignoring me. What's going on? Why all the strife?"

"Back off, Mom! You of all people should understand that not everyone goes running to their mommy about stuff."

Carmen ignored the dig, "Stuff? What stuff exactly? All I know is you ditched your old friends and started hanging out with a crowd that causes you to be rebellious and cruel. You quit water polo, your grades have dropped, you're cutting, and our property is getting vandalized. Excuse me for wanting to know what the heck is going on!"

Amelia picked at a thread on the side of her tank. "Mom, just leave it alone." She was completely on edge, on the brink of unraveling along with her stitching.

"Not a chance. It's my responsibility as your mother to make your life my business. You may not understand or appreciate it now, but someday you will realize I love you too much to turn my back and make believe everything is okay when it's clearly not."

Penelope's chest heaved with each breath, she looked pissed, and that scared Carmen. She didn't want to add culpability to her brittle state, yet she refused to let up. If there was anything Carmen would cram in her daughters' faces, it would be that she loved them fiercely and would do everything in her power to teach them not to take life, or each other, for granted.

"I'm sick of the rifts in this house. Done dealing with the constant poison you two fill it up with. What happened to the fun and cheerful atmosphere of our household? I miss the days when we laughed, joked, and enjoyed each other's company. You two used to beg for family dates, dinner out, sledding, movies, corn mazes, counting turtles down at the dam."

Penelope scoffed.

"We're not eight years old anymore, Mom," Amelia said defensively.

"Age has nothing to do with it. Attitude has everything to do with it. You two walk around here, looking for a reason to be miserable as if you're under a cloud of inescapable doom. Quite frankly, I think you should both get over yourselves and start thinking of how your actions affect everyone around you."

Carmen could feel herself winding up. Controversy broke her. What she would have given to grow up in a loving and stable environment like she was trying to provide her children. Yet they took it for granted, and Carmen was beginning to resent them for it.

"Penelope, you act as if I'm meddling in your business. I'm not asking for every detail of your life. I'm only asking for some insight as to why the gracious and bright girl I once called Sweet P woke up one day and decided to become defiant and vicious. Don't you think you owe me that? I'm not sorry that I ask about your old friends. Forgive me for wanting you to hang out with non-toxic girls who bring out the best in you."

Penelope's glare bore through Carmen. Tears filled her eyes and slid silently down her cheeks. Carmen's heart plummeted into her stomach. She had gone too far.

Amelia's cheeks were ablaze as she shifted from one foot to another, winding her finger around the thread, undoing the hem.

The three of them stood in an uncanny silence.

As if on cue, Victor walked in. "How are my ladies?" Headed for the bathroom, he stopped short, melodrama hitting his radar. "What's going on?"

"What's going on is I've had enough. I can't take it anymore."

Victor looked from Carmen to the girls while nodding, clearly at a loss of how to coolly intervene, keeping all tempers at bay. *Back me up,* her inner voice begged him.

"Clarify how we've gotten here," Carmen barked. "Now!"

"You mean like you and Grandma?" retorted Penelope. "You went two decades without speaking to your mom. Cut her out of your life. Now that she's dead, you think you have the right to demand we confide every detail of our lives to you?"

Victor stepped towards them. "Whoa, Penelope, watch how you talk to your mother."

Carmen drew in a deep breath, noting the look of superiority Penelope gave her. "Good point, Penelope. So, let me tell you why I chose to set boundaries against my mother. She had severe mental issues. First, she was diagnosed with a mental impairment, then bi-polar, later as schizophrenic. Regardless of what her true diagnosis was, she physically and verbally abused me."

Visions flooded Carmen so clearly it was as if she were back in the moment: their pristine house, permanent vacuum marks in the beige carpet, the cheery yellow kitchen that always smelled of lemons, the mauve flowers climbing the wallpaper in the bathroom with fluffy matching mauve rugs and towels, and the grandfather clock in the corner of the great room that chimed every quarter hour and rang out with a series of dongs on the hour.

The house spoke of upper middle-class southern charm: a handsome pilot, his gorgeous Columbian wife, and their daughter who spent endless hours swinging on the metal playset in the backyard. The story that took place inside was far different than the deceiving cover boasted.

Carmen fixed her eyes on the corner of the banister in a daze as the haunting images played in her head. "She'd be in the middle of folding laundry and explode into a rant, fling clothes at my head, throw the basket at the chandelier, and then chase me to my bedroom where I'd lock my door until my dad got home from work.

"On the days I wasn't fast enough, she would push me up against the wall and call me names, spitting in my face, flicking at my head with her fingers, and tell me I was dense. When she went totally berserk, she'd pinch me, tickle me until my skin was scratched and swollen, or kick me in the shins so my bruises looked as if I'd bumped my leg while riding my bike.

"Most of her abuse took place when my dad was at work, leaving no physical signs that couldn't be explained away as an accident. I fell off the tire swing, I bit it while roller-skating in the driveway, or I shut my own hand in the door. One minute she would be tickling me, teasing playfully while laughing, and the next she had me pinned to the floor, kneeing me in my side, screeching in my ear, "You're worthless, a slob, lazy," berating me, and blaming me for her migraines."

Carmen continued in a trance-like state. "After shutting the trunk down on my forearm while I loaded the groceries in the car, she'd spend the rest of the day making me believe I'd done it myself so that, when my dad asked what happened, her lies *actually* became my truth. After a while, the lines were so blurred I doubted the abuse. I began to believe every encounter *was* my fault, at the least, I was so rotten that I deserved to be treated cruelly.

"Every so often, she would go completely mad when my dad was home, and he would try and restrain her. She would hit, claw, and kick him too. He never fought back, always got her help, and told me he would keep me safe. He lived in denial. He was a loving, gentle man, and I didn't want to make things worse for him, so I pretended nothing ever happened."

Penelope and Amelia stood like statues as they listened to Carmen. For the first time in ages, she saw their eyes shift towards each other and lock, sharing their secret perception, that long lost look that bonded them in their younger years.

Carmen's heart was racing, and sweat trickled down her back. "My entire life was spent avoiding my mother, staying out of her way, trying not to upset her."

Vivid backgrounds that evoked so much pain flooded Carmen. Mary's face when it transformed from radiant to wicked if Carmen had so much as left a single crumb on the table after finishing her lunch; the disgusted look she gave Carmen for saying ouch if she had stubbed her toe. The look had led to hours of scolding Carmen for being wimpy, blind, and an idiot for walking into the couch.

Involuntarily, Carmen's hand went to her head. "She would insist on braiding my hair. She'd be singing, telling me I had the thickest, prettiest hair, and then, like a switch, she'd snap, smack my head, jerk my neck, and yell at me to hold still. She'd tell me that the kids at school thought I was ugly so she was doing me a favor trying to make me pretty, and since I couldn't hold still, the braid was full of bumps. 'Ugly, ugly, ugly,' she'd snarl in my ear.

"If she couldn't open the jar of pickles, it was my fault for sucking all the strength from her body, or if I didn't fold a towel her way, she would go ballistic, dumping the folded linens on the floor, demanding I do it over. I lived in a petrified state of apprehension my entire childhood.

"My dad checked her in and out of rehabilitation facilities. I prayed my heart out, that after those weeks, or if I was lucky, sometimes months, she would come back changed, sweet and kind. Often, she did, for a few weeks, sometimes months, but she always slid back. She abused her medication or would flush it down the toilet. She smoked like a chimney and would blow cigarette smoke in my face, laughing wickedly, and say, 'Those doctors are all part of a cult, trying to drug me. Prescribing me medication for the sake of job security.'

"I played sports for the sole purpose of having to stay after school. The summer I turned fourteen I rode my bike to my first job at the corner store to stock shelves to escape my mom.

"I couldn't have a social life outside of school because I couldn't bring anyone into our home. I rarely accepted invites to friends' houses for fear they would want me to reciprocate or ask personal questions about my family. Because of my mother, I've shunned women from my life, haven't cared for them, labeled them all crazy and abusive, and have avoided any meaningful friendships."

With a sob, Carmen fell to the steps. She had never broken down to this degree, not even to Victor. Amelia darted down the stairs and wrapped her arms around Carmen's back. Penelope sunk on the steps next to them, held her head in her hands, and wept.

Carmen had not wanted her daughters to know about her childhood, the type of woman their grandmother was. Even though ludicrous, to this day Carmen couldn't escape the feeling that she was in some way responsible for her mother's behavior. It had been drilled in her head, constant accusations that Carmen was to blame for her mother's erratic mood swings. Did she truly suck the life out of her? Drive Mary to insanity?

Victor plopped down on the steps as well. Although embarrassed, a surge of relief swept over Carmen, the burden of her secrets finally aired. They all scooched in and surrounded Carmen, reminding her of a big pile of stained, dirty crumpled laundry.

Absorbed in the moment, Penelope's shorts had slid up her thigh, revealing two fresh cuts. Carmen was at a loss for words to even comment. A moan somewhere from deep within escaped. She didn't get it. With everything she had gone through as a child, she didn't go around cutting herself, allow her grades to slip, quit sports, sneak boys into her room, drink and do drugs. No, she had trudged forward, worked diligently to overcome, escape her circumstances. She got out of her house as fast as she could, figured out how to survive on her own, and didn't make her issues everyone else's problem. Or had she?

Carmen vowed at their births not to be their best friend, but a parent that loved them unconditionally, teaching them morals and values, raising them to be independent, loyal, and trustworthy. Instead, she feared she'd taken it too far, creating fluffy, self-absorbed, entitled lives for her daughters.

The pendulum swung Carmen's feelings back and forth. One minute she was sympathetic, wanting to hold Penelope and rehabilitate her with gentleness. The next, she wanted to tell Penelope to suck it up, grow up, get over herself, give back, volunteer, and figure out how to be a well-adjusted, productive citizen.

CHAPTER 22

*When people treat you like an option, help them narrow their
selection by removing yourself from their equation.*

Gabriella

The knot formed in Gabby's stomach before she opened her eyes.
She slipped out from under Greg's arm, the weight of it feeling
claustrophobic. She tiptoed to the bathroom, changed into her
running clothes, vigorously brushed her teeth, and rubbed the dark
circles under her eyes with no luck at erasing them.

Countless bodies were strewn all over the house. All the beds
and couches were occupied, and even a few stragglers slept on air
mattresses on the living room floor. Peeking in Stella's room, Gabby
found her and Preston sound asleep. It was an odd sight, her
daughter and her boyfriend sharing a bed, but she found it pointless
to argue otherwise.

She snuck out without waking a soul. The self-loathing began
the second her feet hit the pavement. Her weakness disgusted her,
even if she was trying to prove something.

Yesterday, with Greg by her side, surrounded by all the kids
and their friends, Gabby had been thrown back into her old life. No
denying the thick tension between her and Greg, she spent half the
day wishing he'd disappear. Big picture though, she had missed her
tribe, together, their connection. Dozens of times she'd pointed out
to clients that it was the fear of change that drove them back to their
relationships. Even if that relationship was abusive, the uncertainty
of their future was worse, so they clung to the dysfunctional rhythm
of their mayhem.

Whether it was mistrust, cheating, physical or emotional abuse,
at least they knew what they were going to live with for the rest of
their lives. Divorcing Greg meant letting go of a predictable lifestyle.
Even though he was the cause of the deepest pain she'd ever felt,
the idea that her concrete vision for the future would crumble if she
left him, terrified her.

Sleeping with Greg was Gabby's test. Could she be intimate with him without being repulsed for the rest of her life? More than that, was she willing to live a life continuously questioning his faithfulness?

Dark clouds hung low, threatening to crack open and drench her. A rumble of thunder in the distance only forced her to run faster, farther. She needed this endorphin rush to flush out the war swirling within: to free her of herself if that were possible.

Her thoughts darted back and forth from yesterday's scare: from rushing Stella to emergency, to her mounting anguish over inviting Greg back into their bed.

Thankfully, Stella's bleeding had subsided after a short time, but she was far from out of the woods. It was rare to develop preeclampsia in the second trimester, but it confirmed why she'd been having headaches and blurred vision. Her blood pressure was high, her ankles and fingers swollen.

Stella was put on bed rest and informed of the countless risks. Stroke, seizures, heart failure, and bleeding from the liver were added to the list of complications that could result from preeclampsia. Another knot in Gabby's stomach.

After an ultrasound and four hours monitoring the baby's heart rate, they were sent home. Stella was given medication to lower her blood pressure with instructions to stay in bed, allowed to get up only to use the bathroom.

It felt like the old days as Gabby informed Greg and the other three kids, via group texts, with updates while they were at the hospital. How long had it been since the six of them kept a string of group texts alive?

Gabby looked both ways and crossed the deserted street to the township trail, relieved she could run and completely lose herself in her thoughts of the previous night without worrying about traffic.

Admittedly, walking into Greg's arms was more than a test. She was scared and emotionally spent upon returning from the hospital. As soon as she and Preston got Stella settled into bed, her tears fell easily: tears for the health and safety of her daughter and unborn grandchild, for the mess of her marriage, for the risk she was considering if she turned her cheek and went along with Greg and Holly's charades. The weight of it all seemed unbearable.

Falling into Greg's arms was natural; she'd been comforted by them for her entire adult life. She craved his embrace as much as she felt revolted by it. Greg held her tight, massaged her knotted shoulders, and led her to the bedroom to lie down.

Greg's voice was sincere. "I'm worried about Stella."

"Me too, and not just about the preeclampsia." Gabby heard her voice crack. "They haven't dated long, and I don't want their relationship to evolve around a child," she said, fully realizing how parallel her statement was to Greg's situation. He shifted and reached for Gabby's hand, which she grudgingly let him take, entwining his fingers with hers.

"I know, and with only one year of school left . . ." He shook his head. "It seemed doable, but now with her being on bed rest, she won't be able to complete her internship."

Greg caressed her hand and let his fingers trail up Gabby's arm. She both recoiled at his touch and yearned for it. Part of her wanted to disclose her conversation with Holly, throw in his face that he had been used, but it felt needy, like a desperate plea to fight with another woman over her husband. She wouldn't.

"Let's not forget that their relationship isn't based solely on what Preston wants. What if Stella doesn't see a future with him? Just because he's the father of her child doesn't mean he's the one she desires to spend the rest of her life with." Gabby heard the edge in her voice and, from the look on Greg's face, he connected the dots.

Gabby's watch chimed, signaling three miles in twenty minutes, thirty-eight seconds. She hadn't run three consecutive miles under seven minutes each in ages. Her legs burned as she crested the top of the steepest hill on her route. She kept her speed, told herself she was halfway, and wondered: Was Greg eager to save their marriage because Holly had pushed him in that direction, or would he genuinely choose his wife over his mistress? Or were they both a bunch of scheming liars, crossing her, or crossing each other? A shout of frustration escaped her lips, sending a chipmunk to scurry into a bush.

Greg's words echoed in her head. "I've missed you so much, Gabby. I've missed us and our discussions, our routines, the way you make the coffee, how your hair smells, and the way you throw your leg over mine when we sleep. I miss being able to discuss what's going on with the kids at any given moment or the mundane and quirky things that happen throughout the day."

Gabby had missed those things as well, only missing them also angered her. Gabby felt her pace increase to a near sprint as she envisioned Greg's pleading eyes, which both sickened and seduced her. These weeks had left her weak and weary, emotionally and physically exhausted. She had missed his support, missed being able to vent her concerns over the kids to her husband, the one and only who truly understood.

Greg had caressed her so gently. "I've missed the feel of your skin, your laugh, and the crease that forms between your eyes when you're deep in thought." He then placed his finger there as he often had to get her to relax.

She did relax and then it occurred to her that his touch wasn't all that bad. Could she have sex with her husband and not feel revolted? Be intimate without thinking of how he and Holly made love together? Because really, how could she be intimate with her husband if all she envisioned was the two of them together.

Gabby admittedly knew that, on some level, having sex with him the one time could be used as ammunition in the future to prove to Holly that she had the right to her husband, it was her decision, and she held the power. If the tables were to turn, Gabby could use the encounter in her favor.

~*~

Gabby had always started her day with a quote to reflect on. While she sipped her coffee each morning, she'd find something inspirational that spoke to whatever she was facing and repeat it throughout the day. Today's mantra was, *You make mistakes; mistakes don't make you.*

Perfect. It was also fitting for Penelope. She jotted it down on a sticky note, retrieved a guava-flavored iced tea from the fridge, and placed it on the desk for when Penelope arrived. Gabby was surprised with how Penelope had adhered to using the journal as an outlet. If it was difficult or awkward to find something to write about, she could jot down a few sentences from Gabby's daily quotes.

Penelope seemed to enjoy the quotes as much as Gabby. One morning, Penelope retrieved her journal from her backpack with a huge grin. Sticky notes clung to each sheet of paper, and when Penelope fanned the pages with her thumb, Gabby could see they were filled with her elegant, loopy handwriting.

Finally, the house had emptied out, leaving only Stella and Gabby. Stella had wanted to go back to her apartment in East Lansing, promising she would stay in bed, that between Lottie and their other two roommates she had plenty of people to look after her.

Preston, working full-time and only able to care for her at night, was worried she'd try and get out of bed and do too much. He and Gabby convinced Stella she should be home where Gabby could be with her all day. Even if Gabby was with a client, she was still available at a moment's notice.

Greg had made the trip to Stella's apartment and brought back her list of essentials, which happened to fill his entire back seat and trunk. He had been dropping in unexpectedly, bringing Stella and Gabby lunch. For Stella's sake, Gabby hadn't balked.

Stella was his daughter, and he was concerned about her. He had been texting to check in on her, asking what she was craving; then he'd show up with lunch, books, and magazines. Stella wasn't exactly softening toward him, but she showed appreciation for his efforts.

Gabby saw her last client out the door, poured two glasses of raspberry lemonade, and went to the living room where she'd propped Stella for the afternoon.

Stella was tapping her foot to whatever was thumping in her earbuds, madly texting away, her thumbs a blur. She removed the earbuds and placed her phone, screen down, on her belly. "Done working?"

"Yes, I'm all yours for the rest of the evening. I was thinking I'd make us a blackened salmon salad and then we can do some binge gaming. I'm in the mood to ruin you in Scrabble." Gabby held the straw to Stella's lips and grinned deviously.

Stella's reciprocating smile was far from gleeful. "Sounds fab," she said, her melancholic tone drab and depressing.

Gabby patted Stella's leg. "Cheer up. In hindsight, these months will be a tiny blip on your radar."

Stella frowned as she let out an exasperated sigh. "My radar reads worthless. I'm going crazy over losing my internship, not knowing if I'll get the same opportunity again. Finishing my degree with a baby is going to take forever, and my chances of landing my dream job seem rather slim now."

"I'm not undermining your feelings, Stella. They're perfectly valid, and it's okay to have a little pity party . . . for a day or two." She squeezed Stella's hand. "But don't forget you're growing a child inside you right now, and being a mother, nurturing a human creation to be released into the world, is the most important profession in the universe. Far from worthless."

Stella did her best at being sarcastically jovial. "Deep, Mom. I feel awe-inspired to throw away all my dreams and be a stay-at-home mother. Wait, I need a husband to support me in order to do that."

Gabby didn't have to state her disapproval; it was written on her face. "You know that's not what I meant. Maybe you won't be on the fast track, and it'll take you an extra two years to get through school. You still have the next sixty years of your life to pursue your career. Plenty of reporters and women in journalism have children, Stella. You won't be the first."

"I know. I've watched them on TV through their pregnancies. The difference is they made something of themselves *first* and then they became mothers."

Gabby sat up straight and looked her daughter in the eye, taking her turn at sarcasm. "Well, darn, I guess you'll be the first woman to do it backwards. Wow, what a role model and inspiration you'll be to others and your child."

Stella let out a growl. "Fine! Get over myself! Is that what you're saying?"

"Not entirely."

"But mostly," Stella offered with a sheepish grin. "Can you bring me outside to the lounge chair?"

"Absolutely. Fresh air will do you wonders."

Gabby attempted to carry Stella baby style with no luck. "Piggy back?"

"Seriously, Mom? No. I think I can walk outside. It's no farther than the bathroom."

Gabby helped her stand. "Walk to the door and then you can ride on my back down the steps."

"You're being ridiculous."

"No, I'm not." Gabby closed the door behind them and sat down on the top step. "Climb on."

Stella did as she was told. Laughing uncontrollably, she wrapped her arms around Gabby's neck and pressed her bulging belly into Gabby's back.

Gabby slowly rose to her feet, giggling at how silly they must look. She wobbled one way and then another as she slowly descended the steps. "Stop moving, Stella!"

Stella broke into hysterics, which only made Gabby's legs weaker as she laughed along.

"Are you drunk, Mom?"

"This is serious, Stella. I'm going to drop you if you don't stop wiggling."

Stella's laughter bellowed. "I'm going to wet my pants. Take me to the bathroom, quick."

Gabby froze. "What? Turn around? Are you joking?"

"Not in the slightest. Hurry," she said through gulps of crying laughter.

They had just reached the bottom of the steps, only thirty feet from the lounge. "Wet yourself. Changing you will be easier."

Stella kicked the side of Gabby's leg as if she were a horse. "Giddy up. I gotta go!"

"You actually are worthless," she teased. "Remind me to put your diaper on next time before we go outside. Either that or I'm dumping you in the lake."

Gabby swiveled around, ready to head back up the steps when Greg came out the door.

"What is going on out here?" He trotted down the steps toward them and lifted Stella off Gabby's back. Stella was wiping the tears from the corners of her eyes as Gabby dropped to the steps.

"I could hear you two from inside the house. Are you *both* trying to be bedridden?" Greg eyed Gabby with a smirk.

She felt her lips curve in a sardonic twist, ready to hurl insults for barging in uninvited, killing the mood, killing *her* mood. As if Greg knew what was coming, his eyes flashed at her with desperation. Her emotions, always conflicting, hovered somewhere between fury and consideration.

Greg took advantage of her momentary waver and slipped inside with Stella to the bathroom. He convinced Gabby to let him stay for dinner and help with Stella for the evening. He grilled the salmon while they played Scrabble, added a bag of salt to the softener, and fixed a couple of sprinkler heads that were gushing like geysers.

Gabby was irritated with how he came over spontaneously and weaseled his way into their evening, only she knew for Stella's sake she needed to fake it and set an optimistic tone. Stella's disposition was teetering. The last thing Gabby wanted was Stella flipping out on Greg. She simply couldn't deal with it tonight.

He insisted on carrying Stella down to the boat where he laid towels for her to sprawl out on the back while they trolled around watching the setting sun. Gabby saw Stella's mood improving and knew the fresh air and boat ride were doing wonders for her spirit.

When Preston called, she exuberantly recounted their night to him. Gabby would have to put aside the fact that Greg was taking advantage of Stella's situation to schmooze his way back into their lives.

She knew Stella was watching them closely and dreaded the questions she would be drilled with after he left. *Are you two working things out? Does he talk to Holly? Have you talked with Holly?*

Gabby wanted to answer all the questions honestly. She was telling lies without opening her mouth. The dishonesty of withholding information from her children cursed her.

Once Greg got Stella back upstairs and settled into her bedroom for the night with her latest series on Netflix, he came down to find Gabby sitting on the bar stool in the kitchen, her head in her hands.

"It's all so superficial, Greg." He froze a few feet behind her. "We faked normalcy on the fourth for the sake of the kids and our guests. I made an unwise, emotionally impulsive decision to sleep with you. You've been very helpful in getting Stella settled, collecting her things, and comforting her nerves, but now"—Gabby hesitated—"I don't think you should be stopping by so often, especially unannounced."

Greg hesitantly took a seat next to her. "I can't stand to be away from you, Gabby. These last few days have given me hope. I think you feel it too."

"Greg, I feel a lot of things, some of which are hurt, anger, betrayal, shame, and embarrassment. That's not all going to go away because we slept together and have had a few civil encounters. Right now, my adverse feelings far overshadow the hope you're feeling. If anything, it's been a temporary distraction from the real focus."

"So let's begin right now. Let's focus on us. Gabby, I want to spend the rest of my life with you. I screwed up. I hurt you. I lied." Greg's voice began to crack. He placed his hand on her back, and she could feel the sweat from his palm through her shirt. "I never knew I was capable of cheating. You should feel no shame. I'm ashamed. I'm remorseful and mortified for what I'm putting you and the kids through."

Greg raked his hands through his hair. "Jeez, Gabby, I've cried myself to sleep a dozen times. A minute doesn't pass that I don't regret my actions. I took you for granted. I see that now."

Gabby had so much to say, had countless conversations, or rather screaming matches, with Greg in her head, and yet she couldn't articulate what angle she wanted to take. *Jouska*. She'd learned the term from a professor in college and often attributed it to her patients when they described how they compulsively had hypothetical conversations with others in their heads.

Yet, when it came time to articulating all that garbage, she had nothing. Her mind was void of sensible communication.

She wanted to chew him out, she wanted to wrap her arms around him, but most of all she just wanted it to all go away. Impossible. None of this could ever be undone. She could never un-see the ultrasound picture stuck to Greg's phone, she could never un-feel the blow to her core being, and she could never undo remaining silent to the mounting secrets. Or could she?

"Are you willing to try, Gabby?"

"Greg, we've had this conversation. There's a child involved. This isn't a circumstance you can just walk away from. Don't you at the least feel any sort of moral obligation?"

Greg looked out the window, spoke nothing.

"You have no interest in this child's life? Do you plan on being in the delivery room?"

Greg groaned and rubbed his hands over his face. "Holly suggested I focus on saving my marriage, that she and the baby would be fine on their own. Eventually, the transfer will go through. I'm willing to let them go, for you and our family. I just need you to agree."

Gabby couldn't help but chuckle, as if it were that simple. "You're comfortable with never knowing your daughter? And down the road, what if she comes looking for you, then what?"

He shrugged. "Holly and I have decided to remain open, to take each day, each situation as it comes."

"As it comes?" Gabby scoffed. "Well, it's coming in about two months."

"I've offered to help out in any way I can, be it financially or whatever kind of support Holly and the baby need. I can do it confidentially."

"And what if that suddenly leads to childrearing duties such as doctor visits, overnights, or otherwise? Suddenly, you're living a double life with two families. If she proposed the idea of marriage, would you help out with that too?"

"Gabby, you're my wife."

"On paper." With that, Gabby stood and headed towards her bedroom. "See yourself out and lock up please. Next time ask permission before dropping by."

CHAPTER 23

None are so empty than those who are so full of themselves.

Monica

"Sweet Jesus, are you pregnant?" Gabby asked, as she, Monica, and Carmen sat outside at Juliet's for a late lunch. After wandering through the art fair in the blazing afternoon sun, Carmen and Gabby had ordered a cold beer and Monica water with lemon.

Monica blushed. "Possibly . . . in a cell division sort of way."

Carmen poured her beer into a frosted glass. "Meaning what exactly?"

"Meaning we've decided to try for another, and I'm currently ovulating, so anything is possible."

Gabby held up her bottle. "Cheers to that! Please tell me you're not thinking of getting pregnant too, Carmen. I don't think I could handle one more expectant woman in my life."

Carmen scoffed. "Ha! I can't parent the two I have. What a disaster that would be."

They all laughed, knowing Carmen wasn't looking for sympathy, only mocking the reality of parenting teenagers.

"In case you haven't noticed, your job as a parent is never finished," Gabby pointed out. "I wouldn't have it any other way, but having Stella home is like raising a demanding toddler all over again. If Preston hadn't come for the weekend shift, I'd be on house arrest or would have had to line up a sitter to leave today."

Carmen nodded. "Even when they're teenagers and self-sufficient, you question whether it's safe leaving them home alone. Who knows what kids are sneaking into your house, what substance they are abusing or stealing from your laundry room or medicine cabinet? Whatever they are searching on your laptop could get them abducted or you arrested." Carmen leaned back in her chair and took a sip of ice-cold beer.

"Well, this has been a great pep talk," Monica joked. "Getting pregnant sounds so enticing now."

"Calvin butt-dialed me last night at two thirty in the morning, and the commotion and bits and pieces of conversation I heard on the other end of the phone were enough to keep me awake worrying for two hours. When I finally dozed off, I heard the toilet from upstairs flush, so I ran upstairs to check on Stella. My kids are adults, and I'm not sleeping through the night yet," joked Gabby.

Carmen's cheeks rose elatedly. "When the girls were little, they would tackle me, smothering me with hugs and kisses as I walked in the door after work. Now when I walk in, I hold my breath, trying to analyze the mood or rather who's attacking whom. Who wore the other's clothing without asking, who ate all the pizza rolls, or whose turn was it to take the dumpster to the end of the driveway after missing it for the second week in a row," she went on with an eye roll that looked more like a gorgeous flutter of her lashes.

"I remember those days, when the smallest nuances created the biggest fights," said Gabby. "The other day I raced fifty-seven miles to Calvin's rescue. As he was walking out of his apartment door to go to the airport to fly to Scotland, he realized his passport was in the side pocket of a duffel bag he had left when home for the fourth of July."

Monica grunted with a face full of sarcastic pity. "You two are awful! You're absolutely no support in my quest to get pregnant."

"You know we're only teasing. Parenting is the toughest yet most rewarding job in the world," Gabby said sincerely, patting Monica's forearm. "Klay will hug me anywhere, in front of anyone, and tell me he loves me and I'm the best mom in the world. Ever since Calvin turned sixteen, he would often come home with my favorite truffles, a single flower, or a coffee for me. Stella has always been the one to clean the entire kitchen after dinner or vacuum the house without being asked. Lottie, well, Lottie is my grateful one, I guess." She laughed. "I've never had to prompt her to say please or thank you when we are shopping together. Somehow Lottie is extremely clever at getting me sucked into shopping trips where my purse strings seem to fall wide open. Regardless, she's very grateful for the loads of money I dump on her."

"Gabby's right," agreed Carmen. "I wouldn't trade it for anything. Whenever I'm at my wit's end, I remind myself of the simple fact that we are all healthy and the only boundaries are the ones we place upon ourselves." She poured the rest of her beer from its bottle into her glass. "Kids will test the waters, rebel, fight, and screw up; it's the nature of the parenting beast."

Monica cocked her head to the side. "If you could do it all over again, you'd have more kids?"

Both Gabby and Carmen shook their heads. "Heavens no! Carmen hollered. I have a timer set on my phone ticking down the minutes until Penelope goes off to college. Once that timer dings, I'll set it for Amelia." Carmen took her phone out of her purse. "Whew, I've roughly 2,102,400 minutes left, but really, all I'm focusing on at the moment is the 65,000 or so minutes until summer vacation is over and they have zero spare time to sit and stare at their phones and record and post every breath they take as if it's an accomplishment.

"They're more obsessed with counting likes than they are blackheads; that's so backwards!" Carmen roared at her own joke.

Monica noticed Carmen's face faulter mid-laugh as she turned toward a woman sitting alone at the table next to them snickering, mumbling rather loudly to herself or possibly her drink. "Who do you think you are to criticize my friend?" snipped Carmen.

Carmen stood, propped her hands on her hips, and peered down at the woman cradling what looked like straight booze. Monica, oblivious to what Carmen had overheard, was shocked by her forwardness.

"Criticizing?" scoffed a curvaceous woman whose face hardened.

"Yes, it sounded critical to me. You made a skinny joke about my friend. For a moment while she laughed, she had a piece of salad dangling from her lip. I clearly heard your comment referring to"—Carmen held up her fingers for air quotes—"obnoxious, cackling, skinny bitch in need of a burger. That's rude. Do you make it a point to go around ridiculing women?"

The woman stood abruptly, bumping the table, causing her chair to skid across the floor behind her and the drink to slosh over the rim of the glass. The racket triggered a cluster of heads to turn their way as she approached their table.

She peered down at Monica, prompting Carmen to inch closer, protectively placing herself by Monica's side. "As if a skinny reference really offends you, boohoo in all your thin glory. Shallow women like you live for comments like that!"

Carmen bolted from her seat, towering over the woman.

The woman eyed Carmen from head to toe. "You as well, easily offended with your designer labels and two-hundred-dollar highlights and blow-out. Give me a break. As if you don't seek, bask in, and relish the attention."

Carmen crinkled her face at the woman. "Let me get this straight. It's okay for you to call her an obnoxious, cackling, skinny bitch in need of a burger, fries, and chocolate shake. Ya, I heard you mumbling that too. What if I were sitting here telling my friends you were an obnoxious, cackling, overweight bitch in need of a detox, salad, and green drink?"

Monica felt sweat ooze from every gland in her body. Was this really happening? A waitress watched anxiously as she filled water glasses nearby. They were going to get kicked out if Carmen didn't reel it in. Monica patted her mouth with her napkin in case she still had greens on her lip and stood. "Carmen, it's okay, really. Let it go. Her comments don't offend me."

The woman eyed Monica with vehemence and huffed in disgust. Okay, perhaps Carmen wasn't overreacting.

"Really, Carmen, I couldn't care less what this woman thinks of me." Monica turned to her. "All is forgiven. Are you okay? Do you need a ride someplace?"

The woman used her arm to nudge Carmen out of the way and took a step closer to Monica. "Forgive me?" she slurred. "I don't remember offering you an apology."

Monica felt Gabby's hand nudge her thigh. "Monica, sit down and don't respond," she urged.

Gabby turned to Carmen and told her to do the same. Monica obeyed the order and took her seat while Carmen remained, frozen and unyielding. Jeez, Carmen was intimidating.

"I pity you. Mean people suck," Carmen snarled in the woman's face and plopped down in her chair with a huff.

The waitress swooped in with a tray of water and offered the woman a glass, inconspicuously leading her back to her table.

Carmen leaned in towards Monica. "I'm sorry. I don't know what came over me. Women can be so cruel to each other. I have zero tolerance is all. It bothers me that it's socially acceptable for someone to bash a thin person, and since I'm larger than that woman is, well, I guess I felt entitled to speak up.

"Personally, I love my curves. You should love your shape, Monica, and she, hers. Amelia has gotten called gangly and anorexic dozens of times by a group of girls from school, and when I brought it up to one of her teachers at conferences, the teacher smirked and said, 'Hardly something for a teenage girl to fret about. She should be flattered.' It floored me because, if Amelia were to call those same girls chubby, she'd be suspended for bullying."

"No worries. I'm grateful that you stood up for me. And you looked so damn hot when you did, you know with your designer labels, fancy highlights, and blow-out," Monica teased with a wink.

Carmen rolled her eyes. "Exactly. My fancy drug store flat iron. And how dare that woman judge my character based on the labels I wear."

Monica rubbed her hand over Tiffany. "We've got your back, sweetie," she purred to the purse.

"The studs in my ears are fake," Carmen said defensively, touching her left earlobe. "My Meijer tank cost $12.99."

"You wear it so well it only looks expensive," Gabby affirmed.

Carmen tucked her feet under her chair with a smirk. "Thank God she didn't see my Jimmy Choo's."

Monica peered under the table, "Really?"

Carmen yanked her head up by her hair. "Don't make it obvious. Victor, feeling guilty, brought these back from Vegas for me last week. If he keeps bringing me similar gifts, I'll let him travel all he wants."

Monica nodded admiringly. "Well, even though you're obviously flamboyant with those shoes and that purse, you balance it nicely with economy brands. Well played."

The woman stood again, threw back the last swallow of her booze, and flung her purse over her shoulder, almost hitting Carmen in the head. "For the record, I did not, and will not, apologize for voicing my opinion of you. That's the beauty of freedom of speech, and quite frankly, I get sick and tired of women like you walking around like you're the center of the universe. You think you're superior—that just because you're thin, beautiful, and have money to throw around, the rest of us are beneath you."

Carmen opened her mouth to speak, but Monica kicked her under the table before she was able to get a word out. She made the zip-it motion, sliding her pinched fingers across her lips, as she often did to the kids when they were being too noisy.

Sauntering past their table, the woman sneered. "Anorexic bitch."

Monica gasped and felt her adrenaline shift into high gear as tears filled her eyes. "I'm so humiliated. Does this woman realize my faulty body can't even keep a baby alive?"

Carmen looked at Monica pointedly. "Don't go there!"

"Let it go," Gabby reassured. "Never rip yourself to pieces to keep someone else whole. It always pays to take the high road, even when you'd rather slap someone in the face. It isn't being fake. It's sucking it up, acting like an adult, and swallowing your pride."

~*~

Monica had been on a roll around the house. She had completed the stone walkway. Dex had restained the deck, and currently she was building a locker system for the garage. Her grandfather could turn any piece of wood into a sturdy, fantastic-looking piece of furniture. She had spent endless hours alongside him in the garage, working the bandsaw and sander.

She'd also hung around the woodshop room at the high school over the past few years, refreshing her skills, and felt comfortable building something herself. Her grandfather would be proud.

Dex offered to help her with the project in the evenings, but Monica was both impatient and too independent to seek his help. She needed to measure and cut the wood, sand it, feel the power of the nail gun in her hand and finish it off with paint from start to finish.

Partly, she needed to prove to Janice that she was a capable woman, that just because she hated to cook and be overly domestic didn't mean she wasn't handy, useful. Gabby kept reminding her that she didn't need to prove her worth to Janice. Deep down, she agreed, but still felt compelled to do so.

She bought four hard hats and four pair of goggles for Beck, Kenzie, Trixie, and Reese. The kids were good helpers in the garage, sweeping saw dust and throwing scraps of wood into the wheelbarrow to be saved for their fire pit.

Monica wasn't a slave to the kitchen, but she had morphed into a certified health-crazed fitness junkie, thanks to the help of Gabby, and she was decent at chopping things. She set up a picnic on the beach for lunch, serving her kids lettuce wraps filled with veggies, fruit smoothies that she'd sneak spinach into, and water with frozen fruit for ice cubes.

She let the kids bury her in the sand, accumulating it in every crevice of her body. Kenzie had formed a mermaid tail on her and placed two large plastic shells on her chest. Monica laughed until she cried. All the while, Janice peered down at them from the deck above, her cell phone in her hand, playing *Words with Friends*.

They were bobbing in the water, rinsing off the sand before heading in for a nap when Monica caught the familiar look in Kenzie's eye. She was paddling around in the water, her penguin life vest snug around her chest when her face glazed over, oblivious to her present world.

"Mommy, can you pick up Trixie and Reese and take us to get Pont Puppies?"

"Not right now, but sometime soon, sweetie. Pronto Pups are in Grand Haven."

"But Trixie and Reese is waiting fer me right now." Kenzie started to get whiney, and Monica knew this was the price she paid for not getting her down for her nap on time.

"No, sweetie, Daddy will be sad if we go without him."

"Pleeease, Mommy." Kenzie began to splash at the water with her open palms, spraying Monica in the eyes. "We wanna go now!" she wailed.

"Sorry, sweetie, but it's nap time." Monica guided Beck, in the island-shaped floatie complete with a palm tree for shade, towards the shore and asked Kenzie to follow.

"No! I not getting out less you take Trixie and Reese to get Pont Puppies!" Kenzie demanded in her botched language, which Monica found adorable when she was behaving. At times like this, she was silently correcting her in a violent tone PRONTO PUPS!

Monica lifted Beck from the floatie, wrapped him in a towel, and set him on the beach. She waded back in the water to try and coax Kenzie out with minimal drama. She took hold of her hands and began twirling her, singing, "You are my sunshine, my only sunshine. You make me happy," gritting the word *happy* through her teeth. As she sang, Monica inched closer to the shore with each twirl.

Kenzie, fully aware of Monica's tactics, flailed her arms and threw her head back. A surge of water flooded over the top of her face, and sure enough, she gulped, choked, panicked, and gasped for breath. Great. So much for cheerful distraction.

This was what sucked about living on a small lake where you were on exhibit. Every wail echoed and drew attention. Even though Monica wasn't the type to portray that her children were golden nuggets, she was still mortified.

Kenzie was usually an easygoing girl. However, to all the watchful eyes, she was probably being branded as a melodramatic, intolerable child. Monica felt like she carried a label ever since she went missing for half the night with her imaginary friends. Now, she was out of control, throwing a tantrum and making a scene in the water.

Disturbed, disobedient, wild child, whatever the label may be, Monica could almost hear the whispers, and it infuriated her because that was the furthest from the truth. Kenzie was imaginative, adventuresome, independent, and determined. Currently, she was a normal child throwing a typical fit about taking a nap. Right?

"Trixie, Reese," Kenzie shrieked as she reached for them over Monica's shoulder, grasping for them in the air. Monica hauled

Kenzie out of the water and plopped her down on the towel next to Beck with a huff.

Monica resisted the urge to look over her shoulder as she'd done thousands of times, expecting to catch a glimpse of the ever-present Trixie and Reese in the flesh.

"Kenzie, they aren't here. You just asked me to go pick them up for Pronto Pups, remember?"

"They are too!"

"Ta, Reee?" Beck repeated, looking sad for his sister.

Ugh, not you too. Monica took off their life vests, "Nap time." She hoisted Beck up in her arms while Kenzie sat firmly planted, digging her heels into the sand.

"Now, Kenzie," Monica warned in a low growl.

Kenzie hmphed. "Trixie and Reese don't take naps and neither does me."

"Kenzie Kay Colburn, you have two seconds to get up and start walking inside." *Or else what? Think quickly. Think rationally.*

Kenzie shook her head and flung her foot, throwing sand at Monica's leg. On second thought, maybe it was a blessing that they were on display so Monica wouldn't go completely ballistic. No, instead, she would go against the rules of proper parenting and bargain with her daughter.

"You do not have to take a nap, Kenzie, but you do need to take a rest in your bedroom, so please get up," *before I drag you by your big toe.* "Ask Trixie and Reese to come inside and rest with you."

"They not here, Mom. I told you!"

"You were just talking to them, Kenzie! They can't be here one minute and disappear the next!" Monica shouted, instantly mortified to be arguing with her toddler about whether two imaginary people were or weren't present. Beck was rubbing his eyes and getting restless in her arms, rocking back and forth, making it difficult to hang on to the little tyke.

"Look. If you get up right now, then we can pick Trixie and Reese up after your nap—"

Kenzie interrupted with a sob, "You said me only rest."

"After your *rest,* we will pick the girls up and go to Grand Haven for Pronto Pups," Monica barked.

"With Daddy too?"

"Maybe with just Daddy," Monica grumbled.

"What? No, Mommy. You not come?" she wailed.

"Okay, quiet! All of us, but I will change my mind and stay home if you don't follow me inside this instant."

With that, Monica turned on her heel and prayed Kenzie was following. She had been so wrapped up in the neighbors witnessing their little outburst she had forgotten Janice was observing from the deck above. Unlike the neighbors, Janice could hear the low growls of her voice and the bargaining.

Monica stripped Kenzie and Beck, leaving their bathing suits in a wet, sandy heap by the door. She hadn't the energy left to bathe them, so she doused them in baby powder and rubbed the sand off their skin with a towel.

Beck was falling asleep as she tucked him in his crib, wearing only diapers. She quickly kissed Kenzie and left her to rest in her room, or swing from the ceiling fan for all Monica cared.

She went upstairs to the kitchen for her afternoon iced tea and spotted Janice's tall glass of diet Pepsi on the counter next to the MiraLAX she'd been giving Beck. Feeling emboldened, Monica dumped a sizeable amount into the drink and gave it a swirl.

Forgive me, sweet Jesus, she pleaded, but then, thinking of the scenario at the restaurant, an immediate wave of guilt washed over her so intense she drained it in the sink. She plucked her sunglasses, with a fresh scratch and full of fingerprints, from the back of Beck's dump truck on the living room floor, and grabbed her Kindle, while avoiding Janice by going out the basement door leading directly to the beach and her awaiting chair.

As she walked, she could feel Janice's eyes on her back. Janice would most certainly have insight as to how Monica handled Kenzie all wrong and how she should have handled her.

Monica plopped down in her beach chair with little energy left to open her Kindle. She tilted her head back and closed her eyes. Was she crazy for thinking about having a third child? Was she still in panic mode over Kenzie's wandering off? Was she more in love with the fantasy of having another baby rather than the reality?

Monica typed out a text to Dex.

Please hurry home after work so we can go to GH for PP. Need to pick up T & R on the way. Not so sure another baby is a good idea.

A text from Dex landed on her screen immediately.

??? It might be too late for that, Mon!

Monica broke into a sweat. She could take a pregnancy test in a matter of four days. She could be pregnant right now. Maybe that's why she had such a short fuse with Kenzie.

Unlikely to happen that fast, Dex.

Why unlikely, Mon? I've rocked your world for 10 consecutive
days!

You're so full of yourself! We should give it a rest and talk about it
more.

Why talk about sex when you can just do it?

Ha, ha, Dexter, talk more about having a baby.

You lost a bet! We are having sex every day for a month.

I'm trying to be serious, Dex.

Me too! We can talk about it while we are doing it.

Are you, like, eighteen?

When we're talking sex, yes.

Forget I texted you and get back to work.

Can't, too hot and bothered now.

Me too, sweating in my bikini and bothered by you! Good-bye!

Janice startled Monica when she sat down in the beach chair
next to her. Monica hadn't meant to let an exasperated sigh escape
her, but it did, and she immediately regretted it. Janice had changed
into her swimsuit and flowy white cover-up and pulled her shoulder
length hair back into a short, but rather cute ponytail. Janice was
very young and trendy, possibly more stylish than Monica these
days.

She had some sort of obsession with sunglasses, today's pick,
a metal Tory Burch. Noticing Janice's perfectly soft and manicured
feet, Monica dug her own feet, with their cracked heels and thick
calloused toes from running, under a layer of sand.

"I hope I'm not interrupting your *me* time."

Monica reached for her Kindle. "No, not at all."

"You know, Monica Dear, if you need my help with the kids, all
you have to do is ask. Sometimes, when we don't get a break, we
get cranky, and everyone else around us suffers.

"When Dex and Chase were young, we moms banded together
at the country club. We utilized the daycare while we played tennis
and made sure the lifeguards were attentive at the pool so we could
relax and have uninterrupted conversation. We even shared
nannies and dropped the kids at one house while we met for lunch,

book club, or even those silly Tupperware and makeup parties from back in the day." Janice grinned.

"Sounds luxurious."

Where was she going with this? Monica rolled her eyes behind her sunglasses and took a sip of her tea. Was she offering to pay for nannies and a country club membership? Suggesting hosting a Tupperware party?

"Now that I'm familiar with your way of parenting, Monica Dear, I'd be fine with the kids if you wanted to run your errands or run an insane number of miles *after* Dex leaves for work. Possibly you could initiate a weekly lunch with your girlfriends."

Janice flung her hand casually, all the while assessing Monica, probably scheming on ways to get her out of her own house so she could brainwash her children. How was Monica supposed to get over this ever-present level of agitation that underlined their conversations when Janice spoke to her like this? Eyed her like that?

"I'd like that, thank you." And she would; she was willing to give Janice another chance. "It does get exhausting getting up at the crack of dawn," admitted Monica with a yawn.

"I remember those days when I was so fatigued and the boys would act out. My patience would be spent in a matter of seconds. I'd end up giving into their ridiculous demands, allowing them to walk all over me. Before I knew it, they ruled the roost." Janice patted Monica's shoulder. "No worries though, I can establish boundaries for Kenzie and Beck while you get some much-needed Monica time."

Monica closed her eyes. This was why they remained on their disgruntled level. Janice wasn't offering to watch her grandchildren out of love and sincerity to give Monica the gift of a little sanity and freedom. She had an ulterior motive, and that was to shoo Monica away and parent her grandchildren in the way she saw fit.

"Are you referring to the fact that I gave into Kenzie's tantrum?"

"Monica Dear, we mothers are all guilty of bargaining with our children from time to time to get them to obey. It's when we overindulge and constantly follow through with their silly requests and allow the cycle of manipulation, that we lose control. Before you know it, your children are calling all the shots."

"So, you're saying that I should break my promise to Kenzie and not take her to Grand Haven? Because frankly, a night eating greasy corndogs, strolling the pier hand in hand, and sitting on the beach next to my husband, watching the sunset while my kids run around in the sand chasing seagulls sounds magnificent."

"Well, I'm not saying you wouldn't benefit, but don't you think cruising around and pulling into random driveways, picking up imaginary friends, and buying those imaginary friends corn dogs is taking it too far?"

Janice rested her hand on top of Monica's in a fake attempt to be sincere. "I mean, after all, it *was* Trixie and Reese that led Kenzie to wander from her home. To think she could have wound up at the bottom of the lake, hit by a car, or picked up by a pedophile."

She paused for effect and brought her hand to her chest. "Monica Dear, constantly indulging in Kenzie's imaginary friends isn't healthy. She needs a playgroup with *real* girls her age."

Monica reached for her spray oil and discreetly loosened the cap as she pulled it out of the side pocket of her chair. She gave it a ferocious shake, sending the cap, and a slew of oil all over Janice's swimsuit and gorgeous white cover-up she'd draped over the arm of her chair.

Her hand flew to her mouth. "Oops, my bad. Sorry."

CHAPTER 24

Give without allowing yourself to be taken advantage of.
Love without being abused. Trust without being naïve.
Listen without losing your own voice.

Carmen

They found their rollerblades on a shelf in the garage behind a bag of bird seed. After dumping out the chipmunks' winter supply of food and wiping off the cobwebs, Carmen and Penelope tossed their gear in the trunk and took off for the trail.

Carmen had no idea what Gabby plugged in Penelope's head, but she had suggested Carmen ask Penelope to go do something physical together. Carmen initially balked at Gabby, claiming she'd tried countless times to get Penelope to hang out with her and that Penelope showed more enthusiasm over studying for a physics test. "Never stop trying," Gabby had advised.

"I'm going to kill myself. This was the stupidest idea ever!" Carmen confessed as she lurched forward, then back, her arms flailing and finally landing on Penelope's shoulders for support.

Penelope shrieked gleefully, "Get your hands off me, you maniac!"

For the most part, the trail was fairly flat and smooth. They'd gone a solid twelve minutes, Carmen wobbling about, Penelope effortlessly graceful, until the warning sign appeared in the distance.

They careened forward, gaining speed down a slight slope, totally missing the curve in the trail. "Whoa, holy mother of—"

"Rollerblades!" Penelope shouted. "Holy mother of rollerblades," her voice echoed in terror.

Carmen braced herself and tried to fall graciously, failing miserably. She hit shoulder first, head second, and with a thud, she felt her hip kiss the cement. Thank God she was wearing a helmet and wrist guards.

She moaned and laughed at the same time, while Penelope, the caring daughter she was, doubled over in hysterics at the sight of Carmen flattened across the trail, her skin embedded with gravel and dirt.

"I'm seriously going to wet my pants, Mom." Penelope had giant tears running down her cheeks; she could barely get her words out, she was laughing so hard.

Carmen stayed, sprawled out on the pavement, dirt smeared across her face, looking like the amateur she was. She did a quick physical check to make sure she could move her limbs and decided nothing significant was broken. Okay, maybe her pride, a little.

"My gosh, Mom, hurry, get up! Some bikers are coming. This is so embarrassing!"

"Are you for real, Penelope? I'm half dead, bleeding, probably with a concussion and a host of internal injuries. The bikers can ride *around* me."

"What if they stop?"

"And what? Help me? Unlike my daughter?"

A look of horror crossed Penelope's face. "Am I supposed to pull you up or something?"

Carmen lifted her arm weakly. "That would be accommodating."

Penelope stifled her laughter and extended her hand without so much as leaning forward. Carmen was going to be battered, but the sound of Penelope's laughter and sarcastic jubilance were worth every inch of black and blue. She pushed herself to a sitting position and slowly placed her rollerblades squarely underneath her. She took Penelope's hand and fought against her wavering balance as she slowly stood.

The cyclists, in full biker regalia with goggles, aerodynamic helmets, and neon Lycra were closing in on them at speeds Carmen drove her car down the freeway. With their mouths set, the veins in their forearms popping, and their legs pumping in a frenzied blur, they gave no indication of slipping into a single file line as they approached.

"Move back!" Penelope nudged while still holding her hand.

Carmen heard the bikers shout proper trail etiquette, *on your left,* which really translates to *get the fu—k out of the way,* which in turn sent her into a panic, causing her blades to slip back into a moonwalk pattern. She clenched Penelope's arms in a last-ditch effort at catching her balance, but the slick wheels threw them both backwards.

Never mind that Penelope landed on top of Carmen. It was the stick wedged between her shoulder blades that sucked the air from her lungs. She clenched Penelope in an attempt to brace herself and shield her daughter from the tires that were about to trample them.

~*~

Over dinner they could hardly contain themselves as they analyzed the near fatal crash. The first biker swerved and hit a massive rock, sending him over his handlebars. The two men trailing behind careened into each other, creating one big mass of Lycra.

The sounds of tires squealing, grunts, groans, and cursing all filled the air, which now sent them into full-on unruffled laughter as they mimicked and recalled the crash.

Penelope bellowed a deep belly laugh and dabbed the tears from the corner of her eyes. "They were so pissed at us, Mom."

"What makes you think that?" Carmen joked, rubbing her cheekbone where the skin was raw and swollen.

"Ugh, let's see. Well, it could have been the swearing as they lay there tangled in their bikes with their feet still stuck to their pedals. Or maybe the way the dude with the man bun threw his helmet at the tree in a fit of rage. Or possibly the fact that the guy that hit the rock popped his tire and bent his frame."

It was hard to chew their crepes and laugh at the same time without spitting food at each other, which made them laugh even more.

"That will teach them to slow down and use proper trail etiquette from now on. Nothing but a bunch of biker bullies." Carmen sniggered in false anger.

"The look on man bun's face when you asked if there was anything you could do to help . . . 'You've done enough,'" Penelope mimicked with a snarl. "Seriously, he was baring his teeth at you like a pit bull!"

Carmen tossed her head back. "Priceless!"

Penelope threw her hand over her mouth and nervously glanced around the eatery. "Seriously, Mom, close your mouth. You have a huge hunk of green between your teeth."

Carmen pointed to Penelope. "The look of repulsion on your face is exactly how those guys were looking at us. Besides, it's sweet pickle."

Disgust flashed across Penelope's face, but they continued to reminisce, and in that moment, Carmen didn't care if she had broken several bones. Their little mishap was the best thing that could have happened. It not only replaced Penelope's brashness and lack of enthusiasm for their forced bonding session, but they were laughing together, and what an incredible story to bring home along with a memory that would be revisited for years to come.

Carmen knew full well that Gabby had something to do with Penelope agreeing to go rollerblading with her. Also, she was still in the honeymoon phase of feeling sorry for the way Carmen's mother had treated her as a child. Ever since Carmen had broken down, both girls had been overly sweet, doting. Carmen was relishing the attention they were giving her, knowing it could vanish in an instant. Both girls would hang out in the kitchen while she cooked, initiating a hug now and again for no reason.

Penelope must have registered the look of alarm on Carmen's face as the door to Flavors on the Promenade opened and in waltzed Liz, Leila, and Tara. Penelope followed Carmen's gaze and looked over her shoulder and then back at her mother in one fluid movement.

"Let's go."

Boom, their jovial mood dissipated in an instant. "We aren't near being finished," Carmen responded, looking past Penelope as the three girls, upon their recognition, slipped into a booth by the door instead of walking past their table to order at the counter.

Carmen could sense the animosity amongst the girls, their haughtiness, hushed whispers, and conceited look of smugness.

"I'm full," said Penelope as she began to fold the paper wrapper over her half-eaten Thai crepe.

"Okay." Carmen followed suit and wrapped her dinner as well, silently cursing the trio that had killed the mood of a perfect outing. Penelope had been the one to suggest going to the creperie; she loved the rolled ice cream and knew Carmen gave the Cuban crepe a thumbs-up. Now, their perfect night was compromised.

The girls were all on one bench, Liz holding her phone high enough for a group selfie. Penelope started to get up, so Carmen quickly collected her purse and let out a slight moan when her stiff leg was reluctant to follow. Penelope's eyes bore into her, a warning not to make a scene.

As Carmen trailed behind Penelope toward the door, she waited for an exchange between the girls. There was none, not even the slightest glance of acknowledgment. The girls were all staring intently at Liz's phone, acting as if they hadn't seen Penelope. Penelope did the same, her eyes fixed ahead as she blew past them, pushing the door with a force that sent the greeting bells crashing on the glass.

Fury filled Carmen from deep within, words momentarily escaping her as she fought with herself as to which angle, haste or civility, she would take. She decided civility and walked past the girls, arms outstretched ready to push through the door and leave without a word. Something deep within pulled her back. Carmen twirled around. She would at least say hi to the girls. That was the grown-up thing to do, and possibly a tad intimidating for them, she mused maliciously.

And then, she caught a glimpse of Liz's phone. The picture was awful, Carmen obviously mid-sentence with a skewed mouth, eyes half closed, looking as hideous as the shots on the front page of the tabloids. Thankfully, the back of Penelope's head was picture perfect, her long braided caramel-colored hair wrapping around the nape of her neck.

Carmen squinted. On Tara's phone was a picture of Penelope walking towards the girls on her way out of the restaurant. Her eyes were straight ahead, chin up, her face set hard. Penelope looked well enough. It was the hashtags that infuriated Carmen: #momdate, #nofriends, #whore.

Mama bear roared to life in Carmen before she had a second to register that she was about to attack. She swooped in from behind the girls and snagged both their phones.

The shock factor on their faces as they leapt up from the booth was enough to make Carmen want to pull out her phone and snap their picture. They were freaking out. Carmen gloated and felt equally mortified for stooping to their level.

There was a beat of uncomfortable silence which Carmen basked in. In those seconds, she had this moment of brazen clarity. Penelope hadn't woken up one day and decided to ditch her friends. Penelope was barred from their little group. These were the same girls Carmen had spent endless hours doing crafts with when they were eight, making forts for them to sleep in, and playing DJ to impromptu dance parties in the living room. Countless times she'd made midnight runs to the convenience store for ice cream or had given pep talks when their boyfriends broke up with them. The very same girls she'd pulled around the lake, squealing on tubes. Now they were giving her the stink eye and bullying her daughter.

Carmen wanted to give the girls a piece of her mind. Instead, she shook her head disapprovingly. "Your cruelty speaks volumes about your character. I always thought better of you."

She tossed their phones on the hard surface of the table, they landed with a thud, and she hoped she hadn't cracked their screens. Carmen sauntered out of the eatery, feeling regret for every time she'd pushed Penelope to reconnect with those brats.

Penelope's eyes blazed with anger as Carmen slid into the car. There was no saving herself from the wrath she was about to receive from her daughter.

"Why did you stop and talk to them?"

Carmen eased into the traffic, irritated with the extreme highs and lows of emotions that ruled their life. "I was only going to say hi, acknowledge the fact that we all saw each other."

"Now I'm going to deal with the wrath of that too."

Carmen's heart broke for what she had to tell Penelope. "They were taking pictures of us."

"What's new? If Liz isn't posting pictures of me, she's leaving hate notes under my windshield wipers or spreading rumors that I have std's."

"Are you kidding me?" Carmen screamed, throwing her arms up in the air. "Okay, it's obvious you girls had a huge falling out. Will you please tell me why? I want to help you, Penelope."

Penelope pressed her head to the passenger window. "Stay out of it."

"Look. I promise I'll only listen. I won't give advice, I won't judge, I won't place blame, I won't call names, and I won't call parents," she promised. "Please don't shut me out."

Penelope ignored her.

"Jeez, Penelope." Carmen tried to keep her voice steady as she pulled over into an empty parking lot. "I don't get it. First, I don't know why you'd put up with Liz. Second, do you have any idea what I would have given to have a relationship like this with my mother? A mom that cared enough, that could see anything past her mental illness to stop spitting venom at me for a single day, be concerned and ask about what was going on in my life."

She dug her fingers in her hair and held her head. "I love you girls so much, and I'm trying so hard to be the best mom that I know how to be, but Penelope you make it hard. My mom rejected me, and I feel like my daughters are too."

Penelope bit her quivering lip, trying to hold back tears. "They hate me, okay, Mom. Is that what you want to know? They are the *damaged* ones, the *insignificant* ones. Don't you get it?"

Carmen's thoughts raced. *Damaged and insignificant*, those were her words. When had she said them? Then, like a slap in the face, she could see the pile of shit in their yard, the words whore and bitch spray-painted in neon pink, her flowers pulled from their beds.

"Are you telling me that Liz and Leila, your best friends since elementary, are responsible for the vandalism?"

Penelope's head fell to her chest as tears rolled down her cheeks. Carmen was outraged, but more so, her heart was breaking for her daughter. How cruel.

"Please don't say anything, Mom, please."

"We need to back up, back *waaay* up. What happened? How did a bunch of girls that were inseparable from the age of eight, go from being tight as glue to enemies?"

"Polo," Penelope spat.

"Water polo?"

"My surgery gave Liz the opportunity to steal my position, actually get playing time."

"So, that should be a good thing for her. Why would she hate *you* for that?"

"You don't remember how competitive it was getting? Best friends rivaling over who was the best center-forward?"

"Yes, of course, but I thought it was all handled fairly well. You remained best friends, regardless of playing time, points, and stats. Right?"

"Up until our freshman year maybe. Then I would say more like best frenemies. We still hung out, but she was a total bitch to me at practice, and if I ever screwed up, she'd point it out to everyone and to Coach West.

"Then I caught her spilling tea—"

"Spilling Tea?" Carmen interrupted.

"Talking smack about me behind my back, trying to get everyone to turn against me, saying I thought I was better than everyone else, saying that I was spreading rumors about Leila and other people when I wasn't."

"That's splashing of her! Get it, splash?"

Penelope glared at Carmen, but the corner of her mouth curled up in a smirk. "That was stupid, Mom."

"Oh, and spilling tea isn't?"

"Anyway, do you remember when Liz and Leila came to visit me the day I came home from the hospital after my surgery?"

"Yes, they brought you cookies and haven't been over since." Carmen cringed. "Please tell me you didn't rub it in her face that she was only getting playing time because of your injury and absence?"

Carmen had many conversations with Penelope about encouraging and complimenting Liz and never gloating when the coach favored her over Liz, which was often the case. Liz had been benched unless they were up a monstrous amount of points. Finally, Victor told Carmen she should back off because Penelope was starting to feel guilty for her accomplishments.

Penelope's face twisted. "No, Mom, I would never intentionally point out the obvious."

Her tone was curt. Carmen had offended her, but Carmen, like all parents, knew her child on their home turf, in their environment. What most parents failed to recognize and accept was that their sweet and innocent children could be entirely different people around their peers. They could mock, bully, be deceitful, and talk nasty trash to each other's faces or behind their backs while engaging in behavior parents never fathomed their children would.

"Sorry, I didn't think you would, but when attacked we are all guilty of saying things we shouldn't. Sometimes it's hard to reel it in." Carmen chuckled at her own pun. "Go on, what happened when they came over?"

"Ya, well, Liz basically told me how shitty everyone on the team was playing, criticizing everyone as usual, and trying to get me to agree and talk smack when I wasn't even there to witness it. They gossiped about a bunch of other things that had happened at a party I wasn't even at. The two-faced bitch left our house and went around spreading the gossip she had filled *me* in on, and flipped it, saying she heard it from me, and I was spreading it."

Penelope tugged at her braid and took a deep breath. "Long story short, by the time I returned to school and figured out what had happened, she had not only the whole team hating me, but most of our friends too, for one reason or another."

Carmen gripped the steering wheel in an attempt to control her anger. Thank goodness she wasn't driving, or she'd be breaking some serious speed limits.

"I'm so sorry. Didn't Leila stick up for you? She was there. She knew the truth." Carmen knew out of the three girls Leila was the passive one, always trying to please others and not make waves.

"Ha! Are you kidding? And risk the chance of losing all her friends too? I may have been queen in the pool, Mom, but Liz has always been queen of manipulation. Liz is a ringleader, renders everyone defenseless. Typical Leila went right along with it, not so much by spreading lies along with Liz, but by not sticking up for me and the truth. She knows, if she did, she'd lose all her friends, and she thinks it's better to have a bunch of conniving bitchy friends than none."

This was the problem Carmen had with so many women. Instead of empowering one another, they tore each other to shreds to better their insecure, shallow selves.

"I still don't get it. Liz had already taken your position for the season. Why would she have to turn everyone against you?"

"Exactly, for the *season,* Mom."

At that moment, it clicked with Carmen. "So, therefore, she made sure all the girls on the team hated you so you would be too intimidated to try out for the next season after your leg was healed."

Penelope nodded as she dug in the center console and retrieved a tissue. "The team has been working out together all summer. Tryouts were last week, and they're going on a team-building trip to Sleeping Bear Dunes next month."

"That's bullshit, Penelope!" Carmen slapped her hands on the steering wheel, causing Penelope to jump. "You were the star player on that team, on your way to a full-ride scholarship to your pick of several universities. How could you let someone like that rule over you and ruin your chances of playing in college?"

Penelope sobbed. "Mom, stop!"

Carmen took a deep breath and tried to extinguish the inferno burning inside her. She wished Gabby were with them. Gabby would know the right way to talk through this, logically, emotions removed. Right now, Carmen was livid, close to calling up Liz, the voracious wolf, and giving her a piece of her mind and demanding Penelope get herself back on the team.

"I'm this close"—she held her thumb and index finger an inch apart—"to exploding." Carmen leaned in towards Penelope and put her hand on her knee. Gabby had warned her about coming across as accusatory, so she inhaled a deep calming breath while she articulated her words.

"It's hard for me to wrap my brain around the fact that you allowed a jealous little schemer to take away your number one passion in life. I refuse to allow Liz Jensen to steal the last two seasons of your high school career and a shot at playing for a Big Ten university."

"There's a ton of layers to it, Mom."

"Well, I should hope so, because I thought I was raising an independent, strong young woman that stood up for herself."

Penelope wailed. Carmen had never had a way with words. When she meant to encourage, she belittled.

"Look. I'm sorry. I'm not implying that you're weak. I'm simply having a hard time digesting all this. I'm so upset with Liz and this situation. Why didn't you come to me? I could have talked to Coach West or Mrs. Jensen."

"No! That's exactly why I don't tell you anything. I don't need you running around creating a scene. I can fight my own battles!"

"Oh ya? Then show me, Penelope, because as far as I'm concerned, you've thrown in the towel and handed your dream over to Liz on a silver platter."

Carmen put the car in drive, peeled out of the parking lot, and sped home, crushed and angry at Liz, Leila, Penelope, and most of all, herself for failing her daughter.

~*~

Amelia and Piper were in the kitchen making slushies when they arrived home. Carmen had completely forgotten Piper was getting dropped off for a sleepover. Penelope glared at Liz's sister, stormed past the two girls, took the stairs two at a time, and slammed her bedroom door. The light click of the lock sent Carmen into panic mode.

Amelia and Piper shared a sly look. Did they already know what took place at the eatery? Had they viewed pictures on Snapchat, Instagram?

Carmen had this overwhelming sense of dread that Amelia had found her alliance with Piper, which in turn meant an alliance with Liz, which ultimately meant betraying her sister. It was slowly dawning on Carmen that Amelia was withholding a tremendous amount of information from her. Amelia knew full well Penelope and Liz had a blowout.

Carmen plastered on a fake smile and greeted both girls cheerfully.

"What the heck happened to you?"

Carmen touched her cheek. "Penelope and I went rollerblading. I took a few cyclists down."

They giggled, and Carmen accompanied them with forced laughter, the easy banter she and Penelope shared now shattered. They should have walked in the door retelling their story through tears of laughter. "Say, I hate to be a buzz kill, but we've had a few things come up, and I'm going to have to take you home, Piper."

Carmen saw both their faces flush. They knew.

"But we were just about to watch a movie, Mom." Amelia gestured at the snacks they were gathering to take to the basement.

"No worries, Amelia," Piper spoke up. "I'm not feeling very good anyway. I'll just have my mom come get me, Mrs. Fletcher." Piper's body was tense; she couldn't wait to make a run for it.

"Okay, sure." Carmen nodded, knowing full well Piper was too nervous to be in the car with her.

Retreating to her bathroom for a shower, Carmen tried to call Victor four times. On the fifth, she decided to leave a sweet rant. She followed up with a text. He was needed at home. Now.

He was in Vegas, again, for his last extended trip. If she were to ask why she kept getting his voicemail, she knew the answer would be because he was either in the middle of a lesson or he had accepted another invite to a country club dinner or a night on the strip. Two excuses she was sick of hearing.

Once again, he wasn't home to deal with the latest crisis, and she was finding it extremely difficult not to be agitated with him. Quite honestly, her mind was starting to wander and obsess. She couldn't ignore Victor's edginess, the way he always seemed distracted and overly eager to hop on a plane to Vegas.

CHAPTER 25

Allow your passion to become your purpose,
and it will become your profession.

Gabriella

Why was it that Gabby found counseling her clients fulfilling, yet when it came to her family and friends, she often found their issues draining? She supposed it was that she remained emotionally unattached to her clients and that was near impossible with family and friends. Sometimes she wished she didn't care so much, that she'd become numb, losing all empathy.

Every so often she found herself irritated. Instead of being their support, giving proper counsel, she found it difficult to have patience with the people she cared about the most. A time or two she'd gotten so frustrated that she'd barked out orders, harshly blurted that they, themselves, were their own problem, that she was sick of hearing them grumble if they weren't willing to do anything about their tribulations, or in simple terms, move on already. As if life were that easy.

It wasn't that she didn't want to care for Stella as she lay on bed rest. She was privileged to have the flexibility to do so, but Stella was on an extreme emotional rollercoaster this past week. She was being down right pissy and irrational.

After her last doctor visit, Stella was sure she would be granted the privilege of movement, to abandon the confines of bed rest. Stella was convinced that she felt well enough to at least work a half day at her internship. Stella's argument was that she sat at a desk all day, a far cry from the truth since she often was out on assignment, shadowing reporters.

Her doctor pointed out that getting to her place of work required an enormous amount of effort. Showering, dressing, driving, even walking through parking lots was too much movement and would put her and the baby at risk.

Disappointment was a mild analogy for Stella's reaction. Gabby feared her mental state as much as her physical, wondering if she was also developing pre-partum depression. Stella was incredibly driven, and the fact that her life had come to a screeching halt was, in Stella's words, making her go *cray cray!*

Then there was Preston. He was a nervous wreck, fielding his concerns over Stella onto Gabby, texting daily, leaving her to question whether he was capable of handling Stella's strong personality, not to mention a baby.

A soft knock on her office door was a welcome interruption to her thoughts. Penelope had taken on the duty of greeting clients and offering them something to drink.

"Mrs. Maycomb is here," Penelope announced as she pushed open the door.

Gabby took a deep breath. Shannon was in an emotionally abusive marriage. She was a sweet little doormat, always taking the blame for the way her narcissist husband treated her.

Shannon usually sobbed all the way through their sessions. Normally, tears didn't faze Gabby; they were a typical occurrence in her profession. With Gabby's current circumstances, she prayed she could keep her own emotions at bay. Shannon spoke of things that were far too parallel to her own life.

"Last time we met, I asked you to make a brag list. Are you ready to share your pages of astronomical character traits?" Gabby smiled widely as they got comfortable in the new furniture. She had given Shannon this assignment so she could see every morsel of goodness she possessed because she was so beaten down by her husband she believed she was worthless.

Shannon's head shook and fell to her chest as the tears began to roll. Gabby looked at the clock. Shannon hadn't made it two minutes.

"He found my list. Told me I was a self-absorbed, conceited bitch, and then wadded it up into a ball and threw it in my face."

"Shannon, you are not selfish. You are not to blame for his actions. He's only playing victim to the circumstances he created."

"I don't know. I think he has a point. I mean, after my company's downsizing, I was upset. I was out of work for ten months before I took another job."

Shannon twisted the tissues in her shaking hands and sucked in a sharp breath. "I was so consumed with finding another job that I wasn't attentive to him, and so he strayed. He was under a lot of stress when we were living solely on his income."

"Didn't you turn down several job offers because he told you to?"

"Well, yes, but one was in a very male-dominated field, the other I'd have to travel to San Francisco six or seven times each year, and the other, well . . ."

Shannon looked out the window, her mascara running down her blotchy face.

"What, Shannon? Why wouldn't Austin let you accept the third job offer?"

"I'd be making twice as much money as him," she said weakly.

Gabby nodded. "He felt threatened by that."

Shannon shrugged and wailed, her upper body convulsing.

"Austin is insecure and unhappy with himself, and until he can alleviate his own anguish, he's going to continue to inflict suffering on you."

Gabby saw Shannon's shoulders shrug, as if to say, *maybe*.

"He didn't trust you to work with other men, Shannon, because he's a cheat himself."

Shannon's head waivered from side to side in contemplation. "He's always been jealous, a little possessive. In the beginning, I found it flattering. You know, he wanted me all to himself."

"Were *you* leery about working with mostly men?"

"No." Shannon chuckled. "I like the challenge. We scientists, we are a brainy, nerdy bunch. I find our conversations stimulating. However, I've never been physically attracted to those types of men."

"Were *you* willing to travel to San Francisco for the other job?"

Gabby knew the answer to this question. Shannon had been excited when they spoke after she interviewed for the position.

"Sure, why not? I'd love to spread my wings and see California. But Austin and I are a team, and it would have been wrong to accept the job without his consent."

The defeat on Shannon's face was distressing.

"Marriage is a partnership, and I agree that you shouldn't make major decisions without talking it through with Austin, but I don't really think that's the issue, Shannon. It sounds more like you have to ask his permission."

"Austin is very sensitive; he'd worry so much if I traveled. He said he was concerned the men in my field would dominate over me."

Gabby tilted her head to the side. "Shannon, I know you don't really believe that."

Shannon ignored her comment, and Gabby chastised herself for not wording it as a question.

"Austin has insomnia, and his sales at the car dealership are at an all-time low. The stress I've created in our marriage has affected his job performance. I've done enough damage to our relationship. I wasn't going to add culpability and start flying across the country."

Gabby's heart squeezed agonizingly as Shannon spoke. "Putting Austin on a pedestal, sacrificing yourself to cater to his outlandish needs isn't healthy for either one of you. He is damaged, and he's damaging your self-worth."

"He says as his wife I should respect his feelings."

"His *feelings* are irrational and come from insecurity." Gabby's voice wavered; she cleared her throat to hide it. "If he respected your feelings, he wouldn't treat you unfairly."

Shannon leaned forward and placed her elbows on her knees, burying her face in her hands.

"You've been married eight years, correct?" asked Gabby.

Shannon nodded. "Nine next month."

"Do you see yourself as the same or a different person than you were before you got married?"

Shannon made no hesitation. "Different."

"How so?"

Shannon sat up and looked Gabby in the eyes. "I'm too embarrassed to answer that question."

"I admire honesty. Strong, fearless women face the truth, Shannon, even if it's ugly and hard to admit. Denial doesn't make the issues invisible."

"I'm a frazzled, spineless mess," Shannon blurted. "I feel like I tiptoe around trying to please Austin. Everything upsets him or hurts his feelings."

"Do you feel as though it's your responsibility to make him happy?"

Shannon shrugged and whispered meekly, "I guess so."

"Look. You're an incredibly smart, lovable, ambitious woman. You've allowed your husband to take his inadequacies out on you. Austin doesn't get to decide who you should be, how you should feel. He doesn't have the privilege of altering your dreams or how you view yourself."

"I just unleashed on him, yet, I'm no better. I promised him I didn't want kids, and now I do. I really, really do, and he still doesn't. Everything I do stresses him out. How can I not take blame for his misery?"

"Has he ever hit you?"

Shannon sucked in a sharp breath. "Just once, it was an accident."

Gabby screamed inside. She would love to wring Austin's neck. Which reminded her that she'd love to wring Greg's neck. At some point you need to open your eyes to reality rather than cling to some bogus illusion. One can only live in the cloud of falsity for so long.

"And look at me." Shannon grabbed her hair and mussed it before Gabby could respond. "I've totally let myself go. I have three-inch roots, my clothes hang on me because my stomach is too sick to eat, I look run down, and I have dark circles under my eyes. I used to take care of myself, get facials, manicures, wear clothes that fit, and now . . . Now, I don't know. I've been in a funk for years. I can't blame him for being upset that I'm no longer the woman he married."

"Go do it."

Shannon looked at her with confusion. "Do what?"

"Get a facial, manicure, go to the salon, buy new clothes, take care of yourself. For Shannon. Not Austin."

Shannon crossed and uncrossed her legs. "Austin says all that is a waste of money, and he starts questioning whom I'm trying to impress when I do those things."

For goodness' sake, does this woman listen to herself?

"So, he criticizes your looks, but faults you when you do something to improve it?"

"I guess so."

The silence hung in the air between the two of them as Gabby calmed her nerves. Greg was no Austin, but Shannon's circumstances were making her upset with her own. She was surprised when Shannon spoke without being prompted.

"When we were first dating, he told me I was the only woman he'd ever been with that met all of his expectations. Now he tells me I have no standards."

Shannon took hold of the throw pillow and placed it on her lap and picked at a corner thread. Gabby waited patiently, knowing from years of experience when to ask questions and when to let the silence chase the answers.

"Whatever I do, nothing pleases him. He disliked my friends and their husbands, so I let them go soon after we were married. I turned down the job in San Francisco making double what we were making combined. I left the gym I loved and joined his. I sold my Mustang because he said it attracted men. He won't allow me to have any social media accounts because he says it's not healthy for our marriage and, if I loved him, I'd support his decisions. I've become another person, the person he wanted me to be, and now it's not good enough for him."

"Sounds like you've suffered a slow, insidious breakdown of your sense of self. The only person's expectations you need to meet are your own. Austin doesn't get the privilege to make all your decisions. Shannon gets to pick her friends, her career, the car she drives, and whether she gets a manicure.

"He's changed you from a vibrant, outgoing woman to a self-loathing, spiritless person. Shannon deserves to be loved for who she is. You can start by loving and respecting yourself."

Shannon's face brightened. "You sound like my dad."

Gabby laughed. "I like him already. How so?"

"He doesn't like the way Austin treats me. He thinks I can do better and says Austin holds me back."

"Is Austin aware of this?"

Shannon nodded. "He's never liked my parents, especially my dad because we've always been close. Austin says our relationship is creepy, that my dad shouldn't hug or kiss me at my age. It's only a peck on my forehead."

"Sounds sweet to me," said Gabby as she pictured how tender Greg had always been with Stella and Lottie.

A wind chime sounded, signaling Shannon's hour was up.

Shannon's eyes widened. "I can't wait until next week. Can we talk again tomorrow?"

Gabby stood and opened her arms, signaling a hug. "Absolutely. Penelope will get you scheduled."

Gabby walked to the window in a daze of her own thoughts. So much of their conversation was on replay in her head. Her own words rang out. *At some point, you need to open your eyes to the truth rather than cling to the illusion that everything is okay.*

Every word that Gabby spoke to Shannon she spoke to herself.

Greg had been persistent in his attempts to save their marriage. In an odd sense, his efforts upset her as much as the affair itself. She wondered if it would be easier if he had simply left her for Holly, leaving her with no choices.

Greg had the affair. Gabby was left to decide whether she would allow it to tear her family apart. All she could think about was the consequences that would lie ahead for everyone *else* if she chose divorce.

She wasn't going to lie. She missed their life, the familiarity of it. What she was questioning was if she would really miss Greg. Possibly she was only chasing after an image of a lifestyle she dreamed their future life might be.

~*~

Gabby jumped as she heard a loud thud followed by a screech from the garage. Stella was on the couch, watching Netflix as Gabby was digging through the pantry, pondering what to make Stella to squelch her salty/sweet craving.

As she walked closer to the garage, she could hear the spray of the hose and opened the door to find Greg spraying the trash dumpster. "Jeez, Greg, you scared me," she said, putting her hand to her chest, feeling it was caked with sand from the last hour of weeding the beach.

His eyebrows rose in a flirtatious manor as he eyed her from head to toe as he'd done a thousand times. A silent compliment he no longer had the right to deliver.

"Sorry, I pulled the dumpster in from the end of the driveway and almost lost my stomach over the stench."

Gabby folded her arms. "Is that why you stopped by unannounced, to pull the dumpster in?"

"I texted an hour ago to see how Stella was and if I could swing by." He stopped squirting the hose to avoid yelling over the noise of the water hitting the plastic. His face had fallen from the playfulness a minute ago.

"I've been on the beach the last couple of hours, my phone inside . . . " She stopped. She didn't owe him an explanation. "Look, Greg. I need space, time to process and think. Your insistent texting and unannounced drop-ins aren't working in your favor."

Greg dropped the hose by his feet. It was shortly after nine o'clock, and he was still in his work clothes, an outfit Gabby had purchased for him. He looked tired, miserable. He was hurting deeply.

The counseling session with Shannon was replaying heavily in Gabby's head. It gave her such clarity, a pain she understood, a pain that she knew she wanted to end, not one she wanted to be reminded of every day. "You know, Greg. I've given this a lot of thought, and our children are adults. They deserve the truth from you."

Panic surged Greg's face. "Gabby, no, please don't do this to me. Don't tell them Holly is pregnant. It would break them."

"I said *from you*. I'm not going to tell them about the baby. I'm also not going to play along with any charades that you and Holly conjure up."

"I don't think they need to know."

"I *wish* they wouldn't have to know either, Greg, but they are adults, and the truth will set us all free."

Greg shook his head violently. "No. You're only using our children to try and destroy me. Only a cruel person would do such a thing."

"Don't you dare portray me as a bad person just so you can escape your own guilt," Gabby snarled.

"Mom!" Stella hollered from inside.

Gabby quickly ran in, Greg on her heels. "Is everything okay?"

Stella's face was skeptical at the sight of Greg. "I heard all this banging and voices, so I wondered what was going on." Stella's eyes shifted towards Gabby. "Are you okay, Mom?"

Remorsefully, Gabby knew her face was filled with angst. She didn't want Stella getting upset on her part. "I'm fine. Dad only stopped by for a second." Her eyes shifted to meet his. "He's on his way out."

"Do you need anything, Stella? I can run to the store and grab a puzzle for you two, maybe some ice cream?" His voice rose like he was buttering up a small child.

Stella turned from her side to her back with a sigh. "I'm good, thanks."

Her curt voice settled uncomfortably between the three of them. A wave of nausea washed over Gabby. She hated this. However, she would no longer step in and smooth things over between Greg and every person he betrayed.

His demeanor crumbled, and Gabby couldn't help her heart from aching. To be blatantly rebuked by your kids sucked. Gabby knew Greg was absorbing the rejection he'd receive for fathering another child.

Greg walked over to Stella and patted the top of her head. "Love you, Stella. I'll check in with you tomorrow."

~*~

"Do you have a few minutes to stay for coffee?" asked Monica as they dragged their worn-out bodies to the shore. "You seem overly preoccupied. I mean not that you shouldn't be, with Greg and Stella and all, but it's time for me to be here for you, not that I've got great advice or anything."

Gabby interrupted Monica by placing her finger over her rambling mouth with a smile. "I'd love a cup of coffee and a venting session."

Monica returned with two cups of iced coffee, their coined drink of champions. They sat on the end of Monica's dock, looking out toward the flat, un-rippled lake. It was Tuesday, so the lake would remain quiet until mid-afternoon when the teens rolled out of their beds, piled on their parents' boats, blared music, and drove recklessly without a care in the world.

"You two are insane for getting up at this hour. And let me guess you've swum around the lake five times already." Carmen yawned from behind as she approached Gabby and Monica perched on the edge of Monica's dock, their feet dangling in the water.

Gabby scooted over while patting the dock for Carmen to sit. "Hardly, just once." She laughed, noticing the wet imprint of her tush. "Sorry about that."

"My imprint is going to swallow yours up!" Carmen sipped from her steaming mug, eyeing their tumblers of cold brew they sipped with straws. "Iced coffee? You two really are cut from a different thread."

"Keeps my muscles from seizing up," joked Monica.

"What's wrong with less vigorous exercise? Like yoga?"

Monica moaned. "She forces me to do that too."

"Whoa, wait." Carmen leaned forward and peered over to Monica. "You're saying you'd rather do all that crazy intense cardio versus a peaceful yoga session on the beach?"

"You've obviously never had Gabby as your instructor. Running ten miles is easier than holding crow for two minutes or twisting your body into scorpion, holding various planks and warriors for five minutes."

"In my defense"—Gabby held up her hand—"because of me, you've not only mastered the poses, but you've slashed your nine-minute mile down to eight and you can swim in the lake without a panic attack."

"Panic attack over swimming?" questioned Carmen.

"As if you've never worried about weeds getting tangled around your ankles and pulling you under?"

Carmen stifled her chuckle by taking a sip from her mug. Gabby followed suit and sipped her iced coffee to suffocate her giggle.

Monica splashed water at the two of them with her foot. "Okay, saying it out loud makes it sound a bit ridiculous, but it's possible."

Gabby and Carmen snickered again. "Maybe in 1979 at a summer camp in Blairstown, NJ!" Gabby chuckled.

"What?" Monica and Carmen asked in an oblivious unison.

"Ugh, you two are such babies. Jason. *Friday the 13th* movies. Ever heard of them?"

"Ah, yes, of course," said Carmen.

A cell rang behind them. They all turned in unison to the pile of phones lying on the towel. It was Gabby's.

She quickly reached for it, assuming Stella needed her. Unfortunately, it wasn't Stella's sweet face that appeared on the screen. It was the dreaded number.

"It's Holly."

"Answer," demanded Monica, "on speaker."

Gabby gave her a sly look, accepted the call, and pressed the speaker button.

"Hi, Gabby, I realize this is an outlandish request, but Greg is pretty upset about your suggesting telling the kids about the baby. I was wondering if you'd be willing to meet and discuss a few things in person."

Gabby eyed Carmen and Monica. Carmen was shaking her head no, and Monica was nodding her head yes. Gabby agreed; she was the master of speaking in person, after all.

She ended the call with a feeling of supremacy.

"Why is it that I can't bear to be in the presence of my husband and yet I'm drawn to sit face to face with his mistress?"

"Ya, that's weird." Monica snorted.

"You're intrigued," guessed Carmen.

They sat in silence for a beat.

"I like you, ladies. I'm grateful to share our wonderfully messy, imperfect, chaotic lives together." Carmen initiated a group hug, dumped the remainder of her coffee in the lake, and excused herself to go get ready for work.

CHAPTER 26

*Sometimes your heart needs more time to accept what your mind
already knows.*

Monica

Mid-stream of collecting laundry, Monica dropped the heaping
basket in Beck's room with a brilliant idea. Today was a glorious day
to fly the coop. Janice's face registered panic before pleasure at the
idea, yet she agreed.

Monica wandered the streets of Saugatuck, her hair and
makeup done for what seemed like the first time in weeks. Living on
a lake with summers off, she tended to forgo eyeliner and mascara
for sunscreen and lip balm. A café miel in her hand, her purse slung
diagonally across her chest, she was fully armed to shop.

She swung open the door of her favorite boutique, giving
herself the approval to buy whatever she felt like. It was her day,
she declared, blissfully alone, no one tugging at her legs, grabbing
for the display of necklaces, clearing the neatly folded stacks of
blouses from the display tables with sticky little fingers, or peeking
under the velvet curtains in the dressing room. She felt so free and
cheerful. Whimsical, she thought. *I feel whimsical*, even though she
had no idea what that truly entailed.

Ding!

Monica Dear – We are currently at Flavors On The Promenade
having rolled ice cream. What a divine place! Kenzie ordered Unicorn
Dreams and Beck and I are splitting #ClubCaramel. We had a lovely time
in Aunt Candy's Toy Company. I splurged on several things. However,
Kenzie gave me quite the trouble because I wouldn't buy toys for Trix
and Teressa. I really think it would be best to limit, and eventually
remove, these imaginary friends. Overindulging Kenzie isn't healthy.

Trixie and Reese, Monica wanted to correct. Her stomach
clenched, knowing Kenzie's heart was probably broken when Janice
denied Trixie and Reese a toy. What was the harm in grabbing a

tiny trinket that cost a buck or two? Her instinct was to fire off a text, reminding Janice that these girls were very real to Kenzie and that she and Dex made it a point to fuel her imagination, not hinder it.

Dex was always telling Monica that his mother meant well but she only had poor delivery. Which, she supposed, was also true of herself. She was a good person, but Janice constantly provoked her, and she often slipped and retorted in devious ways.

Thanks for showing them a fun time. I'm so grateful!

Monica zipped her phone in her purse, expecting that to be the end of their conversation. Why couldn't she focus on spoiling them with toys and leave the parenting to the parents?

Monica's phone chirped again. Digging it back out, she cursed under her breath.

For your comfort's sake, I wanted you to know we are at the park.
I'm encouraging Kenzie to play with the other children instead of
conversing with those silly girls she sees floating in thin air.

This time the foul language escaped her lips. The sales associate's eyes darted towards Monica in alarm.

Monica cringed—"Sorry"—and held up her phone in explanation.

It was rare for Monica to splurge on herself. Usually, if she dropped money on frivolous things, it was something for their house, not clothes, nor handbags.

She spent an hour, trying on numerous trendy dresses, tanks, shorts, and ended up with a black romper, flowy white linen pants with a turquoise tank, a pair of wedge sandals, and a slinky dress for her and Dex's next dinner date. On the way to check out, two bracelets, a few pair of earrings, and a papaya-scented candle caught her eye. She was finished. Whew.

The salon she walked by was luring her, the gravitational pull so strong it would be rude not to escape inside. The deluxe pedicure was seventy-five dollars but included a cucumber soak, hot stone massage, paraffin wax, and sea salt scrub. How could one pass that up, even if it was frivolous and a good chunk of their grocery bill?

She could get used to this lifestyle: wandering the streets, buying trinkets, pampering herself. She'd have to go back to work. They could survive on one income, but living on a lake wasn't cheap. The property taxes alone required a full-time job, and their place was old—they'd been fixing it up since the day they'd moved in. Besides, Dex, unlike his mother, was frugal, a simple man.

Monica, for the most part, didn't mind. The challenge to stay in the budget was usually a thrill, probably because she knew they had a nest egg to fall back on, so it wasn't like they were going to get behind on payments if she splurged here or there. For some reason, this made her want to stay thrifty even more.

Janice was a free babysitter, she reminded herself, and chuckled, realizing that was such a Dex way of rationalizing. She closed her eyes, cleared her head, and enjoyed the calf massage. *Ding!*

> We are home from the park, but no rush getting back, Monica Dear.

> Perfect! I won't rush. See you in a few hours!

Monica took a selfie of her feet in the pedi bowl and hit send.

> You'll be thrilled to know I exchanged numbers with the mother of a darling little girl at the park. Kenzie and Adel hit it off fabulously. We've already set up a playdate for Thursday morning at Adel's house.

Beads of sweat sprang from Monica's pores. *Where does she get the audacity?* She fanned her face with a magazine that had been lying on the chair next to her and asked for a bottle of water. Gabby. She needed to talk to Gabby before she fired off a text telling Janice to pack her things and get out.

"Hey there," Gabby greeted with forced jubilance.

Monica knew Gabby was masking her grief for the sake of others and wondered how she did it. Monica, on the other hand, wore her emotions on her sleeve, every strike against her throughout the day brazenly standing out like splattered ketchup on a white shirt.

"Hey. Do you have a second?"

"Twelve minutes until my next client."

"Good, because I need you. Never mind the fact that I sense you're having a rough day, we'll get to you later." Monica chuckled as did Gabby. "Right now, I need you to deal with *my* crisis."

"Sounds far better than dealing with mine."

Monica's smile sounded through her words. "And that, my friend, is why I love you. You're always here for me, and I'm rarely any help to you."

"That's why our friendship works. You suck all the time away from me that I could be wallowing in my own pity. You're down to eleven minutes. Talk."

"My sweet mother-in-law agreed to babysit, took the kids to the park, and set up a playdate for Kenzie with a complete stranger, at the complete stranger's house."

Monica went on to explain Kenzie's temper tantrum the other day, how she finally bribed her out of the water with promises of taking Trixie and Reese to Grand Haven, and how Janice had accused Monica of playing into Kenzie's imaginary friends too much.

Sure, it had taken them an extra twenty minutes to get to Grand Haven because they had gone in and out of four different driveways until Kenzie was certain her friends had gotten in the car. Of course, Dex didn't order any of his own Pronto Pups and held out for Trixie's and Reese's, which were cold by the time Kenzie handed him her friend's leftovers.

True, Monica had talked Dex into not ordering an Oreo Flurry so Trixie and Reese could order a Blue Moon sundae with marshmallow topping and sprinkles. Once the sundaes were half-melted, Kenzie told them that Trixie and Reese were finished and Monica and Dex could have them. One bite of the concoction made her and Dex gag. Monica tossed them in the trash and went back to the window and bought Dex an Oreo flurry.

Beck and Kenzie had been running in and out of the waves as the sun set. Instead of being content with their evening, Monica's stomach was in knots. Cold corn dogs, ten dollars' worth of melted blue goo in the trash. Trixie and Reese, or rather Kenzie, was controlling their entire family. "Your mom advised me we should stop catering to Kenzie's imaginary friends," she'd told Dex, unable to look him in the eyes for fear he held her same view.

"What do you think about that?" Dex had asked cautiously.

Monica had shrugged. "Maybe we do accommodate Trixie and Reese a bit much."

He laughed at her analogy. "So we need to set boundaries for Trixie and Reese but not Kenzie?"

Monica had laughed too, but it wasn't a bad approach. "That's a brilliant angle, don't you think? Set boundaries for Trixie and Reese." She reached into the towel bag and pulled out her phone. "Call me and hang up when I answer."

Dex gave her a look of exasperation as he always did when she was up to something but did as he was told. As Monica's phone rang, she picked up Kenzie's towel and waded in the water next to the kids.

"Hello," she answered speaking loudly to get Kenzie's attention. "Yes, this is Kenzie's mom. Oh, hi, it's nice of you to call and check in, Mrs. Trixie and Reese. Yes, we've had a lovely time tonight. The girls are being chased by the waves right now."

Monica had Kenzie's attention. She was looking from Monica to the space in front of her that occupied her little companions. Monica whispered to Kenzie that she was talking to their mother.

"I see, yes. Okay, we will dry off and bring them home immediately. Yia Yia's cottage? Yes, for sure, we will be there as soon as we can. Thanks for calling, Mrs. Trixie and Reese. Bye."

Kenzie was looking at Monica with skeptical eyes. She had begun to speak into the air at her friends when Dex jumped up and announced they had better respect Mrs. Trixie and Reese otherwise she might not let the girls play again.

Even Beck had sensed the urgency to get Trixie and Reese home. They packed their things and trudged through the thick sand to their car in record speed with no protests from either child.

"Mrs. Trixie and Reese?" Dex whispered as they got in the car. "That's the best you could come up with?"

Monica gave him a loving glare. "Worked like a charm."

"So where is Yia Yia's cottage, Miss Charm?"

"Gloriously close." Monica pointed to the quaint cottage just down from where they exited the beach parking lot. As they had plenty of times, they pulled into the driveway of a stranger's home.

Monica took a breath. "Are you following all this Gabby?"

"Yep, I'm with you. Go on."

"As I speak, I feel ridiculous. What are you thinking so far? Do you think I cater to Kenzie's imaginary friends too much?"

"Right now, I'm only curious how you got the girls out of the car and into a stranger's house."

"Of course," Monica continued, fully aware of the expression on the pedicurist's face. She too was fully engrossed in the story. "Let's just say we did not get away with the ritual of opening the back door and letting Trixie and Reese slip out inconspicuously. The front porch was occupied by, no doubt, Yia Yia and her big fat Greek family. Not saying they were fat, just using the term from the movie to describe the large family."

"Got it. Go on."

"Picture this. There were small kids filling up water balloons, a handful of middle-school-age boys doing tricks on their skateboards, adults clustered in chairs, conversing in lighthearted chatter, and a few teens all sitting in a circle staring at their phones.

"A dozen heads turned my way as I got out of the car. *'Don't mind us. We're only dropping off my daughter's two imaginary friends to their Yia Yia's house,'* I said, and then I winked heavily with added animation to get my point across.

"Then Kenzie rolled down her window, and I panicked, hollering to the crowd, *'Their mama called and said Yia Yia wanted them for a sleepover tonight.'* All I could do was plead with my eyes for the crowd of adults to play along.

"Then, from a chair in the corner of the porch, came a voice, *'Yes, of course,'* and a slight woman popped up and walked toward the railing. *'I'm Yia Yia. I've been expecting . . .'*

"'Trixie and Reese,' I called, both to Yia Yia and into the back of the car as I opened the door. 'C'mon girls, time to get out. Your Yia Yia is excited to see you,' I said, as this sweet old woman played along beautifully and air-hugged Trixie and Reese.

"Whoa, Gabby, that was a really long story. How many minutes do I have left for you to tell me I'm mentally damaging my daughter?"

"Two minutes," reported the pedicurist.

"My client just arrived, so I can't say too much right now, but I will tell you I've observed Kenzie with her imaginary friends for the past nine months, and I believe they have many benefits. Kenzie doesn't watch much TV. With that unstructured time, she can be creative. I'm going to give you a few things to think about and we'll talk later."

Monica moaned, fearing Gabby would mirror Janice's opinion.

"Don't be alarmed by this," Gabby stated in her soothing therapist voice. "Sometimes children invent imaginary friends to cope with a traumatic experience. Pretend friends can be a source of comfort; it does not mean the child is troubled."

"Cade," Monica said softly, trying to swallow the anguish percolating in her chest. Of course, Kenzie was using Trixie and Reese to cope with losing her baby brother. Kenzie had constantly been kissing Monica's pregnant belly, coming up with crazy baby names like Bubba, Gilly, and Rocket. She was convinced that Cade was going to sleep in her bed. She was excited to suck him his bottles in da midl a night and change his stink pant. Kenzie had picked outfits for Cade, drew pictures, and taped them to the wall of the nursery.

"Poor thing is still grieving. I damaged Kenzie. She saw me crying all the time. She's jealous of the attention Cade's death took away from her. To her, my pregnancy and the baby were imaginary. Kenzie never saw him."

"Stop berating yourself, Monica. Seriously." Gabby sighed. "I have to go. Bert is here. Come over later and we'll talk. Your grieving is normal and healthy, and so is Kenzie's. I would have spoken up if I were worried. An imaginary friend is a unique and magical expression of Kenzie's imagination. Embrace it; have fun with it if it feels right to you. However," Gabby's voice rose, "you need to know when to lay down the law. Dex eating cold Pronto Pups is his choice. I do feel ordering two ice cream sundaes and throwing them in the trash is taking it too far. Rather, ask for two extra spoons and tell Kenzie that she has to share her ice cream with Trixie and Reese. You need to say no sometimes, a firm no.

"When it's convenient, setting a place at the dinner table and pulling into random driveways to pick up and drop off are great family memories you will laugh about years down the road," assured Gabby.

Monica moaned. "I know, yet Janice is blaming Kenzie's disappearing act solely on her imaginary friends, specifically blaming me for encouraging them."

"Playing the blame game won't change the past. I'm so sorry, Monica, but I must hang up. Come over later today if you can. In the meantime, stop worrying. Kenzie is a well-adjusted, bright girl, and you're a wonderful mother. The fact that you care this much confirms it. Got it?"

"Got it," Monica mumbled despairingly.

The pedicurist eyed her with a raised brow.

Watch it. Your tip is on the line. After her pedicure, Monica didn't know what to do with herself. She was determined to let Janice eat her words, so she needed to find something to occupy another couple of hours. It was four o'clock, so she pondered a glass of wine on the patio at Mermaid Bar & Grill, watching the boats motor by in the channel but wondered if she should be downing wine if she could possibly be pregnant.

Pregnant. A tingling sensation ran through her body. No wonder she was so emotional. She ducked into the C-store for a pregnancy test and was about to enter the dingy unisex bathroom then had a better idea.

She was seated at a two top on the deck, the empty chair piled high with her shopping bags. "A glass of Riesling and an order of Seared Ahi Tuna please. Oh wait, mercury-tainted, raw fish probably isn't the best choice since there's a chance . . . um, *Bruschette Funghi* please."

The server cocked her head to the side. "Riesling or just the water?"

Monica sighed. "Iced tea, please."

An hour, three glasses of iced tea, an overindulgence of *bruschette* later, Monica paid her bill, ducked into the bathroom with a full bladder, and locked the stall door. She opened the box and held the stick in her hand for a minute, realizing the small piece of plastic would reveal her future.

Her heart fluttered in anticipation at the thought of another baby. Her stomach also knotted at the enormity of it.

She flushed, wrapped the stick in toilet paper, and set it on the bathroom counter while she washed her hands. She was holding her phone, watching the time when it rang.

"Hey, Dex, what's up?"

"I just got home from work, and my mom said you've been out but didn't know where, so I was just checking in. Is everything okay?"

Monica giggled. "Yes, Dex, everything is okay. Your mom offered to watch the kids while I got out for a bit is all."

"She said you've been gone all day. Why didn't you call me? We could have had lunch."

Monica smiled. Dex was so predictable, and that was exactly why she didn't call him. Strolling the streets solo was refreshing. "Oh, ya know, I was shopping, got my toes done. I didn't take time out for lunch."

"Are you on your way home? I'll start dinner."

"That would be great. I'll be forty minutes."

Monica could hear Kenzie and Beck screaming in the background but couldn't tell if it was screams of laughter or if someone was hurt or upset.

"Where are you, Mon? It sounds all echoey."

"Er, um, do you really want to know?"

Dex's voice hesitated for a beat. "You're not about ready to board a plane, are you?"

"Ha! Had I thought of it earlier . . ." she teased.

It suddenly got quiet, and Monica knew Dex had moved away from the kids, probably into their bedroom. She could see his face, half amused, half fearful of where she was and what she was up to.

"Seriously, Mon, you took off all day to be alone, and now you're acting all sketchy. What's going on?"

She caught a glimpse of her guilty grin in the mirror. "Listen to yourself! This only proves I need to leave the house and my family more often. I'm in Saugatuck, specifically the bathroom at Mermaid. I've got a pregnancy test wrapped in toilet paper, waiting to be exposed."

"I'm not even going to ask what prompted you to take a test in the public bathroom of a restaurant. I thought you weren't supposed to get your, your um, your . . ."

"Jeez, Dexter, say the word, *period*," she emphasized. He'd never been comfortable talking about such issues.

"Ya, that, I thought you said you weren't supposed to get it until tomorrow. Isn't it too soon to take a test?"

"Probably, no, I don't know, they say as soon as you miss your period, so what does a few hours matter?"

"So, are you going to look?"

Monica took a deep breath. Did she really want to find out in a public restroom and give Dex the news over the phone? She grabbed the bundled-up stick and tucked it in the side pocket of her purse.

"I'll bring it home and we'll look together."

~*~

Dex was hovering over the grill while Janice sat at the table next to him, babbling away. Kenzie and Beck were playing with a bucket of scattered toys in the grass side by side but in their own little worlds.

They hadn't heard her walk up, so she took advantage of the opportunity to hang back and eavesdrop since it was clear from Janice's mannerisms that she was ranting about something.

"It's strange, Dexter. Look at her." Janice waved her hand toward Kenzie, who was obviously entertaining Trixie and Reese: pulling a stethoscope out of her doctor's bag and pretending to hold it on an imaginary child's chest.

"Kenzie should have a friend she can see and touch, someone that talks back to her."

"She *can* see them, Mom, and they do talk back to her."

Monica could hear Kenzie demanding that Reese hold still as she broke a twig off the tree and wrapped a blood pressure cuff on an imaginary arm.

"Real little girls, Dexter," Janice hissed, "at the very least, a doll. Maybe you should get her a dog."

Dex shoved his hands in the pockets of his shorts with agitation. "I've read that kids with imaginary friends have above average intelligence. Besides, she turns four next month, not fourteen. It's harmless."

"I'm going to call my friend Sally. Do you remember Sally?" Janice didn't wait for Dex to answer. "She has a five-year-old granddaughter. I'll arrange a playdate. This"—Janice waived her hand towards Kenzie again—"can't go on any longer. She'll be teased in school, she won't have friends, and people will think she talks to spirits or something. You *know* how people talk."

Monica was furious. How dare she speak about Kenzie like that?

"Mom, you're making a bigger deal out of it than it is."

"Good grief, Dexter, she wandered away from the house in the middle of the night. She could have been hit by a car or abducted, all because Monica Dear"—she sneered—"glamorizes Kenzie's imaginary world and has you sucked in as well."

Somehow, Monica squelched the undeniably fierce urge to pounce on Janice and claw her eyes out. Instead, she restrained herself, patiently waiting for Dex to put his mother in her place. His face twisted in anger, and he opened his mouth to speak, but then he looked toward his kids, Beck smashing the heads of two super hero figures together and Kenzie talking into space, instructing her friends to stick out their tongues so she could look at their throats while she poked at the air with a stick.

Dex turned his back on all of them and opened the grill.

Monica had a side view of his defeated face. If he didn't stand up for their children, for her, she would, and it wouldn't be pretty. One, two, three, Monica ticked off the seconds, waiting for Dex to retort. His jaw clenched, he flipped the pineapple slices hastily, and rotated the asparagus across the grill with force. Monica cheered him on. There you go, buddy, get mad and stick up for us.

He closed the grill and checked his watch. "Salmon is ready. Mon should be home any minute."

Monica stood there, deflated. He wasn't going to stand up to his mother. He wouldn't defend his sweet, creative, imaginative daughter or his wife. Last she knew they were trying to open-mindedly parent their child in a loving and supportive environment, an atmosphere they'd both been on board with since Kenzie befriended Trixie and Reese.

Monica quietly retreated inside and pulled the pregnancy test from her purse. After a quick glance, she stomped on the foot pedal of the trash can to deposit the toilet paper wrapping. This time she made her entrance well-known. She slid past Dex and tossed the pink stick on the table in front of Janice, causing her to jump as it slid to a halt next to her fork.

"Well, it's a damned good thing the test is negative because I certainly suck as a mother."

CHAPTER 27

Power isn't controlling people or situations.
Power is how you react to people and situations.

Carmen

Carmen, Penelope, and Amelia awkwardly settled on the living room sofa for a mandatory meeting, Penelope looking beaten down, Amelia defensive.

"Girls, we have some serious issues to discuss," Carmen opened. "Amelia, I'm sure you're aware that we bumped into Liz tonight and I caught her taking pictures of us."

Irritation registered on Amelia's face as silent tears rolled down Penelope's flaming red cheeks. Carmen's heart ached for Penelope, but Amelia's flippant attitude broke her heart even more.

"Liz has been harassing Penelope."

Silence. Worse, Amelia didn't seem stunned or sorry for her sister.

"I'm confused that neither of you felt you could confide in me. This tormenting has been going on for months, creating havoc around here, and between you two."

Amelia scoffed. "I'm not getting caught up in their drama. It's no secret they all hate each other, Mom."

Carmen pressed her palms together and held them at her lips in attempts to slow herself down and prepare her delivery. "That doesn't give Liz the right to torment Penelope."

Penelope kept her head down and picked at her fingernails while Amelia shrugged like she could care less, confirming where her alliance stood.

"The way Liz has been treating your sister doesn't bother you, Amelia?"

"I have no control over what Liz and her friends do," Amelia stated curtly. "I try and stay out of it."

"Hardly," scoffed Penelope.

Amelia glared at her sister. "As if it's my fault they don't like you. I can't control what people say about you, Penelope." Her voice rose. "Do you expect me to lose all my friends just because you have?"

"All you care about is your reputation. That, and trying to be Miss Popularity amongst a tribe of backstabbing bitches. Your friends are all self-entitled snots. Don't think for a second they won't throw you under the bus when given the chance."

"Ha! I won't give them a valid reason!" retorted Amelia.

Carmen's innards felt like a snake had coiled around them and squeezed. "Amelia, you've been aware that Liz has been mistreating Penelope for months?"

"Of course she has!" Penelope interrupted. "She's a sell-out that will do anything to avoid losing her friends."

Amelia stood up and put her hands on her hips. "I've protected you by keeping my mouth shut. You can twist it any way you like, but I've been doing you a favor by remaining friends with Piper. And for the record, I do stick up for you when I'm around Liz. If I didn't, you'd be in a shitload of trouble."

"Shut up, Amelia!" Penelope spat.

"Watch your language!" Carmen intervened, ordering her daughters to calm down. "What kind of trouble? What are you talking about, Amelia?"

The sisters glared at each other, lips pressed firmly together.

"Penelope, what is she talking about? What are you keeping from me?"

Penelope sank into the couch and buried her head in her hands and cried. Carmen couldn't help but have a flash back to a few weeks ago when Victor caught her and Landon. Here they were again, new day, different saga, more tears.

Carmen moved next to Penelope on the couch and pulled her close, trying to soothe her. Penelope winced when Carmen squeezed her shoulder, her fingers slipping under Penelope's cap sleeve, revealing yet another fresh cut, still sticky with blood.

"Jesus help me," Carmen cried out knowing Penelope did this the second they got home from running into Liz. "Cutting is how you choose to deal with Liz?"

Amelia stifled a sob and bit her quivering lip as Penelope pulled her sleeve over the cut and covered her face with a throw pillow. Carmen needed Victor, here, parenting alongside her.

"Please trust me, Sweet P," Carmen pleaded, at a loss for any other words.

"There are topless pictures of me," she blurted out through gulps of tears.

Carmen was confused. "Topless pictures? What exactly do you mean?" she asked, tugging the pillow free from Penelope's grasp so she could see her face.

"It was a joke. Liz, Leila, and I were at Leila's house and wanted to go in the hot tub. Liz and I didn't have our swimsuits, so we decided to go in our underwear and bras. Once in the hot tub, we ditched our bras.

"We took some selfies. They didn't show anything, just our heads. It was no big deal. Liz sent those pictures to Justin and Mack and told them we were naked."

Penelope took a deep breath and let out a louder wail. "Justin and Mack kept texting Liz back, asking for boob shots."

Carmen, stunned, closed her eyes, knowing where this was going, and wondered how her daughter could be so senseless. How many times had they had conversations about the dangers of snapping inappropriate pictures or texting and posting questionable things? She loathed this aspect of social media and would argue to her grave that it was abolishing our youth.

"Then we were screwing around, dancing to music, flashing the camera. Liz took some video and some pics. I know it was stupid, Mom. It was a long time ago. We were dumb little freshman."

"So"—Carmen exhaled her anguish—"you girls sent topless pictures to Justin and Mack and then—"

"No! Liz swore she deleted all the topless pictures we took, way back when it happened. When Liz and Leila came over after my surgery, she lied to me, made up the story that Justin West had snagged her phone at a party. She claimed he was looking through her pictures and found one of me posing topless, one that she must have forgotten to delete."

Carmen cringed.

"She told me he texted it to himself without her knowing at the time."

"So why is Liz harassing *you* over this?"

"Duh, Mom, Justin's dad is my water polo coach. If Coach West saw the picture, I'd be kicked off the team for sexting topless photos! It would be all over the district, all over the news."

"But YOU didn't text it!" Carmen screamed, feeling herself coming undone. She knew it didn't matter.

Penelope dug her fingernails into her thighs, leaving marks. "I was so pissed about what I thought happened that . . . ugh . . . Mom, you wouldn't understand. There are so many layers to it."

"So peel the layers for me, please."

Carmen tilted her head in Amelia's direction, where she sat on the edge of the chair, looking ready to bolt. "Have you known about all of this?"

Amelia shrugged.

"Damn it, Amelia," Carmen hollered. "Answer me honestly."

Amelia's head fell. "A little."

Carmen knew that was a stretch, a pathetic answer for a big fat yes, but anyway . . . She rubbed her palms up and down her thighs, trying to keep her cool. "I'm so confused, Penelope. Liz has lied about you, turned your friends against you, forced you into quitting water polo. How does someone get so much power over you?"

Penelope grunted, ran her hands through her hair, and tugged it. "Ugh, Mom! You're going to think I'm the worst person in the world if I tell you what I did."

"Never, Penelope. I may not always like what you do, but I love you unconditionally, forever. Quite honestly, I don't think anything can phase me at this point."

Carmen waited patiently while gently rubbing Penelope's back. She wished she could take all the sadness and hurt away from her, protect her from any pain.

"I was so mad at Liz for sending the picture to Justin."

"Hold up." Carmen interrupted, raising her hand. "I thought Justin sent it to himself without Liz knowing?"

"It was all a lie, no pictures were ever sent, but I didn't know that for a few days. At the time, I thought she purposely sent a picture to Justin and covered herself by telling me he *found* it on her phone. None of that happened, but that's Liz. She was always fabricating stories and lies and doing stuff like that, so I didn't know what to believe. You know she was always trying to compete with me, throwing shade at me any chance she could and trying to turn people against me even though we were"—Penelope made quotations with her fingers—"best friends."

Carmen had known, but she was clueless as to how deceitful Liz was. She felt horrible as she'd remembered countless times trying to teach Penelope to ignore and not respond to the berating: *Let it go* and *keep the peace. Liz is just insecure.* She wanted her daughters to have the friendships she'd always denied herself.

Penelope wiped her eyes. "I remembered that Liz had texted me those pictures as we took them that night, so I scrolled back and found they were still on my phone. I wanted to get back at her." Penelope bit her lip. "I actually *did* text a topless shot of *her* to Justin when I knew he was hanging out with a bunch of people, including Kyra, his girlfriend. Liz has been in love with Justin forever. Liz hates Kyra."

Penelope bit her trembling lip.

"Along with the picture, I texted something like*, to Justin, the tit picture you requested—love Liz*, with a bunch of red heart and kissy

298

emojis. Kyra saw it and went ballistic on Justin, claiming he was cheating on her with Liz."

Carmen moaned, but patiently listened.

"Later that night, when Liz showed up at the party, clueless to what I'd done, Kyra went off on Liz in front of everyone. A bunch of people found out about it, so not only does that give everyone more reason to hate me, because obviously it was sent from my phone and I lied saying Liz was with me when I sent it, but Liz threatened to tell Coach West, and the principal, parents . . . you name it."

Carmen shook her head, trying to process it all. "But obviously she hasn't . . ."

Penelope shook her head.

"Why not?"

"Landon."

The name alone made Carmen's skin crawl. "What about Landon?"

"Just . . . stuff that happened with Landon."

Every millimeter of Carmen's body was on hyper alert. *What had that little punk done?* "Penelope, we've come this far. I'm pretty sure I can handle anything you throw at me, so let's not resort back to *stuff*."

A few beats went by and Carmen braced herself. It was as if her daughters were two different people, leading different lives when they left the house. Was this normal? Did every parent see their children through naïve goggles? Goggles with a prescription fit with a fabricated image, sprinkled with fairy dust, of the person you thought you raised them to be?

Hadn't it become the norm for parents to cram the internet with pictures and excessive praise of their children being formed and poured like plaster creatures into the mold they'd created for them? Oops, there's a crack in the plaster, a corner has broken off and crumbled. They're human.

"Stuff that happened to Liz, not me."

"Penelope. Honesty. Please."

Penelope flung her hand towards Amelia. "Not with her around."

"Amelia, give us some privacy, please." Carmen tilted her head towards the stairs. "I'll come up to your room when I'm done talking with Penelope."

Clutching her phone tightly, Amelia let out a huff as she stood.

"Leave the phone here, please."

"What? No, Mom!"

"Excuse me?"

"I mean, why?" Amelia attempted to soften her tone. "What did I do?"

"Because I'm your mother and I asked you to. Because it's my phone on loan to you. Because it's a privilege, not a right for you to use. Because I'll take it away without giving it a second thought. Because cell phones and teenagers suck!"

Amelia tossed it on the coffee table with a clunk and stomped upstairs, slamming her door.

Really? Her too?

Penelope's tears had subsided, an occasional hiccup escaped.

"I gave you my word, Penelope. You're safe telling me." She wrapped her fingers around Penelope's sweaty hand, but Penelope wiggled free.

"No offense, but that's weird, Mom."

Carmen let out a snort. "Ya, it kinda was, and your hands are sticky."

Penelope acted offended, but Carmen saw her grin. "Mom!"

"Just saying."

"So, Liz and Landon hooked up once at a party," Penelope blurted.

"Hooked up?"

"Duh, Mom, had sex."

"Yes. Only wanted to be clear."

"Liz got pregnant."

Penelope propped her elbows on her thighs and hung her head in her hands to avoid Carmen's shock as her mouth fell to the floor.

"Long story short, she decided to have an abortion. I swear I had nothing to do with her decision, but I agreed to drive her there, and she actually spent two nights here after she had it done."

Silence hung in the air as Carmen processed what she had just learned. "Um, okay," Carmen spoke coolly.

"Landon had no idea. Liz never told him she got pregnant. When things got ugly between us, I threatened that I would spill her secret if she ever told Coach West about me sending the pics of her to Justin."

Basic blackmail. How does this stuff happen under a parent's nose? Carmen and Victor were oblivious to the fact that Liz had occupied Penelope's bed while recovering from an abortion. Countless times the girls binge-watched Netflix on a gloomy winter weekend, polishing off an entire bag of sour cream and onion potato chips and a super-size box of Swedish fish. It was their thing. Now, to learn on one of those occasions Liz had been recuperating from an abortion . . .

"As if I didn't suck enough, I went and told Landon everything. That's how we started talking, and I don't know, our relationship just sort of evolved. He was one of the few people that could see Liz for who she really was. She's so malicious, yet somehow I fell prey and committed the crimes."

"Whoa." Carmen exhaled as she processed the enormity of information.

Penelope let her head fall into her mother's chest. "I'm so sorry, Mom. Liz is a horrible, rotten person, but I stooped to the same level and am no better than she is."

~*~

The birds were chirping when Carmen opened her eyes. She rolled over and observed Victor while he slept. He had snuck between the sheets in the middle of the night, his hands rousing her as they slid underneath her silk camisole.

Without greeting, he had undressed her and sealed her mouth with his before she could protest. Carmen found herself trapped somewhere in the gray area of rage and relief at his touch, pulled between desire and aversion.

She started to push him away, words filled with ferocity clawing at the back of her throat. Where had he been when she needed him by her side? Why did her calls always go straight to voicemail? Who was more important in Las Vegas than his family?

Sensing her rebuff, his hands trailed down past her navel and found the very spot that made her melt. She succumbed to the yearning that pulsed through her veins and traveled to her limbs. He had that familiar glint in his eye, the one that made Carmen feel like she was the most desirable thing he'd ever laid eyes on.

Their hunger for each other was apparent in the urgency of their lovemaking, as if they were fulfilling a primal need, conflicting emotions aside. All the drama of the day, of the past several months, had drained her emotionally. She desperately sought to be wrapped in her husband's arms, to feel his skin on hers, the weight of him on top of her.

The release helped her sleep like a rock, six solid hours. She rolled over with hopes at logging another, but as soon as her eyes landed on Victor, she knew her slumber was squashed.

Her mind raced while she watched him sleep peacefully, like he hadn't a care in the world while she felt like hers was imploding. The release she had felt while he'd held her in his arms only hours ago, evaporated as she slept.

He opened his eyes and caught her staring at him. "Good morning, sunshine."

She forced a smile. Makeup sex worked best *after* you'd had a chance to duke it out. "I want us to wake up like this every day, Victor."

He closed his eyes, rested his arm over his face, and moaned. Obviously, her tone didn't match her words. It was lackluster and accusatory, no hint of romance.

"When's the last time we showered together?"

His arm slid off, and he turned on his side to face her. His eyes instinctively trailed down to her chest. She hadn't bothered to put her pajamas back on last night, so she was gracing him with a shot of cleavage.

He shook his head. "Why do I get the feeling there's only a wrong answer to this question?"

"We used to shower together almost every morning. We'd discuss our day, figure out how we'd manage the kids' schedules, even knock out a quickie from time to time."

Victor's eyebrows shot up eagerly. "I could really use a shower."

Carmen scowled. "We don't have enough hot water for everything we need to discuss."

Victor rubbed his eyes. "I'm so sorry. I know. You've been running the circus solo. I'll scale back the lessons to—"

"Three days a week," Carmen finished for him. "So you've said."

Their eyes locked for several beats, and Carmen knew Victor was hiding something. She was so spent that she hadn't the energy to dispute whatever it was. Something in the way he looked at her assured her she was still the center of his universe, and she clung to it, wishful thinking or not.

On impulse, she wrapped her arms around him and buried her head in the warmth of his chest and asked him to hold her as she spewed out the complicated mess Penelope had gotten herself into.

"Penelope cried in my arms and promised me she would stop cutting, but I could feel the emptiness in her words. Cutting has been her way of punishing herself."

Victor pulled her close and kissed her forehead and told her they would figure it out. Even though she knew he was more clueless than she was, she absorbed his words with certainty. They would figure it out. They always had, he assured.

Their morning conversation put Carmen behind schedule. She'd have to walk straight into her managerial meeting without a chance to review her notes. She slung Tiffany over her shoulder and squeezed Victor tight. "I'm kind of sad I made dinner plans with Gabby and Monica tonight. We could use a date night."

She smoothed his trim fit Jared Lang shirt across his chest. He looked so sexy in it, which she guessed was why he wore it today. Victor knew she loved it on him. He was sucking up to her, and she greedily accepted it.

"Since I'm a woman of my word, I don't want to bail on my new friends." She smiled a bit, embarrassed. "Why don't you take the girls out tonight? They could use some alone time with you."

Victor fidgeted uncomfortably. "Uh . . ." He hesitated, raked a hand through his hair, and gripped his skull. "I've got a bit of a crisis. Derek is sick, fever of 102. I'm sorry, but I need to fly out this afternoon and cover his lessons, but only for two, three days at the most."

Carmen pushed away from him. "Damn it, Victor, no! A golf lesson is not a crisis. We are in the middle of a crisis in our very own home," she shouted. "What's going on? Who or what is there that is worth neglecting your family?"

Victor turned his back on Carmen and walked to the window. He looked out over the sleepy lake in a trance.

Holy shit, he's got another woman. A hollow, sinking feeling washed over her, and she wondered if this was how Gabby felt when she found out about Greg's affair? She was paralyzed, standing by the door, fearing what came next. Was she going to hold the door for him while he left for Vegas and to another woman?

He spoke to the window. "Carmen"—he paused for what felt like an eternity but was only a few seconds—"I've gambled away over three hundred thousand dollars."

CHAPTER 28

You are free to choose your actions.
You are not free from the consequences of your actions.

Gabriella

When Holly walked into the coffee shop, Gabby's first instinct was to look the other way. It was brutal to look at the bulging belly that held her husband's child, her children's half-sister. Holly wasn't specific about why she wanted to meet, but Gabby figured it was the pressure she was putting on Greg to be honest with the kids. Quite frankly, Gabby wanted to read her body language.

Greg hadn't spoken a word about Gabby's nasty phone call to Holly nor about their previous meeting by the dam. Either Holly hadn't mentioned the instances to him because she truly did use him and was detaching herself, or they had discussed both instances and Gabby was being played. Gabby only knew one thing for certain: she didn't trust either one of them. For all she knew, they could be involved in a heated tryst, playing Gabby for a fool.

The extent to Greg's involvement beleaguered her every thought. How often did they speak? Did Greg check in with Holly frequently to see how she was feeling? Was he still accompanying her to doctor visits? Did Holly consult him when shopping for a car seat or crib? By not allowing Greg to live at home, was Gabby giving him free rein to rendezvous?

Holly slid into the chair opposite Gabby with ease. She was thirty-five weeks pregnant and still walked gracefully in heels, no waddling with the trademark, painstaking pregnancy expression, so commonly glued to women's faces.

Pregnancy suited her. Her skin glowed, and every curve was accented in a fitted Kelly green-and-white checkered sleeveless dress. Gabby wasn't insecure, never wasted time sizing other women up or comparing herself to them. Instead, she admired the differences between the long and lean, petite, curvaceous, flat-chested, well-endowed, strong, and soft shapes of women.

Had she passed Holly on the sidewalk, she would have complimented her beautifully bulging belly. It had always bothered Gabby when women scrutinized each other when they were only jealous, criticizing the very things in other women they so desperately sought after and couldn't achieve.

How disconcerting it felt when the woman you'd normally admire was sleeping with your husband. An impending threat to her marriage, her family, left Gabby teetering on the edge of detestation.

"I love your romper," Holly complimented Gabby as a longtime friend would have.

"I was admiring your dress as well," Gabby said with forced politeness.

Holly's face brightened. "We have similar taste. In fashion," she quickly added.

And Greg, Gabby thought, trying and failing to stifle a sneer. "I bought this after I found out about you. Greg's side of the closet was empty, so I decided to go on a shopping spree out of spite." Gabby touched the smooth fabric. It was a bright cobalt-blue-and-coral colored print from Lilly Pulitzer. "I usually don't wear such loud prints, but I wasn't thinking rationally the day I bought it."

"Well, it's stunning on you."

"Here it is August, and I only cut the tags off this morning. I haven't worn a fraction of the clothes I splurged on. I don't go out much, so I don't see the point in getting dressed up."

"When you look good, you feel good," Holly stated frankly.

They looked to one another for a beat before the barista called out Holly's name and delivered her decaf hazelnut latte to their table.

Gabby wrapped her hands around her mug. She didn't want to sit here and make pleasantries with this woman. "Can I ask you something?"

"Yes, of course, anything." Holly took a sip of her coffee, and Gabby noticed a solid silver band on her right ring finger. She wondered what it symbolized, who it was from, and twisted the anniversary band she'd slipped on before coming today for reasons she wasn't quite sure. To prove Greg was hers until she decided otherwise?

"Can you tell me, with honesty, your feelings for Greg, now that time has passed, and you've been carrying his child? After disclosing your reason for pursuing the affair, I imagine your feelings have changed toward him."

Holly nodded thoughtfully and examined the heart the barista had formed with the light froth on the surface of her coffee. Her dark hair was pulled tight and smooth away from her face. A large thick bun formed at the base of her neck. She possessed a graceful beauty that Gabby found herself both admiring and loathing.

"Greg's not a horrible man, Gabby. He was lured into a sticky trap, a trap I set, a garish move I'm not proud of, but what's done is done and . . ."

Holly stopped mid-sentence, and Gabby waited for her to admit she had fallen in love with Greg. Gabby closed her eyes, preparing herself for the blow. She had always been *taught* that the truth will set you free. She'd always *known* that often the truth was harder to accept than lies. If Holly had a change of heart towards Greg, would he still be pleading to save their marriage?

"I felt a strong connection to Greg the minute I met him. That's why I pursued him so heavily. Gabby, this is hard for me to admit, because this whole situation creates an image of a person I'm truly not, or rather, a weak person portraying a less-than-stellar representation of my true self. Regardless, it's a dark side in myself I never knew existed."

Gabby nodded, wanting to believe Holly, but she was obviously a woman who went after what she wanted. The question was whether she was sincere, playing a sympathy card. Her words described a brazen side of herself most people wouldn't admit possessing.

"I care for Greg. I'm deeply fond of him. A deep admiration if you will. He's given me such a gift, the"—Holly paused—"the child I've dreamed about for years," she said, instinctively touching her belly.

An engulfing nausea washed over Gabby, hardly new at this point, although feeling as treacherous as it had when Gabby first laid eyes on the ultrasound picture. Gabby didn't think she'd ever be immune to the tsunami of feelings it washed up, only hoped someday they would fade.

"I'm dealing with an incredible amount of guilt. I don't regret this child," Holly said, now patting her belly, making Gabby wonder how often Greg placed his hands on her belly to feel his little girl move, "not at all, but I regret the circumstances, and"—Holly paused again, her face remorseful—"I've been really struggling with accepting what I've done to you and your family, the reality and weight of it all."

Holly cradled her mug between her hands and looked at Gabby with sad eyes.

"I can't sleep. I can't focus at work. My appetite is gone, well, except for green olives." She snickered. "You'll be happy to know that I've not only stolen your joy, but much of mine has been squelched as well.

"I'm not sure how that makes you feel. Possibly, you're pleased that I'm in a way suffering for what I've done. Possibly, you think my suffering is petty compared to the suffering you're going through. At least I'm gaining something whereas you're"—Holly's head dropped—"you've lost trust, possibly your dignity, and countless other aspects of your marriage," she said barely above a whisper.

Gabby wouldn't be human if she didn't feel slightly liberated, but she didn't fully trust Holly's admission. She'd been in the counseling business long enough to know that sometimes those seeking therapy are merely on a quest to validate their immoralities. The best narcissists can fool therapists, even law enforcement. It was prudent Gabby not be naïve.

Was Holly scheming, playing the right cards to ensure Gabby sought divorce?

"I apologize for what I've done to you and your family, Gabby. I wish I could somehow make it right with you."

Gabby bit the inside of her cheek. "You know, Holly, sometimes I wish I had never found out about the affair. Possibly, it would be better to live in a lie that dictated our decisions, so we didn't have to turn a blind eye, making it easier to protect our loved ones."

Holly sat up in her chair and traced her finger around the rim of her mug. "I considered using a sperm donor . . . in the traditional way"—Holly smirked—"but it felt so *laboratory* if that makes sense. I never thought I would get tangled up in a mess to this degree, hurting so many people.

"I've done a lot of thinking about the transfer situation." Holly drummed her fingers on the table nervously. "I've decided to stay in the area. My employer is offering me incentives and flexibility I can't refuse. I've got to consider the baby first. It's such a wonderful place to raise a child. You know that." Holly touched Gabby's forearm with a smile.

Gabby flinched, her recoil brazenly displayed. This woman had seduced a married man to conceive a child, covered up the truth about the father, and has now been rewarded with a raise and extra perks from her employer. Ridiculous.

Holly sensed her disdain. "No worries, I've found a perfect subdivision near the lakeshore, so it's not like we'll be bumping into each other at the local boutiques.

"What I'm getting at is"—Holly paused, glancing at the decadent goodies in the chocolate case—"I really think the fewer people that know about this child the better. We could save everyone from further anguish and hurt."

Obviously, Greg had asked Holly to meet with Gabby to beg for her silence. Why should she protect either of them from their wrongdoing? Gabby was only considering keeping silent about the baby for the sake of her children, the pain it would cause them. She feared they would disown their father, hunt Holly down.

The urge to come clean and reveal the truth was getting stronger by the minute, yet Gabby didn't want the impulse to come from a spiteful place.

"Remaining in the area also means constant contact with Greg," Gabby pointed out.

"That's unavoidable; however, our relationship would be strictly professional."

Gabby noted the hint of defensiveness in Holly's tone. "Of course, all business, you'd never discuss the child you share. However, should you somehow need him to be a father figure, he'd be in the vicinity?"

"No!" Holly was shaken. She sat upright and pushed her mug away.

"Holly, one thing I know is people. I'm not saying I can predict future behaviors. I do, however, have a keen sense of reality and how feelings continuously evolve. We don't always act on our feelings as we foresee we will."

Holly placed her palms firmly on the table, clearly flustered and appalled by Gabby's words. She opened her mouth to speak, sighed, and closed it again.

A few silent beats passed between them until the bells hanging on the coffee shop door jingled and clanked against the glass. A young couple walked in, an infant strapped to his mommy's chest, his little head bobbing as she walked, eyes wide with curiosity.

Gabby could still envision her and Greg when Stella and Lottie were first born, pushing an oversized double stroller everywhere they went, occasionally wearing the babies strapped to their bodies.

Had anyone told her she would go on to have another set of twins and years down the road be in the predicament she was in, she might have walked out on Greg right then. Or not? Had the years between still been good? Hadn't she at least been given over twenty-three, not perfect, but fulfilling years and four healthy children to be grateful for?

Yes, she had, and she wasn't about to hand all that over to this woman on a silver platter. Gabby could suddenly see the writing on the wall. Holly's moral self was willing her to walk away. However, she was now wrestling with her deep *admiration* for Greg and her maternal instincts to latch on to the father of her child.

If Gabby divorced Greg, would Holly slither in and snatch up her family?

"Holly, despite whatever Greg is portraying to you, he is pleading with me to save our marriage," Gabby threw out, solely to read her reaction.

Holly's features hardened. Clearly, she was threatened. Gabby's head swirled. Were all three of them playing mind games with each other?

~*~

Gabby slid into her chair at Whiskey Warehouse out of breath. "Sorry I'm late. It's been . . . a day," she said, flinging her hand in the air, "and I'm parked three blocks away."

"I'd say it's been a day." Monica grabbed her hand. "What is this?"

Monica's and Carmen's eyes drilled into her. She pulled her hand back as the server approached, asking for a drink order.

"A shot of Buffalo Trace White Dog, please."

"Oh, jeez, this is too much." Monica cringed. "I suppose I'll have the same."

"I'm new to the friendship ring," Carmen confessed to the young metro-sexual-looking server. "Whisky bar or not, I'm feeling peer pressure."

"No pressure!" said Gabby in an awkward high-pitched voice, teetering on the verge of a breakdown.

"Yes, pressure!" Monica settled. "We'll take a round please."

"And bring a pitcher of Farmhouse Punch as well, please," Gabby said to the server and then turned toward Carmen. "Gin, rum, brandy, curacao, and fruit juices." She waived her hand in the air. "It's light."

The server walked away before he had to listen to any further banter.

"For the record, I never counsel solving your problems with a few drinks. Also, for the record, I don't counsel friends. Only give massive amounts of advice."

Carmen eyed them inquisitively. "What's the deal with the whisky?"

"It's Gabby's crisis drink is what it is. But the real question is what the heck is the anniversary band doing on your finger?"

"Ugh, I meant to leave it in the cup holder, but the lack of parking distracted me, and I forgot."

"I'd say. So, you're taking Greg back and you weren't going to tell us?"

The server returned with their shots and poured them each a glass of punch from the pitcher, muttering he'd be back shortly for their order as he backed away.

Gabby held up her shot glass and downed it without waiting for Monica or Carmen.

"Whoa!" Carmen unrolled her silverware and perfectly aligned them next to her plate, stalling for Gabby. "Monica, maybe Gabby isn't ready to talk. We should respect her privacy."

Monica rolled her eyes and scoffed. "Right. Wrong. Talk, Gabby."

Gabby laughed wholeheartedly. "No worries, Carmen. I'd only hoped we'd get through our pitcher before divulging, but Monica here is on a need-to-know basis, the need to know everything."

"Not fair," said Monica.

"Fair and true," Gabby pointed out.

Monica hmphed. "Fine."

Carmen shifted in her seat uncomfortably and slid her hand over her purse. Nothing was off limits with these two.

"Don't flee, Carmen. Despite Monica's hunger for information, I know my life is safe with her, and it won't go anywhere. So, you and Tiffany stay put. She can be miffed about my decision. I can handle her." She chuckled.

Carmen looked shocked. "I hadn't noticed my hand was on my purse. I promise I wasn't going to grab her and run."

"Gabby's right, Carmen. I'm nosy and have strong opinions and won't hesitate to give my two cents when it comes to my friends' welfare, but my mouth is a vault, I promise. Anything you do or say, legal or illegal, will go no further, and I don't judge . . . most of the time."

"It's true. I fully trust Monica."

"Thanks, Gabby."

"You're welcome."

Gabby took another long sip of her drink, feeling herself relax in the company of her friends. It had been a long and emotional day, and she was tired.

"Waaaaiting," Monica said in her singsong voice as she tapped the back of her wedding band on her glass.

The server approached their table cautiously. "Are you ladies ready to order?"

"No!" Monica stated rather curtly, but then giggled.

"Another pitcher of punch, please," Carmen said as she drained the rest in their glasses. The server looked at them with concern; Farmhouse Punch was no froufrou drink. "No worries, we'll call an Uber." He shrugged and left.

"Holly's not being transferred. Instead, she's received a promotion at work and is moving by the lakeshore."

"She's totally going to sink her claws into Greg!" Monica sneered.

"Monica!" Carmen reprimanded.

Gabby held up her hand. "No worries. Valid point."

Carmen squirmed uncomfortably. "She probably wants the kids to know about the baby so she can break up your family."

Gabby shrugged. "She encouraged me to keep silent to avoid further hurt to everyone, but I don't know if that's just a ploy. She could totally be playing me and, boom, somehow the truth slips."

Gabby closed her eyes and pinched the bridge of her nose. "I'm confused. I don't know if I'm ready to give up on my family. The thought of every birthday, holiday, and the numerous ordinary events that pull us all together, whether it be weekly dinners or meeting for monthly college football or basketball games, the thought of being divided . . .

"When one of the kids calls and spontaneously asks Greg and me to drive to Lansing and take them to dinner, I want us to do that together. I don't want them to have to choose between us. If they call sharing exciting news about grades, or a new job, or asking for help or advice, I want us to share that together not separately.

"I wore the anniversary band to meet with Holly today to prove to her Greg was mine until I decided otherwise. Suddenly, it became a reminder of the bond connecting all of us. I want my kids to bring their future spouses and grandchildren to *our* house, not my house for a couple of hours and then Greg and Holl"—she caught herself—"his house."

"There it is," Monica pointed out. "You won't divorce him if there's a chance he and Holly will end up together. All that other garbage, you'd figure it out."

"Monica!" Carmen chastised.

Gabby closed her eyes and exhaled. "It's okay. Monica's partially right. I guess I don't want to look back five, ten, or thirty years from now and regret not at least *trying* to make it work. Our marriage is so much more than just the two of us, and it's multiplying with a grandchild on the way."

"So what are you going to do when Holly decides she wants Greg to be a part of his daughter's life and starts demanding child support and wants to dump the kid off at your house every other weekend?"

"Monica!" Carmen reprimanded again. "Too far."

Gabby shook her head. "No, it's okay. These are the things I need to consider. Maybe use the next year as a trial period."

Monica sneered and Carmen elbowed her.

"Ya, ya, ya, I know what you think I should do, Monica." Gabby smirked.

Monica patted the top of Gabby's arm. "I can't stand to see you hurting is all. I don't mean to come across as insensitive. If there weren't a child involved . . ."

Carmen rested her chin on the palm of her hand and sighed. "Husbands . . . bastards!"

"Time to place your order, ladies?" the server asked with a frightened look.

"Max?" Monica asked, peering closer at his name tag. He nodded. "We really are an easygoing group of women, regardless of what you've witnessed tonight. You only have bad timing."

Max nodded again, but this time his face crept up into a smile. "Typically, all the groups of women loosen up as they drink and bitch about their husbands and children. Night after night, I see it repeatedly. I've learned to tread lightly until halfway through the second drink."

They all roared in agreement.

Monica held up her finger. "In our own defense, we return home better than when we left."

"I hope I'm not bringing up a sensitive subject, Monica, but you're drinking, so I assume no baby yet?" asked Gabby.

Monica sighed with relief and informed them of the scene that unfolded with Janice: that, after throwing the negative pregnancy test on the table and spending days defending Kenzie's imaginary friends, she and Dex had decided not to try for another baby. The timing wasn't right and quite frankly it might never be.

The conversation bounced through dinner from tales of Janice and her relentless Monica Dear pestering, to Penelope's cutting, sexting, and blackmail dilemma, and now Victor's gambling crisis.

Regarding her tattered marriage, Gabby shared her concerns for Stella's future as a young mother, admitted she worried the boys' relationship with Greg would be permanently strained, and was concerned with how Lottie would cope with sharing Stella with a baby. Lottie had called her in tears about an issue with her roommates, and Gabby quickly realized the reality of Lottie being without her twin for the first time in her life was terrifying and lonely.

"We need a vacation to get away from it all for a few days, or weeks," said Monica longingly.

"I could use a mental break from life." Gabby nodded in agreement. "We should plan something this fall, maybe wine-tasting in Traverse City."

Carmen raised one eyebrow and looked at them contemplatively. "I've just booked a flight to North Carolina to stay with my dad for ten days. There's plenty of room at his house, and it's right on the Atlantic: tranquil, quiet, a good place to reflect."

Monica pushed her empty plate out of the way and leaned forward. "Are you asking us to join you?"

"Ya, I guess I am. I mean . . . don't feel obligated." Carmen fidgeted with the centerpiece candle. "I get it if we aren't at the vacation-together level."

"Stop," ordered Gabby. "I'm in. Between Preston and Greg, they can work out a schedule and stay with Stella. I'll have Penelope reschedule my clients. That only leaves me to pack a bag."

"Dex, and I daresay Janice, can do life without me for a week," exclaimed Monica. "When do we leave?"

"Four days. As soon as Victor gets back from Vegas. My flight departs an hour before Victor's flight arrives." Carmen hesitated. "I haven't told him I'm going."

Carmen flagged down Max and ordered the chocolate mousse cake and three spoons while Monica and Gabby pulled out their phones to check availability on Carmen's flight.

"He told me to give him one more chance to go gamble some money back. I gave him an ultimatum. If he left, I would be gone when he got back. Not gone, gone, but somewhere. He left. I was going to grab the girls and go to my dad's for the rest of the summer, but then I stopped and tried to think sensibly." Carmen sighed.

"That's when I decided I needed time away and he needed to be immersed in fatherhood. I booked my ticket to leave the day he comes back so we won't cross paths."

CHAPTER 29

Show respect to people who don't deserve it,
not as a reflection of their character, as a reflection of your
character.

Monica

Monica had been scurrying around the house like a manic since the sun came up. She'd gone to the grocery store, stocking the refrigerator, freezer, and pantry with more food than her family could possibly consume in a week. She was folding her sixth and final load of laundry, stopping to scribble yet one more reminder on the three-page lesson plan she was leaving her substitutes, Dex and Janice.

To say she wasn't a bit anxious about leaving her family for nine days would be a lie, but the truth was, she was far more excited to get away with Carmen and Gabby than consumed with the *what if's*. Dex and Janice would probably ignore her lists, which made her cringe. However, they would be okay, if she didn't know about it.

"Monica Dear, Kenzie must have tied knots in her hair after you brushed it this morning," Janice chided from the living room where Monica had placed her children for a comatose dose of cartoons to keep them occupied for the past hour.

"No, Janice, I've been busy and haven't bothered to brush her hair. Be a dear and do it for me please," Monica hollered from the laundry room and muttered her belligerence under her breath.

"Relax. We'll be fine," Dex whispered in her ear. He had snuck up behind her and rested his chin on her shoulder.

Monica tossed Beck's "Captain America" pajamas on the counter and turned toward Dex. She wrapped her arms around him and kissed the side of his neck, the soft spot that always smelled good and gave her comfort.

"You're home early. We don't have to leave for the airport for two hours."

"I wanted time for this," he said as he squeezed her. "Ten days is a long time to go without touching you."

"You should have warned me. I don't have time to stand around and play kissy face, Dex. I still have to set out the kids' outfits, empty the dishwasher, make more sunscreen. Please don't use store-bought sunscreen on Beck; he'll break out in a rash. I need to put their vitamins in little Dixie cups—they love that—and cut up the watermelon, mango, and carrots so they eat fruit and veggies while I'm gone. Oh, and I promised Kenzie I would play a quick game of hide and go seek before I left, and . . ."

Dex shushed her in his usual manner by placing his finger over her lips. "You don't *have* to do any of that. I've got it covered. Relax. We will be—"

"Fine," they both said together.

"Oh, Dex, thanks for being supportive of this trip. I know it's a long time and you're taking off half days from work, and we never even got around to taking our own family vacation this summer, and here I am flying the coop."

"Stop it! Seriously, Mon, I'm looking forward to the time with the kids. It forces me to step away from the office and play. We'll be having our own vacation. I've got a few things planned. Besides, I'm excited for you. You deserve this time away."

"No matter what I've said in the past"—Monica giggled—"you're an amazing dad and an even better husband." She squeezed his butt and gave him a teasing spanking.

"Whoa, maybe we should sneak to the bedroom so I can help you zip your suitcase?"

"Wow, that's a suggestion I've never heard before. You're the most predictable person I know, Dexter."

"The predictability of always trying to lure my wife into the bedroom is a bad thing?"

Monica shook her head. "No, I suppose not." She looked him in the eye and felt a surge of emotion.

"We've got it good, Dex. It's not perfect. You're slightly flawed and annoy me all the time"—she grinned— "and I annoy you on occasion"—she kissed his neck— "especially when it comes to your mother."

"Ugh, Mon, don't go there right now, please."

"I know. I know. I'm not. I'm just saying with Greg's cheating and Victor's gambling . . . I guess what I'm saying is I realize Janice is who she is, and you react how you react because you're caught in the middle and I get that. But it's petty to dwell on in the big grand scheme of life. Soon she'll be gone, and we'll have to find something new to grumble about." She chuckled.

Dex nuzzled Monica with his nose. "I love you."

"I know, and that makes me love you even more."

~*~

Dex tossed Monica's suitcase in the back of the Explorer, asking if she packed for a month. Here she thought she had packed conservatively since they were welcome to use the washer and dryer.

They had twenty minutes before they had to pick up Carmen and Gabby for their flight out of Grand Rapids. Dex had offered to drop them off so they didn't have to deal with parking.

Dex joined Monica and Kenzie in a game of hide and go seek while Janice cuddled a sleepy Beck, who'd just woken from his nap.

"Seven, nine, four, ten, ready, here I come, or not!" Kenzie shouted.

Wait, what? Monica smiled at the jumbled numbers and words. She would miss her babies incredibly. Kenzie's fourth birthday was two days after she returned, so Monica planned on scouring Pinterest while on the beach, for the perfect, intricate, over-the-top cake . . . that Dex would make.

"Mom," Kenzie scolded with her hands on her hips, "that's a super easy spot hiding."

"Hiding spot," Monica corrected as she sat up and straddled the tree limb she was lying on. Ridiculous! What mom climbs trees to play hide and seek and their daughter condemns her for it? Easy? Easy for whom? To boot, chances were Kenzie would have no appreciation or recollection of these games by the time she was sixteen.

Monica hopped off the limb, scraping away the first four layers of skin from her inner thigh. With a stifled whimper, she continued to help Kenzie search for another ten minutes before finding Dex in the sand toy box with the lid closed over him. He was a sweaty mess with sand stuck to his forehead and an imprint on his cheek where his skin had been pressed against the side of a beach pail.

"Me turn to hide!" announced Kenzie as she jumped up and down.

"Okay, but promise if you hear me or Daddy yell that it's time to leave for the airport you'll come out of hiding. Mommy can't be late."

"Promise," Kenzie squealed. "Mom find me. Dad finds Trixie and Reese," instructed Kenzie before she ran off.

Monica and Dex meandered around the yard together, nonchalantly looking for Kenzie, Trixie, and Reese, but mostly using the time to go over the checklist one last time. Monica couldn't stress how important it was to keep the kids on a schedule, that they needed as much normalcy as possible while she was gone; otherwise, they would act out.

"So, you're saying that if I put them down for a nap at 1:00 instead of 12:45, and only read three books instead of four, or they don't get seven servings of fruits and vegetables from various tongue-twisting veggies such as edamame, arugula, and quinoa, then they are going to be little monsters and have melt-downs?"

"It's a grain."

Dex pinched the bridge of his nose. "What?"

"Quinoa, it's a grain, Dex, not a vegetable. And yes, that's exactly what I'm saying. They're going to really start missing me by day three or four. If you don't stick to their routine, it's only going to make it harder on them, on you."

Dex stopped and spread apart the tall purple fountain grasses while Monica looked under the mini wheelbarrow.

"We're eating frozen pizzas, Stouffer's mac n' cheese, and hot dogs charred over the fire pit. I'm pitching a tent in the yard to sleep in, and we are going to stay up late enough to gaze at the stars and make scary faces with flashlights held under our chins. They will be having so much fun they won't even have time to think about you, so why don't you try to stop worrying and do the same."

Monica checked her watch. "Ugh, we need to leave in two minutes, where is she?"

"Kenzie," Dex yelled, "wherever you are, come out and say good-bye. I have to take Mommy to the airport."

"Trixie, Reese, come out from hiding," Monica hollered. She saw Janice's left eyebrow peak as she peered down at Dex from the deck above at the mention of Trixie and Reese. Beck lifted his head from Janice's chest and looked around, no doubt trying to find Trixie and Reese.

"Go say your good-byes to Beck while I find her," Dex offered while continuously calling out Kenzie's name, his eyes scouring the yard.

Monica held Beck tight, kissing and burying her nose in his soft and squishy flesh. His pudgy little arms, a light golden brown claiming a summer spent on the water, were wrapped around her neck. She traced her finger around the light-colored skin in the crease of his wrist and elbow. It looked like he was wearing white rubber bands.

"Call or text me anytime, Janice. I'll Facetime the kids every morning around eight o'clock," Monica said as they walked around the house to the driveway where she found Dex looking exasperated.

"I can't find her anywhere."

Dex looked concerned, which sent a wave of panic through Monica.

Janice scoffed. "She probably ran off with that Trixie and Reese again."

"Save it, Janice. Talk like that will not make her appear, but it will certainly get me riled up." Monica turned away and yelled for Kenzie at the top of her lungs, Dex and Janice following suit.

Suddenly, they all heard a little knock and turned to see Kenzie peering back at them through the driver's side window with a wide grin on her face.

Dex opened the door quickly. The car was a hot box. He pulled a sticky Kenzie out with a sigh of relief.

"I win. I win," Kenzie gloated while Dex explained that it was too dangerous to hide in a hot car.

Monica couldn't help but wonder if this was a sign that she needed to stay at home. How quickly something could go from being fun and games to disaster. Lord knows what she went through the last time she was eager to fly the coop.

Dex dismissed Monica's worried face and wiped the beads of sweat from Kenzie's upper lip before handing her to Monica to say their good-byes.

"I'm taking Mommy and her friends to the airport, and when I get back, we'll go for a boat ride."

"Can we swim in da deep?" asked Kenzie.

"Wim dee," Beck echoed.

Monica gave the kids one last kiss and was trying to shake Beck off her leg and get in the car when Janice's cell rang.

Monica rolled her eyes in annoyance when Janice dug it out of the pocket in her tennis skirt and answered. As if she didn't know they were on a time crunch.

"What? Nooo!" Janice's hand went to her mouth with a gasp. "Up in flames? Severe smoke and water damage?"

Monica let her head fall back on the head rest, the car door wide open, inviting both Kenzie and Beck inside to crawl on her. "For the love of God, I'm going to miss my plane."

"Dexter!" Janice shrieked, covering the bottom of her phone. "My house caught fire. The damage is extensive."

Monica turned to Dex. "There's nothing you can do. I'm begging you, please, get me out of here. Now."

CHAPTER 30

*Today I decided to forgive you, not because you apologized,
or took ownership for the pain you've caused,
but because my soul deserves peace.*

Bald Head Island

The three women took their seats on the plane with a sigh of relief
and sat in a comfortable silence for a moment before Carmen asked
if it was time for the in-flight beverage service.

They all roared. "I'm guessing we need to be *in-flight* before
they serve the in-flight cocktails," Gabby responded, opening a bag
of peanut M&M's.

Upon arriving to the airport, Carmen had double-checked the
monitor to be sure Victor's incoming flight was on time and sighed
with relief that it was. She had never done anything like this before,
booked a flight without telling him. It was dirty, she knew, but she
convinced herself it was small on the severity scale. She only texted
him a snapshot of her itinerary when she knew his flight had taken
off. By the time he landed and turned his phone on, she'd be in the
air.

She didn't let on to the girls how upset she was with Victor.
Instead, she explained to them that Grandpa needed her and she
wanted some time with him. Which was true.

They taxied onto the runway and pinched themselves
simultaneously because it all seemed dreamlike. Only days ago,
they were having dinner and came up with this wild idea, and now,
here they were, schedules rearranged, bags packed, good-byes
said, wheels up.

After claiming their baggage, they took an Uber to Deep Point
Marina in Southport and boarded the ferry to Bald Head Island. They
sat on the upper deck and took in the scent of the salty ocean air,
so different from the fresh water of their little inland lake and that of
Lake Michigan.

Dusk had set in, cooling the intense August heat to a tolerable
temperature.

"It would be odd living on the Atlantic Ocean and not having a sunset over the water," admitted Gabby. "It's second nature to watch the sun dip into Lake Michigan."

"I suppose you two will have to catch the sunrise each morning. As for me, I plan on sleeping until I'm good and ready to get up," Carmen said wistfully.

Monica closed her eyes and exhaled all her cares. "Heaven, a morning run along the beach while the sun rises." Like a switch, her eyes shot open, and she went into drill-sergeant mode. "Then I'm going to swim in the ocean, after that drink coffee and eat a cinnamon roll. We need to find a place that sells cinnamon rolls. I only eat them while on vacation. Then we can stroll the streets, shop, and have lunch at some quaint restaurant, be on the beach by 1:30 with a book, and say, hmm, about 3:30 take a walk and collect shells. Cocktail time should begin about 4:30. No, wait. We should take a swim after our walk—we'll be sweaty—then plop back in our beach chairs, refreshed with a cocktail about five o'clock."

"You're so high-strung, Monica. Can't you tone it down a notch and relax?" teased Carmen. "No schedules."

"Hello! I allocated down time from 1:30 to 3:30," Monica replied with mocked sarcasm.

"Yoga session on the beach?" offered Gabby.

"Absolutely, as long as it's well after the sun comes up and I've had my fill of coffee and cinnamon rolls." Carmen chuckled. "I'm not opposed to any of your ideas, Monica." She squeezed her shoulders with a side hug. "I only prefer to stretch them out over several days. I see no reason coffee and cinnamon rolls can't take up an entire morning, shopping the next . . ."

Monica fluttered her lashes. "You two are so grounding. It must come with age." She grinned.

The ferry docked, and they collected their suitcases and strolled off to find Chet waiting for them. He and Carmen embraced, Chet's eyes filling with tears at the sight of his daughter. Gabby noticed Carmen return a tight squeeze although avoiding eye contact.

Both Gabby and Monica had been asking Carmen if she wanted to talk about her mother's death. She had refused, claiming she was fine, that she had mourned the loss of her mother decades ago. The subject was closed. Off limits.

Chet greeted Monica and Gabby with the same warm embrace and led them to his golf cart, where he piled their luggage on the back.

Gabby and Monica were facing backwards, the hems of their summer dresses flowing in the breeze. They took in the peaceful ambiance of Bald Head Island, the quaint harbor with a few restaurants. They passed Maritime Market and a string of small shops already closed for the evening, including a post office that looked more like a cottage with its flower box on the window and two rocking chairs anchoring an inviting porch.

They'd only been on the island a few minutes, and already Monica envisioned moving there. She could see herself strolling the quiet streets with her family, running errands on her bike with Kenzie and Beck in tow. They would no doubt buy lemonades and stop to relax at the post office and lounge in the rockers while watching the foot traffic.

Chet wound the golf cart around a bend and pulled into the driveway of a picture-perfect east-coast beach house, complete with weathered shakes, white-and-blue trim, and a metal roof.

Chet carried their bags to their rooms, each adorned with large windows and breathtaking views of the ocean. After a brief tour, he led them outside where a simple spread of lump crab dip and crackers awaited on a chilled, pewter dish shaped like a pineapple. A bucket of iced waters, teas, and sodas sat alongside a package of store-bought chocolate-covered pretzels.

"Absolutely charming," admired Gabby, taking in the surroundings.

Carmen opened a diet soda and kissed Chet on the cheek. "Thanks, Dad, this was sweet of you."

"Don't repeat this to Dex." Monica scooped a generous portion of crab dip on her cracker. "This vacation may outdo my honeymoon!" Leave it to Monica's sarcasm to bring on the laughter that would carry them through the night. The roll of the waves crashing to shore lured them to the Adirondack chairs looking out to the Atlantic.

Dusk settled as they got acquainted with Chet. His bright green eyes flanked by generous crow's-feet, appeared to give his face a permanent smile. He had thick, silver hair, styled by the wind. His deeply tanned skin boasted hours on the water, fishing.

He was inquisitive of Gabby's and Monica's hobbies, their lines of work, their husbands and children. He was the sort of guy who captivated you in conversation, so genuinely interested in you that, without conscious effort, you'd spill details of your existence you'd never bothered to communicate to those you'd known for years.

~*~

The rising sun filled the room with both light and heat. Carmen kicked back the sheet, opened her eyes, and squinted. Her bedroom, which had spectacular views of the ocean, lacked any sort of window treatment. Most likely, her mother hadn't bothered with blinds, figuring she'd never have an overnight guest.

It was after nine o'clock, but she felt no shame. Sleep hadn't come easily in months. Upon landing and seeing the itinerary text Carmen had sent Victor, he had called, panic in his voice, explaining he'd had a great win in Vegas. He promised no more going back and begged Carmen to call him. She decided on a text, informing him she wasn't ready for a conversation. They'd talk when she returned. She was going to focus on her relationship with her father, and he should immerse himself in his children while she was gone.

She retrieved her cell from the bedside table to find several long apologetic texts, a picture of Victor and the girls out at dinner last night, and already another of the breakfast casserole currently baking in the oven. Not that she was keeping tally marks, okay possibly, but this earned him two. She wasn't one to play the silent-treatment game—that was obvious to anyone that knew her—yet she was adamant they would have no conversations until she returned home. Carmen desperately needed a breather from her family and work. It would all be there when she got back.

She texted a kissy face emoji in attempts to silence some of Victor's apologetic texting, and put her phone facedown where she vowed it would remain most of her trip.

She walked over to the second-story window to see her dad sitting on the beach, having coffee with Monica and Gabby. He was a hospitable host, her friends embracing him as if he were their own. Already she was aware of the good that was coming out of the bad. Had Victor not gotten himself in a gambling mess, she wouldn't be here, and neither would her friends. Friends. Thank you, God.

She brushed her teeth, propped her sunglasses on her head, poured a cup of coffee from the kitchen, and went to the beach in her pajamas. Gabby and Monica had already been swimming, their hair still damp, bathing suits under their cover-ups.

As she approached, she heard her father's deep voice trail off and a howling of laughter fill its place. Carmen had a hunch as to what story her dad was reminiscing about.

"Hey," Carmen called out as she took a seat in the vacant beach chair that had been set up for her. "What's so funny?"

"I was retelling my favorite story of all time . . ."

"The mermaid story," they both finished together.

Carmen had been ten when she decided she wanted to see what it felt like to be a real mermaid. She had concocted a mermaid tail, using bubble wrap, duct tape, and spray paint.

While fishing on *Hooked* one afternoon, Carmen put it to the test. Without telling her father, she slipped the tail on and dove in the ocean. He had heard the splash and rushed to the side of the boat to find Carmen floating on her back, trying to flop her tail.

Carmen was ecstatic at how well she could move around the water with her tail shimmering in the sunlight. With her father closely watching, she swam around the boat between their fishing lines, feeling as free and peaceful as she envisioned mermaid life to be. If only she could dive down and live under the sea, anything would have been better than living on land with her mother.

When Carmen was finished swimming, she tried climbing up the ladder on the back of the boat with no success. Chet was unable to pull his daughter up by her hands without the fear of falling in himself, so he did what any smart fisherman would have done and fished his daughter out of the water using a fish net.

Carmen was never able to use the mermaid tail again because, once it got wet, they couldn't pull it off. Chet had to slice it down the middle with one of the knives he used to clean fish.

"What a great story," said Gabby, still giggling. She noticed Carmen's eyes tear up before removing her sunglasses from the top of her head and placing them over her eyes.

Gabby could sense the enormous amount of pain from Carmen's childhood. Clearly, the love that Carmen had for her father was abundant yet guarded.

"Your dad is the best. He drove me on the golf cart this morning to Maritime Market for the ultimate sticky buns." Monica opened the box and passed it to Carmen. "Between the sugar and the coffee buzz, you're going to have to tie me to the beach chair to relax."

Two sticky buns later, Gabby led them through a yoga session, Chet included. He wobbled and groaned through the warrior poses, while Monica stole the show with her crow and headstand, and Carmen with her smooth and fluid vinyasa flow. Several minutes in, a straggler, whom Chet introduced as Tully from a few doors down, joined in, more for the eye candy than anything.

Their first two days consisted mostly of lounging their tired souls. They started their routine every morning with walking or running on the beach or around the island, followed by coffee and breakfast. They talked and laughed all afternoon until their cheeks hurt. Then they went long stretches in silence, napping, reading, or contemplating their lives, mesmerized by the waves crashing to shore.

The stretches of silence often stimulated deep conversation. Carmen tried to untangle the knots in her stomach caused by Victor's gambling, worried sick Penelope was home cutting and punishing herself over the debacle she'd gotten herself into with Liz.

Victor had assured her he had been keeping the girls busy with projects and chores around the house. He texted her pictures of them cleaning out the garage, mowing the grass and pulling weeds, and power washing the dock. Much to their dismay, he'd told them they weren't going to be hanging with friends while Carmen was away. Naturally, texts of retaliation landed on Carmen's screen like seagulls dive-bombing an open bag of chips on the beach. They were begging, rather, demanding, she talk Victor into letting them escape with their friends, at the very least, however boring, allow them to have friends over. It was so freeing to reply with a simple answer:

Sorry, can't overrule Dad's decisions.

He had promised he was keeping a close eye on Penelope, monitoring her for cuts, and he'd even had a few meaningful conversations with both his daughters. Carmen tried to relax as Gabby assured her this time away was good for all of them, and now that Penelope disclosed the truth, when she returned, it was best for Carmen to sit down together with both Penelope and Liz.

Carmen groaned. "I'm so not good at that sort of talk. You know me. My tongue tends to go all snake: hiss and rattle."

"You'll be fine," Gabby said with a wink before fishing her dinging phone out of the side pocket of her tote.

Mom, I'm going all sorts of crazy!!! Dad took the afternoon off work, and he's like a bee on honey. And I'm in no mood to be sweet towards him.

Gabby laughed out loud as she read the text from Stella to Carmen and Monica. Stella was far from honey these days, and Greg, well, he deserved every morsel of backlash. Gabby inquired without asking specifics:

Full on 007 mode?

Off the charts. His doting has gone too far. I've gained forty pounds just by looking at all the takeout boxes piling up. What am I supposed to do with two dozen yellow frosted cupcakes arranged like the sun?

Say thank you, Stella, and lick the frosting off a few of them.

In other words, be respectful and compliant when I really feel like hurling the box across the room. Do you always have to model moral behavior?

Gabby thought of her phone call to Holly along with all the nasty, conflicting thoughts that had swirled in her head, the secrets she was keeping.

Moral. If only that were true.

Meaning?

Gabby had half a wit to call Stella right then. Was this a sign, an omen, that the right thing to do was be wholeheartedly honest with her children?

Instead, Gabby snapped a picture of her feet nestled in the sand and thumbed out an exit text.

I wish I could rescue you; however, I'm stranded on an island.

You wish nothing of the sort! Love you, Mom. I'll let you enjoy your vacation. Tell Monica and Carmen hi.

Chet had gone fishing and had come back with a treasure chest of fresh fish for dinner. While he grilled black sea bass and tuna, the trio engaged in a fierce game of Scrabble. Chet dusted off the box of an old puzzle boasting one thousand pieces of marine life. Never did their conversations and roars of healing laughter lull for a moment as the sky painted itself a gorgeous shade of orange sherbet.

By the third day, they mustered up enough energy to venture out. They had borrowed extra bikes from the neighbor and set out to explore the island. With Chet as their guide, they looped down quaint streets boasting breathtaking beachfront bungalows, Monica declaring at least ten of which she would own someday. They weaved down streets lined with huge banyan trees that led to marshy areas, and to the adorable island chapel full of charm.

Ditching their bikes, they climbed the one hundred eight steps in Bald Head lighthouse. The 360-degree views of the state's southernmost barrier island were spectacular.

"Fun fact, ya'll, Old Baldy was built in 1817, and it was in the movie *Weekend at Bernie's*. The teacher in me is always thirsting for knowledge," Monica announced proudly as she gathered them for a selfie.

~*~

Carmen picked up a piece of green sea glass and dropped it into the bucket her father was carrying. Chet and Carmen had been walking for nearly thirty minutes, strolling mostly in silence, merely commenting on the shells or sea glass they encountered. They had yet to speak of her mother other than Carmen asking how he was getting by without her, and Chet showing her where he had spread Mary's ashes along the shore where they took daily walks.

"I think we should talk about it, Carmen, about your mom, her life, her death, your childhood."

Carmen nodded and looked out to the water, feeling her insides twist up with all sorts of emotion. She bit her tongue so as not to admit she felt no remorse over her mother's death and didn't really see the point in talking about her. She had been dead to Carmen for decades. It upset her that her father didn't feel the same way.

"I know I've let you down, Carmen. In no way am I making excuses for the way I failed you as a parent, and I've spent a lifetime trying to convince myself I did the best I could under the circumstances."

Teetering on the edge of tears, Chet paused. He picked up a piece of sea glass and threw it far out into the ocean, the iridescence catching in the sunlight. Carmen felt like that glass, thrown out to the sea for years, the treacherous waves tossing her around in a battered and uncertain world before washing her ashore in Michigan, where she invented a new life for herself.

Carmen liked to think she had softened over the years just like the sea glass. However, being in her dad's presence opened her eyes to her deeply burrowed, jagged, and sharp edges of anger and bitterness.

"I was lying to myself." Chet's voice wobbled. "When I think of your childhood, I try only to see the weekends we spent together on the boat, the countless fish we reeled in together. I picture you running into my arms, your pigtails swinging side to side when you got off the bus, squealing with delight as you told me about doing flips off the monkey bars and how you were the fastest in your class with your multiplication facts."

Carmen remembered that too, remembered the feeling that washed over her when her dad was excited for her, told her she was smart, and rubbed his knuckles on the top of her head and said, "Way to go, kiddo."

"Most of all, I remember the carefree weeks we had when your mom was admitted to the mental facility." He sighed heavily. "Your spirit soared.

"In between were the long stretches when your mom was home. She would come back vibrant and stable, faithfully taking her meds, but then, like a switch . . ."

They both spoke together, "She would *regress*."

She said the word *regress* laced with resentment. How often had Carmen heard that term growing up? To her, it meant watch your back. Be cautious. Mom could snap any second. What a way to grow up, fearfully on edge.

"The wheels would hit the runway at the end of the day, and I would be praying all the way home that she hadn't . . . hurt you." He tried to swallow back the tears unsuccessfully and broke down, drawing his grown daughter into his arms while he wept.

They stood in an embrace in a desolate part of the beach, their feet and calves submerged by waves.

"I told myself that, when she spat her nasty words, they bounced off your thick skin, that you knew it was her mental illness talking. I bought into the garbage that kids were resilient—a stupid cop-out phrase that adults use to comfort themselves, excuse themselves from their own failures as parents. I know your mother mistreated you and I failed to protect you, and yes, the destruction is still among us decades later.

"Do you remember me explaining to you at night when I tucked you in that she was sick, that her words were not the truth? That you were smart, ambitious, kind, and the best first mate ever?"

Carmen didn't answer, even though she remembered him explaining how sick her mother was and that her behavior was not Carmen's fault. Of course she thought she was to blame. Carmen squeezed her dad so tight she could feel his racing heart.

"Why didn't you leave her? Why didn't you take me away from her? Why didn't you protect me? She was emotionally and physically abusive, Dad."

"When she got physical with you, I always admitted her, and when she was released, well, I was sure it would never happen again. When she was taking her meds and she was stable, she was so good to you." Chet's voice trailed off as their eyes met, both knowing how short-lived that was.

"The thing is, Dad, it hurts more now that I'm an adult with my own kids because I know I would cut off my left arm for them. Knowing you weren't willing to do that for me is so hurtful. I've gone through life, feeling rejected by both of you."

"If Victor ever"—she waived her arm in the air—"did anything remotely damaging to our girls, verbal or physical, I would flee with them in a heartbeat. I can't wrap my brain around the fact that you wouldn't do that for me."

"Your mother had no one, Carmen. You know that. Her father had left when she was a baby. Your grandma wasn't any better off than your mother. She was a drug addict that led a string of men through their welfare apartment on a regular basis. Your mother was sexually abused by those dirt bags from the time she was eight years old until she left at sixteen."

Looking exasperated, Chet put his hands on the top of his head. "I'm not making excuses for her, Carmen, but she never had contact with any of her family while growing up. I couldn't abandon her. She had no siblings, and I wasn't about to look up her deadbeat extended family. If I left her"—Chet closed his eyes and raked his fingers through his thick silver hair—"she wouldn't have survived. I felt obliged to take care of her, get her treatment. Till death do us part. I was all she had."

We, Carmen wanted to correct him. We were all she had.

"Funny thing was, when people met your mother, she drew people in. She had this magnetic, alluring aura about her, her best quality, which I've always believed you inherited."

Carmen cringed. In no way did she want to be compared to that sadistic demon. To this day, Carmen could still see the way her mother's hollowed eyes would glaze over, her face would transform, and she would unleash a crazed venom until she wore herself out enough to collapse in her bedroom.

When she woke hours later, she'd swoop in with vigor where she left off, or emerge exuberantly vivacious, as if she was the most cheerfully spirited woman to walk Planet Earth. With a smile glued to her heavily painted face and matte red lips, she'd say, "I bet you can't wait to tell Daddy about all the fun we had at the roller rink today."

Carmen never dared bring up the outlandish events from only hours prior and wondered if her mother had truly convinced herself that they had, in fact, gone to the roller rink, rendering Carmen defenseless to argue otherwise. She spoke in such bogus detail about erroneous events that sometimes Carmen couldn't decipher truth from lies, especially when it came to her own misbehavior.

"She formed friendships with anyone she met," Chet interrupted her thoughts. "They would flourish to the point where your mom would latch on. She was intense and became needy. Soon enough, something as simple as a phone call not returned would set her off on a tirade, and she would lose the friendship as quickly as she'd gained it.

"She had burned every bridge, Carmen. If I'd abandoned her, she would have rotted in a mental facility or taken the path of self-destruction. I couldn't be responsible for that."

Chet sat down near the shore and patted the sand next to him for Carmen to do the same. He pulled his feet in and rested his elbows on top of his knees. A large, scabbed-over cut ran down his deeply tanned shin.

Carmen's voice was hesitant. "Did she ever try . . .?"

"To kill herself?"

Carmen nodded and avoided eye contact by fixing her gaze on a pelican swooping down for a fish. She tried not to think about how she would feel if her mother ever succeeded.

Chet inhaled a sharp breath. "Yes." He paused and exhaled slowly. "Twice. Once when you were ten and then again a month after you left."

Again, it was dangerous territory for Carmen to entertain any thoughts. Chet, sensing her trepidation, changed the subject.

"Do you remember going to Miss Lisa's?"

Carmen nodded. She remembered playing G.I. Joe figures with Miss Lisa's youngest son Gabe, drinking grape Kool-Aid, and eating chocolate and vanilla swirl Pudding Pops on a blanket in their yard. When the older two brothers got home from school, they would all play kick ball and capture the flag in the yard with a few of the other neighbor kids. Miss Lisa kissed and hugged her every day, quizzed her on her spelling words, and stuck her pictures on their refrigerator next to her own children's artwork, something her own mother had never done.

"I loved Miss Lisa." Carmen used to fall asleep praying that she and her dad could move in with Miss Lisa's family.

"Me too." Chet nodded. "She was a godsend. Her husband Jeremy unloaded cargo planes at the airport. He was a funny guy, drank Lisa's Tab instead of coffee, and ate peanut butter and grape jelly sandwiches with the crusts cut off.

"In casual conversation, Jeremy mentioned Lisa might have to look for a job to make ends meet. I asked if she could babysit you while I worked to give your mom a break. The very next day I dropped you off. You were so brave, adopted those boys like they'd been your brothers for life." Chet chuckled. "You even started asking for *Star Wars* and *Spiderman* paraphernalia for Christmas. You started watching *He-Man* and *The A-Team*."

"Until Mom showed up and practically ripped off Lisa's head for *stealing* me." Carmen bit her tongue. Her dad knew what had happened. The fingerprint bruises on Carmen's arm told the story of how her mother dragged her to the car in hysterics, sped ninety miles away to a cheap motel, and hid for three days, claiming Lisa would try and kidnap her again. Carmen never questioned how Chet found them. She was only relieved that Mary was admitted to the mental facility for the next six months.

Carmen had been going to the Potter's house for well over a year, every day after school and for the first two months of summer vacation. She thought of the fourth of July parade that she and the boys decorated their bikes for, rode through town with hundreds of other kids, red, white, and blue streamers flowing from their bikes, flags sticking out of their handle bars, horns and bells making a lovely racket of noise. They wore crazy Uncle Sam hats, blue sunglasses with white stars and red stripes, and Lisa had painted their foreheads blue, one cheek red, and one cheek white, USA drawn in block letters from their forehead to nose to chin.

Closing her eyes, Carmen could still feel an intense sense of pride for her country as she pedaled along with the Potter boys. Only now, she recognized it for what it truly stood for, pride for belonging, being loved and accepted in a family, and the gentleness with which Lisa had brushed Carmen's hair, pulled it into a ponytail, and held her chin like she was a breakable china doll as she painted her face.

She'd thought of the Potter family often, yet never had the courage to reconnect. It may have only been two years of her life, but Carmen believed that time with them saved her in so many ways. If anything, it explained why she'd always preferred male friendships. Had it not been for Lisa, Carmen would never have become a mother. It was those months, those memories, that shaped the vision of family for Carmen.

Carmen and Chet rested their elbows on their knees and let the waves roll over their feet. Above, two seagulls were ganging up on a third, cawing loudly as they dove toward the water and shot back up in the air inches before careening into a wave.

Chet placed his hand on Carmen's and apologized, but Carmen wasn't sure if he was apologizing for his wife, or for the fact that Carmen remembered the kidnapping incident.

"When they sent her to the facility for six months, a long stretch compared to her usual two, she had made such good progress. You were able to go back to the Potter's during her stay and for a few more months after her release, and I always tried to be home when you got off the bus." Chet's voice trailed off with the realization that his explanations were futile.

"Dad." Carmen drew a deep breath. She couldn't suppress her words any longer. She'd been choking on the bitterness since she was eighteen. "I feel so rejected by you. Sure, I was the one that took off, but you had already abandoned me. Every time mom came home *rehabilitated,* a conflicting switch flipped. You went from being this doting dad who made me feel loved and safe to this doting husband who catered to an abusive woman.

"You didn't come to my wedding, weren't there to walk me down the aisle." Carmen's head dipped to her knees as she pulled them into her chest, buying her a few seconds to nix the tremble in her voice. "You fabricated that story, telling Mom I eloped." Her head shook. "Since I walked out the door as an eighteen-year-old kid, I've been pushing a swirling myriad of hostile visions from my head. Unfortunately, I've done a lousy job. They're still vivid, raw and painful."

Carmen turned and looked at him now. His dark weathered skin, bright sea green eyes, and silver hair made him look strong, but Carmen saw a weak man. She knew her mother had attacked him physically on many occasions: hit him, clawed at him, and threw things at him.

"Dad, no part of me wanted her at my wedding, but I did need you. I wanted you to hop on a plane and come to my wedding, alone. You could have easily left her for a few days every couple of years to visit us, especially when she was getting treatment.

"I wanted you in my life when my babies were born. I wanted you there to watch them take their first steps, take them for ice cream when they got their braces on, pick them up from school just so you could ask about their day and what their favorite subjects were. To show interest in us.

"Have you any idea how often I've wished for you to show up on my doorstep? Give me a fraction of the attention you gave Mom? I've fantasized about you sitting in the bleachers, cheering next to Victor and me while the girls played sports. Most of all, I wanted you to visit *me* on my little lake and fish with me and build memories with your granddaughters. Instead, you devoted all your time and energy to *her.*"

Carmen was so upset she found herself trembling. Chet took her hand and stroked the back of it with his thumb as he did when she was little. She loved the way her hand still felt so small in his, so protected, unlike the weapon of her mother's hand.

"Mom's mental disorder made her absent and cruel. Once I moved out, you chose to be absent, and that has felt equally as cruel. No matter how old, I've wanted you to love me enough to leave her from time to time and show up on my doorstep, to call me more often and ask about my life, to act interested. I only want to matter to you."

"Oh Carmen," Chet said with anguish. "I figured you were better off without us in your life. In my eyes, I was doing you a favor, sparing you, not abandoning you."

"I was better off without *her,* Dad, not you. I realize that I need to forgive her, but your disinterest has only made that harder. Over the years, the resentment has shifted to include you, and it's built to this level where I have so much anger in my heart towards both of you."

Chet pulled Carmen closer, and even though she wanted to resist, she rested her head on his shoulder. "If I could only explain how much I've missed you and wanted to be a part of your family. I felt like I did such a horrible job at shielding you from her . . . abuse." He paused, and when the next word left his lips, several tears followed. "The least I could do was keep her away from you as an adult. I love you, Carmen."

Carmen wanted to tell her father she loved him but couldn't muster the words. "I pour my heart and soul into my girls, and I don't understand how I was so easily dismissed. As they grow up, it stirs so many memories, so much emotion. It aches, Dad."

"I'm sorry, Carmen. I'm very, very sorry. So, the theory that kids are resilient isn't true?"

"Total bullshit," she said rather accusatory.

He sat up straighter and rubbed the back of his neck, his face pained.

"Sorry, Dad. I didn't mean to be disrespectful. That was harsh."

"No, no, that's okay. You're only speaking the truth. You moved out, entered college, met Victor, and married, and I chose to believe that you made it through your childhood unscathed. I convinced myself that you were better off without either of us and kept my distance. I see now I was hiding from reality, being a coward. I only hurt you further."

He took the hem of his shirt, stretched it up to Carmen's eyes, and blotted at her tears. "Blow your nose."

"What? On your shirt?" Her nose crinkled in question. "That's gross."

"Come on. You used to do it all the time as a kid. I can handle a little snot."

Carmen laughed through her tears and wiped her nose on the shoulder strap of her beach cover-up.

Now Chet crinkled his nose. "That's gross." He took his shirt off, exposing an awful tattoo of a WWII fighter jet that he had gotten when he was a drunken nineteen-year-old. He handed his shirt to Carmen with which she blew her nose and dried her tear-streaked face.

"Can I ask you something, Carmen?"

"Sure," she said with a sigh of relief for getting years' worth of pent up aggression off her chest.

"Do you think someday you could find it in your heart to forgive me?"

The flood of tears came again as she hugged him. "I've already begun."

CHAPTER 31

FEAR ~ Forget Everything and Run or Face Everything and Rise?

The fire pit was nestled just off the patio on the beach between several patches of dune grass swaying in the breeze. They sat in the most amazing cocoon chairs with thick cushions and plush pillows.

"Mary had exquisite taste in luxury furniture." Monica sighed, pushing herself deep in the chair.

Chet smiled in appreciation while giving a sideward glance toward Carmen. Carmen caught the wary look on his face at the mention of a compliment towards Mary and asked in comfort, "Did the two of you sit out here often, Dad?"

Chet's frame relaxed. "Yes. We were homebodies, so to mix things up, we created many different spaces to retreat to."

"I've a hard time figuring out where I like to be the most," admitted Gabby, "the patio Adirondack chairs with a cup of coffee in the morning watching the sun rise, the beach chairs in the afternoon, or the settee by the windows in my room in my robe with a book, cocooning it under the stars by the fire . . ."

"Don't forget the south-facing deck where Chef Chet serves ceviche for lunch! Really, Chet, you're a fantastic cook; you'd give Dex a challenge."

Chet's face blushed through his deeply tanned skin. "Thanks, Monica Dear."

Monica waved her finger, ready to reprimand Chet; however, it sounded so sweet when Chet called her Monica Dear. Instead, she teased in response, "You're quite the prankster, Mr. Moreno." She waived her finger. "Watch it or I'll insist on making dinner, and I'm warning you I have no business being in the kitchen."

Carmen coughed to suppress the laugh/cry desperately trying to escape her throat. Was it possible to actually feel resentment dissolving? Evaporating off her skin as the early morning fog rises off the water? Forgiveness was taking place each day, with moments like this. Her eyes welled up with profound awareness at the impact Monica and Gabby played in her transition.

"Every nook and cranny of the house is charming, Dad, but hands down . . ." She stifled a cry, and all their eyes darted her way. This was so out of her comfort zone, but she felt so compelled to voice her thoughts that she powered on, "Your hospitality has been outstanding. The way you've opened your home and catered to us, while you're grieving, I"—she fluttered her hand towards Monica and Gabby— "*we* appreciate it so much. Thank you."

Monica and Gabby thanked Chet as Carmen wiped her tears with a chuckle. "Sorry, I'm getting rather emotional on ya'll."

Chet reached over and squeezed Carmen's hand. "I love you, sweetheart."

"I love you too, Dad."

It wouldn't have been real life if technology didn't interrupt a significant moment. Monica's phone lit up, signaling a Facetime call.

"Sorry," she apologized.

Carmen's cheeks rose. "More like I should be thanking you for saving me in a jiffy from a delicate moment lingering into awkwardness."

Monica pressed accept on her phone, and Beck's face filled the screen for two seconds. Then a bucket of frogs jumping haphazardly came into view, before it swung once again toward Dex hunched near the edge of the pond.

"Catchin' toads, Mom," Kenzie announced with glee. She whirled the phone once again toward Beck, who had a large brown toad cupped in his hands so tight Monica was sure the little bugger's eyes were going to shoot out and splatter the screen.

"Beck, little buddy, be gentle." Monica cringed, turning her phone towards Chet, Gabby, and Carmen, who all broke into hysterics over the strangled toad captured via Facetime.

"Time to break out the cherry pie filling," declared Chet as he rose for the hobo pie maker.

"Disgusting, Dad," Carmen said as she helped him butter the bread for their fireside treat.

Kenzie had handed the phone back to Dex, far more interested in the toads than her mother. "Do the kids even miss me?"

"Not really," Dex teased. "Hi, everybody," Dex hollered.

Monica rotated the phone to show Dex her surroundings, and everyone waved and greeted him.

When Monica's phone rested on Chet for an introduction, Dex said, "Thanks for taking my wife off our hands. We've had great fun over here playing with insects, rodents, and wild game, and eating carcinogen-tainted, packaged food, with ingredients we can't pronounce."

Chet appreciated Dex's sarcastic humor. "That a boy! You're a fine daddy." He winked.

Dex took the opportunity provided by the jovial mood, and the cushion of three additional sets of eyes and ears, to update Monica on the status of Janice's home. "So . . . the fire damage is expected to take four months to repair."

Monica growled, ready to sling a litany of cussing Dex's way. She had to admit, although calculated, his move was slick. Everyone zeroed in on her. Carmen's eyes widened, Gabby's face curled in a smirk, and even Chet looked alarmed for he had been on the receiving end of Janice commentary the last few days.

A screech from Kenzie prompted Dex to end the call quickly. "Did Dex pinch her?" joked Carmen.

"Janice will be with us through Christmas," seethed Monica. "No worries," Monica assured them as she took a deep breath. "I refuse to borrow trouble from around the bend."

Carmen had a sympathetic look on her face. "Now that Janice has been with the kids in your absence, I'm sure she'll be better when we get back. Possibly you'll feel comfortable going back to work and leaving the kids with her?"

Monica looked at Carmen as if she were nuts, but pondered the thought.

"Are you getting homesick for Kenzie and Beck?" asked Carmen. "It's such a long time to be away from your kids when they are young."

"Puhlease! The peacefulness has been blissfully intoxicating. It has been magnificent not to be needed every second of the day. No whining, complaining, temper tantrums, or demands to play make-believe. I haven't missed cutting up two plates of food before taking a bite of my own dinner only to have it be cold.

"My patience hasn't been tested for forty-five minutes every night while they dilly dally getting their pajamas on, find misplaced blankies, beg for longer back rubs, extra songs, and books, while I just want the day to be over so I can have an hour of peace and quiet before exhaustion claims me."

Monica covered her face with her hands and stifled a sob. "Who am I kidding? I miss them so much! I miss holding and kissing them. I miss their scent. I miss massaging their little feet after their bath, reading, and building sand castles."

Carmen handed Monica a golden-brown cherry pie fresh from the hobo pie maker. "You're not booking an early ticket home, are you?"

Monica's yearning ceased abruptly. "I said I miss them. In no way does that mean I'm senseless!"

"You're in the thick of the toddler years. Being needed every second of the day is draining," Gabby empathized. "A break is warranted, and anyone who acts like motherhood never catches up to them is a liar."

"How did you do it with four?" asked Monica.

"More like what didn't I do." Gabby winked at Monica. "I couldn't micromanage."

"Ouch, that was blunt."

Gabby smiled lovingly. "You asked. I answered. Seriously though, don't be so hard on yourself. Problem was I set my bar so high that I stressed myself out. If I could go back and give myself any advice, it would be to relax more. Give yourself a break for not being the perfect mom. Persistence, not perfection.

"You're not a failure if your kids bicker, burp in public, don't make the honor roll, or they get caught stealing a case of beer and sneaking it to the shed." Gabby frowned. "That stirred an uproar with a few parents when Klay and his buddies got shitfaced while we slept in ignorant bliss."

Gabby rolled her eyes. "Anyway, when the aide scolds your child for calling someone a fart factory on the playground, or most recently your daughter shows up on your doorstep and tells you she's pregnant . . . you've got to learn to throw your arms in the air and ride the rollercoaster in all its wild, scary, thrilling uncertainness. Avoiding life's unpredictable tragedies is impossible. Freaking out doesn't solve anything. Trying to make sense only causes you to obsess on the negative."

"Freaking out makes me feel better!" Carmen declared and they all roared.

Gabby looked pointedly at Carmen. "I realized early on that you were doing more harm than good, constantly striving to fix everything for your kids. They need to make mistakes and learn from them, and you're doing them a disservice swooping in and always bailing them out.

"Their slip-ups are not a negative reflection on your parenting. And it's not always everyone else's kids in the wrong. Plenty of times it's your unperfect child. Parents have a hard time accepting that."

Gabby's gaze landed on Monica. "I know people tell you all the time how fast it will go and that you need to enjoy it. At this point in time, you feel like rolling your eyes and telling them to save it."

Monica nodded. "Yes!"

"Truth is it does go fast. Okay, elementary may have dragged, but middle school was a blur, and by high school, they've replaced you with their friends. In four years, both of your kids will be in school, Monica." Gabby turned to Carmen. "In four years, you and Victor could be empty nesters."

Carmen did a sarcastic mini clap, and Monica followed suit.

"Save the applause, ladies. Did you forget Stella's currently living at home, and I'm constantly receiving SOS texts from the other three, driving forgotten passports to the airport, getting middle-of-the-night phone calls on how to handle less-than-stellar roommates, proofreading term papers, and driving care packages halfway across the state? Parenting doesn't cease when they turn eighteen."

Carmen twirled her foot in the cool sand. "I've never admitted this out loud, but when the girls were young, I was envious of another mom at Amelia's dance studio because she traveled for work. She'd hop on a plane and have a hotel room to herself for two or three nights at a time, long enough to get a break, uninterrupted sleep, dining out, shopping, reading, or watching mindless TV at night, use of the hotel's fitness center, spa, and room service at her disposal. Rarely confessing for fear of being judged, every mom has their secret admissions and fantasies. They're being dishonest if they act like they don't."

"Either that or there is something totally wrong with them." Gabby snorted. "Seriously though, if you live solely for your kids, you've made them your idols. I know I'm preaching, but I could write a book about how unhealthy that is."

"As you should!" declared Monica, holding up her pointer finger.

Carmen sighed heavily. "Never in a million years did I think Penelope's path would have taken the turn it has. You always assume it's your child on the receiving end, and for much of it, Penelope is, but wow, the moment you realize your children are capable of making astronomical mistakes"—Carmen shook her head— "it sucks."

"Are you saying I shouldn't have flown off the handle when Beck stuck his tongue out at the cashier last week? Or beat myself up for an entire day about the way I forcefully tied Kenzie's shoes, probably cutting off the circulation to her toes, after she kicked me in the face when I asked her five times to stop swinging her feet!"

"Oh, how the memories come flooding back," Gabby remembered. "A mom called me consistently, explaining how Lottie's group of friends always snubbed her daughter, stopped inviting her for sleepovers, and created new group chats excluding her, blah, blah. True, Lottie was avoiding this girl because she was trouble, sleeping around, and getting high in the school parking lot. I had half a mind to tell the mother, but I refrained while she made Lottie out to be a bitch. Lottie was free to choose her own friends, regardless of whether that girl was trouble or not."

Gabby shifted and threw her legs over the side of the chair. Another mom made comments to me at lacrosse games that she'd heard how a group of boys were getting tanked on the weekends. Puking in buckets in the basement took place at my house while I slept. She claimed her son had never drank a drop and listed the names of the rotten kids, leaving Calvin's and Klay's names out, but accusing me with her eyes. As if I was stupid enough not to understand her point.

"When I confronted the boys, lo and behold, it was *her* son that had supplied the booze every weekend! He'd only ratted out his friends to his mommy to save his own sorry ass. She went around gossiping, throwing kids' names around the community, that they got drunk every weekend, while the parents turned their backs."

Monica's jaw fell slack. "Did you call her out on it?"

"Nope! Warning. The ones that constantly justify how wonderful their kids are . . . those are the ones to watch out for. They love to trash-talk other kids. Steer clear of those drama mamas. Never react. They'll dig their own grave."

"If only there were do-overs," said Carmen, gazing into the crackling fire, confessing she was so wrapped up in getting her business off the ground, proving that she would never be dependent on anyone, that she often wished the toddler years away.

"No doubt," agreed Monica.

"Forget the past. Obsessing over the rewind button is a waste of time," Gabby said while nodding as if she were also convincing herself. "Just make better use of the pause button, ladies. The rewind button becomes insignificant."

Carmen pretended she had a remote in her hand and pressed her thumb down. "Could we pause right here for a couple of months?"

~*~

Gabby stretched and allowed herself to linger in bed for a couple of more minutes before changing into her running clothes. She loved everything about her cheery little lake house in Michigan, but waking up to second-story views of the sun rising over the ocean . . . wow. She could definitely retreat here on occasion.

She slathered her shoulders with sunscreen, donned a baseball cap, and double-knotted her laces before tiptoeing downstairs. Gabby had quickly adapted an island running route over the past several days and had even started seeing familiar faces of fellow runners, walkers, and bikers. She ran effortlessly, knowing it had everything to do with distancing herself from her troubled life at home and immersing herself in the peace of the island.

The humidity had skyrocketed, leaving Gabby drenched. Between the salt in the air and the salt she excreted, she felt like a hot, soft pretzel. After five miles, she slowed to a walk, causing the sweat to ooze madly from her pores, drizzling down and stinging her eyes and pink chest.

She guzzled a bottle of fancy Ph water Chet stored in a refrigerator in the garage and settled into a runner's lunge. She wondered if there would come a day she would cease to run. Like *Forrest Gump*, would she abruptly stop and go home? Give in to the plea of her chronic sore muscles and achy joints? No amount of yoga loosened her these days.

Upon entering the house, she was greeted with a blast of cool air and the scent of coffee. Chet prepped the coffee each night before he went to bed, setting the timer so the pot was hot and ready at precisely 6:02 a.m. He placed four mugs next to the pot. Gabby had found the gesture sweet, wondering if this had also been his role when Mary was alive.

The thought assaulted her with such visions of the gestures she and Greg were accustomed to doing for each other. She plopped a few ice cubes in her mug and meandered to the back porch to find Monica, Carmen, and Chet sitting in the rockers, reeling over crazy stories from the VRBO rental house a few doors down.

"Thanks for the coffee, Chet." Gabby raised her mug as she strolled by to the ocean for her saltwater bath. "Not that I smell, but I'm doing y'all a favor going for a swim. Anyone want to join?"

"It's my off day," said Monica, taking another sip of coffee.

Carmen bounded out of her rocker. "I'm in."

"You ladies enjoy. I'll play chef and make omelets," offered Chet, retreating to the house. He'd quickly become resort chef, soaking up every compliment to the fullest.

Monica crossed her tan, muscled legs with a sigh. "I'll kick back and perfect the art of doing nothing. I could get used to this life of luxury, breakfast made to order, no one demanding my attention."

Perfectly on cue, Monica's phone signaled a Facetime call. Kenzie was holding the phone an inch from her left nostril.

"Hey, sweetie, how are you?"

The phone bounced to a shot of Kenzie's knee and then her toes, finally sweeping back up and landing on her eyebrow. "Mom," Kenzie said, sounding like she'd aged several years since Monica had been gone. Her insides instantly went gooey with yearning. "I not find my Easter dress to Adel's house."

"Who's Adel?"

"Adel be Kenzie's friend. I wear my Easter dress to Adel's, and I can't find it." The phone spun around to Kenzie's closet, revealing piles of clothes on the floor, shirts dangling from their hangers. "Do see it, Mom?" Another blur of colors swept across the screen.

"Kenzie, where are you going?"

"Adel's."

"Who's Adel?" Monica asked a purple sweater dress.

"Mom. See it?" Kenzie's voice had a hint of impatience.

"I'm pretty sure your Easter dress was tossed in the chest with your princess costumes, but Kenzie, who is going to Adel's with you?"

Kenzie set the phone on the floor, giving Monica a view of the ceiling as she dug through the chest. Monica raised her voice and questioned Kenzie about Adel again.

"Told you, Mom. Kenzie and Adel have playdate. Mémé said no Trixie and Reese come either."

Monica's toes curled, gripping the sand as the fury shot through her body. "Sweetie, can you give the phone to Grandma, please." Monica couldn't wait to see the look on Janice's face when she questioned her about the top-secret playdate she'd received no memo about. How dare she drop Kenzie off somewhere without asking Monica's permission.

"It's *Mémé*, Mom."

"Yes, of course, *Mémé*. Where is she? Please bring her the phone."

Kenzie squealed in delight. "Found it, Mom." She picked the phone up and zoomed in on the wrinkled Easter dress. "Mémé is giving Beck bath, and we hustle cuz she gots a play tennis with hers friends."

Monica's heart felt like it was going to beat out of her chest. "Where is Beck going while Grandma plays tennis?"

Kenzie huffed, and the phone spun to her exasperated face. "Adel's!"

"You're *both* having a playdate at Adel's while Grandma plays tennis?"

"Yesss!" Kenzie exaggerated, making the s sound more like a z. Her wide-eyed expression mimicked Monica's when she was at her wit's end from explaining things to her kids for the umpteenth time.

"Gots to go, Mom." Kenzie's lips encompassed the screen with a kiss, and the call ended halfway through "Love y—."

Monica frantically dialed Dex and was sent straight to voicemail. "Dexter, call me pronto." She immediately dialed Janice's number and growled when it went straight to voicemail. Monica slammed her phone down. Gabby obviously had severe memory lapses regarding the consequences when you don't micromanage your children.

Monica was pacing in circles, kicking sand, Dex and Janice ignoring her redials. She pounced on her phone when the familiar ding came through, ready to rant and instruct Dex to intercept the playdate, but her phone was void of a text. It was Gabby's phone suddenly blowing up with messages. One ding after another soon turned into insistent ringing and the pings of voicemails.

Gabby and Carmen trudged back through the sand to the house, breathless. Droplets of glistening water trailed down their sun-kissed skin.

"That was amazing," Carmen declared, wringing out her hair.

"Breakfast!" announced Chet, walking out with a tray of omelets and a stack of paper plates and plastic forks.

Monica closed her eyes and took a deep breath. "Gabby, your phone was blowing up so I peeked at it in case there was an emergency."

She bit her lip and held the phone towards Gabby. "I think you should have a look."

Fear flashed across Gabby's face. "Is Stella okay?"

Monica nodded. "Stella's fine."

Chet had set their breakfast on the table while they all stood waiting for Gabby to fill them in.

Gabby's exuberant mood crumbled as she scrolled through a slew of texts. "Oh my gosh, they know. The kids know about the baby. Greg's phone was on the counter, and Stella read a text from Holly that her water broke and she wanted him to meet her at the hospital."

Simultaneously, Carmen and Monica engulfed her in a hug.

"Go ahead and eat without me. I'm going to collect myself for a bit and call the kids." Gabby walked to the shore and sat down in the sand. She wasn't anywhere near prepared for the rush of emotions she was experiencing.

She felt like she could vomit, cry, scream, kick, even throw sand, and yet she sat paralyzed. Numb.

Her phone rang again. Stella.

"I'm so sorry, sweetie." Her voice trembled as the first trickle of a tear meandered down her cheek.

Lottie spoke first. "We're both on the phone, Mom. Holly had the baby."

Gabby wished she could dissolve in the sand as she was informed that Lily May was born at 6:12 a.m. Gabby almost laughed out loud. How uncanny the timing was! Her and Greg's anniversary was June 12th. On 6/12, Gabby had carried a bundle of lilies down the aisle.

Had the time of the birth and their anniversary date occurred to Greg?

Greg hadn't called Gabby. That fact alone killed her. Was it because he thought it inappropriate? That maybe the news was better coming from the girls? Or was it simply because he hadn't had a chance to think about calling her because he was so wrapped up in the intimacy of Holly giving birth to his child? At this moment, was he holding Lily in his arms, looking for signs of his angular nose and long fingers?

Gabby thought back to the delivery of their four children: the seventeen-hour labor with the girls, the four hours of pushing. Three days of on-and-off labor with the boys spared her to a mere twenty minutes of pushing. What plagued Gabby the most though was the intimacy in the delivery room between her and Greg and the babies they each held.

The bond that formed during the delivery of a child and those hours afterward were some of the best moments of Gabby's life. She really couldn't think of any other moments that were as crystal clear, right down to the words that were spoken, the looks on the doctors' faces, the look on Greg's face, the way his voice wobbled and his eyes filled with tears as he declared the sex of their babies before cutting the cord.

Gabby could still hear the pride in Greg's voice as he called their parents and informed them of the births of their grandchildren. Knowing he had just experienced that with another woman broke her to the core. The single act they had only shared with each other until now . . . Greg now shared that experience with another woman.

People could doubt her all they wanted, but she could close her eyes and hear the first cries of her babies, feel their skin on hers, and if she really concentrated, she could smell their sweet scent. For Gabby, it was those private moments that defined what life is about. The moments that are worth so much that years later you can hear them, smell them, taste them, feel them and no one can connect with those feelings other than the one you shared them with.

How many times had she described that to her kids? Sometimes, meaningful life experiences are more sacred when kept close and not spread through social media where they are open to judgment and scrutiny, often hampering your perception. The recollection only posed more questions.

Would Holly post the birth? Would Holly's family and friends be gushing, liking, and congratulating? Would the affair be unveiled to coworkers and clients? Would the nameless father eventually be included in the pictures?

Gabby was so overwhelmed with the uncertainties, her thoughts, and all the unanswered questions. She looked out to the rolling waves, cresting, breaking effortlessly, and thought how easy it would be to stay on the island, seclude herself from the pain. Her kids could visit for long stretches, and between those stretches, she wouldn't have to stare in the face of the ache.

Lottie and Stella slung a litany of interrogating questions at Gabby. When had she found out about the baby? Why had she and Greg hidden the truth? Were they ever going to tell them? Were they going to get a divorce? Were Greg and Holly actually a couple? All Gabby's fears were being manifested angrily through the speaker. As predicted.

Gabby started from the beginning with the truth: how she found the ultrasound picture stuck to Greg's phone, how she and Greg went back and forth about whether to tell the kids, and about Gabby's final proclamation for Greg to disclose the truth. She even came clean with her anxiety over losing her family to Holly if she divorced Greg.

She and her daughters talked and cried for the better part of an hour before Gabby hung up, feeling as broken as she had that fateful day on the front porch. A weight had been lifted off her chest, and another, equally heavy, added. She feared her next calls to Klay and Calvin.

She hadn't heard Monica and Carmen approach from behind. They sat down on either side of her and each rested a head on a shoulder. A flashback to the three of them sitting, same order, on the dock a short while ago popped into Gabby's head. She'd be lost without these two.

"They named her Lily."

Carmen winced. "I don't have anything to say except I'm sorry for you, Gabby, and if I could take away your pain, I would."

"Same," said Monica bleakly.

Gabby swayed her hips in the sand side to side, bumping them with her shoulders. "You've no idea how much your presence has softened the blow."

"She wasn't due for several weeks. Is the baby okay?" Monica asked cautiously.

Gabby's head fell. "Everything is fine. Everyone is just fine."

They sat in silence for several minutes, life's tribulations unfolding with the waves, kissing their toes, reminding them no one makes it through life unscathed.

"Get up!" declared Carmen. "We're going boating for the day. We're motoring to Beaufort, Morehead, Kitty Hawk, and wherever else Captain Chet takes us. We're exploring the coast port to port, stopping for retail therapy and divine cuisine."

Monica shoved a cold omelet on a soggy paper plate at Gabby. "Eat this before you pass out."

"We aren't talking about any of our issues all day. I'm not going to vent about my husband's gambling or the ongoing torture my teenage daughters put me through. Monica isn't going to bitch about Janice or yak and contemplate for hours whether to abolish Kenzie's imaginary friends and worry how she measures up as a mother, and *you*," Carmen said, giving Gabby's leg a nudge, "aren't going to speak a word about your cheating husband, the baby, or Stella's pregnancy. All of it, off limits, even your outstanding advice. The only thing we need to contemplate today is whether to buy the shoes in every color, and that, my dear friends, is a definite yes!"

Gabby tried to look enthusiastic, only her face stubbornly disobeyed. She didn't want to go boating and be the one to bring the mood down and ruin everyone's day. She was fine with hanging back by herself. She needed to call the boys, speak with Greg. Her mouth opened in protest, but Monica's hand reacted faster and covered her lips.

"Carmen's right. We need to go and leave our crazy issues behind, go and live despite our circumstances." Monica bounded up, placing her hands on her hips. "On more than one occasion, you've told me that we are not defined by our problems. Regardless of what they are, we need to rise above them and be"—Monica shrugged—"happy."

"My life is such a mess," muttered Gabby.

"Yep, it sure is. Mine too!" Carmen retorted. "Dwelling doesn't solve it."

Gabby nodded knowingly. Easier said than done. "Was I drinking last night when I said that?"

"Nope!" they both yelped.

"Janice is a thorn in my foot, but my life isn't nearly as muddled as the two of yours!" Monica declared, giving way to a melancholy of pathetic chortling.

Carmen let out a snort, and they all laughed even harder. Monica fell to the sand with laughter and farted, and they completely unraveled in a fit of hilarity. They were rolling in the sand, covered head to toe in the sticky stuff. Gabby picked up the gooey cheese-and-mushroom-filled omelet with her bare hands, tore it in two, and rubbed it in Carmen's and Monica's hair.

"What the heck!" Carmen screamed and threw a chunk back at Gabby.

Monica grabbed two fistfuls of omelet coagulated with sand and chucked it at her friends. Seagulls swooped in, dive-bombing their food fight.

Chet hollered from behind them, "So, shall I gas the boat?"

"Yes!" they gleefully shouted in unison.

CHAPTER 32

Dear friend, if you're alone, I'll be your shadow. If you need to vent, I'll be your sounding board. If you need to cry, I'll supply the tissue. If you need to laugh, I'll tell the joke.

"Dinner is served." Chet retrieved the lobsters, crab legs, and shrimp from the boiling pot perched over the fire and placed the spread on the table. He'd ridden his bike to the market for loaves of crusty bread and tossed a simple salad in a vinaigrette dressing.

"This, my lovely ladies," he said, setting the melted butter before them, "isn't simply melted butter. It's ghee. Ghee is quite possibly the finest butter to ever reach your palate. So don't go all health crazy on me. Shellfish are meant to be dripping in this golden richness."

Chet had been calling them his lovely ladies for the past nine days. Tomorrow they were flying home, and he had insisted on going all out for their final meal: four lobsters, larger than their heads, a dozen crab legs, and several pounds of scallops.

Carmen cut a crab leg lengthwise, lifted out a perfect four-inch piece, and dipped it in the garlic ghee. "You outdid yourself, Dad."

"A-ma-zing," agreed Monica after her first bite of lobster.

"Excellent," agreed Gabby, licking butter off her fingers. "I'm not afraid to admit that I'm a total food snob. My foodie standards are high, and you never disappoint. Have you always loved to cook?"

"I surprised Mary with a couple's cooking class after one of her long stints away. She flourished. We both did. It evolved into therapy."

Gabby nodded. "I completely understand. Cooking has always felt soothing to me."

Monica guffawed. "Sorry, can't relate whatsoever."

Chet's eyes glassed over. "I sure will miss you three," he said, taking Carmen's hand in his, "especially this one right here." He smoothed his thumb across the top of her knuckles.

"Stay at my house, Dad. There're only a few weeks before Penelope and Amelia go back to school. You can visit as long as you want."

"Oh, I don't want to be a bother, honey. I know you have a lot on your plate right now."

Carmen gripped Chet's hand tighter. "Bother me? I'm begging you. That's what family is for, to support one another through the good, bad, and ugly. Things are kind of ugly right now, but so what. We'll survive." Carmen chortled. "In fact, your presence will force everyone to behave better."

Chet brought her hand up to his lips and kissed it. "Okay, give me a few days to wrap things up around here, and I'll book a flight."

"Sorry we brought so much baggage with us, Chet, and no, I don't mean luggage," Gabby teased. "There's no other place I would rather have been when I found out the news of Lily's arrival. Had I been at home, without all of you as my support system . . ." Gabby shuddered at the thought.

Monica tore off a piece of bread. "The past eight days with all of you, talking through our struggles, has been eye-opening for me too. I'm sick of being angry at Janice all the time; it takes too much energy. I've realized I'm ignoring the big picture and focusing on everything that's wrong when she's around.

"Drum roll, please." She paused while they all fluttered their tongues, looking ridiculous. "With every ounce of my being, I'm going to try and accept Janice for who she is and love her wholeheartedly. She can be nasty all she wants, but I won't allow it to affect me. I'm stronger than that, and up until this vacation, I thought that meant fighting back, proving how rotten she is, getting Dex on my side, but I was wrong."

Carmen spoke up with understanding, "It's letting *her* go. You can't let someone else's demons take residence in your head."

Gabby spoke next. "What you allow is what will continue."

"Exactly!" agreed Monica.

Their wise words resonated as they finished their meal, lit candles, and welcomed dusk and the evening breeze off the ocean.

Although submerged in their stories over the past week, Chet had remained a quiet, supportive listener, but spoke up now. "No one escapes life unscathed." Chet looked to Carmen before he continued. "Sometimes you need to stop licking your own wounds. Whether your wound is betrayal, disappointment, abuse, or rejection, don't keep probing it. Take your hands off and stop trying to fix the situation or yourself. Hand it off and trust a higher power."

As if on cue, they looked out towards the dark ocean, soaking up the words of wisdom. Each wave held a silver lining from the moon as it crested.

Monica bolted from her chair, beaming with excitement. She pointed towards the starry sky. "Did ya'll see that?"

A shooting star had zipped across the sky. All four of them had witnessed the magnificent sight: a gift for each of them to perceive in their own way.

"All our discussions have been rather heavy," Gabby announced as they sat comfortably watching storm clouds move across the sky, one by one snuffing out the stars. "Let's end this trip laughing so hard our cheeks hurt. Who has a story they can tell?"

Chet raised his hand. "Pick me. Pick me!"

His gesture alone sent them into a fit of giggles. He went on to tell a story about renters down the road, sinking a golf cart at high tide, and another of a woman who'd untied her bikini top and fell asleep facedown. "She was out like a light and rolled over; unfortunately, or fortunately, her top hadn't rolled with her. Everyone on the beach was snickering as they walked by. Finally, after a half hour of gawking, Tully from two houses down volunteered to give her a gentle shake, claiming he was worried she'd burn her breasts to a crisp."

Chet was near crying as he retold the tale. "Even Mary had been spying through binoculars from the window."

They all cracked up and continued to fill the air with lighthearted cackling into the wee hours of the night.

Gabby tilted her head in thought. "We need a mantra to remember this trip."

"I'll never forget this trip. It will always remind me of the time I chose to forgive"—Carmen looked lovingly at Chet—"and fully accept the friendship of two amazing women," she said, shifting her gaze towards Gabby and Monica.

"Totally, this trip will always be a reminder that I'm never alone and I have you two to lean on. BEACH ~ Best Escape Anyone Can Have!" Monica declared.

"Well said!" Gabby took each of their hands in hers and lured them to the shore.

"The waves of the sea help me get back to me," Gabby chanted. "That's our mantra; say it with me."

They stood, hand in hand. "The waves of the sea help me get back to me."

Thunder rumbled in the sky as a streak of lightning lit up the ocean.

"How fitting," Monica joked. "Just in time to go home and weather our own storms."

"Those storms too shall pass," reminded Gabby.

Carmen, standing in the middle, raised their clasped hands in the air. "Us three!"

CHAPTER 33

Actions prove who someone is; words portray who they want you to believe them to be.

Gabby bounced four-month-old Annabelle on her lap as she sang, "You Are My Sunshine." Annabelle sucked on her little fist and cooed and giggled as Gabby hummed and nuzzled her nose against Annabelle's. She smothered her cheeks with kisses, gracing her smooth warm skin with her lips. She'd fallen hard for her granddaughter, couldn't imagine life without this bundle of joy.

Annabelle arrived almost three weeks early on November 8th, relieving Stella from bedrest not a moment too soon. After a long pregnancy, she was spared any complications and had a fairly mild labor and delivery, thanks to an epidural.

"That must be your mommy checking in on us for the fourth time today," Gabby said in her singsong voice to Annabelle as her phone chirped from the kitchen.

Per their request, Gabby had sent Stella and Preston hourly updates with pictures of Annabelle's daily schedule. She sent pictures of Annabelle napping, Annabelle sucking away on her bottle, Annabelle giggling as Gabby tickled her, and most recently, videos of Annabelle while she rolled from back to tummy and screeched with delight.

Stella and Annabelle were living with Gabby while Stella finished up her last semester at MSU. Stella made the seventy-five-mile drive to campus Monday thru Thursday, and most weekends Preston came back with Stella.

The two were going strong, loosely flirting with marriage several years down the road, but mainly focusing on earning their bachelor's degrees and landing jobs. They were both madly in love with their daughter, which was the most important thing.

Gabby's cell chimed again with the reminder that she had an awaiting text. She scooped Annabelle up in her arms and went to look for her phone, finding it nestled between a stack of diapers and ointment on the changing table.

Greg: Can I bring lunch?

Sure, thanks.

Gabby texted back, fully realizing she would never have to give Greg her order. He knew what she liked from every local restaurant.

Greg stopped by every Wednesday to spend time with his granddaughter. Regardless of their future together, Gabby wanted Annabelle to grow up making the connection that they were her maternal grandparents. They agreed to this standing lunch date. It had felt strained to Gabby. She wanted to look forward to spending time with Greg, desperately wanted to connect with the notion that their marriage could survive. Instead, she felt forced to tolerate him, found it hard to look him in the eye after all these months.

It gave them time to talk, with Annabelle as a buffer, during their agreed upon one-year trial period. Greg had remained in the penthouse, until recently, when he informed Gabby his lease was almost up, and he had held out on securing another place, anticipating moving back home.

Gabby denied his request. His and Holly's relationship stood uncertain in her eyes, regardless of how Greg portrayed it.

For the sake of their kids, Gabby was willing to keep their relationship on the best terms possible. Greg stopped by for dinner if the kids were home on weekends. They had all spent Christmas together, honoring the exact traditions they had since Stella and Lottie were born.

Christmas Eve consisted of a small crowd with the inclusion of Preston and Annabelle. Both Lottie and Klay brought dates home, *prospects*, Calvin had coined them. He was nowhere near ready to bring a girlfriend home for the holidays.

They had gone to church and come home to their usual feast of steamed crab legs. They each opened their first gift, always Christmas pajamas, by the fire with hot chocolate. Gabby had gotten all the kids, and their significant others, matching striped footed pajamas, with reindeer hooves. They were rolling on the floor in laughter as they rocked the hideous attire.

Christmas Day was the usual fun of opening presents, eating enormous amounts of food, ice skating and ice fishing on the lake, and playing board games in between to thaw their fingers and toes.

Greg had given Gabby a bracelet with Annabelle's name engraved on a charm with room to add charms for her future grandchildren. The thoughtful gesture brought tears to Gabby's eyes, but she couldn't help wondering if he had given Holly the same bracelet with Lily's name engraved on it.

Gabby was aware she set the tone when they were all together. The kids' attitude toward Greg varied. Mostly, they fed off her, so she was adamant to be as jovial as she could be when around him. The girls were coming around, mostly because Gabby had been guiding them, and they were receptive towards mending their relationship with their father.

According to Lottie, the boys only talked to Greg when they were gathered at the house. Gabby only hoped, with time, they could restore a relationship with their father. She wanted that very much for the boys, for Greg.

And then, on a moment's notice, he had to be out of the penthouse.

"It's not what it looks like, Gabby. It'll only be a couple of weeks until I find a place of my own. I'm staying in the guest bedroom."

Greg had been living with Holly for three weeks now, solely as roommates. That familiar feeling in the pit of her stomach rushed in. Should she have agreed for him to move back home? Then there was that little voice reminding her that he hadn't asked her a second time before moving his things to Holly's. He'd moved out of the penthouse and had been living with Holly for three days before communicating it to Gabby.

Stella had slipped and began to explain how Annabelle and Lily were carrying on a cooing conversation when she stopped by Holly's to get some of Lily's clothes that she'd outgrown. Gabby's heart skipped several beats, and Stella, fumbling apologies, took Gabby in her arms.

"I promise, Mom, we don't have a relationship or anything. Dad mentioned Holly had set aside a bag of Lily's newborn clothes. I was getting them off the porch, and Holly opened the door with Lily in her arms."

Convenient, thought Gabby, but only assured Stella that it would be wonderful for her to get to know her half-sister and Annabelle to get to know her Aunt Lily.

Greg knocked softly on the door and let himself in. He placed the takeout on the counter, hung his coat by the door, washed his hands, and immediately took Annabelle in his arms.

His easy camaraderie with Annabelle evoked an unsettling picture in Gabby's mind of him and his own infant daughter. Gabby wondered if Lily and Annabelle would eventually become as close as sisters.

Greg and Holly's relationship was still baffling. Greg swore it was temporary, living together out of mere convenience until he found a place of his own. Gabby hadn't asked for repeated explanations. He often felt compelled to offer them, acting as if he were living in limbo, waiting on Gabby to let him move back home. Sure, live with your mistress while we work on our marriage, Greg. Fantastic idea.

Gabby thanked him for lunch and busied herself with pulling the contents out of the to-go bag. "I'm glad you brought something hot. I've cranked the heat to seventy-four and I'm still cold." She shivered.

"I figured as much," Greg said as he looked over Annabelle's head and winked.

Gabby faked a smile. It was a compliment on Greg's part that she didn't want to accept for fear of breaking her courage; so instead, she turned back to the bag and pulled out two Reubens she had no appetite for. She knew one was pastrami with coleslaw for Greg and one was turkey with extra Thousand Island for herself. The simple, predictable fashion of their lunch put her on the verge of a breakdown.

Some days it felt bearable to be civil with Greg. Today the sky was a thick, heavy gray blanket. The wind howled and blew in one direction and then another, causing the snow to swirl like mini tornados. The drifts barricaded their driveways and doors, creating both a haven from the elements and a claustrophobic restlessness. She wanted to hurl the sandwich at Greg, tell him she no longer liked Reubens, that he didn't deserve to know the details that made her who she was.

Conversely, she wanted nothing more than to turn back time to when her family was intact: for Greg to come home, forget the past, rebuild their marriage, and plot their future. But Greg had a daughter. Her children had a half-sister. It made all the difference. Gabby knew if she didn't release Greg from her heart, sadness and envy would engulf her. It would be a constant struggle not to succumb to resentment and bitterness. She couldn't live that way.

Gabby retrieved the divorce papers from the desk, and with a heavy heart, she slid them across the table to Greg.

~*~

Monica, Janice, and Gabby sat at Monica's kitchen table piled high with samples of tile, wood, granite, and carpet. Janice's guest house, connected to Dex and Monica's by a breezeway, would be complete at the end of April.

The construction had started in the fall after Monica had returned from Bald Head Island and suggested to Dex that Janice sell her home in Palm Springs to live with them permanently. She wanted to go back to work part-time and proposed the idea for Janice to live with them and care for Kenzie and Beck three days each week.

Dex first thought Monica had gotten lost on the island and a Monica look-alike returned in her place. Second, he thought the idea was ludicrous. There was no way he would ever tolerate his mother living with them.

Even Janice was appalled at Monica's suggestion. Monica agreed to let the topic die while Janice worried over the renovations of her charred Palm Springs house, flying back and forth to meet with contractors.

The stress was getting to Janice. She had been laying the *Monica Dear* charade on thick. Janice thrived on attention and getting Monica riled up. She bombarded Monica with child psychologist pamphlets for Kenzie, showed Monica the correct way her dishes should be arranged in the cupboards, corrected the way Monica folded the laundry and mopped the floor, even insisted Dex should walk in the door to a hot meal on the table.

Monica was sticking to her vow and not reacting to Janice negatively. Instead, she would thank Janice for the advice and even asked Janice to rearrange the dishes in the cupboards, properly. Monica also agreed to let Janice make the appointments she felt Kenzie needed. And Monica graciously accepted the tutorial on how to mop the kitchen floor . . . before the tile police knocked on the door and issued her a ticket.

"Janice, I've had a revelation. Your life is in a state of chaos and uncertainty. Hence, you channel your anxiety on me. I know you love me—that's why you consistently give me great advice—only, without your knowledge, it often feels condescending and accusatory."

Janice, ready to retaliate, took in a sharp breath, immediately on the defense, so Monica talked faster before she could get a word in. "I understand your need to feel in control of something since your own life is in disarray. I feel awful I didn't recognize it sooner. I'm sorry for reacting harshly. What you really need is understanding, acceptance, and a hug." Monica dove in and squeezed Janice's stiff torso.

"Your advice really is superb. I've only been stubborn. You know I grew up extremely independent. My mother was big on self-reliance. Being a single mother, working full-time at the university, she wanted to be certain I could survive on my own if I had to. She's more of the intellectual type, values work ethics and worldly concerns above clean floors and dinner on the table at six."

Janice's eyes narrowed critically. Monica queued herself to reel it in. She vowed to submit to the daughter-in-law damsel-in-distress. "Where I struggle, and thank God I have you, Janice, is with typical domesticity. I'm so appreciative you're willing to mold me into Martha Stewart, aka, Janice Colburn."

Monica scoured the pins on her dinner board, which were few, but came up with four recipes she was willing to make. Janice agreed, and the two of them cooked together with a minimum of ten *Monica Dear, not like that, like this,* speeches. Janice would huff as she took the spatula from Monica or grabbed the liquid measuring cup from her hand and replaced it with the dry measuring cup.

On the fourth night of cooking together, Monica could tell Janice had had enough. Monica stayed chipper, gloating over her magnificent plan. She sang annoyingly off-key to the music she had thumping through the speakers as she diced the sweet peppers and onion for the fajitas.

"What are you doing to the peppers?" Janice huffed.

"Chopping them."

Janice grabbed the knife from Monica. "You slice, not dice, peppers for fajitas. For the love of God, Monica Dear, when have you ever eaten a fajita with diced peppers and onions?" Janice reprimanded.

"Umm, here. That's the way I always make them. I dice the chicken too. It's easier for the kids to eat."

Janice huffed again. She did that a lot when they cooked. Huff. Huff. Huff. "Well, that's not the proper way, but I suppose it's best for the kids." With that, Janice set her mouth in a straight line and fiercely chopped the tomatoes and basil for the salsa.

The fire alarm screeched, sending Kenzie and Beck into panic mode. They jumped up from the floor where they were drawing on their Aqua Doodle and began screaming, "Fire, fire!" Monica calmed them down with a reassuring giggle. "No fire, but the chicken is done! Oopsie daisy, the rice is boiling over too."

"For the love of God, Monica Dear, all you have to do is put the lid on the rice and turn the flame off!"

Dex walked in with caution, overhearing his mother, prepared for his wife's vengeance. Monica greeted him with a wide smile and a lingering kiss that forced Janice to look away. She still liked to score a few points, for a giggle, where she could, making Janice uncomfortable. Monica swatted his butt. "Welcome home, honey. Dinner is ready."

He coughed from the smoke. "Seriously, can we just go back to the way things were?"

"And what's that, dear?" Monica purred.

"It's a nice gesture and all, and you two cooking together has been a good bonding experience, but . . ."

Monica nodded a little too eagerly as she looked at Janice, who rolled her eyes and huffed again. Nineteen. Nineteen huffs while preparing dinner.

"But, well"—Dex fingered the button on his shirt—"I like coming home and playing with the kids for a bit then having a beer while I grill. You know it's kind of our routine. You throw together a *salad* . . ." Dex accentuated the word salad but then trailed off, not wanting to offend Monica's lack of cooking skills.

Dex was completely oblivious, but for the first time ever, he was standing up for his wife, putting Janice in her place.

Janice lifted her chin as she spoke. "Well, if the alarms weren't going off and dinner wasn't scorched, it would be pleasant to walk in the door to a meal on the table after a long, hard day at work, Dexter."

Janice was notorious for telling Dex what he liked, what he didn't like, forcing him into compliance.

"Your mom is right, Dex. You deserve a meal of appreciation for all you do for our family and the way you work so hard and provide for us."

Janice was nodding, totally buying into Monica's sarcasm. Dex crinkled his nose and forehead and pulled Monica into his arms. "Monica works. She cares for our children, and she cleans, does the laundry, makes sure the bills are paid on time, builds shelving in the garage, and even lays stone walkways. We are *both* exhausted at the end of the day. When it comes to cooking, Monica and I both enjoy when I take over."

Janice's smile faded as Dex continued, "Mom, Dad liked walking in the door to a meal on the table. Monica and I, well, we enjoy a conversation while we hang out and cook at a relaxing pace. It helps me unwind."

"Well, I just figured . . ." Huff.

Monica cut her off by touching her arm. "It's okay, Janice. You were only acting out of love for Dex and me. Why don't we pick one night each week that the two of us cook together?"

She turned to Dex. "Is that okay, sweetie? Can your mother and I prepare you a meal, say, every Tuesday?"

Dex nodded in agreement, suddenly aware from Monica's tone of voice that this was part of her pledge, her sudden one-eighty since returning from her girls' trip. Janice's guarded posture softened, she huffed lightly, and reluctantly agreed.

~*~

Chet had flown to Michigan to stay with Carmen for three weeks. On the second night of his stay, she hosted a dinner party so he could reunite with Monica and Gabby and meet their families. Janice declined the extended invitation as it landed on the same day as her monthly massage and facial appointment. Her friend Barbara was joining her, and they were having dinner after the spa.

It wasn't five minutes after their conversation that Monica saw Chet walking down Carmen's dock with a tackle box, Penelope and Amelia following with fishing poles in hand. Monica was so excited to see him she barreled through the neighbors' beaches, hollering his name.

He engulfed her in a tight fatherly hug and kissed her cheek. "How's my Monica Dear?" he asked cheerfully with a wink.

Monica peered over her shoulder, knowing how sound traveled across water. Sure enough, Janice stood erect on the deck, eyebrow arched, eyeing their interaction. Guilt swept over her. Not only had Janice overheard, she'd never greeted her mother-in-law in such a loving manner. Janice had never made her want to.

"I'm good, really good." She squeezed back, filled with an emotion she'd never felt. She couldn't quite describe the feeling, only compared it to that of the love she'd felt for her grandfather. She felt a tremendous rush of sentiment for Carmen. After twenty years, she and Chet were rebuilding their bond.

Monica saw the trio off and returned to an interrogation of sorts from Janice. Her sudden interest in Chet was apparent, no matter how she tried acting nonchalant.

"Mr. Moreno is in town for three weeks, you say?"

"Yep."

"Does he leave Bald Head Island much?"

"I don't think so." Monica elaborated on Mary's illness a bit to explain.

"So he's a fan of the east coast. I've always been more of a Cali girl myself. You know I summered in Cali as a child."

"Yep." Monica smiled. She'd only been told a thousand times.

Janice's gaze was fixed on the fishing boat. "He's quite the fisherman." Chet was standing in the boat, gripping a fish, trying to release a hook from a large mouth bass.

Their conversation went on another fifteen minutes, Janice inquiring and Monica divulging little tidbits of Chet's life back home on the island. Monica retrieved her phone, and for the first time since Monica's return from Bald Head Island, Janice was interested in looking at the pictures.

Janice's eyebrow arched with interest instead of the usual disapproval, as she oohed and aahed over Bald Head Island and Chet.

"I'll reschedule dinner with Barbara. I suppose it would only be polite to attend the dinner party at Carmen's."

Monica nodded and stifled a laugh. "I suppose."

Janice reached for her phone. "I'm sure Barbara won't mind going an hour early to the spa as well."

Monica's grin let loose. "For sure."

The sparks between Janice and Chet flared into uncontained flames the second they laid eyes on each other. Within seconds of a formal introduction, they struck up a conversation about boating then moved to talk of Chet's guitar playing and their shared interest for traveling, dancing, and antiquing. Over dinner, Janice had purred about how *her* Monica Dear bragged about what a beautiful house Chet had on the serene Bald Head Island.

By dessert, they had plans to go antiquing the following morning. During the rest of Chet's three-week stay, they had gone bike riding together, fishing, and out on two dinner dates.

Three days after Chet flew back to North Carolina, Janice was suddenly inquisitive about the guest-house idea, pondering the proposition of watching Kenzie and Beck when Monica went back to work. Twenty-four hours after that, she listed her Palm Springs property and took them up on the offer of the guest house if it still stood.

Dex thought Monica was crazy and warned her that her new-found fondness of how to handle his mother would wear off before the foundation was poured, but despite the odds, they hired an architect, began drawing up plans, and met with their project manager, Gabby.

In November, Janice flew to Bald Head Island and stayed with Chet for two weeks. Chet visited for three weeks over Christmas, and the two vacationed in Siesta Key together in February.

"Chet doesn't like subway tile in the kitchen, so we need to go with the mosaic glass," Janice confirmed. "He also prefers this sea mist paint over the blue lagoon with the shiplap in the master bath," said Janice, handing the paint swatch to Gabby.

Janice pointed to the picture she had saved on Pinterest. "This, this right here, the dark flooring with the vintage fixtures and a coastal flair . . . absolutely stunning!"

Gabby and Monica shared a grin before Gabby went back to her punch list and they moved on to sink and faucet selections.

Monica looked at her watch. "Kenzie, it's time to get your shoes on; you have an appointment with Mrs. Price."

"No!" Kenzie shouted from the playroom.

Monica sighed. "Ever since she turned four, she tells me no. Will everything always be a battle from now on?"

Gabby nodded. "Pretty much. Yes."

"That's encouraging. C'mon, Kenzie, it's rude to be late, and I was planning on stopping by the bakery for doughnuts on the way home, but if we don't stay on schedule, the bakery will be closed."

Janice's signature left eyebrow arched. "Bribery?"

"At its finest," Monica retorted.

"Trixie and Reese don't want talk to Mrs. Price, she boring, and Mrs. Price says they not allowed in our sessions anymore."

Monica chuckled at the word "allowed." Kenzie was using Mrs. Price's words verbatim.

"I like Mrs. Price only when she let Trixie and Reese go too," Kenzie hollered from the playroom before slamming the door. A small click from the door handle signaled Kenzie had locked it.

Monica rose from her chair at the table. "I'm going to get Dex. He can deal with her, starting with switching the locks around."

Janice put her hand on Monica's and sighed. "Monica Dear, let her be. She doesn't need counseling because she has imaginary friends."

Monica looked at Janice quizzically. After weeks of Janice drilling them that Kenzie needed her head checked to be sure the visions and voices of the two little girls weren't demonic spirits, Monica had caved compliantly. Monica suggested booking an appointment with Gabby, but Janice scoffed at the idea, insisting Kenzie needed the top child psychologist in the area and offered to pay.

Gabby had assured Monica that Trixie and Reese were healthy, so if Janice wanted to hand out big bucks to squelch any doubt that Kenzie wasn't cursed, so be it. Monica acted overly enthusiastic, graciously accepting Janice's offer, knowing full well Janice only wanted control.

Janice waved her hand in the air. "I know. I know. Say I told you so. You were right, Monica Dear. She's just fine, and she is a smart girl with a very vivid imagination and an enormous amount of curiosity. I've spoken to Mrs. Price several times. Kenzie is brilliant. My granddaughter will be valedictorian of her class someday."

Janice said this with such certainty that Monica suddenly felt responsible for seeing it happen. Monica stood, not knowing whether to submit to Janice or follow through with a few more appointments. "Mrs. Price is expecting us. It's not right to be a no-show, and I think Kenzie has benefitted from seeing her. Trixie and Reese helped her cope with losing Cade and have sort of evolved to become part of our family."

"Mrs. Price will bill me whether you show up or not. The only way Kenzie has benefitted is because, every time she leaves Mrs. Price's office, you take her for ice cream, doughnuts, and trips to the zoo or the children's museum."

Gabby looked up from the lighting catalogue, waiting to see how Monica would respond.

"That's because she doesn't throw a temper tantrum at the ice cream window anymore when I refuse to buy extra cones for Trixie and Reese. It's actually enjoyable to do fun things without the dreaded war."

Janice hung her head, defeated. "That's because I told her, if she stopped asking for extras when she was with you and Dexter, that I would take her, Trixie, and Reese to the inflatable bounce place."

"You bribed her under the conditions you insisted she needed treatment for?"

"Yes, Monica Dear, same as you."

Monica rolled her eyes for effect, secretly relishing in her glory. "For God's sake, now she does need therapy."

"About that"—Janice waved her manicured finger—"I don't think Esther Price is really all that great of a therapist." Janice looked to Gabby. "Gabriella is far superior."

~*~

Some days Carmen wished her ten-minute drive home from work was twenty so she could have a few extra minutes to decompress from the three-ring circus at the office before walking into the three-ring circus at home. Today, however, was not one of those days.

When the meteorologist defined the accumulating eight inches of blowing snow as *blizzard-like* conditions, she wasn't joking. Crawling down the road, white-knuckled, at twenty-four miles an hour felt dangerously fast. It was hard to decipher whether she was sliding on the ice or if her vehicle was being blown into the center line by the thirty-five-mile-an-hour gusts.

At least the storm brought cancelations, giving her a free night from racing between Penelope's water polo match and getting Amelia to and from hip-hop practice. She also used the snow as an excuse to drive past the market. Groceries could wait one more night. At the very least, she could whip up grilled cheese sandwiches.

She inched into the driveway where Victor was snow blowing, achieving little as the snow swirled up in the air and for the most part settled right back where it had been. He greeted her in the garage with a kiss, his lips covered in a face mask, revealing only a set of eyes. She suggested he wait a couple of hours until the snow let up, but he was adamant to stay on top of the storm, to keep pacing up and down the driveway like a snow zombie. Carmen was glad he enjoyed the manual labor of shoveling the walkways and snow blowing the drive. She'd always found self-sufficient, handy men, those who could build and fix things, sexy.

The heat had been turned up, no doubt by Amelia. She insisted on wearing short shorts and a midriff, notoriously cranking the thermostat to a balmy seventy-seven degrees, oblivious as to how much it cost to heat a home in the winter.

Carmen was blasted by the heat as she entered. The kitchen was full of girls, and it smelled like a mixture of garlic, chocolate, and baking bread. Amelia and Piper were cutting into a pan of brownies, the crumbs falling on the counter and floor because they were too impatient to let them cool before digging out the gooey mess with their hands, tossing them around yelling, "Hot, hot, hot!" At least Carmen didn't have to worry about overindulging on brownies.

Carmen was instantly warmed at the sight of Penelope's new friends, Tessa and Erin, whom she also played water polo with. Erin was sitting on the counter, phone in hand, thumbing away while Penelope stirred a pot of chicken noodle soup on the stove. Tessa scraped overly baked crescent rolls off a sheet pan.

"Hey, Mrs. Fletcher," Tessa said, looking up from her phone, and all the girls followed suit with "hi" or "hey."

"Wow, dinner! I'm impressed!"

"Dessert too," Amelia mumbled, brownie falling out of her mouth, landing back into the pan.

Penelope scoffed. "Disgusting, Amelia, as if no one else wanted any brownies?"

Erin scooped out a steaming hunk and shoved it in her mouth. "Doesn't bother me!"

"Me either," said Tessa, following suit. "Hot, hot"—she opened her mouth wide, showing off black teeth—"probs should have let them cool off first."

After the entire pan of brownies was eaten, the girls ladled soup in their bowls and gathered around the table. They checked the snow day indicator and saw it was at 99% for tomorrow.

"Can we spend the night, Mrs. Fletcher?" asked Tessa. "There's no way we'll have school. They're calling for a boatload of snow, and it's only going to be four degrees."

"Fine with me as long as you girls clean up the kitchen and don't keep me up all night, screeching while you record yourselves plunging in the snow in your bikinis." She winked. Last weekend she caught them doing just that as well as ice skating in their bikinis at two in the morning.

Tessa wrapped her arms around Carmen and squeezed. The girl was all legs; she had at least four inches on Carmen. "Promise. And you'll be happy to know I brought my one-piece this time."

"I won't be a bother. However, I'll probably eat all your food," exclaimed Erin as she dug into the cupboards and pulled out the peanut butter, a bag of chips, and chocolate morsels. Erin scooped the peanut butter on a chip and topped it with a few chocolates and handed it to Carmen. "Tell me this isn't the bomb."

Carmen couldn't help but love these girls. Her eyes went wide as she chewed. "It's like salty, sweet, creamy, and crunchy all in one!"

Erin was already handing Carmen another chip. "I know, right!"

The girls were pulling random items from the pantry and putting together concoctions that made Carmen's stomach flip. At the same time, her heart was flooded with gratefulness that Penelope had adjusted quickly at her new school and walked on the water polo team with ease. She clicked with the girls on her team, and even though drama was inevitable in all high schools, it was minimal compared to what she'd previously dealt with.

In many ways, Penelope was thriving. Her grades quickly returned to A's. She enrolled in honors and AP classes and placed high demands on herself both in academics and in the pool.

The trouble was, when Penelope didn't reach her level of perfection, she cut. It was her way of punishing her imperfectness. When she screwed up, whether it be her grades, a water polo match, saying or acting the wrong way with her friends, or in general, disappointing herself, she cut. Erin held a special place in Carmen's heart. She had been a cutter in middle school and had called

Carmen, concerned, when she noticed some cuts on Penelope in the locker room.

Everyday Carmen thanked God for putting Erin in their lives. Erin often showed up at their house at random hours, slipping into Penelope's room after a shared, concerned look. Erin could obtrude in a way Carmen couldn't, without Penelope flaring up in hostile defense.

Penelope was still working for Gabby after school and agreed to regular counseling sessions. Carmen was trying to be patient. If she had to pick, she'd want Penelope to stop the self-destructive behavior and slide through school with a D average. Even engaging in normal teenage rebelliousness at parties, breaking curfew, sneaking out, being mouthy, and ignoring her chore list all fell to the wayside in comparison to cutting.

Gabby had also been a godsend, helping Carmen retreat from going into problem-solving mode too eagerly, thinking that she must *fix* everything for her daughters, for Victor. It had always been an automatic, habitual response for Carmen, bypassing any conscious discernment, often coming across as bossy and harsh instead of her loving intentions of being supportive and caring.

Carmen reminded herself every day that she needed to let go of self-reliance and trust in her faith. This was an ongoing struggle. Carmen couldn't comprehend why someone would self-mutilate. Her mother's mental illness always lurked in the back of her mind, made Carmen hypersensitive. Penelope was predisposed. She had Mary's genes.

"Difficulties are inescapable, woven into the fabric of our lives," Gabby reminded her.

These words empowered Carmen to accept her difficulties with grace and thankfulness. She was growing. As a family, they were growing, and with that growth came great virtues.

Carmen had insisted on a meeting with Penelope and Liz. What started as raised voices and accusatory comments rolled into tears, which crumbled barriers, opening the spigot and allowing honesty from both girls to spill out. Carmen assured Liz she wasn't going to tell her parents about the abortion; instead, she assured her, if she ever needed someone to talk to, she'd be happy to help and gave her Gabby's number, offering to pay for her visits, no questions asked.

With coaching from Carmen, the girls both confessed their wrongdoings and apologized, promising no more future drama. Liz admitted to orchestrating the group of five who vandalized their house. For now, pretend the other doesn't exist, Carmen advised, asserting zero social media tolerance. Carmen made it clear the circle of viciousness had to cease immediately. By the end of their meeting, the girls were cordial, and although forced, they hugged before parting ways.

Shortly after their meeting, Carmen received a card in the mail from Liz, apologizing for the damage along with a gift certificate to a nearby greenhouse. Last month, Carmen had been sitting in her office, taking stock of the progress Penelope had made by talking with Gabby when she thought of Liz. Wondering how Liz was dealing with the repercussions of her abortion, Carmen sent her a text, asking if she wanted to set an appointment up with Gabby.

Liz replied immediately and had faithfully been talking with Gabby twice each week. Although Penelope was annoyed at her mother for arranging the meetings for Liz, she understood the importance and even reported that, when Liz came for her appointments and Penelope was working, their exchanges had been polite.

Carmen retreated to her bedroom to change into her fleece pajamas. That's the way it was with Michigan winters; by the time Carmen got home from work, it was dark and she was chilled to the bone. The energy she had in the summer months to do yard work, take a cruise on the boat, or take a walk around the lake, vanished once winter set in. Getting a load of laundry through the washer and dryer even felt too big of a chore tonight. A mug of hot tea and a book by the fire was all she had energy for.

She wrapped herself in the thick chenille blanket and stretched out in the chaise next to the fire. Barely through the first page, she heard a crash, splatter, and several shrieks. Carmen closed her eyes, willing it not be true.

"Oops, my bad. Sorry. I kinda dropped the pot of chicken noodle soup," Tessa apologized as Carmen leapt from the chaise and peered into the kitchen.

What could she do but laugh? Chunks of carrots stuck to the cupboards, broth and noodles dripped from the stainless-steel refrigerator and dishwasher, celery stuck to the ceiling, and shredded chicken hung from the faucet and littered the floor.

One by one they all broke out in laughter as they looked at each other, their clothing and hair splattered with the soup.

"Is anyone burnt, blistered?"

They all shook their heads.

Carmen sighed with relief, cringed, and broke into her own chortle. "Good luck, girls. There are extra paper towels under the sink," she said and ducked out.

From the living room, she could hear the scraping of the shovel outside, the craziness in the kitchen. The crackle of the fireplace mixed with the strange concoction of scents wafting through the house, all granting a momentary swelling of contentment.

Sure, Victor's gambling had rocked their finances, their marriage. Between a loan from Carmen's company and a personal loan from Chet, Victor was paying his debts. It was going to take time for him to earn her trust back. He had put so much at risk: their home, Carmen's business, the kids' college funds.

Victor resigned from traveling to Las Vegas and went back to work for Callaway. With help from Chet, he'd built a small winter clientele, giving lessons on North Carolina's east coast, staying with Chet for two-to-three-night stints. Carmen convinced him to attend a gambling addict's class, with which he dutifully complied.

Carmen was elated with the blooming relationship between her husband and father. Victor held him in such high regard, and the two could carry on a conversation for hours. It softened her heart. The resentment she'd held towards her father for so long was quickly dissipating. It was also apparent how her bitterness had spilled over into her other relationships. She had a new-found patience and consideration for her daughters. The abundance of love she'd always possessed for them, but often failed to express with mercy and grace because she was hurting so deeply inside, came with ease.

Life could be exhausting and probably boring without all the trials and tribulations. Her girls had a huge impact on the friendships she formed with Gabby and Monica, and her dad had become her rock. Carmen no longer felt like she was drowning in the troubled waters of her life. Rather, she was continuously being cleansed by the swells that surrounded her.

EPILOGUE

Those who shine from within don't need the spotlight.

"Keep your eyes on the road, Penelope," Amelia shouted from the passenger seat, pointing out the windshield as they crossed the center line and then jerked to the other side and rode the rumble strip.

Penelope kept digging in her purse, hunting for her lip gloss as her family white-knuckled whatever they could grasp.

"You're the worst driver ever! Pay attention!" said Amelia, leaning to the left as if she were going to help the vehicle veer back between the lines.

Penelope placed her purse on her lap, dropped her head, and began digging with both hands, guiding the steering wheel with her knee.

"Eyes on the road! Mom, Dad, do you see her?" Amelia turned to face her parents in the seats behind her. Carmen had her laptop open, focused to the point she was completely oblivious to Penelope's reckless driving, and Victor punched away on his iPad with his ear buds in, intentionally blocking out the disturbances of his daughters.

Amelia smacked Victor's knee to get his attention. "Hello, people!" Amelia shouted, "Does anyone care that we're about to die? Grandpa and Janice's wedding is about to turn into a funeral."

Penelope, annoyed that she still couldn't find her lip gloss, chucked her purse at Amelia, sending its contents scattering, the lip gloss hitting the passenger window with a sharp smack.

"There it is!" The car swerved from the left lane into the right as Penelope reached across her sister for it. She was oblivious that they were four inches from sideswiping another vehicle.

Amelia pushed Penelope off, and the car jerked back in its lane.

Penelope shoved Amelia back. "What are you trying to do? Kill us?"

Victor pulled his ear buds out and leaned forward. "You two stop before we get in an accident."

371

Carmen kept silent, choosing to stay out of the battle, reached for a bottle of water from the cooler, and placed it on her cheek. It was a nice gesture to haul a few boxes of Janice's things down, but seriously, what was she thinking when she decided to drive? The traffic was insane, and they only had eight days. Although . . . eight days was probably six too many for all of them to be together on an island. Still, she couldn't wait to share Bald Head Island with her family.

"I don't see why we couldn't fly along with everyone else," said Penelope as she fiddled with filtering her music from her phone to the car.

"Agreed," said Amelia, adjusting the temperature. "Why would anyone in their right mind volunteer to spend twenty hours in a cramped car with their family when you could easily hop on a plane?"

"Don't start, Amelia!" Carmen warned. "Grandpa is being very generous hosting us, Gabby, and the entire Colburn family."

"What if Grandpa gets cold feet and calls off the wedding and we're all staying there and it gets super awkward?" asked Amelia.

"Oh, please, that's ridiculous. Grandpa is smitten with Janice."

"I know. I'm kidding, but really, how weird is it that Monica is going to be like my step-aunt?"

Carmen grinned to herself. Monica had called her yesterday to go over last-minute details and called her "sis." They had several laughs, wondering how Tully, the ordained minister, was going to spice up the nuptials. He was a peculiar man to say the least.

Victor held up his hands. "I still think they're jumping the gun a little."

Penelope laughed proudly. "They're old, Dad. Old people don't have time to date long."

Victor nodded. "True."

Amelia turned up the air and unplugged Penelope's phone, scanning radio stations.

Penelope slapped Amelia's hand. "Turn the air off. It's freezing. What are you doing? Stop touching my phone!"

Amelia slapped Penelope's hand back. Back and forth, slap, slap, slap, the hands went as the cussing started.

"Maybe we should have flown," admitted Victor, frowning.

Carmen gave him a warning look, shushing him, but Penelope had heard.

"Ya think? Finally! You agree what a mistake this was, Dad," snapped Penelope.

"I should have bought my own ticket and met ya'll at the ferry." Amelia sneered.

"Flying is for wusses." Carmen suggested playing the ABC game and got two snarky snickers. She started singing, "Don't go Chasing Waterfalls" as they did in, *We're the Millers*, but no one took the bait. Finally, she pulled out the big guns and reached in her cooler for the bag of no-bake cookies.

Carmen took one out, set the bag on her lap, and dug in without offering them to anyone else. Victor reached for the bag, and she swatted his hand away. "Uh-uh, mine," she mumbled with a full mouth.

He looked stunned. "Jeez, you can't share?"

Carmen shook her head and pulled the bag closer to her body as both girls glanced back at her, simultaneously reaching for the cookies. She swatted their hands away too.

"My cookies. I made them, and I'm not in the mood to share with a bunch of sourpusses."

Victor threw his arms up. "Sourpusses? What did I do?"

"Complain. Then you continued to stay in the slump, refusing to play a game or sing a song. When you act like that, you purposely decide *not* to have fun."

Victor opened his mouth to speak but then closed it. Carmen smiled with victory as she dangled a cookie in front of his nose. "Sing my favorite Tom Petty song."

Victor closed his eyes and shook his head. "Seriously, you're going to play this game?"

"Yep, sing it."

"You have a lot of favorite Tom Petty songs, what if I don't sing your favorite?"

Carmen bit into another cookie. "Then I guess I get this entire bag of cookies to myself, and you'll have to keep singing until you get it right."

Victor started singing, "She's a good girl, loves her mama, loves Jesus and America too. She's a good girl, crazy about Elvis, loves horses, and her boyfriend too . . ." Victor inhaled sharply before diving into the chorus, "Yeah, I'm free, free fallin'."

Carmen did a mini clap and buzzed him, warranting annoyed eye rolls from both Penelope and Amelia.

"A for effort, love that song, but not my favorite. Try again."

Victor sighed, but he powered off his iPad and tossed it in the back with a grin on his face. He pretended he was warming up his vocal chords, making all kinds of weird noises that got more annoyed looks from the girls, but they too turned down their music and waited for Victor to continue.

"Well, I started out down a dirty road, started out, all alone. And the sun went down, as I crossed the hill, and the town lit up, the world got still. I'm learning to fly, but I ain't got wings. Comin' down is the hardest thing."

"Tom would be proud." Another mini clap and loud buzz came from Carmen and echoed from the front seat as both girls mocked her buzzing and mini clap. Their mocking turned into giggles, and finally they told her how ridiculously lame she was. Perfect. Worked like a charm.

Victor caught Carmen off guard and grabbed a cookie. It was two inches from his mouth when she snagged it back, reminding him he had not earned the cookie until he sang her favorite. She hummed a few notes, giving him a hint.

"Well, I won't back down. No, I won't back down. You can stand me up at the gates of hell, but I won't back down. No, I'll stand my ground, won't be turned around, and I'll keep this world from dragging me down. Gonna stand my ground, and I won't back down. Hey, baby, there ain't no easy way out. Hey, I will stand my ground and I won't back down."

Carmen bounced up and down in her seat. "Ding, ding, ding, correct!" She handed Victor a cookie and kissed him on the cheek.

"Wow!" Penelope snorted with sarcasm.

Carmen dangled the bag upfront between the two girls. "Wanna play? It's fun!"

Amelia scoffed. "Not a chance."

"Suit yourself, Mealie." Carmen bit into another cookie. "These are so good."

"Don't eat the whole bag. What is it? Like your third cookie?"

"Fourth, I think," said Carmen, licking her chocolaty fingers.

Amelia begrudgingly searched Tom Petty and started playing YouTube videos. "And you criticize the music videos we watch. What is up with the dead woman in the video of *Mary Jane's Last Dance*?"

It wasn't long before Carmen had them all bellowing out lyrics from Aha, Wang Chung, Tears for Fears, Prince, Wham, Sting, and a small dose of Ratt, Def Leopard, and Guns n' Roses. She insisted her girls needed to take breaks from current music and learn some classics so that they were well-rounded. "Well done," Victor complimented as they devoured the entire bag of no-bakes, singing in chortles together for the next hour.

~*~

"Race ya," Monica challenged as she peeled out of Chet's driveway on Tully's golf cart. Chet's tires squealed as he tagged along behind her.

Monica was in her glory as they made their way around the island to the ferry dock to greet Carmen and her crew. She had fallen in love with this little island and couldn't wait to visit and start making memories with her new, extended family. Janice and Chet's whirlwind romance blossomed quickly. Janice had slowly transformed into a bearable human being, owing Chet an enormous amount of credit for the way he endured her.

Janice was still Janice, always would be, but Monica was no longer her focus, the bullseye on her target. Janice doted on Chet, and he fawned over her, at the same time taming her haughtiness. Chet was a gentle, humble soul. Dex easily accepted him as a stepfather, agreeing he mellowed his mother.

Since completing their little bungalow alongside Dex and Monica's house, they'd had a chance to spend time getting to know one another. He'd grown quite fond of Kenzie and Beck. The kids had even started calling him Pops.

Monica and Chet parked the golf carts side by side and watched the ferry approach. Monica took this opportunity to get a few things off her chest. "Hey, I know last summer, when we girls came for the week, I gave you an earful about Janice. I was pretty fed up with her"—Monica winced—"okay, really fed up with her."

The corners of Chet's mouth turned up knowingly.

"I'm sorry if I've offended you at all. I've changed how I react to Janice, and thankfully"—Monica slid over to sit next to Chet on his golf cart and squeezed his arm— "because of you, Janice has too. We're both softer to each other, lenient with our differences, I suppose."

Monica swallowed. "When Janice treats me poorly and Dex dotes on her, it's like this raging war ignites between Janice and me. You're a good buffer between all of us. And knowing you love Janice makes me want to treat her kindly, because I care a lot about you too."

Chet turned to Monica, his bright green eyes glassy. "Without knowing it, you've given me many gifts too. I know how instrumental you and Gabby were in restoring my relationship with Carmen. Not only have I reconciled with her, I've connected with Victor and bonded with Penelope and Amelia. How I've longed for the day to fish with my granddaughters. And let's not forget, if you hadn't taken Carmen under your wing, I'd never have met Janice." He gave Monica a nudge with his elbow. "Gaining a stepson, two more grandchildren, and the most incredible stepdaughter-in-law is the icing on the cake. A few short months ago, I was looking at a lonely, solitary life on this island, talking to fish."

Chet took Monica's hand and stepped off the golf cart as the ferry docked. "There's no denying Janice can be difficult. She's a firecracker, damn-good looking one too!" He pulled Monica close and embraced her in a hug. "I know you love her. Don't be so hard on yourself."

Chet rubbed the stubble on his chin and gave an off-kilter smile. "On the down-low, she's driving me a little batty right now over the wedding, stressing over petty things as she did when we were building the bungalow."

Monica beamed. "Tell you what, when we get back, why don't you take Victor and Dex fishing for the afternoon. We ladies will have her tamed and tipsy"—Monica winked— "by the time you get back. In three days, you'll be married, saying bon voyage to Paris, and she won't have a worry in the world."

The Fletchers disembarked the ferry with no need of searching for Chet and Monica. They both rushed the family with open arms.

~*~

Janice peered down the beach to Tully's house through the binoculars. "Chet, I've seen Tully wear nothing other than those loud Tommy Bahama printed shirts." She slammed the binoculars down on the table, the silverware bouncing in fright. "If he shows up to officiate our ceremony in one of those, I'm going to have a hissy fit."

Monica and Dex shared an eye across the table, before shifting their gaze to Carmen, Gabby, and Victor. Even Penelope and Amelia joined in on the communal look. Everyone seemed to busy themselves with a bite of chicken, an edgy sip of their drink. Penelope pointed out to the ocean. "Dolphins!"

Kenzie and Beck flew from the table and ran towards the shore in search.

"Really?" Gabby asked.

Penelope shook her head and mouthed, "Sorry" to Monica and Dex.

Dex held up his palm, insinuating not to worry.

Janice shoved back from the table and stood, shaking her head. Taking hold of the binoculars again, she examined the ocean. "If they spot dolphins and dart like that during the ceremony tomorrow . . ."

"What, Mom? We'll all laugh?"

"Dexter!" Janice reprimanded.

"It would be a hoot," Chet mumbled, but not quietly.

He too was reprimanded by Janice, her slack jaw, and furrowed brow. "How can you say such things?"

"He's right, Janice," Gabby spoke up, knowing Janice was very receptive to anything she said. She'd always made it well-known in front of Monica that she valued Gabby's opinion. "It's just us. Relax. Your wedding day is supposed to bring you joy, not angst."

"Us and six of the neighbors, one of which is the most peculiar character, and we've chosen him to unite us. They'll think we're all a bunch of hillbillies getting married in our backyard, children running everywhere, grilling our own food, using decorations we've crafted ourselves, and eating melted chocolate instead of a cake that will surely be filled with sand."

One by one they all spoke up. "Those are your adorable grandchildren," Monica snapped.

"You begged me to prepare beef tenderloin, Janice," reminded Chet.

"And the decorations will be fit for a celebrity wedding, thank you very much," Gabby assured.

"Not to mention I hauled the chocolate fountain nine hundred fifty miles to surprise you after you'd dropped dozens of hints about how exquisite it would be," said Carmen.

Janice threw her arms up in the air and shouted. "I know! You people are truly the best and most likely to screw it all up!" She placed her thumb and middle finger in her mouth and whistled down the beach, catching Tully's attention as he practiced his golf swing. "Tully, get rid of the golf club, grab your Bible, change your shirt, and get down here and marry us. No, wait. Don't change your shirt. Grab your wife and the Snyders and Bartles and tell them the wedding's been moved up. I'm walking down the aisle in sixty minutes."

Everyone looked at one another in fear. What aisle? Nothing was arranged.

Tully looked dumfounded. He pointed the driver in his hand at Janice. "You want me to marry you right now?"

Everyone piped up, "Janice, no." Gabby took hold of Janice's shoulders. "Come sit down."

Dex handed her a glass of water. "Mom, don't be ridiculous."

Monica replaced the water with a glass of wine. "You're just nervous. You'll regret not going through with tomorrow's wedding plans."

"We haven't steamed our dresses yet," reminded Carmen.

Janice ignored all of them. "Dex, go grab the rings from the refrigerator. They're hidden in the butter tin, third shelf, pushed way to the back." She propelled herself out of the chair. "Ya'll stay put. Chet honey, come with me. We're going to change and fix ourselves up and get on with it."

"Mom, Chase was planning on Skyping the wedding tomorrow. What if he's pushing skydivers out of his plane right now?"

"Your brother could care less. He probably doesn't even remember Chet's name." Janice grabbed Chet's hand and kissed it. "Don't take offense, honey."

"Okay fine, you're obviously serious. We'll all change into our wedding attire, wrinkled or not," Monica suggested.

Janice turned on a dime. "Do you always have to steal the show? For once, Monica Dear, can I be the center of attention?"

Monica stifled a laugh, but really, that was the best compliment her mother-in-law had ever given her. "I guess we'll all stay as we are. Do you need help getting in your wedding dress?"

"I've hardly overindulged these past few weeks, Monica Dear. It slips on easily."

Carmen snorted and quickly covered her mouth while Monica stifled the cackle in her throat. "You two go get ready. We'll set up some chairs."

They all busied themselves setting up, hauling the ceremonial pergola from the garage to the beach. Beck and Kenzie lined the aisle with seashells.

Chet flew out the door in panic, his unbuttoned shirt billowing behind him. "The champagne . . . I got a phone call from the market. It's still on the mainland. They promised it would be on the first ferry tomorrow morning. Janice will flip if we don't have champagne for the toast. She has a huge three-page speech planned."

"I'm sure one of the neighbors has champagne," Victor said.

"Not the kind Janice requested. The Market has one bottle. I was waiting for the case to come in."

A communal groan rippled, but not even one of them wanted to deal with the wrath of Janice.

Gabby raised her hand. "I'll go. You're all family. I'm needed least."

"I'll go too," Carmen insisted. "You guys can handle the last few chairs. I need a breather before enduring the next few hours."

Monica waved a finger at them." Uh-uh, no way are you two leaving me here."

"I need gummy worms. Can I go"? asked Amelia.

"Me too," Penelope piped up. "I want chips."

"No!" Carmen barked. "It's just . . ." She looked at Gabby and Monica as if they were a bunch of teenagers desperately fleeing their family. Carmen grabbed their hands and they all shouted in unison . . .

"Us three!"

Behind you, memories. Before you, dreams. Around you, all who love you. Within you, uniqueness.

The End

READERS' DISCUSSION

1. Carmen identifies herself by her wounds. For instance, her general dislike for women. Do you see ways in your own life where your wounds have shaped your identity?

2. Gabby is forced to make the toughest decision of her life. As a therapist, she counsels people to work through and overcome adversities. Were you surprised by her decision to leave Greg? Were you rooting for their marriage to be saved or for her to walk away?

3. Monica continuously struggles with how to handle Janice. She reacts deviously then vows to get a grip and react rationally, lovingly. Do you see yourself reverting in life situations as Monica does? Committing to act or do one thing and doing the opposite?

4. Which character did you relate most to? Why?

5. Monica is in her early thirties, Carmen late thirties, and Gabby mid-forties. Do you think their ages influenced how they responded and dealt with the struggles they faced? If the three women were closer in age, how do you think the dynamics of their friendship would be different?

6. Do you think Carmen should have been more forgiving towards her mother? Do you think Chet could have done anything different to protect Carmen from Mary?

7. Monica and Dex have a strong, loving relationship. Dex often finds himself in the middle of his wife and mother and their woes. Does he react in a way that supports both women? Do you think he would he react differently if his father were alive?

8. Knowing Gabby was a therapist, were you surprised by her interactions with and phone call to Holly? Or did it make her more relatable? Who do you think Gabby placed more of the blame on, Greg or Holly?

9. Carmen and Victor both value family and career. Do you think Victor's gambling and temporary checking out was influenced by Carmen's success?

10. Gabby's independence and the ages of her children influenced her decision to leave Greg. If the kids had been younger, or if Gabby wasn't independent, do you think she would have made the same choice?

11. Monica ridicules the helicopter/lawnmower parents. Do you think she succumbs to being one at times? How do you feel about Kenzie's imaginary friends?

12. When it comes to parenting, Carmen can be intense, whereas Victor is the voice of reason. How is it the same or different in your household? Which do you relate with?

13. Did social media impact Penelope's cutting? Has social media been a positive or negative influence on youth and teenagers?

14. Has social media influenced how we parent our children? Do you think parents posting about their children's achievements on social media adds stress to the lives of their children?

15. Penelope and Amelia were extremely close when they were little. Were you surprised that their relationship turned sour?

ACKNOWLEDGMENTS

Thank you, God, for guiding me and giving me the passion and gift of writing. Thank you for the determination and trust to keep typing on the days I doubt myself and feel like giving it all up.

Much love and thanks to my husband, Jason, for supporting whatever it is I find myself submerged in and loving me through it. I couldn't ask for a better father to our children or man beside me to live life with.

Alex, Tori, Cole, and Miya, thank you for giving me unfiltered material to stimulate my imagination and an abundance of love, laughter, and chaos. Oh, and navigating me through my inadequacies when it comes to social media. The love we share as a family keeps my world spinning.

Thank you to my mom for her feedback and the title "Us Three." Also, thank you to my mother-in-law for being the complete opposite of Janice!

My dear friends who provide much fun, love and support. You know who you are; Beautiful, Brave, Strong, Loved, Enough.

A heartfelt thank-you to the talented Theresa Wegand at TW Proofreading & Editing for catching all my grammatical mistakes and calamities such as characters mysteriously changing eye colors from one chapter to the next or a martini changing to a margarita from one paragraph to the next. You've been instrumental in making this novel immensely better.

Sarah Hansen at Okay Creations, thank you for bringing Carmen, Monica, and Gabriella to life and once again creating the exact cover feel I was imagining. Your talent amazes me.

Thank you to my talented photographer, Tori Berris, for taking my portrait.

Lastly, a big thanks to my readers. A reader lives many lives; those who never read live only one. I hope you were entertained.

ABOUT THE AUTHOR

Jamie Berris is the author of Us Three and Whispering Waves.

Her hobbies include running, reading, writing, boating, camping on the shores of Lake Michigan, and traveling with her family.

She resides in West Michigan with her husband and four children.

Visit her Facebook page: facebook.com/JamieBerrisBooks

Instagram: JamieBerris

www.jamieberrisbooks.com

https://www.bookbub.com/authors/jamie-berris

https://www.goodreads.com/author/show/15957051.Jamie_Berris?
from_search=true

Made in the
USA
Monee, IL